FORTUNE'S WAY

BY

EMILEE HINES

Published by Escarpment Press

Fortune's Way
Copyright © November 2020 by Emilee Hines

FIRST EDITION
10 9 8 7 6 5 4 3 2 1
ALL RIGHTS RESERVED
ISBN: 978-1-7346750-6-1

This book is a work of fiction. Names, characters, places, and incidents either are the product of the author's imagination, or are used fictitiously. James Bonsack, who invented the cigarette rolling machine, and James Buchanan Duke were real people. All others mentioned in the book are fictitious. Any resemblance to actual persons, living or dead, events, or locales is entirely coincidental.

Published in the United States of America by
Escarpment Press, Hendersonville, NC 28739

FORTUNE'S WAY

BY

EMILEE HINES

Chapter 1

"Marry you? A sharecropper's son? What can you offer me?"

Charlotte's words struck Fortune like the hail that destroyed crops and hope.

He wouldn't let himself turn away, but stood meeting her gaze. There was no possible defense. He *was* a sharecropper's son, but that hadn't stopped her from kissing him and making him want her. He felt his face grow hot with anger, and bit down on his tongue to stop his furious words from spilling out.

She was the first to look away, and then back at him. "I have to marry someone rich enough to save Oak Hill."

"I'm going to be rich."

"You may, but not soon enough. And whomever I marry has to be someone my father approves of."

"Then what you've said to me, the look in your eyes, letting me kiss you—it didn't mean anything?"

"It was pleasant."

"Pleasant? Looking at the mountains is pleasant. I love you!"

"I shouldn't have admitted that I'm attracted to you," she acknowledged. "But marriage is more than attraction."

He reached to take her hand, to close the distance between them, but she stepped back and put her hands behind her.

"You're being sold to save the plantation."

"Women have had to do that since the beginning of time. It's just happening more often since we lost the war. What else can my family do? The slaves are gone, the land's worn out, and my father doesn't know anything but being the plantation owner."

Fortune looked around at the bare parlor, which still maintained some of its former splendor. The upholstered sofas and seats of the graceful chairs were worn threadbare, and the carpets were replacements for the opulent originals which had long ago been sold. Tall shutters had been closed to prevent the velvet drapes from further fading, and a weak fire sputtered in the fireplace. It was shabby, but it could be brought back to its former beauty — with enough money. At least it hadn't been burned by the Yankees like so many Virginia plantation houses. "I wouldn't qualify even if I had money, would I?"

"No, probably not," she admitted. "If it's any consolation to you, my husband isn't likely to be a Virginian. There's no money left in the state."

"Chilly Langhorne has money."

"He made it in railroads, not farming, and he has daughters to marry off, no eligible sons. Those daughters will be presented at parties and balls up north and attract rich husbands. I'll be competing with them, but I won't have the money for new ballgowns and entertaining."

She touched the skirt of her faded blue dress and he pitied her, envisioning her standing in a receiving line beside the resplendent Langhorne daughters. But he could offer her nothing better than what she now wore, not for years.

He stood a moment longer, seeing her as the wife of some rich older man. He imagined stained, aging hands touching her, flabby legs straddling her.

"I think you'd better go, Fortune," she said, almost as if she could read his thoughts.

He had already turned away and was halfway to the door, defeated.

"Father wants to see you," she said.

"Why?" *What was the point now?*, he thought.

"He'll tell you."

He shrugged and walked back past her to her father's library. He'd spent a lot of winter afternoons there, reading

2

and talking to "Colonel Bob," as the old man wanted to be called.

Colonel Bob looked up, carefully closed the book he was reading and placed it on the mahogany piecrust table beside his chair. "Come in by the fire, my boy," he said, and Fortune realized how annoying it had always been to be called "my boy."

A small fire burned fitfully in the fireplace, sending up a thin wisp of smoke. It did little to dispel the chill of the library. Fortune walked toward it and stopped by the older man's chair. "You wanted to see me, Colonel Bob?"

"Yes. I suppose Charlotte told you why."

"No, sir. Only that you wanted to see me." What did the man want? Was he about to forbid him from seeing Charlotte again? He wouldn't anyway. She'd made that clear. Fortune glanced around the library, its glass-fronted shelves filled with leather-bound books. A clock on the mantel ticked softly. Fortune wondered if this was the last time he'd ever be in this room.

"I need some work done on the place," Colonel Bob said, breaking into Fortune's thoughts.

Fortune pulled his attention back to Colonel Bob. The Colonel's clothes hung loosely on his skeletal frame, his hair was thin and lank, and red splotches marred his face.

"A lot of work," Colonel Bob went on, "inside the house and outside. Trimming, raking leaves, sanding, varnishing, pointing the bricks. We'll be having guests from up North after a bit, and I want Oak Hill to look prosperous and desirable."

Like Charlotte, Fortune thought. She was already desirable, but it would take a lot of work to make the plantation look anything but dilapidated. He imagined himself pushing a plane across wood, smoothing it ready to replace rotting boards, or squeezing putty into loose window sashes. Colonel Bob hadn't turned a lick of work to

3

keep Oak Hill in shape since he came back from the war, and before the war slaves did his bidding. The Colonel believed that gentlemen didn't do manual labor.

"I can't pay you right now, but I'll give you your choice of my books, one for each day's work you put in. There will be money later, and I'll make it up to you."

After you've sold off your daughter to the highest bidder, Fortune thought. Be damned if he'd work for a few books to attract some old man to Charlotte. "I'm sorry, sir, but I can't do it. Maybe one of my brothers can. I'm leaving Monday."

As soon as the words were out of his mouth, he knew they were true. He was going away, and not coming back until he had something to show for his time and labor. If it took years, so be it.

"I'll still drive you to church, as usual, if you want me to." He didn't want to see either of the Stannards again, not until he could show them that what a man earned mattered more than being born into the "right" family, but he'd made the agreement to drive the carriage, and a deal was a deal. Even if he wasn't a gentleman.

Colonel Bob nodded and picked up his book, opening it to where he'd left off. "Send your next brother over to see me. I may have to make do with him. You're a good worker; maybe it runs in the family."

"He's a good worker, and bigger than I am. But he won't work for books."

Colonel Bob ignored that. "Would you put another stick of wood on the fire before you go out?" He resumed reading.

Fortune took a piece of wood from the hod on the hearth and added it to the coals. He recognized the wood: the remains of a fallen-in shed. He'd sawed it up and stacked it back in the summer. Sparks flew up and flames caught and licked about the wood as he left the library.

Charlotte waited by the door to see him out.

He pulled her against him roughly, desperately, feeling her heartbeat against his chest, and brought his mouth down on hers, branding her with his last kiss.

She tore away. "No, Fortune!"

He released her and plunged out into the late afternoon sunlight.

Behind him he heard her call his name, but he didn't turn back. Damn them both, her and her worthless father.

Colonel Stannard had returned from the war a broken, bitter man, stripped of the slaves that made up most of his wealth. The rest of it was lost in worthless Confederate bonds. He had land. *Ten thousand acres more than my old man ever had*, Fortune thought. *He lost an arm at Antietam defending landowners like Stannard, with their holier-than-thou attitude.*

Everybody in the area knew about the Stannards' situation. They were, after all, one of the old-line Virginia families, related all the way back to the Carters and Randolphs. They were aristocrats even if they were as poor as everybody else. Colonel Bob Stannard had married his second cousin, a Stannard from Tidewater. After a string of babies had died as infants, there was Charlotte. Now she had to save Oak Hill and rebuild the family fortune, and she couldn't do it by marrying a sharecropper's son.

Fortune looked back at the mansion. Paint flaked off the white columns and the mortar had fallen from some of the bricks. Colonel Bob sat in his office reading books about ancient Greece and Rome, lost in the glories of distant worlds instead of doing something to shore up his property.

Colonel Bob had been generous enough with his library, letting Fortune borrow books. Fortune had devoured them, but he wasn't beguiled by the past. He had to make something of himself in the future, and that future was somewhere else, in a city where he could earn money, not just work somebody else's land and end up after the crop was sold with nothing to show for a year's work.

Despite its dilapidation, Oak Hill looked beautiful in the late afternoon, painted gold by the rays of the setting sun. Beyond lay the mountains, the well-named Blue Ridge. He would miss those mountains, but he could always come back after he'd made his fortune. Someday he'd buy Oak Hill, or some other plantation as big, and turn it into a showplace. Never again would a woman reject him because he was poor.

He'd leave on Monday. Tomorrow he still had to see Charlotte at church, would even have to drive the carriage that took her there. And before then he had to tell his parents he was going away.

He spoke up at breakfast on Sunday morning. He wiped up the last bit of gravy with half a biscuit and pushed his plate back. "I reckon I'll be leaving tomorrow morning," he said.

His mother paused in clearing plates. "Leaving?" Her voice was high, her hands still.

"Running out on your duty, boy?" It was more accusation than question from his father.

"No, sir. Tobacco crop's all in, most of it sold, and corn's all shucked."

"Where you headed? Going into the coal mines?" His father gripped his coffee cup, as if it held the answer to his question.

"No, sir. I plan to go to the city, to Richmond."

His mother stood holding his plate, looking stricken. With her free hand she pushed a straggly lock of hair off her forehead.

"Farming's not good enough for you?" his father demanded.

Fortune let his gaze circle the table, studying each of his brothers and sisters in turn. Laura, sixteen and attracting

6

attention with her long-lashed blue eyes, dark hair and sweet smile. Rachel, at ten the baby of the family, who worshipped her oldest brother. Jamie, nineteen and over six feet tall, trim and muscular. Beside him Pete, a year younger and so much like Jamie strangers sometimes took them for twins. Both brothers stared at Fortune, probably realizing that if he left, they'd face their father's wrath as well as the extra work.

Fortune considered letting his father's jibe pass. He'd spent his life ignoring taunts, taking whatever slurs his father threw his way, being the buffer between the old man and the rest of the family. He'd done it long enough, and besides, he was leaving. Somebody else had to be the buffer. "No, sir," he said firmly. "No, it's not. There's no way to make any real money in farming, just getting by from year to year, scratching out a living on this wore out little piece of land."

"What do you think you can do in the city? All you know is farming and driving the carriage for the high-and-mighty Stannards."

"I'm good at figures. Maybe I can work in a bank."

His father laughed, a harsh sound that ended in a rattling cough. "Maybe they'll let you sweep the floor."

"It can't be any worse than spreading manure on fields," Fortune countered. "I'll do whatever I have to. I'm going to make something of myself."

"You don't think you owe your Ma and me something for your raising? Just when you get old enough and big enough to be of some use to me, you high-tail it out of here. Ungrateful, that's what you are."

"I'm grateful for a roof over my head and Ma's good food in my belly. But didn't you ever think I'd be moving out, having a wife and a place of my own?"

His father laughed again. "You always had big ideas. You've been sweet on that Stannard girl all your life, but I could have told you she won't have you. They marry their own kind, not folks like us."

Fortune wanted to hit his father. What he'd said was true, but it hurt to have it said so plainly, without any possible comeback. Fortune pushed back from the table and went to get ready for church. His family walked, but the Stannards rode. In the bedroom he shared with his brothers, he sponged off in icy water, slicked back his hair with more cold water, and put on the one suit he owned.

It took only a few minutes to walk to the Stannard house, but the way was full of possibilities to spoil his church clothes, especially this time of year, when cockleburs, Spanish needles and beggar lice could cling to clothes and socks. Then there was another hazard as he hitched the horse between the shafts of the carriage: the animal might excrete liquid or solids. He was careful to stay clear of spatter.

Before the war, the Stannards would have had a slave to drive the carriage, and they'd had a stable of handsome trotters. Now there was only the one, and the big carriages sat idle in the carriage house, gathering dust. That wasn't his problem.

In minutes he'd climbed up on the seat and driven the carriage to the front of the house. He climbed down and tapped once on the door. After a few minutes the Stannards came out, wearing their usual threadbare Sunday best.

Colonel Bob sported the hat from his Confederate uniform and strode ahead as if he were leading his troops instead of his daughter. Charlotte's hat had once been a vivid blue trimmed in white ermine, but it had faded pale, and when Fortune took her hand to help her into the carriage, he felt the slight lumps in each fingertip that indicated she'd mended her gloves.

As he flicked the reins over the horse's back, he wondered how much longer the animal could hold out.

Long enough, probably, until the intended rich husband could bring his own horses to the Oak Hill stable and pastures. Fortune flicked the reins again and the horse made a valiant effort to walk faster. Fortune was immediately sorry, and relaxed his hold on the reins, slowing the horse's pace to a plod. It wasn't the nag's fault that Charlotte and Colonel Bob scorned him. The horse would go on serving father and daughter as long as it was able, but *he* wouldn't, not after today.

The Stannards took their place in their usual front pew of the little church while Fortune tied the horse to the hitching post and made his way up to the loft where lesser mortals sat. It had been seating for slaves in the time before the war, and it was cramped and uncomfortable, with narrow hard wooden benches instead of the cushioned pews below. There weren't many seats aloft, for few landowners in the mountains had had large groups of slaves. Cotton and tobacco didn't do well in the mountains, and it took fewer people to tend a pasture of beef cattle or sheep than to pick cotton or harvest tobacco.

Fortune vowed when he returned he'd sit down in one of the pews. He'd be rich. Maybe rich enough to buy a plantation of his own, even Oak Hill. That was "pie in the sky," his mother would have said, and it didn't help to daydream about it rather than do something practical.

For the moment he turned his attention to the service. He found the place in the hymn book and stood to sing. He knew he had a good voice, and he sang extra loud, so that Charlotte turned to look up at him, and then quickly back to her own book.

He made himself listen to the readings and the sermon, and was glad to hear the final words of prayer, "Go forth into the world in peace." That meant he could take the Stannards back to Oak Hill, stable the poor nag and be done with the lot.

Back at the mansion, Charlotte laid her hand on his arm and he let it lie, meeting her gaze without smiling. She dropped her hand and went inside.

Colonel Bob said, "Young man, I don't hold it against you for deserting us like this. If you need me to write a reference, I'll comply."

"Thank you, sir. I'll keep that in mind," Fortune said through gritted teeth. What would Colonel Bob write about him—that he could handle a horse? Did Colonel Bob think he was applying to be somebody's carriage driver? *He could say I can read and write*, Fortune thought, *but I can demonstrate that myself. I can also split wood, sand boards and handle a scythe without cutting myself or anybody else, but I'll be damned if I plan to do that for the rest of my life.* He reached to shake hands with Colonel Bob, but the older man had already headed inside.

All afternoon Fortune's family acted as if he hadn't said he was leaving. He washed up for Sunday dinner and took his usual place at the table. His father's blessing droned on as usual, and the younger siblings looked up impatiently. Dishes of chicken, potatoes and turnip greens were passed and the family ate in silence. "Good dinner, Ma," Fortune said, breaking the silence. "I'm going to miss all this good cooking."

His mother smiled and his father gave a short grunt of disgust. Fortune wished he were already on the train, on his way to Richmond.

The next morning he got up while it was still dark outside, dressed in his Sunday suit and rolled up his spare underwear and shirt into a bundle. He left his overalls behind. Let his brothers wear them.

He was at the back door on his way out when his mother stepped from the shadows and handed him a small, cloth-wrapped packet. "You'll need something to eat, Son," she said. "You weren't going to slip out without saying goodbye were you?"

"I said goodbye last night."

"But not to me special. You know you've always been my favorite."

"I know, Ma." He pulled her into a hug, feeling the slightness of her, the ribs poking against his hands.

"It's always the first born and the baby that are a mother's favorite," she said. "The first because you're so happy to be a mother, and the last because you're so glad to be done with bearing babies." She laughed lightly, as if she were joking, but he knew it was true. "I love all my children, but I'm going to miss you special, Fortune."

"I know, Ma. I love you." He kissed her cheek and turned toward the door. "I'll write you as soon as I can."

"Come home for Christmas."

"I will if I can."

She reached into her apron pocked and handed him three coins. "This is all I can spare, Fortune."

"I appreciate it, Ma, but you may need it worse than I do. I've got my share of the crop."

She put her hands behind her, refusing to take back the coins.

Fortune nodded and left. The extra money would help, added onto the pittance his father had doled out to each child after the crops and beef cattle were sold. He didn't look back, but he knew his mother was still standing in the doorway watching him.

The sun was just coming up when he climbed on board the train and found a seat among the sleeping passengers. One was wrapped in a blanket, two others wore rumpled suits and the remainder wore overalls.

As the train began to move, he saw Oak Hill in the distance, sunlight gleaming off its white stucco'ed sides.

From this distance, the neglect didn't show. Oak Hill looked magnificent. When he came back he'd be rich, and someday, no matter how long it took, he'd buy a plantation as big as Oak Hill. Maybe bigger.

Chapter 2

After Oak Hill had long passed from view and the land had flattened, Fortune got up and made his way to the rear of the train car. Just as he pushed open the lavatory door, he saw out of the corner of his eye a man reaching for his bundle.

Fortune let go of the door and lunged for the man, knocking him to the floor. He had a moment of regret, for the man was emaciated and despite the chill, he wore almost no clothing.

"Get up!" Fortune commanded.

The man eyed him fearfully, but said nothing. He pulled himself to his feet and dropped onto the seat opposite Fortune's. "I'm hungry," he said.

"If you'd asked me, I might have shared my ham biscuits with you, but not my clothes. I'll be damned if I'll stand by and let somebody take what's mine. I worked all year for what little I have."

"I worked too, but hail took my crop. I ain't got nothing to show for my year."

Fortune understood how random and unfair weather could be; he relented slightly. "Where you headed?"

"Richmond. Washington. As far as I can get before somebody throws me off this train. Anywhere's got to be better than this god-forsaken state."

"What you plan to do?"

"Work in a factory. Or a mine."

"Coal mine's back the other way."

"There's mines in Pennsylvania too, and pay's better."

"You have family in Virginia?"

"A sister that lives with a family and takes care of the old folks. Brother killed at Antietam, rest of the family took with typhoid. They might have survived if they hadn't been half starved after the Yanks burned everything."

Fortune unwrapped the ham biscuits his mother had prepared and passed one toward the would-be robber. The other shook his head. "Wouldn't be right, after I tried to steal from you."

"Take it. I might have done the same if I was in your shoes."

The man laughed ruefully. "Not much shoes to be in." He held out his feet so Fortune could see the cracked leather held together with twine. He took the proffered biscuit and stuffed it into his mouth. "Thank'ee," he said when he'd swallowed.

"You're welcome." Fortune stood, put his bundle of clothing on the seat and sat on it.

"You don't have to do that. I ain't going to try nothing."

"Someone else might." He'd just have to keep a tight control on his bladder and bowels. All around him men were stirring, and one fell forward at Fortune's feet when the train lurched to a stop at a small station.

Fortune got off in Richmond while most of the passengers in his car stayed on board, seeking more opportunity farther north. *I can succeed here if I can succeed anywhere*, he thought. *This city rose once and it can again. It's got the river and some railroads still. And there's always Petersburg, or what's left of it after the Siege.*

He started walking, with little idea where he was going. Factories were down by the river, where barges brought in tobacco and timber and sand and everything else the factories needed, and trains took away finished products. The rounded stones of the cobbled streets pressed his feet through the flimsy soles of his shoes, and he was hungry. Sharing his ham biscuits had been the Christian thing to do, his mother would have reminded him, but Christian ideals didn't fill an empty stomach.

14

He didn't really have a plan. Making this trip, leaving the farm had been a hasty decision. Where was he to sleep tonight? How would he fill his belly? At least back home he'd had a bed and three good meals a day. Boring meals sometimes, but as good as his mother could make them.

The first three factories he tried didn't even ask his name or what he could do, but just waved him away and pointed to the hand-lettered sign saying 'No Help Wanted' that Fortune had purposely ignored. While mild weather usually accompanied October, the air was growing chill, especially on the shady side of the street, and a cool breeze from the James River buffeted him. If he didn't find something soon, he'd be begging in the streets, or curling up in a doorway to sleep—and maybe be robbed or beaten. He felt the coins hidden in the lining of his suit jacket. He might have to spend one of them to get a room at a boarding house.

Then he spied his opportunity. Through an open doorway he saw a burly, red-faced man shoving stacks of paper aside as he searched for something. As Fortune stood listening, the man said to another standing by his desk, "You're fired!"

"You can't fire me. I already quit," the other returned.

"You'll regret it," the big man said. "Jobs are hard to come by."

"Here, maybe, but not up north, and not at the mines out in western Virginia. Just pay me what you owe me, and you'll never have to see me again."

The big man continued to search without speaking further, and finally produced a key, unlocked a desk drawer and counted out several bills. "There you are. Good luck, and good riddance."

Fortune waited until the man had pocketed his wages and walked off down the street before he knocked on the frame of the open door.

The man at the desk looked up. "What d'ya want?"

"A job."

"I'm not hiring."

Fortune decided he had nothing to lose by being blunt. "You need somebody to do whatever he was doing." He indicated the departing man.

The man's face grew redder, and then he burst out laughing. "If you're brave enough to speak up to me like that after hearing us go at each other, I reckon I ought to give you a chance." He looked Fortune up and down and frowned. "But you don't look strong enough to do what he was doing, and you ain't dressed for it. Can you lift a bag of corn?"

"I've done it many a time, bags of wheat and sticks of green tobacco too, but I don't mean to make my living at it. I can read and write, and I'm good at figures."

"I'm looking for somebody to load barges and sweep up the place. You got any work clothes?"

"I left my overalls on the farm."

"Well, you might find something back in the storeroom. I keep some clothes there for when I need to turn to the heavy work myself."

"Then I'm hired?"

"I'll give you a try. When can you start?"

"Right now."

"Almost quitting time. Tomorrow morning's soon enough. Where you staying?"

"Nowhere yet. I just came in on the train today."

"You can sleep in the store room tonight," the man conceded. "Save your money to buy some proper work clothes."

"Thank you." Fortune couldn't believe his good luck. His coins could remain together and untouched.

"What's your name? I'm Horace Brown, of Brown and Company." He pointed to the sign. "I'm the whole company. I wanted it to be Brown and Sons, but I only have a daughter. Brown and Daughter just doesn't have the right ring to it."

"Fortune Barranger." Fortune stuck out his hand, which was enclosed by Brown's large calloused hand.

"Sit down, Barranger. Have a cigar?" He flipped open the lid of a box and passed it to Fortune.

"No, thank you, sir. I don't smoke."

"You got something against it? We deal mostly in tobacco, after all." He picked up a damp cigar from an ashtray on his littered desk and thrust it into his mouth.

"No, sir. We grew tobacco and my Pa said if we smoked or chewed it, there was less to sell. With three boys and himself, that would have been a substantial amount of tobacco."

Brown laughed. "A right-thinking man. That's one reason I chew on the same cigar all day to make it last. Want to show buyers that I use my own product. I have to give them a sample, but too much cigar smoke would make the place smell bad. At least that's what my daughter Emma says. I don't hold with that necessarily, but she raises holy hell if she comes down to straighten out my desk and the place stinks."

Fortune glanced at the cluttered desk. His fingers itched to get at those papers, arrange them in some orderly fashion and leave a good work surface.

After a few minutes, Brown stood, looked regretfully at his cigar and placed it back in the ashtray. "Time to get home. Emma will be expecting me for dinner. Toilet's out back, and there's a water jug and a bowl for washing up in the storeroom. There's a lantern and matches in the corner there, but be careful of fire. The Yanks burned Richmond and we rebuilt it of bricks instead of wood, but there's still enough lumber and jute bags around to burn, and the flour could explode."

"I will, sir," Fortune said, spotting the lantern.

"I'm going to have to lock you in tonight without a key, until I get so I can trust you, so you really don't want a fire." He laughed at his own remark.

Fortune nodded. "That's all right. I understand you have to keep out thieves, or in my case, to keep one in if I decided to steal a bag of corn."

Fortune went out to use the toilet, came back in and washed up, then lit the lantern under Brown's supervision.

When the key turned in the lock, Fortune felt like a prisoner, which in effect he was. The lantern cast a small steady glow, and he turned it down as low as he could to save Mr. Brown's kerosene. If he blew it out, there would be total darkness, and he wouldn't be able to avoid the scurrying creatures he heard around him.

He clenched his arms tight across his abdomen to stop the growling of his empty stomach, and tried to convince himself that he'd done the right thing by leaving home. Bags of wheat formed his bed, and his bundle of clothing served as a lumpy pillow. It was the first time he'd ever slept alone. Maybe if he thought of something pleasant, he could fall asleep. Charlotte Stannard's image swam into his mind, her pale hair caught up in a smooth knot, her hand lying lightly on his arm while her face turned up for his kiss.

That was the most disturbing image he could conjure up. He shifted position, tugging his pants to ease his erect member. What a fool he was! Twice a fool: once for falling in love with her, then for leaving. No, thrice a fool, the third time for thinking of her. He had to put her out of his mind for good.

A barrel of apples stood in a corner of the storage room, smelling like the ones that grew on the farm, Albemarle pippins. He took two out. He'd have to eat cores and all so there'd be no evidence that he'd swiped apples. But he could do that. He was so hungry he could even eat the seeds. Or maybe he'd toss the seeds and cores further into the storeroom and hope the rats liked apples. What kept them from eating Mr. Brown's flour and cornmeal? His presence tonight might keep them away, at least until he fell asleep.

When morning finally came, he awoke stiff and achy, uncertain whether it was actually morning after all. The lantern had burned all the kerosene and filled the air with a smoky odor. It was dark, but he could hear sounds outside of wheels rolling on the cobblestones, and guttural voices calling back and forth.

He opened the storeroom door and went into the front office, where windows let in light. Not knowing what he was to lift or where to take the burdens, he decided to spend the time until Mr. Brown came in by tidying up the desk. How could the man conduct a business in such clutter?

It took only a few moments to determine that there were two main kinds of papers: bills and receipts. Some were scribbled on, a few were undated, and none seemed to be arranged in any kind of order. Fortune started to throw away the damp cigar with the chewed end, but thought better of it. Mr. Brown should make that decision.

Fortune made two stacks and weighted one down with the box of cigars. His clutter-clearing had exposed a dusty notebook. He flipped it open and saw scribbled, abbreviated entries that made little sense. He was puzzling over this when the outer door was unlocked and a young woman with a basket came in.

Chapter 3

The young lady stopped when she saw Fortune. "What are you doing snooping at my father's desk?"

"Snooping would be near impossible with this mess of papers. I was just straightening up," Fortune said. He closed the notebook and laid it down, while he studied the young woman. She was plump and rosy-faced, with brown curly hair that escaped her blue knitted cap. "Mr. Brown hired me last night. Are you his secretary? If you are, I think you need my help."

"I handle the billing, and I don't need your help, thank you very much!" She set the basket down on a space Fortune had cleared on the desk. "Papa asked me to bring you some breakfast. He'll be in soon, so eat now. Then you'll be ready to work. He's fair, but he works his people hard."

"I appreciate the breakfast, and how early he sent you out for it." Fortune smiled and made himself hold back from tearing off the linen cloth and grabbing whatever was inside. Wonderful smells emanated from the food. Fortune could identify fried meat, probably ham, and coffee. Miss Brown, as he assumed she still was, might be prickly, but food was necessary, and she might also be his way to advance. He couldn't just take over the paperwork, though somebody obviously needed to.

He knew he wasn't supposed to sit while a lady stood, and he must consider his employer's daughter a lady, but how else was he to eat?

He knew by the twitch of her nose and the step she took backward that he must smell rank, but that couldn't be remedied.

"Oh, for goodness sake, sit down and eat while the food's warm," she said. "I'll just take a look at these papers." She picked up a stack, rifled through them, and nodded. "It does help to have them in order."

Fortune realized what a concession it was for her to give him even that compliment. He made no response, but set about eating. The ham had a lot of translucent fat that had flavored the biscuit that enclosed it, and the coffee was real coffee, not the homemade concoction of scorched sweet potatoes and acorns his family usually had. It was hot and sweet. He didn't like sweet coffee, but he gulped it down to the last drop, and wiped his mouth on the napkin she'd brought along. "You're a good cook."

"Oh, I don't cook. I do know how, a little, but Father thinks I'll attract a better class of man for a husband if my hands are white and soft." She spread her hands and Fortune touched her left index finger with his own. Hers was soft and plump, contrasting with his tanned, calloused one. He looked up, met her gaze, and realized she'd wanted him to touch her. He stood, bumping the edge of the desk, putting space between them. Her gestures and words weren't as cruel as Charlotte Stannard's had been, but the effect was the same. He was not suitable as a husband. He didn't want to marry, not for years, but he wanted to plan on its happening.

"I won't insult you by saying you shouldn't trouble yourself with business," he said. "Actually, I respect a woman who understands business. The two of us can succeed better than either one could alone."

He kept distance between them, and half turned toward the storage room where he'd seen the coveralls Mr. Brown had mentioned. "In the meantime, Miss Brown, I'll do the sweeping and loading and heavy lifting and whatever else your father intends for me to do, and in my spare time I'll be glad to work on the accounts."

"Mr. Barranger, Father and I discussed it and he suggested that you could live with us as part of your wages. He left it up to me to decide."

He turned back. "So I passed?"

21

"Yes. And he will advance you some of your wages so you can buy suitable clothes."

"Thank you." He decided not to reveal that he had a little money. He might need it badly later, if this job didn't work out. And if everything did go well, he could return his mother's money to her and use his own to buy Christmas gifts. Still thinking, he went into the storage room and changed into the coveralls, the very clothing he'd sworn to leave behind. But they were temporary, he promised himself.

When he came back out to the office, she was gone, along with the basket, the two stacks of paper and the notebook. Fortune strolled out to the street, which was now filled with horse-drawn carriages and wagons and men pushing wheelbarrows and hand carts. At the head of the street he saw in a carriage turning uphill the flash of red that he knew was Miss Brown's dress.

He took stock of his position: he had a job with so far unknown duties and unknown wages, but a place to stay, food to eat and an employer who trusted him enough to allowed him into his home. Add in a woman who thought she was better than he was. Had he improved his situation? At least he wasn't where he had to see Charlotte and feel the sting of rejection. Miss Emma Brown had made it clear where things stood between them, and he wasn't in love with her.

Eventually the carriage returned and Mr. Brown strode in. From that moment on, Fortune was kept on the run. With the help of a large black man he moved bags of corn and hogsheads of tobacco from barges into two separate warehouses, dragging them across a plant from the decks to the street, then uphill and into the cavernous space. By noon Fortune was gasping for breath, and knew that if this was to be his daily occupation, he'd made a bad bargain. He'd be worn to a skeleton in no time, and would probably have consumption from breathing in the dust from the tobacco crumbs that escaped the canvas covering the hogsheads.

"Dinner time," Mr. Brown announced, as Emma came in with her food basket. She cleared a space on the desk which her father had somehow managed to litter in the short space of a morning. This time she brought a jug of buttermilk and three glasses, wedges of cornbread and baked potatoes still warm.

The black man, who'd told Fortune he was Isaac, took his food and a glass of buttermilk and moved off to one side to eat. Brown waved Fortune to a rickety wooden chair beside his own substantial one. Fortune crammed the buttered cornbread into his mouth, washed it down with buttermilk and stopped when he realized that Mr. Brown had bowed his head and was about to say grace. It was short, and then the three men ate in silence while Emma stood watching.

Fortune glanced up and saw that she was studying him. Probably scorning him for his greedy table manners, he thought. But it didn't matter. She'd already dismissed him as a possible suitor.

To his surprise, she smiled, and then her face was once more impassive, before he had a chance to smile in return.

The afternoon dragged on. There was a brief mid-afternoon respite when the incoming barges had been unloaded and before the outgoing goods were loaded. Fortune discovered he had another task at this time: measuring out cornmeal, sugar and coffee, weighing the bags and calling out the amounts to Mr. Brown, who wrote them down. Isaac carried the items to the customers' barges or wagons.

A few customers bought twists of chewing tobacco, cigars or tiny cloth bags of crumbled tobacco and packets of paper for rolling their own cigarettes. Isaac was sent off to fetch the various items, and Fortune accompanied him, to learn where things were kept. Mr. Brown wrote down purchases or handed out money or papers good for later purchases. It was chaotic, and Fortune longed to bring some order to it. His labor and Isaac's could be put to much better use, and the entire operation could be a lot more efficient. As items were sold, others were moved into their spaces, and spilled items swept up, so Isaac and Fortune were kept busy long after the last customers had departed.

Finally, when the sun began to dip beyond the buildings on the other side of the river, Mr. Brown called a halt and handed a few coins to Isaac, who left.

"Get your things from the back room," he commanded Fortune, as the carriage drew up outside. "Emma told me she'd talked to you and decided it was all right to have you live with us. You'll be in the attic room, where servants would live if we had regular ones. Emma hired a woman to come in by the day to clean and cook. My folks never had slaves, and I don't much like the idea of having the freed ones living under my roof. They don't seem to want to, either. They want their own little piece of land and cabin, and I don't blame them."

"My folks never had slaves either," Fortune volunteered.

"I figured," Brown said.

"How much did you make today?" Fortune asked, as the carriage began to roll.

Brown looked at him sharply. "God knows. You counting or something?"

Fortune regretted asking. It was obviously a sore point with Brown, but once he'd brought it up, he had to go on. "I just wondered which parts of your business are the most profitable. It seemed like a lot of labor for a little money for some of the goods, like corn, but it was easy to sell tobacco."

24

"I can see you've kept your eyes open. You're right about it, but we have to sell all kinds of things, so our customers can come to us and buy everything at one fell swoop."

"But some of your sales are to general stores, aren't they? So you're a wholesaler and a retailer as well."

"Are you trying to take over my business?"

"No, sir, just trying to earn my wages, and move up from hauling bags to keeping records and helping you be more prosperous."

"So, already you don't like lifting and loading?"

"I never did. I'm the smallest of my brothers, but the smartest. I figure I've got to make my way in life by my brains. If I depend on my muscles, by the time I'm your age I'll be all worn out, or missing an arm or leg and useless."

"So what do you plan to be when you're my age?"

"Your partner, or in business for myself."

"In competition with me, no doubt." Brown laughed and slapped Fortune on the knee. "So, it looks like I have a choice: I can fire you right now, or give you some leeway to see if you can make me some more money. You have some brass, talking this way to me your very first day at work, before you've even had a cent in wages. What if I fired you and refused to pay you for today?"

"You'd regret it. I'd find somebody else to work for who would use my talents, and put you out of business."

"I think you mean it."

"I do."

"Fortune, I'm going to try you for a month. This is our busiest time, when the crops all come down the river and the farmers are stocking up on food for the winter. But you've got to keep on doing the heavy work as well as showing me how you'd improve things. I fired the man you replaced because he kept stopping to rest and sneaking twists of chewing tobacco."

Fortune had a tiny flash of guilt over the purloined apples, but Mr. Brown didn't seem to have noticed the loss of two.

The carriage drew up before a sturdy clapboard mansion, two stories above the street, with dormer windows and a broad front door banded on both sides and above by stained glass panels. A railed porch ran across the front and along both sides, reached by a flight of brick steps. It was not half as grand as the Stannards' Oak Hill, but it was in much better condition. However careless Mr. Brown was in recordkeeping, his home was well-maintained. Brilliant maples shed red and yellow leaves onto the lawn, and even as Fortune watched, a few leaves drifted past to the steps. Boxwoods bordered the flagstone front walk.

The driver climbed down and held open the carriage door for the two men to alight, but made no effort to assist them as Fortune had done for the Stannards. It was almost a relief. The Browns weren't putting on any airs. They were prosperous, but made no pretense of being First Families.

Chapter 4

Emma was waiting in the front hallway, and led the way upstairs for Fortune. The stairs were plain and steep, not curving and graceful like the ones at Oak Hill.

He followed her, clutching his bundle of clothing, and in spite of knowing how she felt about him, he admired the sway of her hips as she mounted each step, the swish of her skirt across her buttocks. His fingers itched to reach out and grab a handful of fabric, feel the warm plump flesh beneath, but he knew damn well that would surely get him fired. He wasn't about to risk his opportunity to succeed in business by a crude, pointless gesture. And besides, he judged by the looks of Emma's broad shoulders and ample body that she could take care of herself and knock him back down the stairs if he tried anything stupid with her.

Charlotte was delicate like a tea rose that still struggled to bloom at Oak Hill. Emma was a sunflower, tall and sturdy, the kind of woman who would probably produce a large family.

She came to the top of the stairs, paused to let him catch up and said, "Father's bedroom is toward the front, with a view of the river and the warehouses. Mine is just there." She pointed to a closed door across a narrow hall from the stairs. "Yours is another flight up."

"Yes, your father told me. The servants' quarters."

He followed her up the final flight of stairs, narrower than its predecessor. He kept a few steps below her, conscious that he stank. At the top she flung open a door and stepped back to let him enter. He had to stoop to pass through the low doorway, and across the open space he saw light from dormers and from a tall window at the end of the loft. Three iron beds stood side by side, and across from them, between the dormers, stood a wooden washstand with a bowl and pitcher atop it and a towel hanging from a peg on its side. Above it was a small unframed mirror. An oil lamp took up most of the surface of a tiny piecrust table by one of the beds, the only one, he saw, that had linens on it.

"Come down as soon as you're ready," she said. "We eat supper early, especially from this time of year on, when the days are getting shorter." She didn't wait for his answer.

Fortune heard her footsteps retreating down the stairs. He waited until she had entered her room and closed the door that he closed the attic door and pulled off his sweaty work clothes. He saw that a cake of soap and a small toothbrush and a bowl of baking soda had been laid out for him. He enjoyed lathering, rinsing and drying his body and cleaning his teeth with the baking soda. He finished by slicking down his hair with a bit of water before pouring his bathwater into the slop jar that had been pushed out of sight underneath the washstand. He'd have to ask if he was to empty it or if the woman who came in by the day would do so. He peed into the sudsy bathwater and replaced the slop jar's lid before making his bed.

Afterward, he stood waiting in the unaccustomed silence. It was almost as quiet as the storage room had been. He went to the end window and looked down onto the street below, where a carriage rolled past, harness bells jingling. The sound didn't carry up to the attic, but he knew they were jingling by their movement. Beyond lay the city of Richmond. Several black areas with dark fingers of chimneys and fallen walls still marked where the city had been burned during the war. He wrenched open the window and when a gust of chilly air came in, closed it quickly.

As he made his way down the narrow stairs to the hall below, he looked at the door to Emma Brown's room. It was closed. Had she gone downstairs? Were the Browns waiting for him in the dining room, or was he too early? Was she still bathing and getting dressed?

He found the dining room, which Emma had neglected to indicate, by following the sound of clinking. Father and daughter were already seated and eating when he went in.

They both looked up, gestured to an obvious third place, and went back to eating. Fortune was relieved that supper seemed informal. There were no hovering servants, no elaborate table settings. He was being given the same as they had, nothing fancy but nothing worse either. He pulled out the chair opposite Emma, seated himself and tucked the napkin into his collar as he saw Mr. Brown had done.

"You find everything?" Mr. Brown asked from the head of the table as he passed a platter of fried pork chops and fried potatoes to Fortune.

"Yes, sir," Fortune answered, assuming he meant bathing supplies and bed linens. He speared a pork chop and scraped a heap of fried potatoes onto his plate as Emma passed him a bowl of string beans and followed it with a plate of warm biscuits and butter molded into a mound with a criss-cross pattern on top.

All three were eating silently when Mr. Brown said, "As you can see, Fortune, we don't eat fancy here. Just plain home cooking."

"It's very good, sir," Fortune responded.

Again they ate in silence, and again Brown stopped chewing and spoke. "Just how do you think you can make my business better?"

"I have several ideas."

"Just give me one. If it works, we'll try another one. If it fails, I don't want to hear any more out of you. You'll be a day laborer like Isaac, or you can go somewhere else."

Fortune swallowed a half-chewed lump of pork chop, swilled a drink of water to wash it down, and gulped slightly. He had to win over his employer. Which idea would work the best the quickest and save money too? He plunged in. "I want to install a pulley to move the big bags and hogsheads from the barges into your warehouse, and for the goods that are being sent downriver to Norfolk, it can load the other way around."

"Show me how it would work," Brown said, pushing his plate back. "Emma, find Fortune some paper and a pencil."

Fortune watched as she rose from the table, noticing the slight bounce of her breasts. He dared not look further, lest her father notice. He concentrated on finishing his own supper. Emma came back and as she laid the paper and pencil on the table in front of him, her breasts brushed his shoulder. Was it on purpose? Fortune pushed the question aside and began to sketch out a system of pulleys, ropes, slings and hooks. By the time he'd finished drawing, Emma brought in three small bowls of stewed apples. This was to be dessert, not even apple pie as his mother would have made.

Fortune passed the paper across to his employer, who looked it over and asked, "How much is this gonna cost me?"

"I can't say for sure until I see if all this is available and what it sells for."

"Write down what you need: how many feet of rope, what kind of pulley wheels, and so on, so I could have some idea what I'm letting myself in for."

"The labor would be Isaac's and mine, and you're already paying us," Fortune pointed out.

"I can see how this could help you and Isaac, but how would it help me?"

"I saw that some of the barges that lined up to sell you goods moved on to other warehouses without waiting to unload, and likewise with the buyers. People don't like waiting around. If you get a reputation for unloading efficiently, you'd have your pick of the sellers and buyers."

"And what would you and Isaac be doing while I'm paying you? Resting?"

"One of us would be standing on the barge, the other at the warehouse door. When we finished loading and unloading, we could do other things to make you money, like rolling cigars." He glanced at Emma and saw that she was studying him intently. "Or I could help Miss Brown with the billing. The quicker bills go out, the quicker they're paid."

He saw Emma stiffen at the implied suggestion that she wasn't getting bills out quickly, but he'd already concluded that he needed to please her father, not her.

"Let me think about it," Brown said, rolling up the paper and stuffing it into his pocket." He pulled out a watch, consulted it and announced, "Time we all turned in."

Before Fortune could stand, he felt a small silken clad foot touch his ankle above his boots and push his trouser leg upward. He flicked his eyes toward Mr. Brown, who had noticed nothing, and then met Emma's bold, inviting glance before she withdrew her foot. It had happened quickly and was over. Emma might resent his attention to the company's bills, but she was interested in him otherwise. Fortune met and held her gaze before they both broke contact at the same moment. Chairs were scraped back from the table and Fortune said goodnight and headed up the stairs. He wasn't sure if it was proper for him to leave first, but he thought he'd better get out of Emma's sight before she spotted the erection that had sprung up at her gaze and her touch. Or before her father did, which would be far more disastrous.

For two days Brown didn't mention the plans for pulleys, and Fortune and Isaac continued their arduous labors. Each day went the same, with a shared breakfast of coffee, eggs and something else: one day jowl bacon and hot cakes, the next sweet potato biscuits. Emma stayed away from the breakfast table and the warehouse, and said nothing at dinner. But both nights the foot caressed his ankle, and each time Emma looked across the table at him, a clear signal of her interest. Fortune acknowledged by a look his own interest, but he was too tired from lifting and loading to pursue anything beyond eating, bathing and sleeping.

On the third morning Brown and Fortune set off to the various suppliers, and by the end of the fourth day the pulley system was installed. Fortune and Isaac grinned and shook hands. They had missed a few barges during the day as they worked on the pulleys, but knew they'd make up for the missing goods the next day and from then on.

"I can't wait to see if it works," Brown said at dinner, "or if I've thrown my money down a rat hole."

"I want to come down and watch, Father, if I may," Emma said, her gaze on her father but her foot against Fortune's leg. It moved up to his thigh. He managed not to flinch at the unexpected touch, and put his hand underneath the tablecloth to caress the foot in return. Emma smiled, all the while looking at her father.

"Of course. I'll have the carriage come for you."

"No need. I'll go down when you and Mr. Barranger go."

Fortune almost laughed aloud. She was calling him Mr. Barranger as the same time her toes were touching his crotch.

At breakfast Emma was as sedately dressed as she'd been the first morning, in a gray dress, a bonnet and a gray and rose knitted shawl. The ride to the warehouse was over quickly, and Fortune dismounted first and went to start the unloading process while Emma and her father followed.

It worked perfectly, to Fortune's immense satisfaction. He climbed aboard the first barge in line, hooked the sling under a bag of corn and signaled Isaac. Both men pulled and the bag moved upward with only a few jerks. Isaac guided the cargo into the warehouse, unhooked the sling, deposited the bag onto a rolling cart Fortune had improvised. Fortune pulled on the rope and sent another bag on its upward journey.

Emma clapped her hands, and her father grinned at a small crowd who had gathered to watch the operation. Pulleys were as old as history, but for some reason no one had seen fit to use them on the riverfront.

By the end of the day an extra three barges had been unloaded and the products stored.

"Now what am I going to do with all this extra stuff?" Brown asked. "I extended myself financially to buy it all. You'd better know what you're talking about, or I'll be stuck with it."

"Buyers will come. You'll see," Fortune said. His arms ached, but his back didn't, and he'd accept that change any day. His arm muscles would get accustomed to the different duties. And he didn't plan to do this forever. It was just the start. It was the financial part that he itched to get into.

Meanwhile, there was Emma. Sooner or later there would be an encounter between them. She wasn't Charlotte, and he didn't love her, but she was here, and lush and available. He didn't stop to think how the wrong move with Emma could end his job with her father, but he decided to wait for her to make the first move. That worked in business. Whoever made the first offer was at a disadvantage, and he didn't plan to put himself at a disadvantage.

Chapter 5

In the next few days Fortune went about the second step in his plan: getting himself out of heavy labor altogether. He'd noticed that the owners of the barges stood by idly while he and Isaac hoisted their bags, bales, barrels and hogsheads on and off the water. He went onboard the first craft in line and hooked up the first bag of the day, then turned to the barge owner. "Would you like to try?"

The man nodded, and Fortune instructed him. He stepped aside while the entire barge was unloaded, with no help from him. It worked for other barge owners, who soon realized they could unload their cargo more quickly and with more care than anyone else could. There would be no more complaints of split bags, spilled grain or favoritism at which barge got unloaded first.

Fortune approached Brown, who was writing out tickets and making change out of his desk drawer. "Why don't I open up the retail side?" he suggested. "You've got to sell some of the extra goods, haven't you? The warehouse is about as full as it can get."

"You're right," Brown mumbled, continuing to write laboriously.

"Do you have any plans for that barrel of apples?"

"I thought we could eat on them all winter. They'll keep until March. I got 'em in trade. Poor farmer didn't have enough wheat and corn to pay for all he bought, so he gave me the apples. I got a good deal."

"And that's the way I want our customers to feel." He realized a moment too late that he'd said 'our' when it should have been 'your'. He hoped Brown hadn't noticed. The older man wasn't paying much attention.

"Take all you want. There's plenty," he said.

Fortune dragged the barrel of apples out of the storage room and set it up next to the sales counter. When he pried off the lid, the delicious fragrance poured out, reminding him of times in his childhood when all he'd had between him and raging hunger had been apples. He'd seen children trudging after their parents into Brown's, gaunt and wistful-eyed. Today he was in a position to do something about it. As he tallied each order, he handed an apple to the customer's child, and noted their surprised smile. To those who bought sugar and flour, he asked if they planned to make an apple pie, and when they smelled the fragrance of the apple barrel, most decided to buy apples. "Buy ten and we'll add two to make it an even dozen," he said, and by the of the day the apple barrel was almost empty and the cash drawer overflowing.

"I gotta hand it to you," Brown said.

Fortune smiled and shrugged modestly. "People like to think they're getting more than they pay for, that they're coming out ahead of you on the deal."

"What'll we do now that the apples are gone?"

"We'll think of something else to please your customers." He was careful to say 'your' this time. "Or we'll buy more apples."

Brown was busily stuffing money into his pockets.

"Why don't you put your money in a bank?" Fortune asked.

"Don't trust banks. Banks is government, and in the war my folks lost everything. If they'd kept their money in gold instead of buying Confederate bills, and kept the gold hidden, I'd be rich now."

"Everybody lost in Confederate money," Fortune conceded. "Our side lost the war. But this is a new time. If you put your money in a bank, you'll get interest on it, and the bank will get to know you as a customer so you can borrow when you need it."

"I'll think about it," Brown said, as he had said about the pulley.

"Be careful you don't get robbed while you're thinking about the bank," Fortune said.

Brown thrust a bundle of money at Fortune. "I reckon this is your wages, with a little bonus. Tomorrow go get you some new clothes. Take Emma along. She'll know where to go and she can tell which fabric is the finest."

Fortune laughed. "I need some work clothes, not fine fabrics."

"No, I'm promoting you to the front office. Customers like you. I'll still do the buying and oversee loading and storage."

Fortune turned to see Emma smiling broadly at him. She and her father had obviously discussed the matter while he was selling apples. Something else was afoot too. He'd underestimated the Browns, both father and daughter. He was smart from reading books, but they had the edge on him in other matters, because they controlled his pay, what he ate, where he slept and what his duties were.

Emma was friendlier, different from the first day when she'd made it clear she was repulsed by him. She asked him for an apple from the bottom of the barrel, and when he handed it to her, her fingers closed around his before she let go and held the apple for a moment against her chest, between her breasts. Fortune's gaze followed the apple to its resting place, and up to her mouth when she raised the apple for a crunchy bite.

"Hand me one too," Brown said. "And help yourself, if there are any left."

Fortune reached down into the barrel and when he came up with an apple in each hand, he saw that Emma was staring at his bent body. He felt his face grow hot, and he took a quick bite of his apple. Juice spurted and trickled down his chin. Emma scooped up a few drops of the juice with her fingertip and licked it off her finger.

Fortune was relieved to see the carriage approach, and jerked open the door the moment it stopped, without waiting for the driver to dismount. Emma laid her hand, warm and soft, on his arm as she climbed into the carriage, though he'd seen her enter without assistance, and even drive the carriage herself. Her hand lingered until he boosted her up, and she moved sideways so that her breast brushed against him. Her father clambered in and sat opposite her. Fortune had a choice: beside father or daughter? He sat with Brown, and realized that looking at Emma was as tantalizing as touching her would have been. She lifted her hand to brush back an errant strand of hair and Fortune envisioned that hand touching his own face. Emma appeared to know what he was thinking, for she looked at him for the entire ride, not glancing down modestly as most young women would have done. As Charlotte would have done.

At dinner Brown brought out a half-full bottle of brandy, poured himself a hefty drink and offered the bottle to Fortune. Fortune splashed a small amount into his own glass and passed the bottle back. It wasn't offered to Emma, but she didn't seem offended.

"That all you want?" Brown asked.

"I'm not used to drinking much," Fortune said. "At least not this. Most of what we drink is wild grape wine or homemade corn liquor." He sipped, aware that Emma was watching him across the table, smiling disconcertingly. It burned a trail down his throat, just as the homemade kind did, but it was better tasting.

"More?"

"No thank you." He had a feeling he was being tested, and that he'd just passed. Emma was beaming, and when he met her gaze she passed her tongue over her lips in a way that brought him a partial erection. She licked her lips again, and Fortune knew that it was deliberate both times. She was teasing him.

Fortune could hardly wait for the apple pie to be served so he could escape to his attic room. He was being entrapped by the Browns' silken nets: extra money from his employer and the encompassing attraction of Emma. Brown was doing to him what he'd done to the customers: give him more than he expected, to keep him loyal. And he would keep doing so, Fortune realized, until he could save enough for his own business. That might be a long way off. First, he had to buy clothing—Brown's orders—and he wanted to take gifts home if he was lucky enough to go home for Christmas. That was over two months away, though. Anything could happen in the meantime.

He undressed, brushed his teeth and had just slipped into bed when the door creaked open. In the dim light from the hall below, he saw Emma's silhouette, before she closed the door behind her and in the darkness slid into his narrow bed beside him.

He'd never seen her without stays encasing her, and didn't now, but he could feel her soft, yielding flesh as she pressed against him. A silken robe was all that came between them, and as Emma flung her leg over Fortune's thigh, the robe fell open, exposing her breasts.

After a moment's startled surprise, Fortune put one hand on her cheek, the other tangling itself in her hair, and brought her mouth to his. Emma clasped his head and when he lifted his mouth from hers, brought his face against her chest. Fortune pillowed his face against her smooth, welcoming breasts, rolling his head so that his mouth touched first one and then the other. Charlotte had let him kiss her, and had kissed him back, but she'd never bared her breasts for him, and hers would have been much smaller. The touch of warm, willing flesh against his flesh was exhilarating, and he knew Emma could feel his erection.

Fortune didn't know what he was supposed to do, or what Emma expected him to do, but he knew what he wanted to do. He wanted to push his throbbing penis deep inside her. He'd seen how farm animals came together, but their position was different from this. He wanted to keep touching her breasts at the same time that he entered her, and that meant face to face, body to body. He pushed her leg aside and she rolled over and opened her thighs to him. Fortune knelt over her, his fingers feeling for the place to enter.

Emma took his penis in her hand, and he gasped with the pleasure of it. "Are you sure you want to do this?" he asked.

"That's why I'm here," she whispered, guiding his penis so the tip of it touched where she was soft and moist.

He pressed, and stopped. She seemed closed.

"Go ahead," she urged. "It's my first time, and it may hurt, but just for a moment. Maggie told me all about it."

Fortune had no idea who Maggie was, and he hesitated until Emma lifted her legs and clasped them around his hips. There was no turning back. Fortune pushed in, felt her flinch for just a second before she urged him with her hips to keep on.

It was over quickly. Fortune came with a burst of sperm and after a moment's fatigue that was near death, he rolled over beside her. "Did I hurt you?"

"Not much. It will be better next time."

"Will we have a next time?"

"A lot of next times, I hope. This was my first, and I like it. I've wanted to try it with you for days."

"It was my first time too."

"Really? I thought men were more... active."

"Probably most men are. My brother who's a year younger certainly is. He's been fooling around with Ruth McCarthy for over a year, and he's bragged to me about it, but he keeps worrying about getting her pregnant." Suddenly aware of his own situation, Fortune sat up and asked, "What about us? Will you get pregnant?"

"No, it's the wrong time of the month." She ran her hand across his bare chest, down his thighs and back up to touch his limp penis. "Why haven't you been fooling around?"

"I was saving myself." He almost said, 'for Charlotte,' but stopped himself in time. "I wanted to make something of myself, not get stuck on the farm with a wife and children to support."

She slid out of bed. "I'd better go to my room. It wouldn't do to fall asleep up here with you." Before he could respond, she was gone and Fortune was left to ponder what had just happened.

Chapter 6

Emma wondered if she looked different, if her father and Maggie could tell by her face what she'd done. She certainly felt different. It wasn't supposed to happen to a woman until her wedding night, but who knew when that might happen. Maybe not for years.

Ever since the first night when Fortune came to the supper table after he'd bathed and dressed in his good clothes, she'd been wanting to see and feel his body. She'd sent enough signals and he'd ignored them all, until she'd decided to take matters into her own hands.

Now it was done, and there was no turning back. She'd sensed that Fortune was a virgin, so they could learn together and not be embarrassed if things didn't work out right. It was over too quickly, and that disappointed her. Just when it had begun to feel good to her, when the motion made her feel tingly, Fortune had groaned and quit moving, and that was it. But she'd gone to his bed, and she would again, until she could persuade him that her wide comfortable mattress what a lot better than his thin one filled with corn husks. Quieter too, if they made any noise.

She waited until her father and Fortune were almost finished with breakfast before she came downstairs. They both looked up as she entered the dining room, and she wondered if her embarrassment showed.

"We'd about given you up," her father said. "You all right?"

"I'm fine." She turned her back on them and served her plate from the sideboard, not daring to meet Fortune's gaze. "I think I'll stay behind today and catch up on mending," she said. "Fortune can take care of the accounts, can't you?" She took her place at the table, looking at him, wanting him to realize that she was doing this for him. She knew how he'd been itching to get his hands on the account books.

"I'll do my best," Fortune said, and concentrated on his food.

As soon as the men left, Emma went back to her room, closed the door, pulled down her pantaloons and examined herself with a mirror. She didn't see any blood, and there was no gaping hole as she'd half thought there might be when Fortune thrust his big penis into her. It was a little red and swollen around the opening, and when she touched herself, the tingling sensation told her everything was as it should be, and that she would indeed arrange to have other nights in bed with Fortune.

She was bent over the darning egg, trying to mend a sock so there wouldn't be an annoying lump in the toe when Maggie came in with a feather duster.

"What you up to? You know you can't darn worth shooting. That's part of my job. And why you grinning like the cat that swallowed the canary? What you up to?" She frowned, narrowing her eyes. "Oh, precious Jesus, you done lost your virginity with that boy from the mountains, ain't you?"

Emma nodded at the black cleaning woman. "How can you tell? Can everybody tell?"

"Not everybody, but I can. Nothing else make you grin so silly like that. So it must have been good."

Emma nodded and laid aside the darning egg.

"Then there ain't no holding you back now. Once you've done it, if it good, then you be wanting it more and more and next thing you know you'll be having a baby, and the fun's over."

"Does it have to be like that?"

"Usually. Still, you lucky in a way. Some women get married not knowing nothing about what men gonna do to them and he rough and hurt them so they never enjoy it. But if you like it, you gotta be careful. You gotta make him want you more than you wants him, so you got the power."

Emma laughed. "I was prepared, thanks to you telling me what would happen."

"So he didn't hurt you. Does he got a big one?"

"Big enough," Emma said, and Maggie laughed. "I don't know how big it's supposed to be, since it's the only one I've ever touched."

"Let's see that you keep it that way," Maggie said. "You plan on marrying him sometime, or you just playing around?"

"I don't know. I think Father would be satisfied if I married him. He thinks Fortune is smart as a whip and he wants to keep him on. He used to talk about making enough money so I could attract one of the big plantation owners. Wouldn't it be funny if Fortune helps us make enough money so I can marry somebody else?'

"Funny ain't the word I'd use. Sad, maybe. Dangerous, for sure. If that young man like putting it in you as much as you enjoy it, he's not going to take it lightly if you marry somebody else and have that man making your babies. Child, you done started something that might be hard to finish." Sighing, Maggie went back to her dusting, although Emma could have sworn there was not a speck of dust anywhere in the room.

It was sunny and cool, a lovely October afternoon, when Emma went to the warehouse with the men's lunch. She had the driver wait while they ate, and then set off with Fortune to shop for clothes. Her father wanted Fortune to look good in the office, to make a good impression on the customers, but she didn't want him to look too good to other women. Whether she married him or not, she didn't want to share him with any other woman. Not ever.

Chapter 7

Fortune had never had a new suit. Suits in his family were passed down from father to son then on to younger sons. In his case, the one suit he had now had been inherited from an uncle who died in the Civil War. The war had ended 16 years ago, so the suit was out of fashion.

Looking around him at church when he went with the Brown's, he had seen that others were still wearing outmoded suits. There were a few who had good-looking suits, and he wanted to be one of them. He suggested to Emma that they go to Parson's ready-to-wear store, but after trying on a few suits, he agreed to go to the tailor, though it would mean spending a bit more of his precious money. The cut would be classic, the tailor assured him. It would not go out of style.

When he and Emma went back the following week to get the new suit, he felt like a different person once he put it on, and he saw admiration in Emma's eyes. He bought an extra pair of slacks from the tailor and two shirts from Parson's to wear at work. As it got colder, he wore a sweater Emma had knitted for him.

Even after buying his new clothes, he still had money enough for his train ticket and gifts for the family: socks and underwear for his father and brothers, and lotion, gloves and dress fabric for his mother and sisters. His extravagance for the family was a box of oranges.

When Emma arrived at Brown's at noon on Christmas Eve, both her father and Fortune were still waiting on customers, and Fortune looked especially harried.

"I'll close up," her father said. "You go ahead, Fortune. Here. You'll need this." He thrust money at Fortune. Merry Christmas, my boy." It was all delivered in staccato sentences as he continued weighing, wrapping, smiling and collecting money. Following Fortune's earlier example, he gave each customer an apple, and each child a small candy stick. Emma knew there were candy sticks packed in Fortune's bag along with the gifts he'd bought for his family.

Fortune threw on his overcoat, grabbed his bag and scrambled up into the carriage.

Emma took his hand and lifted it to her lips. He squeezed her hand, then let his palm drop to her thigh. Emma longed to throw her arms around him, to tell him her secret, but he would be back in only two days, and that would be soon enough. "Merry Christmas, dear Fortune," she said. "I hope you enjoy being with your family."

"I will, sweetheart, and Merry Christmas to you. I'll have a gift for you when I get back."

"And I'll have one for you as well," she murmured, but she wasn't sure he heard her for the train's horn blast.

The train was already in the station, steam issuing from its funnel into the chilly December air. Fortune jumped down, slapped his hat on his head, and bent back into the carriage to kiss Emma. She smiled and watched him clamber up the steps into the coach.

He looked grand, she thought. And it was mostly her doing, helping him choose the right clothes, reproving him gently over his table manners, seeing that he got his hair cut in a way that showed the shape of his head to best advantage. He was one of the best looking, best dressed men boarding the train. That other woman, if she existed, might benefit but Emma kept herself from showing jealousy. She'd done what she wanted to, what she had to do where Fortune was concerned.

He wore his new suit on the train. He regretted wearing it when he arrived and had to disembark with his gifts and clothing in a burlap bag, and balance the box of oranges on his shoulder. To his immense relief, his brother Pete stood waiting at the station. "How did you know to meet me?" He asked.

"I reckoned it would be this one, especially after I met the one before it. You look too good for the rest of us, Fortune."

"And you look as if you've grown 4 or 5 inches. Now both you and Jamie are taller than I am."

Fortune wore his new suit to church when he went with the family, and insisted that they all sit on the main floor, not in the loft.

Jamie caught him glancing around for Charlotte. When they were back outside, Jamie said, "No use looking for her. She and Colonel Bob are staying in New York with some kinfolks for what they call 'the social season.' Colonel Bob wrote me that he'll have more instructions for me when he comes and sees the work I've done, and he'll pay me then. I could have used the money now, but I'll still need it when I get it, I'm sure. My guess is Miss Charlotte will stay there until she catches a rich husband."

Fortune's father said little, although he seemed pleased about having something new to wear. "So, you're staying in Richmond, are you?" he asked. His voice was low and scratchy, and Fortune thought that his always thin father was even more gaunt.

"Yes, sir, I am. I have a steady job, and I board with the man who owns the store and warehouse. Someday I'm going into business for myself." After a moment he added, "Are you feeling well, Pa? You don't look so good."

"I get this way every winter, half coughing my insides out. Cold damp weather does this to me, brings back the pleurisy I had during the war, even though it was almost 20 years ago."

Later, Fortune walked with Jamie and Pete over to Oak Hill to see all the work they had done. A white painted railing now ran the length of the front porch, and new front steps and rail shone with fresh paint. Missing boards had been replaced on the stable, and the rusty tin roof painted dark green. A white board fence ran along the pasture edge.

"It looks good, Jamie," he said. "You've done a good job. What about the inside?"

"I'll get to that in the next month or so, when the weather is too bad to work outside."

Fortune had little to say to his mother and sisters. They had never been much of a talking family. He didn't mention Emma, and he couldn't invite them to visit him, because the house was not his. He had a strange feeling of being suspended halfway between his family and the Brown's. He didn't really belong to either place now.

When he was getting ready to leave, his mother said, "We don't have anything to give you, except for what we've grown here. Pete and Jamie have filled up your bag with turnips and turnip greens and some butter and eggs and part of a ham, and I've made you a ham biscuit to eat on the train."

"I'll think of you when I eat those things. And could you put in a piece of your fruitcake?"

She smiled and patted his arm. "You know I didn't just fix one ham biscuit. You've got half a dozen, two slices of fruitcake and two pieces of the fudge with black walnuts. That ought to hold you until you get back to your fancy city food."

Fortune laughed and hugged his mother. "That's gift enough, Ma. Thank you and Merry Christmas."

Chapter 8

As the train eased down the mountains going eastward to Richmond, Fortune stared out at the passing scenery. This Christmas had been different from previous ones, mostly because he was different now, but also because no one was home at Oak Hill.

When the train halted at Richmond, Fortune got down from the car with the burlap bag and started trudging up the hill toward the Browns' house. He had no money to hire a carriage, and wouldn't have spent the money on it even if he had. Walking was good for him; after the long ride on the train, exercising his cramped muscles in the fresh air felt good after the stuffy train car.

Tomorrow was another work day. Mr. Brown's store would be open again, as people still needed to buy food, tobacco and other products, even if it was still the Christmas season. Tomorrow he'd start over.

When he opened the front door to the Brown's house, Emma was there waiting for him, and he knew she'd been watching him walk up the street.

"I have something to tell you, Fortune," she said, but before she could go any further, Mr. Brown called out from the dining room, "Is that Fortune?"

"Yes, Father," Emma called back.

"Well, bring him on in. He doesn't need an invitation. He must be hungry after his train ride, and he knows where the food is."

It wasn't until he'd gone to bed that Emma slipped in beside him, wrapping her arms around him. "I missed you," she said.

"I missed you too," he said, because it seemed the appropriate thing to say. He had scarcely given her a thought while he was gone, and now feeling her body warm and lively against him, he was ashamed that he had not thought more about her.

"We've got to get married, Fortune," she blurted. "I'm going to have a baby."

For an instant, Fortune felt trapped and angry. He hadn't planned on marrying for a long time, and this meant he could never marry Charlotte. But then she was off marrying someone else anyway so that part didn't matter. And he had to admit that he hadn't done anything to not let this happen. He had enjoyed having Emma come to his bed at night and give herself to him. He was as responsible as she was, but she would be the one to carry the burden and to suffer the shame if he didn't marry her. "Of course we'll get married. Have you told your father?"

"No. I was waiting for you. We can tell him tomorrow."

Fortune slept little, and faced speaking to Mr. Brown at breakfast with as much trepidation as he had felt in announcing to his family that he was leaving.

Emma however, seem to feel no such problem. "Father, Fortune and I have an announcement. We're getting married."

"Just like that? When was this decided?"

"Last night after I returned, sir," Fortune said.

"And what if I say no? I had in mind that you would marry up, Emma."

"But Fortune is the one I want, father. Besides, were going to give you a grandchild."

"How soon?"

Emma reached for Fortune's hand and squeezed it then met her father's eyes. In about "in about seven months."

Brown shoved back his plate and stood, turning his anger on Fortune. "You seduced my daughter and ruined her chances of a good marriage, after all I've done for you."

"No he didn't, Father. I went willingly. I love him. And you've said yourself he's a good employee and has helped the business."

Brown sat down slowly. "Very well, we'll have a wedding as soon as possible, and I'll no longer pay you wages, Fortune. I'll give you half the profits. You'll be half owner of my business. Then when I die Emma will get the other half. That way you can't slip out on us, or put anything over on her, and she'll have to consult you before she can make any decisions too."

Fortune waited until after the wedding to write his mother a short letter: "Dear Mama, I have married Emma Brown, the daughter of the warehouse owner. I will bring her to meet you someday, just not right now. Love to you and all the family."

The next he heard from his mother was similar news: "You've started the ball rolling, son. Your brother Jamie got married too, to Ruth McCarthy. They have moved into your room, and she is a big help to me, as your sister Laura seems to have her head in the clouds and may soon marry and move away."

Fortune soon realized that there was no way he could save up money to help his family or even himself. He was now trapped, not just legally but financially as well. If he wasn't to receive wages, how could he amass enough money for even small gifts to his family?

He took it up with Mr. Brown.

As they finished work one afternoon, he said, "Sir, I'd like to go back to being an employee and receiving wages. As it is, I have nothing. You're getting my labor for free on the promise that someday I'll be half owner of the business after you've died. I don't like waiting for you to die."

Brown laughed a little nervously. "But you don't have to pay room and board anymore," he said.

Fortune was undeterred. "I was better off living on the farm with my family. At least then at the end of each harvest, the money would be divided among us and I could do what I wanted with my share. I know from keeping the accounts that we are making a profit, but none of it is going to me. I can't buy myself a drink or buy a gift for Emma, and what kind of father will I be if I can't support my family financially?"

"What do you have in mind, young man?"

"You can call me Fortune. I'm your son-in-law and the father of your coming grandchild, not just any young man. I want us at the end of each month to look at how much profit we have made and you get half and I get half."

"You expect half the profits? I built up the business from nothing, and you walked in as a hired hand."

Fortune bit his tongue to keep from making a sharp remark. He nodded. "What you say is true sir, but you did say you were giving me half the business, and I have increased your profits every month since I arrived. If you have really given me half the business, then I want a contract that says so, and I want half the profits each month to spend or save as I wish. I don't want to have to wait for you to die."

"And if I say no?"

"Then I will leave and find a job somewhere else."

"And what about Emma? What about your responsibility to her?"

"She can go with me if she wishes. I would hope she would, but I can't force her to, and at this point I couldn't support her."

For a few moments Brown said nothing, and fortune waited in silence. Finally, the old man said, "All right, I'll divide the profits with you."

51

Fortune nodded, then went on. "About the ownership, I want a contract that states that I am half owner. I will make two copies of it, one for you and one for me."

"You drive a hard bargain, Fortune," Brown said. "You'll make a successful businessman."

"I think so," Fortune said. "And I'll support Emma and our child or children."

Over the next months, Fortune watched his bank account balance swelling along with his net worth. He attempted to make more decisions about the running of the store and warehouse, but he made little headway with his father-in-law. Brown always retorted that he had been running the store all his adult life and he knew best. "Soon enough, you'll be in charge, and then you and Emma can hash it out."

"That may be decades," Fortune said. "Let us hope so at any rate."

He did succeed in persuading his father-in-law to have more candy for sale. "When people have a penny or two left in change, they're very likely to spend it on something they want rather than something they need or to save it."

Brown agreed to a try, and soon the location became known as a source of penny candy. Profits rose a few pennies at a time, but every one counted.

As summer went on and the heat and humidity became oppressive, Emma stopped coming to the warehouse. She spent her days inside with the shutters drawn, lying in bed and fanning herself. "I'm so big and heavy, I must be carrying twins," she complained. "I can't wait for the birth to be over. If men had to bear children, there would be far fewer of them."

Fortune sympathized, but there was nothing he could do to help, except to bring her ice water after the iceman had delivered his twice-weekly block of ice, or to fan her.

In June, he received a short letter from his mother: "Your father died today. Can you come?"

Fortune withdrew enough money for his train ticket and some extra for unexpected expenses. By the time he arrived, a coffin had been built and his father's body washed and dressed and lying on a row of chairs in the sitting room. Family members sat around in the stifling hot room, making occasional remarks.

Fortune went over to touch his father's still, bony hand. The opposite side was as usual the penned-up sleeve, empty where there was no arm. The face was lined and shrunken. His father looked much older than Fortune knew he was.

"You probably want to know how he died," his mother said, drawing him outside. "I think it were lightning. He had us all busy gathering as much tobacco as we could because he was sure that was going to be hail, and you know how hail is." Fortune knew; in just five minutes, hail could destroy what the family had been working on all summer long, taking away their income for the year.

"We'd cured about half the crop, of course," his mother continued, "but the best leaves were still on the vine. He had all of us out pulling them off and running to put them under the shed before the rain came, or the hail. Then I felt the hairs stand up on the back of my neck as the air kind of shivered."

Her face took on a faraway expression, as if she were reliving the experience. "He made a little cry and fell to the ground. We'd no sooner dragged him under the cover of the barn than the hail began, beating down on the tin roof, tearing everything in its path. More lightning came but it was dry lightning; now that we needed rain, we don't have much of anything."

She shook her head to return to the present. "I've been busy this morning peeling and putting up the tomatoes that the hail split open, and Laura has been busy peeling the damaged apples to make apple butter. Rachel has helped too, but Jamie's wife, as you can see, is going to have a baby, and she's not much help right now. How's your wife?"

It was the most Fortune had ever heard his mother say, and she had covered so much. "She's due sometime soon," he said.

His mother nodded. "I figured you and Jamie both got your women in trouble, and you both did the honorable thing, so I'm going to be a grandmother twice over. Fingers crossed that Laura don't get in no trouble like that."

The funeral was short and simple. Neither of the Stannards attended, to Fortune's mingled relief and disappointment. He knew Charlotte had been married for several months, but wasn't certain he was ready to see her with her new husband.

As he was preparing to leave for the train, he offered his mother money. She shook her head. "Don't need it. Miss Charlotte and her husband have hired Laura and me to work in the big house. You know I'm a good cook, and Laura is a good worker if she gets the right directions, so she cleans and helps me in the kitchen. We've been doing that for some weeks, along with the canning and preserving and working in the tobacco . . ." Her voice trailed off. Fortune could tell how very tired she was, but she was carrying on with determination.

When he got to Richmond, the Brown carriage didn't meet him at the train station so he walked up the hill, carrying his suit jacket over his arm and fanning himself with his hat. Emma wasn't waiting in the front hall either, and when he went looking for her, he met a woman hurrying out of their bedroom carrying a basin and cloth.

She stopped and looked him over. "You must be the father. It's high time you got here. Why don't you go on in and see your wife? She's been calling for you."

Fortune went in and saw Emma lying back in bed with a wrinkled baby cuddled against her. Despite her obvious fatigue, she smiled and said, "We have a son." She paused and added, "There was a girl, too . . ." but her next words were lost in sobbing.

Chapter 9

Mr. Brown seemed prouder of little Simon than either of his parents did. He enjoyed dandling the boy on his knee while making silly hooting sounds, and feeling the grasp of a tiny hand around his finger. He was more than willing, however, to hand Simon back to Emma when it was time for a diaper to be changed.

Fortune and Emma never spoke of the little girl who would have been Simon's twin. In fact, they spoke very little to each other at all for months after the birth, each lost in their grief.

One afternoon as Fortune and his father-in-law were closing up business for the day, he came out to see his sister Laura sitting on the shop's front steps, a scruffy bag beside her. When he appeared, she leapt up and threw her arms around him, exclaiming in joy.

He gave her a great hug, then set her down, laughing. "What are you doing here?"

"Mama sent me to help take care of the baby, but there's more to it than that. I'll tell you everything later, as soon as I've had something to eat and a bath."

After dinner that night, while Emma was resting and Mr. Brown was playing with Simon, Fortune had an opportunity to talk privately with Laura. "Didn't Jamie and his wife need you to take care of their baby? And what about your job?"

At the last question, she burst into sobs. "I lost my job, but it wasn't my fault!"

"What happened?"

"I was helping serve dinner when Miss Charlotte's husband Mr. Bishop reached out and put his hand on me—" she hesitated, blushed, and went on, "in a private place. I knew it wasn't an accident, and I dumped some coffee on him."

Fortune forced himself not to laugh at the image, realizing it was a serious matter for Laura. And for his mother, who needed Laura's income. "So what happened after that?"

"Miss Charlotte—Mrs. Bishop, she is now—said I should go wait for her in the kitchen and for my mother to finish serving. After the longest time she came out and said I was too careless to be a maid, or maybe I meant to pour the coffee on her husband. I said he had done something ungentlemanly and she said I must have done something to tempt him, to make him act like that. But I didn't, cross my heart and hope to die, I didn't!"

She went on, with a slight spiteful frown. "Although I could understand why he might want to look at somebody besides her. She's going to have a baby, and she's all puffy and scraggly looking at the same time, and she has a sour look about her now, not pretty the way you remembered her."

Fortune tried not to think about the way he remembered Charlotte, but concentrated on what Laura was saying. He could easily see why a man might be attracted to his sister. She had black curly hair and long-lashed blue eyes, and her body was slim and gently curved, untouched yet by childbearing or too many years of hard work.

"The next morning, Mr. Bishop himself came to the house and gave me some money. He said he'd had too much to drink the night before, which I was sure he had, but that that was no excuse for what he did. He apologized, and asked me if I would be willing to go with them back to New York when they went and be the serving maid there. I would never trust him anymore, even though I think it would be exciting to go to New York so I said Mama would never let me."

She looked up at Fortune imploringly. "So, can I stay here and help Emma, or help with the business, or do something? Whatever you need, I can help!"

Chapter 10

Later on, Fortune would look back on those early years as a time of waiting for something to happen. Laura began working in the office, while he and Mr. Brown sold items, took inventory and kept the business going and Emma looked after their son.

Mr. Brown reveled in his grandson, a plump, gurgling happy child who delighted in being bounced on his grandfather's knee, crawling around making the dog's life miserable, and toddling to the door to meet his father, grandfather and aunt Laura at the end of the day.

Within 6 months of Simon's birth, Emma became pregnant again but had a miscarriage. When Simon was three, he finally had a little sister who was named Eve. Like Fortune, Simon was a fast learner, and now he had someone to teach.

Fortune himself yearned for something new, some way to earn lots of money so that he could not only provide for his wife and children but see that his mother was comfortable and not dependent on Charlotte Bishop nee Stannard and her husband.

One day Laura came back to the warehouse where Fortune and Brown were taking inventory and re-arranging the stock. "There's a man to see you in the office," she said. "He has a little machine in a bag with him, and says he has an opportunity for you."

Fortune took off the leather apron he'd been wearing to protect his good clothes, and went out into the office, followed by his father-in-law.

The visitor rose and extended his hand. "I'm James Bonsack, and I've come to show you a machine I have invented that can make you a fortune."

Both Fortune and Brown shook hands with the man, and Brown waved him to a chair beside Laura's desk, pulling out boxes for himself and Fortune to sit on. "What's this you say about making us a fortune, and why have you come to see us?" Brown asked, his voice tinged with a bit of suspicion. "If it's going to make someone a fortune, why not keep it for yourself?"

"I've come here because you two have a good reputation in Virginia as honest, hard-working men. As to why I don't keep this invention for myself, well, I need some financing so I can produce more." He reached into the burlap bag beside him and drew out a small machine, placing it on Laura's desk.

"This is a cigarette rolling machine. This little one can be operated by hand, but if it is installed in a larger version, I think it's capable of rolling thousands of cigarettes each day." At this, Fortune and Brown leaned in slightly to see its workings.

As Bonsack spoke, he pointed to the machine's parts. "The ground tobacco is put in here." He took a small pouch of tobacco from his bag and dumped it into a little tray. "Paper goes in this trough." He spread a thin piece of paper in to the trough and poured the tobacco into it.

"As the trough turns, the paper wraps around the tobacco, then the paper is glued together, producing a firm little cylinder, a cigarette." As he turned the handle, the trough revolved, and then dropped back into place as a cigarette was deposited at the end.

"Why would anybody need a machine to roll cigarette?" Brown asked. "They can do it just as well themselves."

Fortune picked up the cigarette. "No one I know produces a cigarette as firm and well packed as this," he said.

"But why would anyone care how neat a cigarette might be?" Brown asked.

"People are always looking for new things, and some people always want nicer things," Fortune said. He turned to Bonsack. "Assuming we wanted to use your machine, how much would it cost us?"

"I could sell it to you outright and some would say that I should, to be sure of getting something out of it, but I think it will succeed and make money for you and thus for me. I want a share of the profits of the cigarettes you sell."

"You trust us to keep accurate records and pay you on time?" Brown asked.

"Another possibility would be paying me a certain amount each month, whether you sell the cigarettes or not," Bonsack suggested.

"So we'd have to pay you for the use of your idea for this machine, as well as building a factory, hiring people to work in it and finding a power supply," Fortune summarized. "Money is hard to come by around here right now."

Bonsack laughed. "You don't have to tell me. I'm short in my pockets myself, but I can invent things, and I know a good idea when I see it, especially when I can make an actual model of my idea. Of course, your machine would have to be many times bigger."

"We're not interested," Brown said. "I don't put much stock in some machine that makes something that people could do for themselves. I've made a comfortable living selling things that people really need."

Fortune put his hand up. "My father-in-law and I need to discuss this. How can we get in touch with you, and how long will you give us to make up their minds?"

Bonsack's face, which had fallen upon hearing Brown's rejection, perked back up at Fortune's words. "Let me know as soon as possible. If you don't buy this, I'm going to try to sell it to James Buchanan Duke. I've heard that he is quick to latch onto any way to make money." He handed Fortune a piece of paper with his name and address written on it.

The three men shook hands. Bonsack thrust the small machine back into his burlap bag and with a bow and a smile at Laura, he took his leave.

As soon as Bonsack was out of earshot, Brown burst out, "Do you trust this fellow? Out of the blue he comes with a little machine that makes one cigarette and wants to sell us his idea. We'd have to put up a fortune, buy a building and find somebody who can make that machine. How long do you think that would take? And in the meantime, what's to keep him from selling the same idea to Duke? Duke already has money and he could put us out of business by making the machine first."

"All the more reason to sign a contract with Mr. Bonsack and get started building our factory."

"I'm not willing to risk it," Brown declared.

"Well, I am. I've saved a little money, though not near enough to build a factory," Fortune admitted. "I'll keep working with you, the same as I have been, and see if I can get a loan from the bank."

Brown looked at his son-in-law thoughtfully. "Well, it might not have to be that way. I could loan you the money and you'd pay me back with interest," Brown said, emphasizing the last two words.

Registering Fortune's surprise, Brown continued, "I can save money by hiring some other young man at the same price I started you out—and not have to split my profits with him. Then when you fail and come back with your tail dragging between your legs, I could take you back as an employee for the sake of Emma and the children. You're a fool to follow such a good-for-nothing idea when you can make a good living running the store as I've done."

Fortune wished that Laura hadn't been sitting there listening to the argument. He bit his tongue to keep from saying anything more before he and Brown agreed on how much money would be loaned.

For the next three days, Brown said not a word to Fortune, and the two men worked side-by-side in dead silence. At the dinner table and again at breakfast, Fortune asked Emma or Laura to pass food to him, or they offered it without being asked.

On the third night Emma curled up next to him and said tentatively, "Fortune, you know Papa has more experience than you do. Don't you think he might be right about not risking everything? If this doesn't work out, what about the children and me?"

Fortune drew back. "So he's talked to you and got you on his side, has he? Aren't you supposed to support your husband ahead of your father? He thinks I'm going to fail, and maybe I will, but I'll never know whether I could have succeeded until I try." He turned over with his back to her pulled the covers close around him and went to sleep.

The next day Brown approached Fortune at breakfast. "So you haven't changed your mind? You still want to give this tomfoolery a try?" He sighed. "I think you're wrong, but I won't go back on my word. I will loan you the money you'll need to make the deal with Mr. Bonsack, and you can see if the bank will finance the factory. At least that way they'll have something to foreclose."

A week later Bonsack arrived and the three men went to the bank and then to a lawyer to draw up the contract. Fortune's stomach churned at the enormity of what he was doing, but his mind told him it was the right thing to do.

Chapter 11

Before Fortune could begin constructing his factory, tragedy struck.

Rain came, heavy and incessant, for five days. The river rose and spread, creeping up the bank toward the pier until it touched the bottom of the pier's planks.

"What are we going to do if the water gets up to the warehouse?" Fortune asked.

"The rain will stop before that happens," Mr. Brown said confidently. "It hasn't risen much in the last two days."

"It's risen enough that I'm worried," Fortune said.

"Where would we move the goods if we did want to move them?" Brown asked with a shrug. "At least in the warehouse they are undercover."

But by the next morning the river had risen alarmingly, completely covering the pier and making its way close to the warehouse itself.

"You may be right," Brown admitted. "I'll hitch up the mule to the wagon and see if we can't move a few things at least up to the house. And Laura can take the cash box and all the records and go on ahead."

Shortly Mr. Brown was standing in the wagon while Fortune dragged bags of flour, corn and other staples out of the warehouse and handed them up to his father-in-law. Brown, a bear of a man, managed to haul each bag up, lay it onto the flat bed of the wagon, and pull a tarp over it so the contents would not get wet.

The two had established a rhythm of work when suddenly a chunk of earth beneath a wheel of the wagon broke free and washed downstream. The wagon wheel dropped and the mule lurched forward, throwing Mr. Brown off the side of the wagon and into the swirling current just as a mound of debris crashed toward him.

Without stopping to think, Fortune dove into the moving stream, and as the water closed over him, he realized he'd made a terrible mistake. His father-in-law was out of sight. Fortune came up downstream choking and spitting the muddy water, trying to clear it from his eyes. Brown was nowhere to be seen, and Fortune himself was in danger of being swept away for good.

He had been washed toward a mound of debris that had gotten caught in a bend in the water, and managed to reach up and grab a limb before the debris broke up and swirled on downstream. He paused a moment to catch his breath, then as he saw another mass of water hurtling toward him, he swam ashore and crawled up onto what he thought might be solid ground beneath him. Still holding on to the branch, he pulled up again, and felt solid pavement beneath his feet. With his last energy he managed to move up to what had been a street, turned sideways and clutched the remains of a building.

Looking back upstream, he saw the warehouse break in collapse, and fall into the swirling water. Had he not managed to pull himself ashore, he would have been struck by the boards that swept past him.

The mule had instinctively moved away from the water, carrying the few bags that had been saved from the flood. All else was beyond retrieval sunk into the river and soon to be covered by mud.

Fortune saw that the mule had managed to pull the wagon forwards a few yards and was standing patiently in the rain. Fortune managed to pull himself up onto the wagon bed and drive slowly to the house.

Emma opened the front door in alarm. "What happened to you?" She asked. "And where's Papa?"

"He's gone," Fortune moaned. "Everything's gone. All we've got is what's on this wagon and in the house." He slid groggily off the wagon and fell at her feet. Laura ran out and took hold of the reins of the mule, leading it around to the carriage house to get the wagon out of the rain before she unhitched the mule and stabled it along with the horse.

Fortune pulled himself to his feet and followed his wife inside. He slumped into a straight-backed wooden chair, not wanting to ruin the upholstered furniture with his soaking muddy clothing.

Emma stood before him. "Now tell me what happened."

"Your father was standing on the wagon when the river bank underneath the back wheel washed away, and he fell off and right into the water. I jumped in after him but I never saw him again. By the time I came to the surface he was out of sight and I was in danger of drowning myself. I couldn't save him, Emma." He sighed. "I need to get off these clothes and take a bath."

Emma watched silently as he made his way up the stairs. When he came back down, clean and dressed, she threw her arms around him. Leaning against his chest, she sobbed, "What are we going to do? "

Fortune didn't answer. He patted her shoulder awkwardly, but he had no experience in dealing with crying women. His mother had been stoic and calm at his father's funeral.

No one ate much supper, and Laura put away the food and got the children to bed. Fortune slid in beside Emma, but she moved away from him. He knew she was grieving, but he'd have liked to hear her at least say that she was glad he had survived.

He awoke to a strange sound. Silence. The rain had stopped. Sunlight streamed in through the open screened window, and when he went to look out, the humidity seemed to weight him down. He was grateful that the rain had ended, but it didn't help his situation or his family's at all. In fact, there would still be at least two more days when streams from the west would dump their watery burden into the river, and it would continue to rise. Then it would slowly recede, carrying its debris of items, animals, and people down-river and out to sea.

The entire city would suffer from the devastation, not just the few merchants and warehousemen in the boat traffic along the river. It wasn't as bad, of course, as the devastation when Union troops burned Richmond, but in some ways it was worse. A fire destroys cleanly, leaving ashes and bricks. A flood leaves muck and slime, and the overwhelming stench of rot and drowned bodies.

But whatever had happened, life must go on. He was now the head of the family, responsible for Emma, the children and Laura, as well as his mother and younger sister back home on the farm. It was a frightening responsibility and yet it eventually came to every man, or at least every man who accepted his due.

At breakfast Emma asked once more, "What are we going to do, Fortune?"

"We'll send word downriver for people to be on the lookout for your father . . . for his body. In the meantime, I plan to start building my cigarette factory."

Emma looked at him in shock. "How can you think of starting a new business when my father has just died not twenty-four hours ago?" She burst into tears again.

"What would you have me do? Shall I sit around here waiting to see if your father might be alive and terribly wounded? Or if he's dead, how long should we wait to find out if anyone locates his body? He may never turn up, you know. Floods bring tons of dirt downstream, and he may already be buried under a pile of it."

She had winced at his descriptions of her father's body. "You're being cruel! You can go get a job, that's what. You've done it before, you can do it again."

"I don't want to get a job," Fortune said. "I've had a job working for your father for more than four years, and what has it gotten me? I certainly can't work for him anymore, can I? I want to build a factory and be my own boss and get rich."

"And you think this machine will make you rich?" She scoffed, wiping her eyes with the back of her hand.

"Well, I plan to get a job," Laura said. "I can keep records almost as good as you can, Fortune, and some business will surely want to hire me. I can be the bookkeeper or the receptionist, and meanwhile I'm going to study how to use a typewriter and take shorthand, so I can move up. I'd already thought about it before this flood happened."

Fortune stared at his sister. She would never go back to the farm, never be dependent on a man.

"You are being cruel!" Emma charged again, ignoring Laura's statement.

"No, I'm being realistic," Fortune returned. "I'm the head of the household now, and I intend to be responsible for you and the children, and the best way I know is to get busy establishing a business just as your father once did long ago so that I'll have the money to take care of the children and you."

"And what do you expect me to do? Give you the money my father left in the bank account? He left you half the business and half the house."

"Well, we all know that half the business is half of nothing," Fortune said. "What I want you to do is to let me have access to the bank account and let me mortgage the house if I have to."

"And what becomes of me and the children if your business fails? You've thrown away the money he loaned you, giving it to that man with the invention you think is going to make you rich.

"Then I'd have to find something else to do," Fortune admitted. "And if you keep the money to spend on yourself and the children, what do you do when it runs out?"

She didn't answer, but turned away. Fortune went to see to the horse and mule, and to unload the few bags of produce that he and his late father-in-law had rescued from the flood. What was he to do with it now? There was no store to sell it in, and who would buy it? It would grow old and moldy in no time. The corn could be fed to the animals, but what of the flour?

What was he to do without financial backing? Somehow he had to persuade Emma to let him have the money.

Chapter 12

The next morning at breakfast Emma was still not speaking to Fortune. At one point she leapt up from the table and after a few minutes came back, her face red and swollen. The children clung to the mother, uncertain in the strange atmosphere.

Then Eve ran around the table and deliberately bumped into her brother. He picked himself up and started running after her, but stopped when he heard his mother's voice.

"Stop it!" Emma screamed. "Behave yourselves. Don't you know your grandfather has died and left us?"

"Of course they don't know. They're just toddlers," Fortune said sharply.

"Then you tell them. You make them behave," Emma said and left the table again.

Fortune started to go after her, but Laura put her hand on his arm pressed him back down. "Give her some time. She's frightened."

"Frightened of me?"

"No. Frightened of the situation. She's afraid that she'll be left with nothing. She's been used to having her father take care of her, and she never had to worry about money or paying bills. There was always food, and I'm sure her father never troubled her with business decisions. It's all too much for her right now, especially with another baby on the way."

"What? She didn't say anything about it to me."

"She hasn't specifically told me, either. I just know the signs. I could be wrong, of course. She's got a lot on her mind and the mind can do strange things to the body."

"It takes a woman to understand another woman, I suppose," Fortune admitted. "What should I do?"

"First of all, tell her you're sorry about her father. I assume you are, but you've been all business and saying harsh things. Tell her you love her and that together you to will be able to take care of everything. I'm sure she loves you. Tell her you need her love and support. Everybody needs to be needed, Fortune."

Laura cleared away the breakfast things, changed and left to catch the streetcar downtown. Fortune walked her to the door. "Wish me luck in finding a job," she said brightly. Then she added softly to Fortune, "And look after the children. They need love and support for their very confused minds. They miss their grandfather. Tell them the truth even though they are only small children. Don't tell them that he's asleep, or they may fear going to sleep themselves."

Fortune walked back to the breakfast table and took a child on each knee. He tried to explain that sometimes bad things happened and we couldn't change them. He saw by the puzzled looks on their faces that they didn't understand death yet, but he knew that eventually they would.

He took the children upstairs and changed them from their night clothes into outdoor garments. Uncertain what else to do, he was about to take them out for ride in the carriage, when Emma appeared behind him. "I'll take over now. You don't know what to do with children, and you probably want to get about your business anyway."

"Emma, I haven't said it, but I'm sorry about your father. He was almost like a father to me too, giving me a job accepting me as your husband, and making me part of the business." He laughed shakily. "Right now there's no business to share, but together I think you and I will succeed, if we help each other and don't fight about it."

Emma managed a small smile, but she made no mention of the finances.

Fortune walked down to the waterfront where two upright posts were all that remained of the dock. The humid air and the stink of mud and filth struck him. He now owned half of this godforsaken piece of land, but of what use was it to him? Would any bank loan him money using this land as security? Emma, he was sure, would have no problem signing over her rights to this land which might after all be a liability instead of an asset. There would be taxes to pay, and he'd have to hire someone to help clear off the accumulation of debris.

His shoulders sagged at the thought. Maybe Laura was the smart one in the family, deciding to get a job and work her way up. But he had already done that, working himself up to own half the business only to have it snatched away by nature. Could he bear to start over as a nobody again?

The next day he made himself dress in his best and take the streetcar downtown when Laura went on her job search. With his contracts in hand, he approached the bank where his savings were deposited, the bank where Mr. Brown had transferred enough money to pay off Bonsack. He was refused a loan, and left determined that he would get the money somehow and succeed, then have no further business with that bank ever.

He went next to the lawyer who had drawn up the contract for him and Mr. Brown with Bonsack. The lawyer waved him to a seat, looked over the papers Fortune had brought, and drew out another from his own file. "You have a copy of this, don't you? Or perhaps your wife has it."

Fortune bit his tongue and said, "She is deep in grief, and I hesitated to ask her to search for her father's will, but I do know the general outlines off it."

"Good, then you know that Mr. Brown was very generous to you, giving you credit for the increase in his business. When he came in to make changes to the will after you and Emma were married, he said as much to me. He made you an equal heir with Emma as you no doubt know. Therefore, you're entitled to half of everything—half the house, half the business and half the money in his savings account. I presume you are here to get on letter from me to show your bank so that you can access the funds which are in his name."

"Yes, of course," Fortune said, hoping he did a passable job of hiding his astonishment at this good luck. With this unexpected windfall, he could surely get a loan from a bank.

Papers in hand, he went to Farmers and Merchants Bank, though he was neither at the moment, introduced himself and asked to see the manager. "I plan to transfer both my account and that of my late father-in-law to your bank on condition that I get a large loan to build a factory. I have the rights to the invention that's going to make my factory productive and profitable." He spread out the Bonsack contract. "Can we talk business?"

"Indeed we can. It's good to see a businessman who wants to rebuild after the devastating flood. It shows faith in our city. I take it you're not planning to rebuild the warehouse?"

"No, I want to start something different, a factory that produces cigarettes."

The bank manager raised his eyebrows. "But people can roll their own cigarettes. Why do they need a machine to do it?"

"This machine will produce a firm tightly packed cigarette, which is much better than the kind anyone can produce by rolling his own. He'll only have to carry one pack, not paper and a bag of tobacco. It's less messy, and it will be something of a novelty. Every smoker will want to try one to see what the difference is, and after that they'll be hooked."

The banker laughed. "You're a good salesman, Mr. Barranger, I'll say that for you. Do you think you can sell your cigarettes as well as your selling the idea to me?"

"I do. My late father-in-law hired me out of the blue and often left me in charge of the business. I was able to sell a lot more to each customer then they came in expecting to buy."

"And why are you planning to build here? I think with a newfangled idea for a factory you'd be moving north, say to New England."

"Virginia has the tobacco and a lot of people without jobs who will be willing to work for low wages. The state has coal to fuel my factory as well as waterpower, and railroads to take my products north and west, especially to cities, which I see as my best market."

"You've convinced me that you know what you're talking about, but what is your plan in case your factory doesn't succeed? Say what about if your machinery breaks down, all people decide not to pay more instead of rolling their own cigarettes? What if you can't repay this loan you want?" The banker's gaze intensified with this last question.

"I'm young and healthy, I'm a hard worker, and I'm good with figures. I might go to work for your bank, or some other manufacturing company, as their bookkeeper. One way or another, I plan to make money."

"And I'm willing to help you, Mr. Barranger. Now let's talk terms. It's probably not necessary, but just to be legal, I'd like to have your wife sign the papers as well."

Fortune wasn't sure how he'd get Emma to sign, but he'd worry about that later. For the time being he could at least transfer his own savings account and half the proceeds of what Mr. Brown had left.

He walked back to his former bank, as he preferred to think of it, to begin the transfer of funds. The banker there protested that it would take some days to get the exact amount in the account and issue a bank draft or a check so that Fortune could redeposit it. "And why are you doing this, Mr. Barranger? We are paying you the standard rate of interest."

"You treated me as if I don't matter. I plan to become very rich, and you have missed your opportunity to handle my funds from now on. As soon as I can get my wife's signature, I'll transfer the remainder of Mr. Brown's account, which is hers."

On the way home he tried to think of various ways he might persuade Emma to transfer the funds, but even if she refused, he had enough backing now to get started on building his cigarette factory.

Chapter 13

It took Laura two days of trudging from business to business before she came home to announce triumphantly, "I have a job. I start two days from now. Emma, as soon as I get my first paycheck, I'll pay you something for room and board, whatever you think is fair." To Fortune she said, "I'll start sending what I can to Mama. I know you won't have anything coming in for a while."

Emma turned from Laura and stared accusingly at Fortune, her expression saying clearly that he too should have gone out to get a job.

"I may have to get a job to, as well as working on the factory," he said.

"So, you're going ahead with that," Emma said.

Fortune nodded. "I'm only using what the lawyer said is legally mine. I'd like you to sign the papers so I can transfer the rest of your father's funds to the Farmers & Merchants Bank, but if you don't want to, I'll manage anyway. I found a banker who trusts me. If I really get desperate for money, I can mortgage my half of the house. And I too will pay you something for room and board, Emma, or pay my half of the expenses."

"Don't be absurd! How can you own half a house?"

"Because your father left everything to us jointly. If you like you can decide which half of the house is mine and which is yours."

"You're being absurd again. You're my husband and we have to live together the best we can for the children's sake, never mind whether I agree with you about the business or not."

Laura slipped away unnoticed as they continued quarreling.

"And do you love me at least a bit?" he asked. "Was what you said at the marriage ceremony all a lie?"

"Of course I love you."

"And I love you, Emma, you and our three children."

"How did you know about the baby?"

"Laura told me."

"But I didn't tell her."

"Laura is observant. It's true, isn't it?"

She nodded. "This is all too much, Fortune. My father dying, the business gone, a baby on the way, and now you're starting something that may fail."

"And it may succeed beyond your wildest dreams. Have faith in me, Emma."

Over the next few weeks, Fortune was so busy with developing the factory that he scarcely noticed Emma's increasing size. He'd come in late from work, tired out, and in no mood to talk. What was there to talk about anyway? She showed no interest in how the factory was coming along, and he was all consumed with that and nothing more.

One evening when he came home, she met him at the door and handed him the bank book. "We can't go on like this, Fortune," she said. "You're my husband and the father of my children, and my whole future lies in your hands. I hope you won't need to use this money, but if you do, here it is."

Fortune made a down payment on a plot of land out near the railroad track, and placed orders for the machinery that Bonsack said would be needed. The brick building that would house the factory went up. Wood would have been cheaper, but he was determined that if Richmond had another devastating fire, his factory would not be the cause of it nor suffer major damage.

Fortune paid little heed to Laura either, or to his mother, sister and brothers back home. Laura arrived on the horse-drawn streetcar that dropped her off two blocks away from the house, and walked the remainder of the distance. On Sundays when the whole family went to church, he did notice that she had bought new clothing, and drew admiring looks from more than one man. She'd soon be married and having babies of her own, Fortune thought.

When all the machinery was in place at the factory and the roof was on the building, Bonsack arrived to observe that his invention did indeed work on a larger scale. "I haven't arranged for electrical or coal for energy yet," Fortune said. "For the time being, it will have to be operated manually." He stripped off his coat and hung it up, rolled up his sleeves, and bent to the task. Bonsack lent a hand, and between them they got the great machine moving, producing cigarettes.

By the end of the first day, Bonsack's theory had been proved right as tarp spread on the floor beneath the machine caught the ever-expanding heap of freshly rolled cigarettes, hundreds and thousands of them.

"Enough!" Fortune announced, straightening from his exertion. "it works, no question."

"Now what do you plan to do with all the cigarettes?" Bonsack asked.

"The state fair will be opening soon, and I plan to demonstrate the cigarettes then, giving everybody who comes by a free one and selling the rest at a penny a piece."

Prior to the state fair opening, Fortune had alerted the newspapers of his demonstration. Always eager for something new, reporters showed up and set up their cameras on stands, waiting to take pictures of someone smoking one of the newly rolled cigarettes.

Laura stood beside the hand-lettered poster offering free cigarettes, and a crowd soon gathered. Fortune was sure that Laura's beauty attracted the crowd almost as much as the idea of having something for free. She was soon passing out free cigarettes and receiving smiles and cheers in return. A reporter stood, pencil poised over his notepad, asking questions about the machine.

Fortune was happy enough to give Bonsack the credit for the invention, but he was careful not to describe the machine in great detail, so that no other manufacturer could make his own machine from the information.

The photographer for the newspaper poked his head under his camera canopy to photograph a group of men standing near the machine smoking their cigarettes. Before he could take the photo, one of the customers said, "These cigarettes are nice enough for ladies to smoke." He gestured toward Laura. "Why don't we have this pretty young lady smoke one?"

"No, it's unseemly for ladies," Fortune objected.

"Oh, I don't mind," Laura said, reaching for one of the cigarettes. Fortune was sure that Laura's picture would be the one featured in the newspaper the next day.

He noted carefully who got free cigarettes, and when some smokers came back for a second free one, he said, "the second one will cost you," and accepted the money they grudgingly passed in.

By the end of the day he had sold out all the cigarettes he brought to the fair. As he had guessed, Laura's picture was on the in the newspaper the following day, and he worked all night to produce enough cigarettes to meet the demand the second day. By the end of the week, he was totally exhausted, but he had proved that people would pay for a neatly rolled cigarette instead of having to roll their own. Several people had suggested that he might put the cigarettes in small boxes and sell enough to each customer to keep them smoking for a good while, and he noted the idea. He'd act on the idea, as soon as he was able.

He gave Emma part of the profits, and knew that she would squirrel the money away in the bank as a guarantee for the future. He didn't care. He had proved to her that his idea would work. He used the profits from the fair to make a down payment on coal-fired power so that his factory could work without a human turning the machinery.

He went every day to his factory, supervising the two people that he'd hired to work, one to strip the stems out of tobacco and chop it up, and the second to pour it in the proper time into the machine and see that the paper and glue were replenished.

As soon as he was sure the cigarette rolling machine was working as he hoped, he knew had to find someone to buy all those thousands of cigarettes. That meant a trip to New York, where there were tobacco shops as well as distributors who could take thousands at the time and sell them to small stores all over America.

He had shown Mr. Brown and everyone else that he could sell things, but the end came to the store looking for something particular. Now things were reversed he would have to go and persuade customers that they wanted ready-made cigarettes.

He decided he needed a new suit, though Emma would think this was an unnecessary cost. She didn't need to know about it; hadn't she said that she had far too much on her mind, especially with the new baby?

The night before he left for New York, he came home early to learn that Maggie had sent for the doctor urgently regarding a problem with Emma's pregnancy, so Fortune was with Emma when the doctor arrived. Dr. Tyler sent Fortune out. "Go look after your children and send Maggie in. She is more help to me now than an anxious father."

Fortune took the children outside, hardly knowing what to do with them. He knew it was too soon for the baby's birth, so he was not surprised when the doctor called him back into the room and told him that Emma had lost the baby.

He took Emma's hand and said he was sorry about the baby and sorry that he would be leaving the next day.

She looked at him in incredulity. "I need you right now. Please stay with me," she begged.

"Maggie can do more for you than I can, and I can't change all my plans for the New York trip," Fortune said, then stood and left the room.

Chapter 14

As Fortune walked along the New York sidewalks, he paused from time to time to admire the items for sale inside the shops, and occasionally to admire himself in the store windows' reflections. The new suit fit him well, and he was tall enough and still slender enough to carry it off. His well-trimmed beard and mustache made him look older and gave him an air of distinction, he thought, which had been his reason for letting them grow. He saw so many New York men wearing hats that he felt out of place, and stepped into a haberdashery to look at hats.

The Homburg he liked was expensive, costing almost as much as his train ticket, but it added just the right touch to his clothing. He turned this way and that before the store mirror, admiring the effect.

"Perhaps a pair of gray kid gloves to finish off monsieur's costume," the salesclerk suggested.

Fortune was tempted. But the gloves cost as much as his first train ride to Richmond. Still, he wanted to look prosperous, and the black Homburg and gray kid gloves made him look just as he wished. Things in New York were expensive, more than he had expected. Or, he thought, perhaps it was just that people in Virginia were so poor that prices had to stay low. He'd already economized by choosing a low-priced hotel, and he decided he'd eat food from street push carts, instead of dining at the fine hotels.

He placed a decorative pack of cigarettes in each front pocket of his suit, and in his inner pocket he had a folded sample contract and the newspaper clipping from the state fair showing Laura smoking one of the cigarettes.

As he reached what he hoped would be his first customer he checked the name on the glass front door and went in and asked for Mr. Berman.

"Do you have an appointment, Sir?" The receptionist asked.

Fortune drew a packet of the cigarettes from his pocket and laid it on her desk. "No, but I would like to give him this. I think he might like to talk to me about it."

He stood waiting while she disappeared into the inner office and came back. "Have a seat, sir. I think Mr. Berman may want to see you."

Fortune had removed his hat and gloves as he entered, and now sat quietly with the Homburg on the chair beside him, his gloves lying atop it. He had a feeling the receptionist had described him to Mr. Berman. That and the packet of cigarettes would win him over — or not.

Mr. Berman came out carrying the opened packet of cigarettes in one hand and a cigarette in the other. "Where did you get these, Mr. . . . ?"

"Fortune Barranger. I manufactured them, and I think you might like to stock them."

"Indeed, I would. These are so much easier to use and give a much better appearance than shaking bits of tobacco into a bit of paper. Come in and let's talk."

The two men talked terms: how much per hundred cigarettes, how soon they could be delivered, and whether they would be in the small decorative packs. Within an hour Fortune had a contract good for six months. If the cigarettes still sold as well as Mr. Berman expected, he indicated he would be renewing the contract and perhaps doubling the amount.

When Fortune rose to go, he extended his hand. Mr. Binder asked, "how about lunch?"

Fortune drew out the watch that had been Horace Brown's, which he found by searching through the bureau dresser. "Thank you, but I have other customers to see."

"Are you planning to sell to my competitors?" Binder asked

Fortune smiled. "I certainly hope to."

"Before you return to Richmond, stop back by here and tell me how many they've ordered, will you?" Binder asked. "Whatever the amount, I'll double it. These cigarettes are going to be a hit, and I want to get in at the beginning. Once a man lights one of these, he'll never want to go back to rolling his own again."

As Fortune left, he thought, that's how you make a deal.

He took the night train back to save an extra night's hotel bill. At the station, he saw a man selling bananas, and bought a dozen, using the last money he had. The children had never seen one, and it would be a nice gift for them and for the rest of the family. As the train began moving southward, he peeled and ate one himself. That would be his supper.

Back home, Fortune let himself in to the front door quietly hoping not to disturb the family. Instead, he found them all seated around the kitchen table, all but Emma.

He laid the bunch of bananas on the worktable. "Peeled two of these and cut them in pieces so everyone can try them. There's something new, and I think you'll all like them."

He went and washed up, carefully hanging up his suit jacket. He knew his eyes were bloodshot from lack of sleep on the train, and splashed water in them. When he got back to the kitchen, Laura and the children were munching on bananas and reaching for more pieces. "Save some for Emma," he said to his sister. "How is she?"

Laura put down her napkin and rose to go. "We'll talk later. Let me get you some breakfast."

Chapter 15

"You're doing what?" Emma demanded, when Fortune confided in her his plans to invest in an electric streetcar system for the city. "Isn't your cigarette factory enough? It's made a fortune for you and for Mr. Bonsack."

"I told you, Emma, that I'm going to be very wealthy, and you'll be right with me, having someone to do the housework for you, living in a beautiful house, and riding around in luxury."

But before he could begin on his latest project, a letter came from his mother with a new problem. "Miss Charlotte and her husband want me to move out. They said they got big plans for this little piece of land that our house stands on. I know it's not really our house, but it's where I've spent my whole marriage and even after your father died. I'm not so sure they want to build something new, or just to get some money."

"We'll see," Fortune muttered to himself and told Emma it was time they took the children to meet his mother and the rest of the family.

She was pregnant again, and not feeling well, but she agreed to go, and went downtown to Parson's department store to buy clothing for the children and herself.

They took the train, and Fortune's brother Jamie met them at the station.

At the house, Fortune hugged his mother and sister, and introduced Emma and the children. "I was hoping Laura could come along too," his mother said. "Is she behaving herself down there?"

"Of course," Fortune responded. "You've raised her well. She wrote you about getting a job in an office, didn't she?"

His mother nodded. "I hope she'll be getting married sometime soon. Working in an office may be very well, when it comes down to it, a woman's place is at home having a family." "My goodness, Emma, you and Fortune are going right along having a family of your own. You be catching up with me before long."

Emma blushed, and shook her head slightly. "I don't know how many we can handle."

For the visit, Fortune's mother moved into the back bedroom with her daughter Rachel, so Fortune and Emma and the children could have the big front bedroom.

The next morning, Fortune set off to see the Colonel, to get to the bottom of this matter of the rental house.

"The mansion looked better than Fortune remembered it, but the Col. did not. He rose shakily from his desk and extended his hand to Fortune "I've been hearing good things about you, young man," he said, waving Fortune to a seat and sitting back down himself. "We hear, that you with that newfangled machine have made yourself rich. That true? "

Fortune nodded, "I've done very well, sir. And I came to see what can be done about the house my mother is living in."

"You interested in buying the house and a couple of acres?" The Col. asked.

"Yes, I am. How much do you want for it?"

The Col. laughed. "You always were quick to make up your mind. The plantation is still in my name, at least for the time being, but that no good son-in-law of mine has borrowed against it until I don't know how much longer I'll can live here myself." He named the figure, and Fortune wrote out a check and passed it across the desk.

The Col. looked at it and nodded. "That should keep the wolf away from the door for a bit longer. I'll get down to the courthouse as soon as I can and draw up the deed for your mother." Fortune couldn't help wondering why money was short. Hadn't Charlotte married a rich man?

Fortune rose and shook the older man's hand. "My mother will be pleased not having to move," he said. He started for the door, and turned back to ask, "How is Charlotte?"

"She and the boy are upstairs. They come down late, and don't spend much time here anyway. Maybe you'll get to see her later in the day. I miss the talks we used to have, Fortune," he admitted.

Fortune's mother offered to have the children stay with her and Rachel so Fortune and Emma could take a walk around and he could show her the church and the mansion house. As they stood on a hill overlooking the mansion, Fortune said, "That's the house we're going to live in someday."

"Way out here away from everything?" Emma protested.

"By the time I buy the place, people will be coming here to see us."

"They'll be coming to see you, not me. And that house looks very run down."

"It is now, because the family lost all its money in the war, and the Col. never had the slightest idea how to make back a fortune. I do, and when I buy the place, I'll fix it up so it will be of showplace."

To his surprise, Fortune saw Charlotte come out of the house, leading a small boy who pulled back, obviously not wanting to take a walk with his mother. She was looking down at him speaking and hadn't noticed Fortune and Emma until the boy looked up and pointed. She half turned away from them, as if she would go back into the house, but this time it was the boy who dragged her along. She was wearing a long tan wool coat trimmed in fur at the wrist and collar, and she had a tan and Brown print shawl thrown about her hair, arranged so that it half shielded her face.

As Fortune introduced the two women, they each studied the other without smiling. Charlotte said, "And this is my son Julian." Emma responded, "We have two, Simon and Eve."

For a brief moment Charlotte's shawl slipped, and Fortune noted that she had a large bruise on her cheek and the flesh around her head had turned from bluish to a yellowish green, a sign of an earlier bruise. She quickly pulled the shawl back into place and said, "Julian and I must be on our way. We are taking a quick walk out to get some fresh air. Papa keeps the fireplace going all the time, and Julian has breathing difficulties with so much smoke. It's nice to have met you, Mrs. Barranger, and to have seen you again, Fortune."

As they watched the pair walk away, Emma said, "she's the one you wanted, isn't she?"

"Yes, I admit it, but not anymore," he said. "And her husband obviously doesn't want her, or at least doesn't appreciate her. I suspect he's been beating her."

Chapter 16

As Fortune began planning for the streetcar system, he soon realized that he was already buying coal-fired electric power to run his cigarette rolling factory, and now would be buying even more. Perhaps it was time to build his own coal-fired generating plant.

Emma wasn't interested in discussing it. Every time he mentioned any future plans, she objected. "Why do you think people want an electric streetcar? Won't they worry about being electrocuted? And what's wrong with horses?"

"One thing at a time, dear. First the horses. The city is growing, and streets will have to be paved farther out, and more horses bought. They have to be fed, and cleaned up after, and the same horses can't work all day long. They have to have a break, so we have to would have to have many pairs of horses. And horses can only pull a limited amount of weight and at a low speed. What I envision is a comfortable close carriage that runs on rails, with the way to close it in when there's rain or snow. At busy times, we could attach a second car to the first. As to electrocution, the wires are overhead, not down where people can touch them. And of course, they will be grounded."

"That all sounds like a lot of money, Fortune. We just got out of debt for the factory and buying the land for your mother's house."

"We're not starving, are we? I promised you I'd take care of you, and I mean to take care of my mother and my sisters as well. Rolled cigarettes have really caught on, and the business will support the building of the trolley system until it starts producing money as well." They were seated at the kitchen table where he continued to drink coffee. Laura had already left for work, riding the smelly horse-drawn trolley. Fortune reached over and touched his wife's belly. "How are you feeling, dear?"

"I'm not sure. Ever since the first weeks of my pregnancy, I can't stand to drink coffee, and some foods make me sick too. This pregnancy isn't going well. I feel so tired that I can barely take care of the children."

"I'm going out to the coalfields to see how much it would take to run my own electrical plant. Shall I arrange for Maggie to come in every day? Will she do or is she getting too old?"

"I'll miss you while you're gone out to the coalfields, but then . . ." she sighed, "I see little enough of you even when you're here and you hardly know our children. You're always busy, either at the factory checking on things, or planning something new."

Fortune had no response to that, but he was careful to hug each of the children as well as Emma the next morning before he left.

Fortune walked the short distance to the trolley that would take him to the railway station. He felt impatient at the slow clip-clop pace of the horses as they made their way along the cobbled streets. Soon there would be iron rails embedded in the streets, and streetcars moving twice this fast to take people downtown to work or out to the edges of town when workday was done.

As he rode the train westward the grade grew steeper, and soon he was passing home and caught a glimpse of the white columns of Oak Hill. Someday he was going to buy it, but not yet. When the time came, he wanted to fix it up the way it deserved, perhaps adding on wings and modern facilities so that it would be of showplace of the mountains. When it passed from view, he returned to the notebook he was jotting figures in.

At the mine, Fortune introduced himself to the owner, but declined the opportunity to go down into the mine itself. "Digging out the coal is your business," he said. "Buying it and putting it to work is my business. I'm going to need lots of coal to run at power plants that will run my factory as well as the streetcar system I plan for Richmond."

The owner smiled. "I'm ready and willing to do business with the man who comes to buy my coal. It's hard times out here. How much do you think you'll need?"

"Can we sit down somewhere so I can show you my figures?" Fortune asked.

"Sure thing, let's walk down to the house. the wife can find something for us to eat as well as a cup of coffee. Or would you rather have a swig of moonshine? Many a day I make more money off that than I do off coal."

Fortune shook his head. "I don't drink the hard stuff, especially when I'm trying to do business. I need to keep a clear head."

At the mine owner's kitchen table, Fortune said, "For what I'm paying somebody else to produce electric power with your coal, I figure in a few years a new coal-fired power plant would pay for itself, and then I'd be able to sell power myself. In the meantime, I need more to run an electric trolley that I have in mind."

"For that much coal, you might be taking half of our output."

"You say you're not making money off your coal as it stands now, but that could be because you're selling it only in Virginia. Business is booming everywhere, even in the South. After all I'm here asking to buy your coal. There's a market for it in the North and in other countries."

The owner shook his head. "I'm just a simple countryman who happen to be lucky enough that his father bought some land a generation ago that had coal underneath it. I have half a mind to sell out and move to town and get an ordinary job, and I'm sure the wife would like that. The big mines are pushing us little ones out, with their machinery and markets."

"If you're serious about that, what do you want for it?" Fortune asked.

The man laughed. "Some days I would give it to you for nothing and just walk away and get rid of the responsibility, but seeing as you have money and have a use for coal, I'll make you a good deal. You want to buy half the mine or the whole thing?"

"The whole thing, if you'll stay and manage it for me, on a salary."

"That's the kind of deal I like. I know the business, so I can manage it for you, and have enough money to build a nice house for the wife. I've been promising it to her for years. Now, seeing as you're buying the coal mine, I think you really ought to go down in it and take a look at what you've just bought."

Reluctantly, Fortune followed the owner to the shaft that led down into the darkness. As they stepped into the cage, it creaked alarmingly. Fortune glanced up at the frayed rope and said a silent prayer that he'd make it down and back safely. The basket descended slowly, brushing against the sides of the shaft think. Down, down, until it stopped with the bump Fortune hadn't realized that he closed his eyes until he opened them and saw that there were faint points of light here and there around him. He glanced up and far above saw a tiny rectangle of sky. He felt claustrophobia overcome him at the darkness all around. How could people live and work like this day after day? And yet they did, producing the tons of glistening black fuel that he had just bought.

"How do the miners light the shaft when they go out of sight of the cage?" He asked.

"Little candles," the owner said.

"Isn't that dangerous?" Fortune asked, laying his hand against the seam of coal for stability.

"I guess it is, but they have to have light of some kind. They make sure they douse the lights at the end of each shift, so there won't be any chance of an explosion during the change of workers."

"I've seen enough," Fortune said, feeling sweat begin to bud on his forehead. "Can we go back up?"

The owner nodded, although Fortune didn't see the gesture in the darkness. A basket of coal was making its way up one side of the shaft, blocking out what little light filtered its way down. A worker at the top of the shaft sent the cage back down, and Fortune gratefully stepped in beside the man who was now the manager of this mine.

As they stepped out of the cage at the top, Fortune pointed up to the frayed rope. "Replace that rope right away."

"It should last another week or so."

"There doesn't seem to be anything we can do to have light in the mine without a certain amount of danger, but we can by God have a safe rope to pull the workers up in case there is a problem. As the new owner, I'm commanding you to replace ropes whenever they show signs of fraying."

"If you say so."

"I'll see that money is sent to you as soon as I get back to Richmond," Fortune said, "And be warned that I may show up here at any time just to see how things are going."

Chapter 17

As the train rumbled its way down the mountain and into the hills, Fortune had time to reflect on what he had just done. Had he acted the fool, buying a coal mine when he didn't know the first thing about how one was operated? Financially, he thought it would be the power plant he needed, plus he could find other markets. Businesses were booming all over America, and railroads and steamships used vast quantities of coal. It could be very profitable indeed.

Very profitable, he thought, but what if something happened? What if there was an explosion that closed the mine? He decided that as soon as he could he would get some better equipment in that mine, something sturdier to transport coal and workers then that creaky little cage.

Either way, it was done, and he was sure if the mine produced more coal than his power plant used, he could find a market for more coal since businesses were booming and factories were going up, especially in the North. But what would Emma say? He'd have to explain once more why he wasn't building a mansion in Richmond.

The hillsides were sprinkled with the pink and white of redbuds and dogwoods, and the first tiny green leaves were emerging on the maples and other trees. On the way to the coal mine, Fortune had been too occupied with thoughts of business to notice, but now it all reminded him of being young and enjoying the coming of springtime.

On impulse, he pulled the cord and the train halted at the station nearest Oak Hill. He got down from the car and started walking toward his mother's cabin. As the train left, he saw there were buggies and carriages and wagons on the other side of the tracks.

Someone called his name, and he recognized it as Charlotte. "Wait, Fortune! I'll give you a ride."

He turned and waved. She was riding in the carriage, which was piled up with packages. His brother Pete was the driver.

His mother hadn't mentioned that Pete was working for the Stannards, but then he hadn't told her much about his own work. Emma wrote her regularly about the children and Laura wrote occasionally as well.

"Hiya, Fortune," Pete greeted him. "Ma didn't say nothing about you coming for a visit, especially not that you'd be all dressed up."

"Hi, Pete. Good to see you too. I hadn't planned this trip, I was just out this way on business."

"Out here on business," Pete mimicked. "That sounds highfalutin."

"Get in, Fortune," Charlotte said. "We haven't had a talk in a long time."

After he was settled in the carriage, she asked, "So what is this business you're on out here?"

"I went to buy some coal, and I bought the coal mine," he said, and they laughed together. "So how did you happen to be at the station, and where is your son? Julian, is it?" He wondered why he could remember her son's name when he sometimes had trouble with his own children's names.

"I had ordered some things from Sears Roebuck, and had to pick them up at the station. Yes, my son is Julian, and he's in New York for the for the time being. His father has him in a special school. He doesn't think the local schools are good enough for him. They will come down here at Easter, and I'll go back with them."

"I wanted to be here right now," she said, looking around at the scenery. "I always loved the early spring. It seems hopes are high highest then, with the whole year to look forward to. Later on, it gets hot and then bad things begin to happen on the farm." She touched his hand. "So, tell me all about your business. You must be doing very well to be buying a coal mine. And why do you want one?"

"My cigarette factory uses a lot of coal and I've agreed to go in with some other investors in putting in an electric powered trolley in the city. Using so much electricity, I decided to build my own power plant, and that of course needs coal. The owner of the mine gave me a good deal." He noticed that she had not asked about his family, but he added anyway, "Emma and the children are doing fine, and Laura has a job in an office and is going to school at night to improve her skills and get a better job."

She made no response to that, and they rode this as they rode silently, he looked from side to side, enjoying the view off the springtime flowering and breathing in the fresh mountain air.

When he disembarked the carriage at his mother's home, Charlotte smiled and said, "Perhaps we'll be seeing each other again while you're here."

"Perhaps we will," Fortune said. "Thanks for the ride."

His mother was delighted to see him, and asked about the family instead of his business. When he told her that Emma was expecting another baby and that she needed help, his mother said, "Why don't you take Rachel back with you for a while until you can find somebody permanent?"

"Don't you need her here to help you? Or to work with the Stannards?"

"They haven't been entertaining much lately. They come and go, and I could count on the fingers of one hand the times Miss Charlotte's husband has been here to stay more than a week. It's like he wanted to be the master of a grand plantation but now he's done that and doesn't want to anymore. You probably saw they still have good horses here to pull the carriage, and Mr. Stannard still has that poor old horse from years back. I expect any day to see the horse wagon come for it, to turn it into glue and such."

"Don't you need Rachel to help you?"

"Not much. You know Jamie and his wife look out for me, and now Pete's thinking of getting married and moving his wife in here too. So Rachel would probably be better off with you instead of in this crowded house."

"Pete's getting married? He hardly seems old enough."

"He's older than you were when you got married. All my children are growing up. And doing well, if I do say so myself, especially you. I'm mighty proud of you, Fortune. It was right for you to go away, even though I miss you so much sometimes it hurts. Life seems so short."

Fortune had never heard his mother talk so seriously, and he asked worriedly, "Are you all right, mama? I mean, you're not ailing, are you?"

She laughed. "Just getting old, son. It happens to all of us if we're lucky to live long enough."

It seemed to be settled. When Fortune left the next day, Rachel was with him, looking forward eagerly to being in the city and seeing her sister again.

When they arrived back in Richmond, Laura met them at the door, to Fortune's surprise. "What are you doing at home? Is something wrong?"

"Yes, there is. Emma's lost the baby. Thank God you're home. She's been calling for you. The doctor was here but he left and said she really needs to stay in bed and have someone take care of the children."

"I brought Rachel," he said unnecessarily.

Laura turned to her sister. "I'm glad to see you, of course, but you may not be much help. You don't know anything about taking care of babies or sick people, and I'll have to show you everything. But I need to get back to my job, so it will be up to you and Maggie will be back soon. Go on in and see Emma, and I'll take care of cleaning up things and help Rachel get settled."

Before Fortune could get to the door to Emma's room, the children ran at him, throwing their arms around his legs and begging him for attention. Fortune squatted down and hugged them each, realizing how frightened and puzzled they must be that their mother was in bed and Laura was at home.

"Can we see mama?" Simon asked.

"Aunt Laura said no," Eve stated.

"But daddy's home now, and he can decide."

"All right, but just for a moment," Fortune conceded, pushing the door open gently.

Emma looked pale and weak. She opened her eyes as her family came in. Fortune had cautioned the children to be extra quiet. "Don't get on the bed," he cautioned. "Just take your mom's hand, and give her a kiss on the forehead. Then go back to your studies."

Simon and Eve went up and did as their father had told them, leaning over carefully to touch their lips lightly to their mother's face. "Is she going to die?" Eve asked.

"No. She just needs rest. And she needs to know that her children are behaving and helping the adults. Go out and see your Aunt Rachel," he said, ushering them to the door. "I need to talk to your mother."

He walked back to Emma's bed, where she looked at him with sad eyes. "I'm glad you're back. I needed you here, but it seems whenever I'm having a baby or having a problem, you are somewhere else."

"I'm sorry, Emma. I didn't know this would happen anymore than you did. But I'm back now, and I stopped off to get Rachel. She's here and I think she will be a good learner and Laura will train her to take care of the children."

"The doctor said we have had too many pregnancies too close together. I need to give my body time to recover. So, Fortune . . ." she hesitated, not finishing her sentence.

Fortune nodded. "I know what the doctor means, Emma. As much as I want to be with you and have more children, I'll abide by what the doctor said."

Chapter 18

Fortune was restless. He needed something to do, needed something interesting to happen. For the first time in his life, nothing actually needed his attention and time, at least not to the degree he was used to.

The cigarette factory was functioning just as he intended, rolling out thousands of cigarettes every day, and he'd arranged promotions and distribution all over America so that all those cigarettes had customers waiting to buy them in their fancy boxes. It was Laura's idea to produce an attractive packet small enough to fit into a man's coat pocket, and the brand had become a mark of distinction for gentlemen.

He'd used most of the cigarette profits to invest in the trolley system, which had been installed and was now bringing in money of its own. Instinct told him it was time to sell the cigarette factory while it was still profitable and before too many competitors got into the field, but the trolley system could continue without competition as far as he could see.

By keeping the cost of a ticket low, people could ride the trolley and get rid of their horses and carriages. People were already doing just that, and he knew that already carriages were being parked permanently in dusty barns, and horses not replaced when they got old. Trolleys didn't have to be fed, groomed or re-shod. The only investment a rider made was the cost of the ticket, and for frequent riders, Fortune had arranged to have a pass that was good for multiple rides. He took the trolley himself when he needed to go to his office, and Laura took it to her job.

Something would come to replace trolleys, he felt sure. Perhaps the motor car, but one of those was much more of an investment than a horse and carriage. Only the very wealthy would choose a motor car over writing the trolley as far as he could see – at least for the next few decades.

With his businesses running so smoothly, Fortune had time to spend with his children, and Emma had noticed. "Fortune, play with the children or at least take them out for a walk," she urged. "They have too much energy to be cooped up in the house all the time."

Fortune had no idea how to play with children. His memories of his father were mostly practical, such as when the old man had taught him how to handle the mule and plow, and do other tasks, including slaughtering pigs, which Fortune had found repulsive. Looking back, Fortune knew that his father had had to work hard and have his family work hard, just to survive from year to year.

Returning to his present task, Fortune set off with the children bundled up for outdoors. Eve and Simon each took one of his hands as he struggled to walk slowly enough for their little legs to keep up.

A trolley clanged by, sparks shooting as it crossed the joining electric lines overhead.

"Let's ride, Papa!" Eve begged.

"How will we get the carriage onto the trolley, Papa?" His son asked.

"With some difficulty," Fortune chuckled. "Let's see if your mother would like to take a ride with us tomorrow."

Back at the house, he told Emma that he and the children would be riding on the trolley to see the cigarette factory.

"They are too young to understand what they're seeing, Fortune, and they might get hurt by the machinery," she said, frowning. "Just take them out to the end of the line and back. They don't have to see everything you own. The trolley will do."

Chapter 19

After taking the children on a short trolley ride, Fortune realized that parenting wasn't one of his greatest talents, and that Emma would never let him be the kind of father he'd like to be. Starting the next day, he returned to the factory, watching with great satisfaction as cigarettes rolled neatly out from the machinery into the tray, then were scooped up and arranged into waiting boxes.

It occurred to him that it would be possible to have a conveyor belt that passed beyond the tray with boxes arranged to catch the cigarettes, but that would take another invention and for right now it was enough to have the cigarettes produced. He hired a woman to gather and pack the cigarettes; she was happy to have a paying job with such light manual labor.

He calculated that with the new orders, the loan for the factory would be paid off that year, even after taking out money to support his family. Next year would be a big profit, big enough so that he could begin thinking about a larger house. Emma would like that. She'd been begging him for a nice big house. He planned to put aside enough money so that when Oak Hill was finally for sale, he could buy it.

Emma wouldn't want to wait that long for a new house, though. Oak Hill was his dream, and who knew how far off into the future it would become available? He wanted Emma to be happy, but he didn't know how to make that happen, other than giving her the new house she wanted. Perhaps she would be satisfied with in addition on to their present house while he waited for Oak Hill. She had been a good wife up until the loss of the baby.

Now whenever he tried to talk to Emma, she either responded angrily and said she didn't want to see him, or else she burst into tears and complained that he didn't care enough to spend time with her. Either way, he was in the wrong.

I can't handle this, he thought. Even with Rachel here, Emma is not getting any better and I don't how to handle it. Maggie is at home taking care of her own sick folks. Of course, Ma has had five children. Maybe she would know what to do about Emma. He sent a telegram to his mother asking her to come to Richmond. She came the following day on the train.

On the way from the train station to the house, Fortune told his mother about Emma and that Maggie was tending sick kin. She told Fortune, "Some women get that way after the birth of a baby, and your Emma is grieving besides. She doesn't even have a baby to show for all the pain."

"Were you like that when we were born?" he asked.

"No, but then I never lost one of my babies. It must be hard to bear. I really didn't want any more children after Laura, but Pete may turn out to be the one who stays home and looks after me in my last days, and there was never a sweeter child on earth than Rachel. Even when you don't want children, most women usually love them anyway."

"What can I do about Emma?"

"It's what we are going to do. I'm going to go in there and get her cleaned up and shampoo her hair and get her up and dressed in something decent instead of those ragged old nightgowns. You're going to help her walk into the kitchen and tell her she looks beautiful and that you've missed her. Then I'm going to go back home."

"Why are you going home so soon?"

"You know the saying, son: no house is big enough for two mothers. She's used to telling people what to do, and she's not used to having her husband's mother here. Laura was welcome, because she helped with the children and was out of the way most of the time at her job. Rachel can stay and look after the twins until Emma is really ready to take over again."

"How do you get along with Jamie's wife?"

"She's used to sharing a kitchen with her mother and sisters, and sometimes I just step back and let her do what she wants to do. Emma is an only child and didn't even have a mother around for the last few years, so she's not used to sharing. You have to keep that in mind, Fortune."

Fortune wasn't sure he could honestly tell Emma she looked beautiful, but he told himself that it was like selling something. To please the other person, you had to complement them and smile. He could do that.

And when Emma came out of the bedroom, walking shakily alongside his mother, she looked much better than the puffy-faced, unkempt woman who screamed at him. He stepped forward and took her arm so she could lean on him and said, "You look lovely today, my dear. And you must be starved. Come into the kitchen and we'll find you something to eat."

During her lunch break, Laura enjoyed walking along Broad Street looking at all the stores. She brought a sandwich from home each day, so that she could eat quickly and have most of her hour free for shopping. Not that she bought anything that she didn't absolutely have to have, at least not yet.

She went into Parsons Ready-to-Wear and climbed the stairs to women's department on the second floor. The store had an elevator, a newfangled thing that she hadn't yet brought herself to try, but the stairs worked.

She went to the rack where her favorite dress—hung dress with long sleeves that ended in ruffles, and the bustle in the back.

"Try it on," a voice said. Laura whirled around, startled, as a young man approached her.

She let her hand drop from the sleeve of the beautiful garment, and shook her head. "I can't afford it."

"You can't persuade your husband to buy it for you?"

"I'm not married."

"Then your father, perhaps." He smiled and came closer.

"I have a job, and I'm saving up to buy new clothes that would be suitable for my job as well as for church on Sundays. This is beautiful, and it's my favorite, but I'm not sure I could sit at my desk with the bustle."

"Perhaps you need to get a new job as well as a new dress," he suggested. He lifted the dress off the rack and handed it to her. "The fitting room is just behind you. I have a feeling the stress was meant for you, and you could be a model for us, and get a discount."

Laura's eyes sparkled at the idea, and she took the dress from him. In a few moments she was back, smoothing the fabric over her hips and walking with the slight sway because of the bustle. She was tall enough to look good in such a dress, and she knew the color became her.

His expression confirmed her thoughts. "I was right," he said. "This dress looks perfect on you."

She looked longingly at her image in the store mirror, and then looked again at the price tag and let it drop. She turned reluctantly back toward the fitting room to take it off.

"Wait! I have a way that you can afford this dress. As you can see, we have it in several sizes. Would you put it on each day and walk around the ladies department so that other women can see the dress and want to buy it. If you sell four, the dress is yours."

"So I'd be getting twenty-five percent commission?"

He nodded. "So you can do math as well as look beautiful."

She blushed in confusion. "Being able to figure runs in the family. My brother is especially good at it, and he taught himself. And I guess how I look runs in the family to, since I had nothing to do with it."

And what family is that?"

"Barranger."

"Fortune Barranger? I sold him a suit. He's becoming a well-known businessman in Richmond. So, do you want to try this on Saturday? If you like it and succeed at it, I can offer you a job. You wouldn't get twenty-five percent commission on everything, but you would have a salary plus ten percent commission, and a discount of twenty-five percent on anything you buy for yourself."

Laura stared at him. Her head whirled with the possibilities. "How can you make me such an offer without even getting to know me? Do you own the store?" He looked too young for that.

"No, but my father does."

"It sounds almost too good to be true," she said. "But I'll be here on Saturday." Reluctantly she took off the dress, put on her own and started down the stairs.

"The elevator's quicker. I wouldn't want you to be late getting back to your job." He took her arm and let her to the elevator. Laura held her breath for a moment as the elevator began to move downward, but nothing bad happened, and soon the operator swung the doors open and she walked out into the sunlight.

As Laura sat at her desk, she kept thinking of the beautiful red dress. Would it be possible that she could earn that dress just by wearing it and telling people they would look good in it? Fortune had told her, back when he and Mr. Brown ran the store and she helped out, that she had a good way of dealing with customers. Now she could find out if that were really true.

She really didn't like her job as receptionist. For most of the day there was nothing to do, so she could read and study the instruction book on how to be a secretary from her mail-order course. Every so often someone would come in and ask to see one of the partners, and she would go to notify that person. She put mail on the partners' desks, and saw to it that the offices were neat and tidy. Wouldn't she enjoy talking with women and helping them to choose clothing more? And Mr. Parsons had complemented her. She couldn't recall that any of the business partners ever complemented her, or even noticed her.

When she told Fortune about the offer that evening, he warned her to be very cautious. "When a man makes an offer that benefits a woman, he almost always wants something in return."

"And what about you, Fortune?" Emma asked. "What do you expect in return?"

"I'm not aware that I have made any offers to any women, not since I asked to marry you. For that, I got a wife."

Despite Fortune's warning, Laura went off happily to the store on Saturday. Fortune went with her, and bought one of the dresses for Emma, but in purple instead of red. "This will get you off to a start," he said. "And Emma could do with some new clothes. She's complained about my buying new clothing, especially the hat and gloves, but I look on them as a business investment. The dress for her will be a gift, with nothing to expect in return."

Laura sold a second dress, also in purple, at midmorning, as well as other items: skirts, lingerie, and even some handkerchiefs. She wasn't getting any rewards for selling those things, but she knew enough to write out the tickets for them, and make the customers happy. That's what Fortune had always told her to do. You never knew when that person might come back for something more expensive.

She cut short her lunch break, not wanting to be away from the store and miss the sale of another dress. She was only halfway to her goal. She sold the third dress, in blue, at midafternoon, and then customers seemed to be staying away. There were no more sales of any kind, and she'd almost given up hope. Then, just a few minutes before closing time, a young woman about her own age rushed in breathlessly, saying, "I've just had an invitation for lunch tomorrow, and I need something gorgeous to wear. Something like what you wearing."

"Yes, this dress would look good on you in any of our four colors. Which do you prefer?"

"Oh, the red, of course, if you have another in my size."

Fortunately, there was a second red dress and the customer decided that she looked perfect and it. "I just hope we won't be going to the same church tomorrow morning," she said with a little laugh. "We go to St. John's," Laura said.

"No problem then," the young woman said reaching for her purse. "And thank you for staying past closing time."

A Laura folded the dress into a large cardboard carton enfolded tissue over it as she'd been taught by Mr. Parsons, she saw him approaching. She thanked the customer who made her way toward the elevator, and then turned to him with a smile.

"Well done, Miss Barranger. The dress is yours. And because you sold a number of other ladies' garments, I'd like you to step over to our shoe department and try on some of our new arrival shoes. I give you the choice of a pair of shoes, or ten percent commission on what you sold today besides the dresses."

Laura did the arithmetic quickly in her head and realized that the shoes would be a much better choice. She tried on a pair that laced up the front to the ankle and had small heels. As she lifted the hem of her skirt to see how they looked, she saw Mr. Parsons also looking at her ankles. She flushed and dropped the skirt. "I can't come in to work here on Monday," she told Mr. Parsons. "I have to tell my boss that I'm leaving, so they can find somebody else to replace me. It's only right."

He nodded. "You have integrity, Miss Barranger. That's a good quality. May I drive you home?"

He was uncomfortably close to her. She stepped away. "No, thank you. My brother is probably already waiting outside for me. Did I leave everything in order here?"

"Yes indeed. Will you let me know just when you can come to work?" Laura nodded.

He went down in the elevator with her, held the door open and helped her get into Fortune's carriage, then bowed slightly as they drove away.

Laura looked back and stared at him. Everything about him seemed to be pale. He wore a gray three-piece suit, and his hair and beard were blonde. His skin was pale too, but she thought that was probably because of his staying inside the store all day. He was only slightly taller than she. But he was kind to give her a job, and generous too. He turned and went back into the store.

"So, you earned enough to pay for the dress, I hope," Fortune commented. When she nodded, he went on, "What about those brand-new boots? Did he make you a deal for those as well?"

Laura hesitated and then said, "I earned the boots too, by all the other things I managed to sell today. He says I'm a natural born saleslady."

"That's all well and good," Fortune said, "but still be wary of anyone who seems too generous. Such people always expect something in return."

Chapter 20

The next morning Laura dressed in her new finery and went to help Emma don the purple dress. Emma turned back and forth before the mirror. "It's a beautiful dress, but I should be wearing black," she fretted.

"No, it's been nearly a year since you lost the baby," Laura said. "It's time for purple, or at least lavender. I think Fortune chose the perfect color for you and he wants to see you wear it to church."

Emma nodded and smiled at her reflection. "I wish he bought me a hat to go with it. My old black bonnet will have to do. But maybe that black will be enough to show that I'm still in mourning."

"It's good you are going back to church, Emma," Laura said. "Some people had begun to think I was Fortunes wife, since you're never there. And some women, when they found out I was his sister, thought perhaps he was single and available. It's time you made it clear you're his wife, and time to *be* his wife."

By the look that crossed over Emma's face, Laura realized she'd said too much, but it was time somebody spoke up to Emma. Her mother had managed to get Emma up and out of bed and doing things around the house, but it was time Emma stopped feeling sorry for herself. She wasn't the first woman in the world to lose a baby, and she wouldn't be the last.

"So, my husband is looking at other women?"

"No, he's not, but he may soon if you don't start being his wife in every way."

"How dare you tell me how to be a wife. You've never been a wife; what do you know?"

"I dare because I love my brother and he loves you, and I don't think you're being fair to him. If you don't want to be his wife, then set him free to find someone else. I know

Rachel and I may be in your way here and as soon as I can earn enough, I'll find a place for the two of us and leave you to be mistress of your own home once more."

"No, don't leave. I don't know how I would manage without you two." She put her hand on Laura's arm.

"Are you ready to go?" Laura asked, going to the door. She didn't look back, but the sound of footsteps told her Emma was following.

Laura climbed carefully into the carriage and sat down beside her sister.

"Both of you look beautiful," Rachel said. "And I don't."

Laura realized it was true. Rachel was wearing a hand-me-down skirt and shirtwaist with a shawl their mother had knitted. Laura patted Rachel's hand. "Just wait, little sister. As soon as I go to work at Parsons I'll buy you some clothes, or have Fortune buy them for you. I can get a discount on anything I buy, and I intend to buy more things for myself as well."

"The children need new clothes too," Emma murmured. "I hadn't noticed how they've grown. They've outgrown everything they have."

As the church service ended, several men came over to introduce themselves to Fortune, who in turn introduced them to his wife and sisters. Jerome Parsons was one of the men, and Laura thought he held her hand a bit longer than was courteous.

"You two ladies look lovely, and show our dresses off to their very best extent. And I think I saw one of the dresses in blue here as well."

"I was careful to suggest different colors, so ladies would not see someone else wearing an identical dress. Each one of us wants to feel that the dress is ours especially," Laura said.

Parsons laughed. "I was right in my judgment that you are a natural sales lady. I shall look forward to seeing you as soon as your employers can find someone to replace you and you are ready to go to work for me."

Laura wore her new dress and boots to work the next day. She hung the shawl on the coat rack and made her way to her desk, enjoying the slight click of the heels of her new boots on the floor. As she had suspected, she had to sit forward in her chair because of the bustle, but that was a small price to pay for the admiring glances she got.

When she told her boss that she was leaving to take another job, he deflated her pride by saying, "Don't worry. We can replace you within a week. Maybe less." He turned to walk away, and turned back to say, "but we shall be sorry to see you go." On Friday Laura received her final pay packet and made her way home. She stopped by the store to tell Jerome Parsons that she was now available for work, starting Monday.

"Why not tomorrow? You did exceedingly well last Saturday. It's one of our biggest shopping days so you can start earning commission." Laura said she'd be delighted to.

Saturday morning, Laura hung the red dress on the screened back porch to rid it of the odor of cigarette smoke from the office so it would smell all right for church the next day. She wore her navy surge skirt and white high-necked long-sleeved blouse. In this outfit she wouldn't be advertising the dresses with the bustle, but she didn't have the same incentive she'd had last week. Today there would be only a ten percent commission on whatever she sold, not twenty-five percent, but she would be getting a small salary as well.

Despite not showing off the dress herself, she managed to sell two of them, both blue, and crossed her fingers that the two purchases didn't attend the same church. She suggested hats, gloves and shoes to "complete the outfit," and even had the boldness to hold out the items and suggest, "something like this, perhaps?"

During her lunch break, Laura selected new clothing for the children: a bright blue jumper and jacket for Eve with a ruffled white blouse, and for Simon, navy surge knickers, long stockings and a navy-blue jacket. Back in the ladies' department, she chose for Rachel a blue velveteen dress with no bustle, and a matching jacket piped in red and white braid. Fortune would probably reimburse her for all of this, but if he didn't, she'd have to work a good while to pay it off.

At the end of the day Jerome Parsons came to her department, smiling. "You have another winning day, Miss Barranger."

Laura laid the family clothing on the counter underneath a ticket she had figured out. She took her pay packet from her purse and counted it into his hand. "This will pay for half the cost of these items minus my ten percent discount. May I take them with me today if you'll trust me to pay the rest as I earn it?"

"Actually, you earn ten percent commission on things you sell, and you get twenty-five percent discount on things you *buy*," he said. "And of course, I'll trust you. I'm sure I'll get my payment. Now, you were so successful in selling those dresses when you were wearing one. Why don't you take the emerald green and wear it to church tomorrow and to work on Monday and let's see if we can't sell the rest of the lot. Oh, and you'll need a hat to go with it. Let's pick out something suitable—perhaps small black straw, all-natural straw and the black ribbons that should go with everything."

"You certainly know a lot about clothing, Mr. Parsons," she said.

113

"It's my business. And I know specifically what would look good on you. The emerald green just matches your eyes." Laura looked away so he wouldn't see her blush. Without meeting his eyes, she said, "I can't afford so many new clothes I'll owe you all my salary for months and months."

"Let me worry about that. I'm sure I can work out a way for you to earn it." His words made Laura nervous, but his earnest smile as he said them allayed her fears.

"Do you think I'm made of money?" Fortune snapped the next morning as his family got into the carriage, dressed in their new garb. "Wouldn't something less expensive have done just as well?"

"I'll pay for the children's clothing," Emma said, to Laura's surprise. "I have money of my own thanks to the repayment of the loan to Fortune to start the cigarette factory. "And I'll pay for Rachel's as well, since she took care of the children when I couldn't."

Fortune turned to Laura. "And what about you. Wearing a new dress two Sundays in a row?"

"I'll be paying for it out of my earnings at the store, and if I wear it to work, it will help me to sell other dresses just like it."

When Jerome approached the family as they exited their pew at St. John's, he shook hands first with Fortune, then bowed to Emma and Rachel, and finally took Laura's hand. "Mr. Barranger, may I have the privilege of taking your sister, Miss Laura, to lunch today?"

Fortune glanced quickly at Laura, and seeing her smile, nodded. "Just bring her home safely right after."

"Of course." He tucked Laura's hand into the crook of his elbow and led her outside to his surrey.

At the restaurant she saw that there were couples dining at small tables, but also several families around larger tables, and wondered why he hadn't invited the whole family. Of course, that would have been very expensive, she realized.

She looked down at the array of silverware on each side of the plate set on a white damask cloth and tried to recall the way the Bishops had handled their cutlery when she'd served them at Oak Hill. Start outside; that was one of the things she remembered. She looked at Mr. Parsons, and decided she'd use whichever piece of silver he used. That seemed to work, and she soon forgot her nervousness.

After lunch, he helped her into the surrey, his hand warm and steady on her back. As soon as she was seated, he went around to the opposite side and climbed in, moving close to her.

It was a lovely sunny afternoon, and Laura relaxed, letting him hold her hand while he handled the horse with the other hand. She closed her eyes and leaned back as far against the cushion as she could with the bustle in place. This was pleasant. Suddenly she realized that the surrey had stopped. Her eyes flew open and she saw that they were stopped in a grove of trees, shadowed and hidden from traffic on the nearby street.

"You look as lovely in green as you did in red," he said as he turned toward her.

"Thank you. I'll pay for it as soon as I can."

"You can pay for it right now," he said. His thigh was tight against hers, and with one hand he pulled her toward him while with the other hand he was fumbling at the fastenings on her dress. His eyes glittered, and his mouth was slightly open, coming toward her with what she was sure was an unwanted kiss.

"Stop! What are you doing?"

Before she could say anymore, his mouth closed over hers, hot and demanding. Laura beat at him with one hand and with the other grabbed for the reins and jerked hard.

The horse reared and this surrey lurched, throwing him off her. Heedless of her new clothing, Laura leapt from the surrey and heard something rip. She started running, back toward where she thought the horse drawn trolley line was.

The surrey caught up with her and he shouted, "Stop running and get in. I'll take you home or to the trolley and buy your fare. I won't touch you again, I swear."

Laura stopped running and let him help her into this surrey. This time his touch was quite different. He might have been handling a fragile ornament as much as a person. She sat down, leaning toward the opposite side of the surrey, as far away from him as she could, and reached for her hat. It was askew on her head, and she suddenly worried he might consider that a reason to touch her and "set it right," so afterward she held that hat in in her hand and close against her chest.

He was as good as his word. He drove in silence passing the horse drawn trolley. He drove faster than Laura would have liked, but she dared not say anything to him. His anger was clear in the way he held the reins and in the set of his jaw, and she felt her own anger matching his.

When he stopped in front of the house, he came around and wordlessly offered her his hand to help her down. "I'll see you at the store tomorrow, then."

Laura watched him drive away in horror. She'd have to face him at the store every day but she had no other job. She couldn't return any of the clothing because it had all been worn, and the green dress was torn besides.

She tried to make her way unseen into the house but unfortunately Fortune opened the door. He started to ask, "How was—" when he saw her disheveled state. Instantly concerned, he asked, "What the devil happened to you? Did you have an accident or take a fall?"

"I jumped out of the surrey after he . . ." she muttered, feeling her face hot in embarrassment.

"I know damn well what he tried to do. Did he...
succeed?"

"No, I got away from him. But I've got to go to the store
every day and see him."

"I'll give him a thrashing and see that he gets fired,"
Fortune declared.

"You can't," Laura sighed miserably. "His father owns
the store. I'll be all right. I learned how to avoid Mr. Bishop
at Oak Hill," — Fortune's eyes widened at this — "and I don't
think Mr. Parsons will bother me anymore.

"I'm going to work at the store and sell as much as I can
to pay off what I bought," she said with grim determination.
"You were right that I should have suspected him when he
offered me beautiful clothing. I don't think he will do
anything against me at work, because I intend to make a lot
of money for the store so they'll need me so much they can't
fire me." Stepping past him, she made her way upstairs
without seeing the rest of the family, changed her dress into
the one she wore around the house, and examined the rip. It
could be mended, and she could borrow a brooch from
Emma to cover the empty space.

The next morning, she was helping a customer at the
dress counter when she saw Jerome approach. He waited
until she finished writing a ticket and the customer had
gone before he drew closer to her. Laura pulled back
slightly to keep him from getting too close.

"I apologize for my behavior, Miss Barranger. I was
mistaken about you," he said in a serious tone.

He doesn't think that what he did was wrong, Laura
thought. *He just thinks he did it to the wrong person.*

"Perhaps you thought that since I'm from the country
and not used to having nice things, I'd be willing to let you
do . . . things to me in return for a dress and a hat," she told
him. "What you might not know is that I've had to work all

my life, and I intend to keep on. I will earn everything I get."

"Again, I apologize. I respect you, and I assure you such an incident will not happen again."

"Oh, it won't," she said firmly.

Chapter 21

Fortune had always liked numbers. He liked the neat shape of them, the way they looked recorded in his ledgers, especially when they added up in his favor. He had a separate section in his big ledger for each of the businesses. He had always instinctively understood that there had to be separate columns for income and expenses, and that there had to be more of the income than expenses, or there would be trouble. And there had to be a certain amount of money kept in reserve in the bank before spending big amounts on personal things.

The coal company was doing better than he had expected. He had definitely made the right decision in buying it. Countries all over the world were awakening to the idea of manufacturing, and that meant coal-powered energy. He had bought some shares in the railroad that hauled coal to his cigarette factory and more to Norfolk to be loaded onto ships going to far-off ports.

He'd been right—very right—about the cigarette-rolling machine. That business was turning such a profit it was almost as if it were printing money with each cigarette rolled. In a few years he might want to sell it, if Buck Duke and some others began to make their own cigarettes.

He was under no illusion that there were other men as smart as he or smarter, who would see the advantages of a cigarette rolling machine, and they weren't above stealing the design. He planned to sell it anyway when Oak Hill became available.

But from his brothers reports, it wasn't about to happen anytime soon, although there were signs that Charlotte's husband, Marvin Bishop, was a heavy drinker, and might make some foolish gambles. Jamie wrote that Bishop had brought some beautiful horses to Oak Hill, which of course cost money for their feeding and care, but he didn't seem to have any use for them. He just liked to show them off when he brought visitors down to the plantation from New York. The mansion had been fixed up, and looked good, although Colonel Bob was the only one staying there full-time.

Fortune gave some thought to Emma's demand for a bigger house. He had to placate her to keep peace in the family. He resented having to spend money on a house, unless it was Oak Hill, but perhaps he could turn this into a profit as well.

On a beautiful fall day, he asked Emma at breakfast if she wanted to take a ride out to look at the site of her future home.

She brightened and smiled. "Of course I do. Have you found something suitable? I didn't even know you were looking at houses."

"Well, it's not a house yet. It's land. Shall we leave in half an hour?"

Her enthusiasm somewhat subdued, she dressed and was quickly ready.

As they got in the carriage, he said, "I didn't want to choose a house that you might not like. I thought you would like to have a say so in exactly what the house would look like."

She smiled and turned to squeeze his arm. "Oh, thank you, Fortune. I do want to choose things for us. I feel so left out. Laura has her job and is earning money, and Rachel looks after the children so well that when they have a stubbed toe or some other problem, they run to her for comfort. I feel useless."

"I thought that's the way you wanted it," he said, not registering how her smile deflated. "Maybe it's time for Rachel to get a paying job outside or go back home."

"Where are we going?" She asked, facing forward now.

"The city is moving westward, and I found a farm just where the residential area ends. You can have a garden and fruit trees and as much land as you want around the house. The rest of it I'll divide into building lots and sell to help pay for the house."

When they arrived at the site he had chosen, she said, "But this is so far out. How will we get to church, and how will I go shopping?"

"I'm investing in trolley lines for the city, and I'll see to it that the main line gets extended all the way out here. That will make this property a lot more valuable, as people come to build houses near us."

"Is everything business for you?" She asked sadly.

"Business is how I make money, so I can support you and the children, and I admit I enjoy business. I'm good at it. You should be glad I don't spend my time drinking or gambling or supporting a mistress."

"Do you want a mistress?" she asked, her eyes wide.

"Sometimes I do, Emma. There had been many times when I haven't thought I had a wife."

She looked down and said nothing. That night she slipped into bed beside him just as she had that first night years before, if not as enthusiastically.

He gathered her into his arms and kissed her, enjoying the soft warmth of her body. After they'd made love, he asked, "Is this just for tonight as a way of thanking me for your future house?"

You have your business and I suppose this is mine, she thought. She said to him, "I'm back to stay. You no longer have to sleep in this little single bed. Come back in with me." She got out and went to the big double bed in the master bedroom, and Fortune joined her.

Chapter 22

Time passed and Fortune's money continued to pile up. Emma was making him happy once again, and he enjoyed the time he spent with his children. His life seemed to be going almost perfectly, until he received a telegraph from the mine: a collapse had killed three men. He left on the train within two hours, first going to the bank to withdraw money.

He arrived to find the mine work at a standstill, as crowds gathered around the opening and rescuers had to regularly shout at them to stay back.

"What's going on?" Fortune asked.

"Oh, Mr. Barranger," the manager said. "It's worse than I told you. Besides the three dead men, there are still some trapped in there."

"What about the dead ones? Did they leave families?"

"Two had wives and children. The third one wasn't married, but he supported his mother who was a widow. His father died in a collapse years ago."

Fortune realized that he could do nothing standing around the mine hoping and waiting, any more than all the other people gathered there. He made arrangements to meet with the men's survivors. He paid for the funerals and gave the two widows and the third man's mother a year's salary.

Afterward, he confronted the manager. "Is this all we're paying these men who risk their lives?"

"Around here it's considered a fair wage," the manager said. "Some of them are immigrants, just come over, and they'll take anything. The rest have lived here all their lives, and they're used to seeing people go down into the mine for this pay."

Fortune recognized his own previous perspective in the man's words. "Well, it's not going to be that way anymore.

I'm raising their wages, and I want new machinery put in and better props for the tunnels."

"Well, you won't make much of a profit that way."

"Maybe not at first, but I think satisfied workers will work better, to show their appreciation. And anyway, I don't want it on my conscience that men are dying because of the conditions in property that I own."

Fortune stayed until the two remaining men had been rescued, and he told all the gathered minors that the mine would be closed until the new equipment could be installed and props put in place.

They glanced nervously at each other, until one man raised a shaky hand to ask, "Does this mean will be out of a job for all that time?"

"No. I'll pay you your regular wages, and as soon as the mine is in better shape, you can go back to work at higher wages." After a surprised silence, there was an outburst of applause.

On the way back home, Fortune got off the train to see his mother and brothers, walking the short distance from the station. *When I own Oak Hill*, he vowed to himself, *I'm going to have the rail line laid right to my property*. He looked at the mansion, its white columns and fences contrasted against the glorious reds and yellows of maples, and the distant blue of the mountains.

He found his brother Jamie just walking home from tending the horses at Oak Hill. "Well, look who's here, the famous Fortune Barranger," his brother greeted him. "What brings you here?"

"I might say that I just wanted to see my family, which is true, but I'm on my way back from the coal mine. You probably read in the newspaper about the mine collapse."

Jamie nodded. "Didn't realize you owned it."

"Is anybody at home at Oak Hill?"

"Charlotte and that no-good husband of hers and the boy? No. Colonel Bob, always. The last time he left was to get Charlotte married off. He asks about you from time to time, and Charlotte does too, like maybe she's looking for something to show that she was right not to marry you."

"What do you tell her?"

"All the good stuff: that you're happily married and about to build a new house, and your businesses are rolling in the money for you." He laughed and slapped Fortune on the back. "And most of it's true. I don't have to make up much."

"Do Charlotte and her husband often come?"

"She comes by herself sometimes, but when he comes, he brings a bunch of rowdy friends with him. They drink well into the night, and act like fools. Sometimes they ride the horses around, and I've even seen them try to jump the fence, which is a bad idea for horses that are not used to jumping. One of these days somebody's going to get killed that way. And some of them puke when they've had too much to drink. The house stinks the next morning. They hire Ma to clean up the mess. Ruth won't go near there."

"Does Ma need money?" Fortune asked, disgusted at the thought of his mother having to clean up after grown men acting like spoiled brats. "She ought to know that I can take care of whatever she needs or wants."

Jamie shrugged. "She says after raising five children, she's used to cleaning up messes, and she wants to have a little money of her own so she can buy gifts for her children and grandchildren. Well, good to see you. You staying overnight?"

"No. I'll catch the late train. Tell Ruth hello for me."

When Fortune arrived at his family's house and told his mother about what he'd done at the coal mine, she smiled and patted him on the shoulder. "I wouldn't expect no less from you, son. I think we brought you up right."

"Jamie told me you've been working for Charlotte and her husband."

She nodded. "I feel sorry for her, even if she did get into this mess by herself. She can't get out of it, that's for sure, and there's no telling how it will end."

He hugged her. "You're a good woman, Ma."

"I tried to be. Now let me fix you something to eat, and you can spend a little time talking to Pete."

As she went off into the kitchen, Fortune turned his attention to his younger brother, who stood shyly smiling. "I don't guess we got much to talk about, Fortune, since I heard all you and Ma said to each other."

"How are things going with you, Pete? Are you still in school?"

Pete nodded. "I'm the oldest one in school, and sometimes it's kind of embarrassing. The teacher calls on me for all kinds of help, acting like I'm almost her own age. But I aim to stay in school as long as I can."

Fortune accepted the packet of food his mother provided, though he knew he could have eaten in the dining car on the train. As wealthy as he was, his mother still thought of him as needing to carry food with him, and he knew that her cooking was better than what he'd have gotten on the train.

As he ate the ham biscuits, he thought about her and Pete and Jamie's little family, and the situation at Oak Hill. His mother's hair was whiter than he remembered, and she was thinner. Jamie seemed satisfied working with horses and keeping up the house and outbuildings at Oak Hill. Pete's situation puzzled him a bit. Was the teacher sweet on him, or he with her? And then he thought about Charlotte, always recalling her as beautiful and aloof.

Back at home, Emma had fallen in love with the idea of their new house. She spent most of her time describing how

125

she wanted the house to look, insisting that Fortune drive with her around Richmond to see the newest houses, though he thought each one was uglier than the one before. He wanted something simple and elegant, something like Oak Hill, with a two-story portico supported by white columns. Emma's dream home had brackets and towers and wraparound porches with wood cutouts that reminded him of trim on someone's dress, not a house.

He was tired of looking at houses, and finally said, "I'll hire an architect. You can tell him what you want, and then you can show me his drawings and we'll talk about how much it's going to cost."

It took months and many consultations with the architect before Emma was satisfied and unrolled the drawings to show him. The exterior was as busy as he had expected, but he said nothing. It was Emma's house and he told her to have it designed the way she wanted. He'd only have to look at it as he entered. He concentrated on what she was saying about the inside. The bottom floor was pretty much what he would expect of any house: kitchen, dining room, parlor, master bedroom, and bath.

She was pointing to the rooms on the second level. "This room is Laura and Rachel's for as long as they want to stay with us. This one is Eve's, this is Simon's, and this is the nursery."

"Do we need a nursery? Daniel is three. He should be having a room of his own."

"True, we can put a small bedroom next to our bedroom for him. But we might still need a nursery because . . . I might be pregnant now. I'm not sure. I thought it might happen before this, as many times as we . . ." she stopped and blushed, then went on, "as many times as we have come together."

"Do you want another baby?" he asked.

"Yes, I do," she said hopefully.

Chapter 23

For several weeks after setting upon her in the surrey, Jerome Parsons avoided Laura. While she was glad not to be around him, she also wished he would come to the ladies' department simply to make certain everything was going well. But of course, he could see by the sales records that she was a good sales lady.

Then one day just before lunch time he showed up. "Miss Barranger, I commend you! Your section of the store is performing better than any other department. I'm raising your commission percent, and I'd like to take you to lunch to celebrate."

"That's good to hear. Where will be going for lunch?" she asked.

He smiled and shrugged. "Wherever you wish. I thought of a place nearby so that we can walk and not have to take the surrey."

Laura relaxed, and nodded. "Yes, thank you I'd be pleased to go for lunch."

While he waited, she got her purse, locked the cash drawer, and put up a small sign that said "Lunch."

She walked with him to the elevator and out the front door. He took her arm and tucked it into crook of his elbow, pressing it close against him. Laura did not withdraw but was immediately wary.

"I hope you don't mind walking two blocks," he said, guiding her gently along the sidewalk.

"No, it's a lovely day." In the restaurant, she noticed immediately that there were only two other women, both of whom were wearing hats. She suddenly realized that she was hatless. She'd been so confused by his invitation that she hadn't thought at all about her hat, although it was right within her reach, under the counter beside the sandwich that she wasn't going to eat.

"What would you like?" he asked.

"I don't know, what are you having?"

"The roast beef sandwich."

"I'll try that too and lemonade."

As the waiter left, she said, "Thank you for increasing my commission, Mr. Parsons."

"You have earned it. I'm very pleased, and so is my father. And please call me Jerome when we're alone. Inside the store, of course, it will have to continue to be Miss Barranger and Mr. Parsons. And may I call you Laura?"

"Yes, Jerome," she concluded, feeling her face warm with the blush. His comments sounded as if he expected them to be alone on other occasions, and she realized that the idea wasn't completely awful to her. Their sandwiches arrived, and she stared down at in dismay. It was huge and cut diagonally into two pieces. She glanced up to find Jerome staring at her, and realized he was waiting for her to begin. She picked up her knife and fork and cut her sandwich into small pieces.

He laughed. "This is not a knife and fork kind of place. You don't have much choice with that one that you've just turned into rubble. You'll have to use a fork for that, but for the other half just pick it up like this." He demonstrated, taking a big bite of the sandwich and chewing vigorously.

Laura bit into her own sandwich and discovered the meat was slathered with mustard and it stung her tongue and it brought tears to her eyes. But she made herself eat it.

When they'd finished eating the sandwiches, he asked if she'd like dessert. She shook her head. "I need to get back to the store."

"You needn't hurry. I'm not going to fire you. If I did, I'd have to answer to my father. You're the best salesperson we have. Is everything in the department to your liking? Or do you have any suggestions on how we could improve things? "

Laura hesitated. It was one thing to be complimented, but if she pointed out things that needed improving, it might appear as if she were complaining. She sat in silence until he said, "Well?"

"We should always have some simple black dresses in stock in all sizes. No bustles or jet beads or feather trim. Slim skirts."

She hesitated. He must think her very forward to be telling him, the son of the store owner, what needed to be in stock. But now that she had started, she plunged on: "I've had women come in red eyed from weeping, looking for a dress to wear to someone's funeral, and when they saw the price of the dress, they turn away and start crying all over again, probably thinking that the money would be sorely needed for every day expenses, now that the person who had supported them had died."

"Very astute observation, Laura. What if I bring you some pictures of dresses we might order and let you pick the style?"

"If you trust me."

"You trusted me enough to come out to lunch after the way I behaved, so in return I trust you to make a decision for the store. And actually, you are the very person who should be making this decision. I don't know anything about women's dresses, and neither does my father except maybe at some of the dresses have too many buttons and hooks so that a woman needs her husband's or maid's help to get dressed." He tentatively reached across the table and took Laura's hand. "So, this really has been a business lunch, although it's been a pleasure for me as well."

The next morning, he brought a paper with drawings of three dresses. It took her only a moment to choose: the model with long sleeves and a high-necked line. It buttoned up the front with simple black buttons, and she envisioned the only jewelry as a small locket or a cameo.

"Are you sure?" He asked.

"I think so, but nothing is ever sure in fashion. If I'm wrong and customers don't buy them, will I have to give up my commission?"

"Of course not. We all make mistakes."

She didn't see Jerome for several days, until he came to her department and invited her out to lunch again.

"Are we going to the same place? What do they have besides roast beef sandwiches?"

"I could tell you didn't like that place," he said. "I thought we'd take the trolley to a hotel dining room."

The trolley was full. A man stood to give Laura a seat, and Jerome stood beside her, holding onto the rail. The horses moved slowly, and the trolley stopped at each block.

The hotel dining room was quiet, and Laura noted that there were more women than at the café where she'd had the roast beef sandwich. She glanced around, noticing that several of the women were wearing dresses from Parsons. This time she didn't order the same thing he had, or even ask what he was having. She chose a small cheese omelet and tomato aspic with a cornmeal muffin.

"This is the kind of food ladies prefer," she said. "Say, why doesn't Parsons open a small dining room so its employees and customers don't have to come so far to find a nice lunch?"

He looked up in surprise from the fried chicken he was just finishing. "We're in clothing, not food."

"Well, of course," she said. "But everyone who works in the store has to eat lunch somewhere, and most of your customers come downtown to shop and then go somewhere else for lunch, or eat lunch at home and then come out to shop in the afternoon. If they had somewhere inside the store to eat, they would stay longer and buy more. They could also enjoy being with their friends, discussing what they might buy." She stopped, embarrassed that she had talked so much.

Jerome nodded slowly. "It's unusual, but you have good reasons for what you say. Would you explain all this to my father? I couldn't make a decision about something like that unless he supported it 100%."

Three days later, Laura found herself in the cluttered office of Mr. Parsons Sr. He was an older version of Jerome: trim and well-dressed, with a small mustache and a short gray beard. He smiled, deepening the wrinkles at both corners of his mouth, and waved her to a seat across the desk from him before he sat back down. He fixed her with a piercing gaze. "Now tell me all the reasons why we should rip up part of the store to make room for a little restaurant. My son seems to be very enthusiastic about it, but then he's enthusiastic about every one of your ideas, while I have reservations."

Laura told the older man what she'd told Jerome and noticed that he had begun to scribble on a pad of paper in front of him and nod as she talked. "I think we would need to buy the building next door and put the café there," he said.

"No, it needs to be part of the store, so the ladies don't have to leave," Laura blurted, and then stopped aghast. He was the man who owned the store and was paying her good money and she was telling him how to handle his business?"

After startling a moment, he laughed. "Ah, a woman who not only has good ideas, but can defend them. I can see your point: once the ladies leave the store, they may not come back in. We could move the men's clothing section into the next-door building and put the dining room where the men's section is now."

He stood and extended his hand; it signaled that Laura's time with him was up. "Thank you for explaining your idea, Miss Barranger. It seems workable. Give me some time to think about it. In the meantime, I'd like to know what kind of food you think we should serve and how the place should be decorated."

Laura left in a daze. Not only was she now expected to keep selling dresses, but to design an eating establishment. She didn't know anything about building or decorating will or even planning menus, but she knew what she liked and didn't like.

Jerome came to her department when the shipment of black dresses arrived.

Laura lifted the black dresses out of the carton, gave them a shake, and hung them up.

"They look rather drab," Jerome said doubtingly.

"That's just the point," Laura said. "A woman doesn't want to look fancy at her husband's funeral. It wouldn't be right. We probably should have some veils to go with their hats as well, some of the widows and orphans can cry away from prying eyes." She held one of the dresses against her. "I think I'll put this aside for myself."

"But you have no husband to mourn," he said.

"No, but my mother is getting along in age. I never know which time I see her will be the last."

Jerome nodded sadly, then said, "Well, I'd better get back to my department. I want to sell as much as I can before we have to move into the new section."

Seeing Laura's interest in the progress of the store development, he added, "Workmen have been getting it ready. It was just a big open warehouse with two levels. We need fitting rooms, display space, hanging racks, and space for the sewing machines where alterations are done and seems closed up. And I've suggested to my father that we move the boy's section of clothing in with the adult men. Boys have pride, and don't want to be trying on clothing in the children's section."

"So, you're coming up with some good ideas for improving the business," she said. "I'm not the only one who deserves compliments and praise. That's good, Jerome."

He smiled, pleased at her compliment. He cleared his throat and then said, "I'd better get back to work to justify your confidence in me."

Chapter 24

Fortune kept busy, going from one of his projects to the next. The cigarette factory was the most satisfactory, producing thousands of cigarettes every day, filling orders and attracting new customers. He had been right that once men experienced neatly packed cigarettes, they never want to go back to carrying around bags of tobacco and paper pieces of paper and rolling their own.

He needed someone to buy tobacco for the factory. So far, he had done all the purchasing himself, but it was a poor use of his time, standing around cold warehouses, inspecting tobacco, and waiting for an auctioneer to start the bidding. It was all he could do to keep up with the progress of the house he was building for Emma, check the laying of the rails for the trolley, and make occasional trips out to the mine to make certain the equipment he paid for was installed.

The quality of tobacco he bought was extremely important. He wanted just the right blend so that buyers could be certain they had the same flavor cigarette from one time to the next.

Perhaps his brother Pete would be the man for the job. He was young and inexperienced, but he could learn, and he was wasting his time sitting in a classroom of younger students, mooning over the teacher, from what he'd said, and eking out a living as a sharecropper on the Stannards' land.

Pete was useful as a companion for their mother, but maybe she would be glad to leave the mountains for the winter and come to Richmond, and Emma could probably use some help when the new baby came. Rachel was good at it, but she, like Laura, wanted to get a job and earn her own money.

By the time he got off the train, Fortune had worked it all out in his mind. Now he just had to convince Pete.

When Fortune got off the train, it was a bleak day in early November, with the chill wind that made him wish he'd worn a topcoat. The mountains were almost bare of color, with just a few bright leaves still clinging to trees here and there. The days had grown short, and the sun was already dropping behind the mountains to the west, sending long shadows across the fields between the station and his mother's home.

As he looked across to Oak Hill, he saw Charlotte walking toward him, clad in a blue cape. Trailing behind her was a young boy swinging a stick in his hand. Fortune waved and went toward her.

"Hello, Fortune, what a surprise to see you!" she extended her hand with a smile.

"Likewise." He took her hand briefly in his, and then let it drop. "How is your father?"

"Not well. I come as often as I can, and I wish I could get him to come back to New York with us, but he says he'll never live leave Oak Hill until it's feet first in a box. He sits and reads and doesn't eat well. Whenever I come, I make sure there's plenty of food in the house, and when I come next, I sometimes find what I purchased is still there."

"I'm sorry. Is there anything I can do to help the situation?" When she shook her head, he turned to the boy. "What's your name, son?"

"Don't call me son," the child snapped. "I have a father, and you are not it. My name is Julian Stannard Bishop. I'm named for both my grandfathers." A brown spotted dog approached and dropped down on its belly. The boy whirled and struck the dog with the stick.

Fortune grabbed it away. "What did you hit that poor dog for?"

"I don't like it," he answered.

"It still wants to be with you, though I don't know why the way you treated it. If you keep on hitting it, it will hate you and someday it may turn on you."

"My father whips his horses and dogs and anybody he wants to whip. If he can do it, so can I, and it's none of your affair."

Charlotte had not spoken, but looked in alarm from one to the other, as if she expected Fortune to hit her son with this stick. She found her voice. "Julian, go to the house and sit with your grandfather. I'll be there in a few minutes, and we'll settle this."

Julian reached for the stick, but Fortune held on. After a moment, the boy turned and started walking toward the house turning back to make a face at Fortune.

"Why do you let him get away with such behavior and such disobedience?" Fortune asked. "Do you want him to grow up to be a monster of a criminal, a man who beats animals — and women?" He was sure he had guessed right, that she had been beaten, when she would not meet his eyes.

"His father allows him to mistreat animals, and when he has too much to drink — " she paused, and then went on in a different tone: "How is your family, Fortune?"

"Fine. My son is as old as your Julian, but not quite as tall. Eve is a little charmer, and Daniel is still a toddler. Laura may be getting married," he sighed, remembering what Jerome had tried to do to his sister. He continued, "Rachel is planning to go to work using her cooking talents. And Emma and I are expecting another child."

She nodded without responding and said, "Come and see Father sometimes. He always liked you and he'd be glad to have company."

Fortune nodded, said good day to her, and turned toward the small house where his mother and his brother Pete lived.

Pete had killed a deer, and his mother had soaked it in her special concoction of coffee, tomato juice, onions and salt-and-pepper, and roasted it. It was delicious and it reminded Fortune of his childhood. No matter how much money he earned, he'd always enjoy the simple food from the mountains. There were turnip greens, and for dessert, baked apples from a tree in the yard.

After they'd eaten, Fortune helped clear the table, and as they sat by the fire, he told Pete his proposition.

"I don't really know that much about buying tobacco, Fortune."

"You can learn. That's why I'm here. The markets are still open, and I want you to go with me to some of the sales and get an idea of what kind of tobacco I want for my cigarettes."

"And you'll pay me?" Pete asked.

"Of course!"

"What about Ma?"

"I'll be all right here by myself," their mother answered. "Jamie and his wife look in on me nearly every day anyway, while you're at school."

The next day Fortune and Pete set off for Lynchburg, and after that to Danville. Sales were held on different days so that buyers and auctioneers could go from one warehouse to another to give all the farmers a fair chance at selling the crop.

Fortune led the way along the row of hogsheads of tobacco that lined the cement floor of the warehouse. Pausing at one, he bent and reached over into the middle of the pile, pulling out a bundle from underneath the top layer.

"Won't they object to you messing up that pile of tobacco like that?" Pete asked.

"You'll have to get used to doing that. Farmers have been known to put trash tobacco underneath or in the middle of a pile, and cover it up with good tobacco. If you judge only by what you see on top, you may be paying top price for trash. I owe it to my customers to keep up the quality of the cigarettes, otherwise they'll stop buying from me and try someone else's brand. Here's what we're looking for: the bright yellow leaf that has been properly cured. If it's dark and thick, it might be good for making cigars all pipe tobacco or even chewing tobacco, but not cigarettes. Cigarette tobacco needs to be easily crumbled."

The next day, Fortune said, "Now it's your turn. Walk down the row until you see tobacco that you think you'd like to buy, then inspect it."

Pete did as he was told, and Fortune smiled with satisfaction when his brother identified just the right kind of tobacco and decided what to pay for it. Fortune clapped him on the shoulder and said, "I think you're ready to leave school and start making your own fortune."

Pete grinned. "I guess I'll have to say goodbye to my teacher, at least for now."

Chapter 25

Laura stood in the clutter of what was to be Parsons dining room, or, as she had decided it would be called, the Tea Room. She had decided on just the right color for the newly-built walls, a rich gold with white trim. She'd known from the first that she didn't want pink, although she liked it, but there would occasionally be men dining there, and they would think it was too childlike. A sunny yellow was her next choice, but when one wall had been painted light yellow, she realized that would not work either. The gold and white struck a balance between masculine and feminine and gave a bit of elegance to the tea room. It would put customers who were dining in the mood for planning parties and dress-up occasions at historic houses. At least, that's what she hoped.

She'd chosen heavy linen napkins with a large "P" monogrammed in a corner. The tables would be just large enough to seat four people to encourage close, friendly conversation. The chairs were white filigree with metal backs, and velveteen cushions that matched the paint color. She was satisfied so far.

She became aware that Jerome was standing nearby, watching her. "When do you think you'll have your grand opening?" he asked.

"Two weeks before Christmas, if all goes well. The china and cutlery have already been ordered and delivered, and I like the looks so much that I think customers may want to buy sets of their own. You might consider ordering extras. We have some for the inevitable breakage, but if it turns out not to be that bad, we can have them available for sale."

"You keep coming up with these good ideas, Laura. I wouldn't have thought of putting a tea room inside the store, but I think it's going to succeed, not just on its own, but also to boost sales. My father says I should marry you quick, before some other business find out how good you are and snatches you from us."

Laura turned to him, clenching her fist slightly. "So, you and your father have worked it all out between you. Do I get a say-so in it? Please tell your father that I will only marry if I love someone and he loves me. I will not be married just because I'm bringing profit to someone. That makes me no better than a servant." She turned to walk past him, then said, "If you want to benefit from my work and my ideas, you and your father can give me a raise or bonus. You don't have to marry me." She left as tears started to well up in her eyes.

Jerome followed her back to the ladies' department, where a newly hired sales lady was helping a customer. He didn't want to make a scene in front of an employee or a customer, much less both. "Please come by the main office after closing, Miss Barranger," he said.

"Yes, Mr. Parsons."

During the rest of the day, Laura had time to think before she met with Mr. Parsons Sr. George, his name was, though she would never refer to him as anything other than Mr. Parsons. She assigned the young sales lady, Miss Freeman, to refold the stacks of lingerie that customers had rumpled, and to re-hang dresses that had been tried on but not sold. She smoothed it out the sheet of paper she'd had in the tea room, and pretended to be studying it to give herself some time to think. By closing time, she was prepared.

She knocked on the office door, heard a mumbled word that sounded like "Enter," and went in. Mr. Parsons half stood, waved her to a seat, and sat back down, staring at her across the desk.

Without waiting for him to speak, she said, "You don't want me to marry your son, do you?"

"No."

"You sent him with that insulting message, knowing how I would react, didn't you?"

"It could have gone either way. I was taking a chance. He's smitten with you, and if he'd had any gumption about him, he'd have phrased a proposal in a way that you would have accepted, and we wouldn't be having this talk."

"But he always does what you tell him to the best of his ability, doesn't he? He wants to please you."

He sighed. "He's been a disappointment to me. He's just not the go-getter that I need to succeed me."

Laura felt hurt on Jerome's behalf. "He's not a natural salesman, that's true, but you've browbeaten what little initiative he has out of him, so all he knows to do is to follow your directions. He's good at other things. He keeps good records and knows how much of everything is in the store, without needing to check the inventory. He even has ideas on how to improve sales, but he hesitates to talk to you about his ideas, because you've quashed so many of them in the past."

"How dare you talk to me this way? Who do you think you are?" He began to rise from his desk, then sat back down. He reached for a cigarette, and Laura saw that it was one of Fortune's.

"I dare because I think you need to hear the truth, and because I have nothing to lose. If you fire me, you'd be losing your best salesperson, as well as the one who has planned the tea room. It's almost ready, but if I walked away you wouldn't know how to carry on."

"So, what is it you want, if you're not interested in marriage?"

"I didn't say I wasn't interested in marriage, just not marrying for money. I want to be accepted and appreciated. And loved. And I want to earn my own money."

"So how much are we talking about?"

141

Laura crossed her fingers at her side where he couldn't see and said, "Double my salary."

His eyebrows rose in surprise. "Double? You're asking a lot."

"Not when you consider that I've been managing the development of the tea room and managing the ladies' department at the same time."

"All right, double, but no more commission."

"Ten percent," Laura said. "I've been making fifteen percent, so it will be less, but it won't be nothing."

"You have a very high opinion of yourself, Miss Barranger."

"Yes, I do. I know how much I've increased sales in my department, and I know there are other employers who might be interested. One man in particular has come several times to the department, browsing and listening in when I have a customer. He pretends he's shopping for his wife, but on my lunch hour I went to his store to see if I was right, and I was."

He frowned and nodded reluctantly. "All right. I wish you could give my son some of your toughness."

"Perhaps I'll try. Now, would you like to hear about what has been done on the tea room? The painting is almost finished, and as soon as it's done, black and white tile will be laid on the floor. The tables and chairs I chose have been ordered and delivered and are stored. Linens and china should arrive next week. Your son approved the purchases, and I think you did too." Without waiting for his answer, she went on, "He did think that I had chosen china that was too expensive and ordered too much, but in the end he decided that we should have extras on hand in case customers like the china and wanted to buy their own.

"What about the food and the people who will prepare and serve it?" He asked.

"I've asked my sister Rachel to be the hostess in the tea room and to plan the menus and do much of the cooking. You and your son, of course, will supervise the whole operation. Would you like to have Rachel come in and meet with you tomorrow?"

"What are her qualifications?"

"She's an excellent cook and has cooked and served for Mr. and Mrs. Marvin Bishop at their Oak Hill plantation."

"And why did she give up that job?"

"They are seldom there. They spend most of that time in New York and sometimes bring along their own servants when they come to Oak Hill. Would you want her to bring in menus and perhaps a sample of the food she'd be serving?"

He waved his hand dismissively. "I'll trust your judgment on that. But you should know that I'm waiting to see if this tea room is succeeds. If not, I'm cutting your salary back to what it was."

"I suppose that's fair." Laura rose, said good night, and left.

She'd gotten the money she wanted. Now she might get the marriage as well. It would take some doing. Well, some women married a man and then try to change him, but she was going to try to change him beforehand. She had an advantage: Jerome was attracted to her, and that was half the battle.

Chapter 26

In early December, Fortune asked Pete to keep an eye on the cigarette factory while he went to New York. According to his records, sales were down, so he had decided to stop production one day each week until he found out the reason why.

He went to New York on the night train, saving a hotel bill, and went first to a tobacco shop rather than a distributor. A New York shop would be in touch with their customers so their insights would be especially welcome. Were his competitors producing cheaper cigarettes? He didn't know. He'd been so busy with the laying of the trolley lines, keeping in touch with the coal mine and building the house for Emma that he'd overlooked what was happening with the cigarettes, and that was still one of his main sources of income.

There was no need to make an appointment to speak to Mr. Van Sant at his tobacco shop. When he went in, Van Sant was busy with a customer, but he looked up at the tinkle of the bill over the door, and his eyes widened in recognition. Fortune waved his hand, indicating that Van Sant was to take his time; there was no rush.

Van Sant came forward, extending his hand. "Good morning, Mr. Barranger. It's good to see you. How can I help you? Do you have a new product to show me?"

"Not with me, but I may have to produce something new. Sales of Barranger's cigarettes have not been good lately. I was hoping you could tell me why."

"I can tell you what my customers have said. They don't like the box."

Fortune glanced at the boxes stacked neatly on a shelf, and took one down. "What's wrong with it? It's attractive to look at, and it keeps the cigarettes fresh."

"It's a good box to put on a table to offer cigarettes to guests, but our customers don't like carrying it around partly because of its weight, and also because it's awkward to remove from their jackets."

Fortune nodded. "Since I don't smoke, I hadn't considered how the packaging would affect the sales. What do you suggest?"

"A lightweight cardboard that can be glued and shaped into a small box that would fit easily into the inner pocket of a man's jacket. Maybe even stiff paper. It should hold maybe a dozen cigarettes."

"That's a lot of package for a few cigarettes," Fortune objected. "And once a paper package is opened, the cigarettes wouldn't stay fresh."

VanSant laughed. "You needn't worry about keeping cigarettes fresh. Even a beginning smoker a will go through a pack a week, and real smokers smoke as many as twenty a day."

"All right, let's make each pack hold twenty, a day's worth. Paper packages will probably cost less, so I'll drop the price to you a little bit and we'll both make more." Fortune liked making deals, seeking a new level where both he and the customer would be satisfied.

He was surprised when Van Sant shook his head. "No. You're going to produce a new kind of cigarette and raise the price."

"What's wrong with the Barranger's? They've been selling well, even with a metal box."

"They sold well when you were the only producer. Now you have competition. You can keep on making the Barranger's, but people always want to try something new and different, especially if they think it's better. We have to give them the impression that a lord or king would have chosen the cigarette."

"But how can I make it better? The Barranger's are excellent."

"Add a little light tobacco, a little more dark. It doesn't matter. If it's a new product and it cost a little more and you tell them it's better, most of them will think that it is. You've put the idea in their minds."

"No wonder you have the most successful tobacco shop in the city. All right, what should we call this new cigarette? I know how to produce things, but you know how to make someone want them."

"We want them to think of it as really special, but we also want them to remember that tobacco products are produced in Virginia. Who was some famous Virginian? And I don't mean Washington and Jefferson. How about some king like King Charles?"

"No, King Charles had his head cut off, and I think there's a dog breed named King Charles. King George won't do, since we fought to get rid of him. None of them came to Virginia, but William and Mary were very well thought off two hundred years ago."

Then King William it is. Put his image on every package and on the advertisements."

"I don't know what he looked like," Fortune admitted.

"Neither do most people, and they wouldn't care. Just pick the portrait of some man who looks as if he would be a king, and have an artist draw his image in the size to fit the package."

"Do I need to advertise here in the newspapers?"

"That would work for New York, and probably Chicago, but if you really want to get the word about your cigarettes out to America, find a well-known performer who's the star of a traveling show to mention your cigarette. I'll have him smoking your cigarettes and mention them when he's interviewed in local places."

"Why do I need a performer? Fortune asked.

"Well, a Vanderbilt would be ideal, but they don't need money. Writers are often old and shabbily dressed, and with the president of the United States or any other politician, you have to figure that nearly half of the people out there voted against him. Performers are usually good-looking, and they like money and publicity. When you have everything ready—the machinery and everything—you might want to put an advertisement in the Saturday Evening Post."

Fortune's head was spinning with the thoughts of all that had to be done. He and Pete would have to experiment with different blends of tobacco, and find some smokers to try out each one. He had to find out what a king would look like and what he'd wear, and have photographs made so the packages could be designed. That meant finding the right paper, all cardboard, and finding someone who could improvise a machine that would cut the paper just right and glue the pieces together. Then the packages would have to be glued and probably the cigarettes hand-packed, unless he could get a machine that would do that. It was going to be down complicated and expensive.

And it meant getting farther behind in the money he was saving to buy Oak Hill.

Aloud he said, "This is going to cost me a pretty penny."

"True, but eventually it's going to make you a lot of money. Or, if you decide not to do this, you can see yourself losing customers, and maybe having to sell out your factory. It's up to you, but I know which way I would choose," Van Sant said.

Fortune nodded. "You're right. There really isn't much choice for me. I appreciate all your advice. How can I reward you?"

"I want my shipment of the King Williams a week ahead of everyone else in New York. I'm not competing with San Francisco or Chicago, just the other tobacco shops here. And I want the first hundred thousand cigarettes free."

"Agreed," Fortune said. "I will be selling to other shops and to wholesalers here, but I'll make some arrangement an explanation for why their shipments might be delayed."

Before Fortune left, Van Sant had agreed to choose the performer who would be their model and symbolic King William, and locate portraits of suitable kings or nobles for Fortune to choose from. And Fortune in his turn, wrote out a check as an advance on the cost of it all.

He took the late train back to Richmond, unable to sleep for the ideas and figures that whirled in his brain. It was not until he had slipped into bed beside Emma and felt her body warm and plump against him, that he finally fell asleep.

Chapter 27

Laura was pleased with the way the team room was progressing, even though it meant she had little time to rest. Until it opened and proved to be a success, she had to work two jobs to earn her double salary. She trusted Rachel to be at work on time and to prepare the foods the ladies might want, but Rachel hadn't had experience in ordering large quantities of the basic ingredients. What if she ran out of something the customers really wanted?

Most of her concern was over Jerome Parsons. She sensed that she needed to flirt with him, but she'd had no experience in flirting with anyone. She also needed to find out just how much he cared for her. Would he defy his father and marry her? Somehow, she had to build up his belief in himself to the point that he would woo her and make a bold proposal of marriage regardless of what his father thought.

And she needed to find out what his mother thought. Jerome was an only son. Were there daughters? If so, how could she arrange to meet them and find out how they felt about her? No, maybe it was better not to get acquainted with the rest of the family. The fewer people who scorned her and wanted to keep her out of the family, the better.

She needed to talk to someone, to get advice on what to do, but there was no one. She dared not discuss Jerome with anyone at the store. Emma had been expecting Simon when she and Fortune were married, and Laura had no intention of getting Jerome to marry her that way. Rachel hadn't married, and might never marry. Her mother probably would say, "If God wants it to happen, it will happen." But that didn't allow for any action on her part, and she thought where Jerome was concerned that God might need a little help.

She asked Jerome to meet her during lunch at the almost finished tea room. He came in eagerly and took the seat she indicated across the table from her. She wanted him to be able to see her face.

"You wanted to see me?" He asked with the tinge of apprehension in his voice.

"Yes, I need your opinion and advice. First, how do you think the half wall turned out? It gives the diners a sense of being in a separate room, and yet they can see clothing in the distance."

"It looks good," he said.

"Yes, that was a good idea you had."

He looked puzzled. "I – I don't remember suggesting it."

"It was one day when you took me to that tea room on the edge of the city for lunch and you pointed it out and said it looked good. But maybe you were paying more attention to me that day and it slipped your memory," she said coyly, reaching across to touch his arm.

He smiled. "I probably was thinking about you. I think about you a lot. Was that what you wanted me for? To see how the tea room looks?"

"No. I want you to sample some of the food Rachel has planned and tell me what you think. Pretend that you don't know who cooked it, that you're in a restaurant, trying it out for the first time."

Rachel set down a plate of tiny sandwiches cut in triangles with the crust removed. She returned quickly with another tray bearing two cups and a dish of lemon, a bowl holding small sugar cubes and small silver tongs. In the center was a silver teapot and a tiny strainer rested on a saucer. She poured two cups of tea and left.

Laura took one of the chicken salad sandwiches, and pushed the tray slightly toward Jerome. He took one of each kind of sandwich and a ham biscuit. She watched expectantly as he ate, waiting for his approval.

He finished the three items and took a large swallow of his tea. "The chicken salad and ham biscuits are excellent. I don't care for the pimento cheese."

Laura laughed. "I don't either, but some people do. We'll print up menu cards, with your permission, and they can choose which two of the three items they prefer. Does that sound all right?"

"You are a better judge than I am in this. Where did you get the silver teapot in the tray?"

"One of my dress customers offered to lend me hers when I told her about the tea room and our plans. I asked her if she'd be willing to sell it. She said no, but she knew that some women, especially older widows, were impoverished, and would be willing to sell. I met with one of them and bought the set."

He looked up in surprise. "You bought it? Yourself?"

"Yes, but I'm considering loaning it to the store until the tea room shows a profit. Then I'll either give it to my sister-in-law, or maybe keep it for myself. Who knows, I may have need of it someday?"

"My mother has a set, but we seldom use it. I'll ask her if she could lend it to the store so you'd have two sets. If the tea room is really busy, wouldn't you need to have two sets?"

"What an excellent idea. Yes, do please ask your mother. I'll see that Rachel takes good care of it."

"Is she doing everything? You Barrangers are hard workers."

"No. She'll be the hostess and the server, but we've engaged a cook. He'll work here at lunch time, and at the hotel in the evenings."

When Rachel brought out a plate of two petit fours and two lemon crisps, he said, "they look too good to eat, but I will eat them. They must appeal to ladies. Give me a big slice of chocolate cake with black walnuts or sweet potato pie any day."

Laura decided to have Rachel make him a cake. She'd have to find out when his birthday was. But for now, there was other business. "So how do we promote this new business?"

"I'll call someone I know at the *Dispatch*. This is business news."

"Oh, that's a good idea. I should have remembered how my brother had a newspaperman come to the fair and take a picture of me with the cigarette," she said.

"I remember that," he said. "I thought you were the most beautiful woman I'd ever seen, and I never thought that I would be sitting here with you." He stopped, embarrassed that he had said so much.

"Were?" She asked, intent on drawing out a present-day compliment.

He took her hand and looked at her so longingly that she knew he was having difficulty expressing his feelings, and that he did have deep feelings for her. "You are still the most beautiful woman I know, Laura."

"Thank you. And you are one of the nicest men that I know," she said. "I depend on you for so much, and I'm grateful that you took a chance on me."

They finished their tea, and after a moment, she asked, "Besides a newspaper article, how can we get customers to actually come to the tea room?"

He set down his cup. "We could give them a discount, maybe for the first week. Maybe free tea or coffee to everyone who comes in to shop, and a free dessert if they buy something."

"What a good idea!", Laura said touching his arm. She quickly withdrew her hand, as if touching him had been impulsive rather than intentional. "How should we handle this so Rachel will know who gets beverage and who gets dessert?" She had her own idea, but she wanted to draw him out, force him to make decisions.

"I can get the cards printed," he said. He dropped his napkin beside his plate. "Well, I'd better go tell my father what we're planning."

She grasped his hand, stopping him from getting up and leaving the table. "No, don't tell him. What if he says no? Then we would never know if your good ideas would have helped the tea room succeed. I want him to see what we can do on our own."

He seemed to relax, and said, "I like that you said we. I enjoy working with you, Laura."

"And I with you," she said with a smile. "Do you have any more ideas and suggestions for the tea room?"

He glanced around. "It's a beautiful room, but it looks a little bare. What about a Christmas tree?"

"A Christmas tree?" She was startled. He did have some ideas of his own, without her prodding.

"Queen Victoria has a Christmas tree in the palace. Why can't we have one here? Just for a week or so, since you're planning to open in time for ladies to shop before Christmas."

"I think that's wonderful. We could put it right over there." She pointed to an area at the back of the room. "I was thinking we needed a potted palm or maybe some indoor plants, but a Christmas tree would be special. Maybe we can find one on my brothers land."

"Shall I come Sunday after church to help you choose it and bring it back to the store? I'll pay for it, of course."

"That would be fine, but I don't think he would charge you for it."

They walked together back to the ladies' department, and when she watched him go off to the new relocated men's department, she felt triumphant. He'd complimented her and taken her hand, and made it clear he was attracted to her. She felt a new respect for him as well. He did have ideas of his own. He only needed encouragement, and that she could give him.

Chapter 28

On Friday just as Laura was getting ready to go to lunch in the tea room, Jerome came in carrying a folded newspaper. "You want to see this," he said. "May I join you for lunch?"

"Of course. Miss Freeman, I'll come back as soon as I can so you can take your lunch hour," she said to her junior sales lady.

After they had ordered sandwiches and coffee, Jerome opened the newspaper. There on the front page was a photo of Fortune standing beside a trolley. The headline read, "Trolley line extended. Opening soon."

Laura took the newspaper and read briefly:

"Mr. Fortune Barranger announced yesterday that the electric trolley will have two new lines westward and one southwestward, beginning January 1. 'People are moving west and southwest of the city,' Mr. Barranger stated. 'I myself am building a new home out to the west just beyond where the trolley line will end. Rides on the new trolley lines will be free on January first.'"

"In addition to his investment in the trolley company, Mr. Fortune Barranger owns a coal mine in western Virginia, which furnishes electricity that powers the trolley and his cigarette factory. He is partial owner of the railroad that hauls the coal and also owns a large tract of land just outside the city limits. He is said to be involved in other beginning enterprises, but he declined to be specific about those."

"That's a wonderful article about Fortune," Laura said. "He always did know how to get publicity when he needed it. What about our tea room?"

"On page three" Jerome said, opening and refolding the paper.

The article about the tea room was much shorter, and there was no photo, but still, it was publicity about Parsons. The headline read "Parsons Expanding."

"Parsons, the well-known ready-to-wear store, has recently bought the adjoining building and installed its menswear department, which is supervised by Mr. Jerome Parsons, son of the founder. In the space vacated, there is now an attractive small café. This is an unusual arrangement, having to go through the ladies' department to reach the café, which is reminiscent of a plantation dining room, though with small tables. It was designed and supervised by Mr. Jerome Parsons and his associate, Miss Laura Barranger, sister of Mr. Fortune Barranger (see page 1).

"Ladies will feel comfortable and safe dining here either alone or in company with other ladies or even occasionally a gentleman. The food is delicious, assorted small sandwiches and dessert served by the charming young hostess, Miss Rachel Barranger, also of that up-and-coming family."

Laura felt for a moment as if she'd been slapped. It seemed from the article is if the tea room had been due to him and she had just helped. But wasn't that what she had wanted—for Jerome to get credit for more things about the store? "That's good for the tea room and the store," she said. "Your father should be very proud of you. When did he come over that I didn't know about it?"

"In the middle of the morning. You were busy with a customer and I didn't see any reason to bother you." He leaned closer to say quietly, "He seemed very interested in Rachel, and he might've been attracted to you as well, and I didn't want that." Laura fought the urge to grimace at the idea. "By the way, he said a gentleman who came along to dine here would want something substantial, like a roast beef sandwich with horseradish. He suggested it to Rachel, and she seemed quite taken with the idea, so don't be surprised if you see it on the menu."

The roast beef sandwich did appear on the menu, and it was Rachel who decided on its name: Gentlemen's Choice.

Emma had been warned that Jerome Parsons might come up for Sunday dinner after church and had prepared extra food. He complimented everything but was eager to go looking for the Christmas tree.

"I'll take you in the carriage," Fortune offered, failing to notice that Laura was shaking her head.

Emma noticed, and said, "I'd like to go too. I want to see how far along the builders are with our house, as I want to be there when the baby was born. Rachel, would you mind the children for me?" She rose awkwardly from the table and without waiting for approval or refusal from anyone, she got her cape from the front hall closet and flung it about her shoulders. The other three rose quickly, put down their napkins and joined her.

Fortune delayed briefly to fetch a hand saw. "You'll need this to cut down the tree," he said, handing it to Jerome.

When they reached in the new house, Jerome took Laura's hand to assist her in alighting. Then he turned back to aid Fortune. Each man took one of Emma's elbows and she laid her hands on their shoulders. Together the two men helped Emma come down from the carriage.

Jerome picked up the saw and he and Laura started walking off across the field where cedars and pines grew. "They look small out here, but inside they'll be too big for the space," Fortune called after them.

Soon they spotted a suitable cedar. Jerome took off his jacket and handed it to Laura, then bent to saw at the trunk of the tree. As the saw teeth bit into the trunk, a small bit of sawdust accumulated on the saw, but Laura saw that he was cutting the tree at a slant and that it would have to be re-cut before it could stand up. She longed to take the saw from him and do the job quickly and properly, but she knew it was important for him to perform manual tasks for her, so she said nothing.

Eventually Jerome managed to saw through the trunk of the small cedar, and held it up triumphantly. "This is going to look perfect in the tea room," he said. He set down the tree for a moment and put on his jacket, then picked up the tree again.

"Can we order some ornaments from New York tomorrow?" She asked.

"Of course."

He turned around and looked across the field. "The land slopes downward from here, so the James River is just over that way," he observed. Laura nodded. Back at the carriage, Jerome tied the tree down firmly and looked at the new house. "It's going to be an impressive home," he said. "Shall we join them inside?"

"I think it's an ugly house on the outside, and so does Fortune."

"Then why is he building it this way?"

"To please Emma. He doesn't plan to live here very long."

"Where is your family going?" He asked in alarm.

"Fortune plans to buy Oak Hill someday. That's what he's worked for since he came to Richmond. He's made a lot of money, but every time he has enough saved up to buy Oak Hill, something happens, like the coal mine collapse and the drop in cigarette sales that made him close down and change everything. And now this house."

"Is Oak Hill for sale? What if someone else buys it before he can get the money together?"

"It's not actually for sale, but the owner is deep in debt and he borrowed against the house. Someday that debt must be paid, and Fortune plans to be the man to pay off the bank loan. Then it will cost a lot more to make the house livable."

"Why does he want it?"

"Well, it comes with a lot of land, and it is a fine old house, and it has beautiful views of the mountains. He thinks of it as his own kingdom. But mainly he wants it because the owners think he's not good enough to live there."

"What?" He said. "I'm astounded that anyone would think Fortune or you or anyone else in your family is not good enough for the finest house in Virginia whatever that is. I hope Fortune is able to buy his Oak Hill."

"I hope so too. I don't think he could bear going back to see Mama knowing someone else owns that house."

"What kind of house do you want, Laura?"

"I'd like mine to be brick with white columns and the front porch upstairs and down. Behind it, I like to have a garden that slopes down to the river, and maybe a pier there where I could have a boat."

He took her arm and turned her toward the front door of the new house. "Let's see the inside. You may like that better. And I must ask your brother how much a lot sloping toward the river would cost."

Laura didn't answer, but she felt a little thrill of triumph. If he was considering buying a lot just like she had described, that must mean that he thought of marrying her.

They walked through the spacious downstairs rooms. Laura was especially interested in the bathroom, which had a deep porcelain hand basin on a pedestal, and a separate compartment which held a flush toilet. It was all very luxurious. Each of the downstairs rooms had a fireplace, set into large stone chimney.

Fortune and Emma were making their way slowly around the downstairs area as well. "What's it like upstairs?" Laura asked.

"One bathroom, three bedrooms," Fortune said. "Emma and I will be downstairs, and upstairs there's a room for each of the children and one for you and Rachel, Laura."

"It looks as if it's almost ready to move in," Jerome observed.

"The floors need to be varnished, and you can see that the mantels haven't been installed. I ordered carved marble ones, and they haven't arrived. The outside has a protective coat of paint on it, but it will have to wait for spring for the second coat."

Laura followed Emma back into the master bedroom, where Emma took a last loving look around. Laura tried not to hear the discussion between Jerome and her brother about the cost of a house.

Chapter 29

When Laura opened the box of ornaments at the store, she saw with dismay that half of them were broken. "What am I going to put on the tree?"

"I'll call New York for more, but I there may not be time for them to arrive."

"A half-bare Christmas tree would look terrible in the tea room, Jerome. Or maybe we can find some things around the store that would do, like beads."

Once she said the words, she realized that was what she wanted all along, that the tree would make an excellent promotional piece by itself. "Can you come along with me, and keep a record of everything I put in the box so we'll know how many items have moved and where they'll go back to?"

Within half an hour they had gathered up cameos and other brooches, strings of inexpensive beads, hair ribbons, men's bowties, watch fobs, cufflinks, and for the very top of the tree, a red bird that had been intended to perch atop a hat. After they decorated it all, they stepped back to look.

"It's unusual but I like it," Jerome said.

"Let's pretend that's what we had in mind all along," Laura said. "And I think we need to put our tree up on a stand or roped off, so our customers don't take a fancy to something and decide to make off with it."

He laughed. "You don't trust our customers?"

"When you have enough people gathered, one or two may be tempted to take something that's not theirs."

Jerome agreed. "I've got the little tickets for a free beverage and the ones for a free beverage and dessert printed," he said, "and those were the last things to do. Now we'll just see how everything works."

On opening day, Laura distributed beverage tickets to everyone who came into her department, whether they purchased anything or not, with a helpful, "Why not go have a sip of something hot in Avenue tea room and finish your shopping later?" To those who had made a purchase, she gave a ticket for beverage and dessert, and told them, "You may leave your parcel here, safely locked up in our closet, and pick it up on your way out."

She was pleased to hear her sales assistant, Miss Freeman, saying the same thing. By the time twelve thirty arrived and Laura went to the tea room, all the ham biscuits and chicken salad sandwiches were gone, as well as the petit fours. Reluctantly, she settled for the pimento cheese sandwich and some lemon crisps along with tea.

She was amused to see a line at the bottom of the menu that read: "To those gentlemen lucky enough to be dining here with a lady, we offer the Gentlemen's Choice roast beef sandwich." A strange man was talking with Rachel. As Laura approached, Rachel said, "Here she is now!" and introduced her to Zachary Todd, reporter for the *Dispatch* newspaper. He stood and bowed slightly, and Laura waved him to his seat.

"Miss Barranger, your sister was just giving you credit for designing and building this tea room. I mentioned to you in my article, which I hope you saw."

Laura nodded, hastily eating her sandwich and drinking tea so that she could be back to her post in time to give shoppers their parcels. It wouldn't matter if they waited a few minutes; they might see something else to purchase. But it wouldn't do for them to get impatient.

"Miss Rachel Barranger, can you stand over beside your sister so I can get a photo of the two of you together. Now that I have seen the tea room in operation, I'd like to do a follow-up article on you too, titling my article 'Successful Sisters'."

Obediently, Laura looked up from her lunch, smiled, and hope she hadn't blinked when the flash went off.

At the end of the day Jerome came by to find out how much the tea room had brought in in food sales as well as in clothing sales.

Rachel was sorting the vouchers. "Over half the people who received a ticket for dessert or beverage also bought lunch," she announced. "We sold out of nearly everything, so I'll know how much to make in the future. Of course, there may not be as many people on what is not the opening day. On the other hand, they may tell their friends and we may have even more customers. Mr. Todd talked with some of them while they were dining, and they said they liked it and might bring their friends to lunch here even when they didn't plan to shop."

Two days later, Laura and Rachel arrived back at the house to see wagons parked outside and men carrying out furniture. "What's going on?" Laura asked as Fortune stepped outside.

"The varnish has dried on the floors and the mantels have been installed, so we're moving."

Inside the house was chaos, and neither sister knew quite where to go or what to do. Wardrobes and chests from upstairs had been brought down and stood in a jumble in the front hallway, almost blocking the way in and out. Linens had been stripped off bids and tied up in bundles, and as each load of furniture was completed, a mattress was tied around it to protect the load during the journey. The dining room and parlor stood empty.

Where do we sleep tonight? Laura asked.

"And what are we going to eat?" Rachel asked.

"At the new house," Fortune announced firmly. "I hired a woman, the wife of one of these wagon drivers, to pack up the kitchen things right after breakfast and take them over to the new house. Then I made sure a comfortable chair and the bed were in the first load of furniture, so

Emma can be comfortable and oversee the unpacking over there. We'll go in the carriage as soon as the last load leaves. I hope we can make it before dark and before any rain or sleet comes."

It was growing dark as Fortune, Laura, and Rachel climbed into the carriage and followed the last two wagons to the new home. Everything was in the new house, but who knew where anything was? Still, Emma would have her wish: they would be in the new house before the baby came.

By Christmas Eve, both sisters were exhausted from sorting out things at home and selling things at the store.

On Christmas morning, Laura sat up with a start, seeing how light it was outside. She was going to be late! And then she realized what day it was and lay back. The store would be closed on Christmas Day and the day after. All she had to do today was get up, get dressed, and go with the family to church. Fortune had even hired the same woman who helped with the move to come in and cook breakfast, so Emma didn't have to, and neither did Rachel.

Fortune had invited his mother to come and be with the family for Christmas, but she had written back: "The other part of my family is here, son. I'll be with Jamie's family and Pete and maybe his teacher girlfriend, unless she goes back home to be with her own family. I'll come there when the new baby arrives, but I won't stay more than two weeks, so you'll be looking for somebody permanent to hire to do the housework and help Emma with the children, now that both my bright daughters are working full-time."

At church, Laura saw the Parson family: the elder Mr. Parson and his wife, Jerome, and his younger sister, who had been away at school. She smiled, but made no effort to approach the family. Mr. Parsons Sr. still thought of her as just an employee, which she was, she admitted. Jerome approached and handed her a small flat box tied up with the red ribbon. "Merry Christmas, Laura. Open this when you

164

get home." He held her hand in both of his for a long moment, and gave her such a passionate look that she almost felt as if she'd been kissed.

When Laura opened the box, she saw a strand of pearls. She knew immediately, both from experience at the store, and by the pearls themselves—lustrous and heavy—that they were genuine and expensive. What did this mean? Should shoe accept such a gift from him?

Fortune had purchased toys for the children, and gloves for Emma and his sisters, soft kid lined with fur, with buttons at the wrists.

As they were thanking him, he announced, "I gave myself the best gifts of all, but we can all use them. I'm having a telephone installed in the small room next to the parlor, which will be my office here. And when we travel, especially out to the mountains, we'll go in comfort. I bought our very own railroad car, which has comfortable seats that turn into beds, and bathroom facilities."

On December 27, Jerome helped Laura take down the Christmas tree and return all the items to their proper department. She put off mentioning the pearls until they finished.

"Jerome, I appreciate the pearls, but they are too expensive. I didn't get you anything."

"I didn't expect you to. I wanted to give you more, but I didn't want to upset you. They are a personal gift for you, my dear Laura, but if it bothers you to think that way, then consider them a thank you for all you have done for the store and for me."

Laura felt her face flush at the term of endearment. It was the first time he had used any such term to her. She waited to see if he said more, but he didn't. He just held her hand in both of his, longer than usual.

Two days later she was taking inventory of the dresses in stock when he came to help. She held up a rust colored crêpe. "It's no wonder this didn't sell. It's awful. We're going to have to mark it down to a very low price to entice anyone to buy it. Who chose it?"

He shrugged. "My father, I'm sure. He sometimes gets a good deal from the clothing warehouse, taking items at a very low price."

"But it's not a good deal if no one wants to buy the dresses. I could sell a lot more if I could choose them myself. I know what our customers want now."

"I'll see if I can arrange for you to go on a dress buying trip to New York next month," he said.

"Oh, I'd like that!" She said. Of course, she thought, some people promise things just to please, but never get around to fulfilling the promise. And some people promise things that aren't theirs to offer.

But to her surprise, some ten days later, the older Mr. Parsons summoned her to his office after work, and said, "My son has persuaded me that we should send you to New York to choose the spring and summer clothing for the store. I think it's a waste of money, but I'm willing to pay for your trip to prove to him what a mistake it is. If we lose money on the dresses you choose, you'll lose your commission and possibly your salary until the loss is made up. Do you still want to go under those circumstances?" He hadn't even asked her to sit down, and wanted an immediate answer.

Laura was angry. This man always made her angry as he considered not only her but his son to be incompetent. Didn't he realize that someday he would be too old to run the business and someday he would die and his son would inherit it—unless he had someone else in mind—and what would happen then if he had not given his son a chance to learn the business and take risks? Hadn't he begun to trust Jerome after the success of the tea room?

Pushing her anger aside, Laura made herself smile and said, "Yes, sir, I do want to go. I think your son and I are capable of making good business decisions for the store. I assume that he is to go with me, since a lady might not be safe alone in New York."

"Yes, of course he will go. He has been before, along with me. I'm the one who has chosen the clothing that you find so difficult to sell. Jerome knows the sellers in the garment district, and he will have control of the line of credit, so you can't buy anything outrageously expensive, or make underhanded deals."

Again, Laura felt her anger rising within her. He was insulting not only her ability to choose clothing, but her honesty and integrity as well. Still, this was a chance. "Yes, I will go." As she left his office, she said to herself, *and I will prove you wrong.*

Jerome came to the ladies' department at closing time the next day. "This trip may not be very pleasant, Laura," he said. "Since sales are usually very slow on Monday, do you suggest that we close the department altogether on Monday, or do you trust Miss Freeman to handle sales while we're gone?"

"Whichever you and your father choose will be satisfactory to me," she said.

"I'll leave it up to him, then. We'll take the train on Sunday evening and I have appointments for us to see all the dressmaking establishments during the day and take the night train back. I know it will be tiring, but it's the best my father would agree to. He's a tightfisted man, and I sometimes think he wants us to fail."

"We'll show him he's wrong," she said.

When they arrived in New York, Laura said, "I want to buy myself a coat, something that's warm enough for this cold weather, and attractive enough to make me look like a suitable dress buyer."

"I'll buy it for you."

Laura shook her head. "No, you won't. I've been saving my salary, and I know what I want." As they walked past a department store, Laura saw just what she wanted on display in the window, and led him inside. Within moments she had purchased a dark green wool coat trimmed in gold braid, fitted at the waist and flaring out just below the knee. She momentarily considered throwing her shabby old coat into a trash bin, but thought better of it. Some poor person back in Virginia might welcome it.

All day they walked among racks of women's dresses, coats, and hats. Laura chose lightweight but serviceable fabrics in pastel shades for spring. Easter would be late, which gave them time to sell lighter clothing for the season instead of dark heavy materials. When they stopped for a late lunch, Laura looked at the list of dresses and other items they had bought, and said, "I think that's enough. If I buy too much and the items don't sell, your father will make me pay a high price, and you as well."

"Do you think this trip was worth spending two nights on the train?"

"Oh, yes," she answered, laying aside the buttered roll. "This way, I was able to feel the fabric. If I like the way the fabric feels against my skin, so will my customers, very likely. And I could see the cut of the dresses. I don't think your father would pay that much attention." She picked up her fork and lifted a bit of fried oyster to her mouth.

"Would you like to see wedding dresses?" Jerome asked.

"Is Parsons planning to start selling wedding dresses?" She asked in surprise.

"Maybe, but I was thinking of getting one for yourself."

She put down her fork and looked at him. Are you proposing?"

"Yes."

"Would you want to marry me if I decided to continue working at the store?"

"Yes, I would."

"Well, what if I decided to stop working?"

"If we have children, I would expect you to, or at least hope that you would want to."

"Why do you want to marry me?" She persisted.

"Because I love you, Laura."

"Then ask me properly."

"Laura Barranger, will you do me the honor to become my wife?" He asked solemnly.

"Yes, I will."

"And why are you agreeing to marry me?" he asked, turning her questions back on her.

"Because I love you, of course."

He reached across the table and took her hand. "Then it's settled. We're engaged. Now, do you want to look at wedding dresses, or perhaps wedding rings? We still have some hours to spare before train time."

By the time they boarded the southbound train, Laura had chosen a slim line white satin dress, and a short veil. She had tried on half a dozen rings, trying to get some idea of what Jerome could afford and wanted to buy for her. They finally settled on an emerald with a small diamond on each side.

They kissed and snuggled in each other's arms in the darkened train car on the way home, discussing possible dates for a wedding, and where they might live. To Laura's dismay, Jerome suggested that they live with his parents until their house was complete, though it hadn't even been begun.

"I've never met your mother, but I know your father doesn't like me. It would be difficult to live with him. Shall we rent a place, or would you prefer to wait until the house is complete before we married?"

"We'll rent, if those are my only two choices," Jerome said. "Perhaps we could rent the house your brother's family just moved out of. Or we could find a small apartment near the store."

Laura eventually fell asleep considering these plans, and awakened when the train jolted to a stop and she saw that it was daylight outside.

"I see the carriage is waiting for us, with the driver," Jerome said. "I'll take you out to your brother's home, and wait while you freshen up and are ready to return to the store."

Laura groaned. She'd been gone only one day and two nights and her whole life was turned upside down. She was exhausted. Still, she had a job to go to.

Chapter 30

Laura opened the front door to a scene of chaos. Rachel met her in the front hallway, dressed for outdoors, in high boots and with a cape thrown about her shoulders. Behind her Simon and Eve stood ready for school—or, at least, partly ready.

"Thank goodness you're here, Laura," Rachel said. "Fortune has gone on the train for Mama, the midwife has another patient to go to, and Mrs. Stanley is late getting here. I would stay, but I'm already late for work, and I don't know anything about looking after babies." She looked as if she were about to burst into tears, and her usually immaculate braided crown of hair hung askew. "You've got to help, Laura." Her voice rose to a high pitch.

Laura put her hand on her sister's arm. "We'll do what we can," she said, indicating Jerome who stood awkwardly behind her. As if waiting for all her signal, he closed the front door, shutting out the cold drizzling rain.

"It's a good thing the trolley is running out this way now," Laura said. "Can you walk over to the line and get to the store that way? Do you have something special that needs to be done at the store, could you accompany the children to school on your way?"

"We don't need anyone to accompany us," Simon said stoutly. "We know where the school is and we're already late. I can look after Eve." He looked at his sister, and gave her a slight nudge to move toward the door." Laura asked, "Where is Daniel?"

Simon responded, "He's still asleep."

Laura looked at the young man with admiration. She'd been so busy with her job that she'd hardly noticed how tall her nephew had grown. He was already taking responsibilities, as his father had always done. "Do you have money for the trolley fare?" She asked.

"We don't need money for a fare," he said. "Father owns the trolley, after all. We have a pass so we can ride anytime and anywhere we want to. And even if he didn't own it, the school would have arranged for us to ride the trolley."

Laura realized how little she knew of the family's arrangements. She and Rachel had been accustomed to going to work early and on their own, and leaving the household to be managed by someone else. She decided to trust Simon, even if it were the first time the children had gone on the trolley alone. They needed to be in school and would only be in the way here with a new baby. "Go on, then," she said. "Will there be a problem if you're late?"

Simon shook his head. "The teachers like us, or else they're afraid that father will buy the school and fire them if they punish us unnecessarily."

Laura laughed uneasily. This child already knew how much power his father had, and that Fortune would have done just that: bought out the place and changed the personnel. "Eve, where are your gloves? And do you two have umbrellas?"

The two children scurried to find the gloves and umbrellas, and Jerome said, "I can take everyone to the trolley, and come back for you, Laura," he offered.

"Yes, thank you. Take them to the trolley and then go for Mrs. Stanley and I will stay here until you get back. Find out if there's a reason she can't come today, and come back with either her or a good reason. I'll stay here until she comes. If she's sick, then I'll have to stay all day. I'm sure Miss Freeman has opened the dress department."

The house was cleared and quiet but for the sound of moaning from Emma's bedroom, and the faint mewing cries of the newborn baby.

Laura went in to see Emma. The midwife had taken care of everything efficiently, and now sat dressed and ready to leave. "Did my brother pay you?" Laura asked.

The midwife nodded. "Most generously, thank you." She stood. "I must be going. There's another woman that needs me right now, so you can be in charge. And I'm most grateful that the trolley runs, so I didn't have to arrange for a buggy to bring me and wait around." She picked up her satchel and started for the door.

"Is the baby a boy or girl?" Laura asked.

"A girl, tiny and helpless but seemingly healthy. She took some time coming, but Mrs. Barranger is going to be all right." Without saying anything further, she left.

Laura went to the crib and looked down at the baby. She looked very much like the others had looked when they were newborns. Her tiny fist was in her mouth. Should she pick her up? She turned to the bed. "Emma, can I do anything to help you?"

Emma stopped moaning. "I'll be all right. I wish Fortune hadn't left. He's never here when I need him the most."

"He wouldn't be much help anyway," Laura said. "Our mother always took care of things, and he's gone for her. Mrs. Stanley should be here soon. I sent Jerome to look for her. What about the baby? She seems to be trying to suck on her fist?"

"She's hungry, and I don't think my milk is coming in. Bring her here and let me try to nurse her."

Laura picked up the baby. She knew to put her hand under her neck and head and the other hand under her buttocks. She laid her gently in Emma's arms, and noted that Emma had stopped moaning, and was looking down at the tiny infant with fondness. She have been scared to try for more children, but she seemed to love this one. She opened her nightgown and brought the infants tiny mouth to her breast. After a moment's hesitation, the baby began to suck, and Emma smiled "we'll be all right now, won't we, Leticia?"

"You're naming her Leticia?"

Emma nodded contentedly, and Laura tiptoed out.

As she made her way upstairs to get cleaned up and changed, she realized how totally fatigued she was. Two nights on the train plus a day of making decisions about clothing had wearied her more than she had expected. And with all the family problems this morning, she realized she hadn't even thought about Jerome's proposal. This didn't seem the time to tell the family.

By the time he returned with Mrs. Stanley she was ready to go to the store and after he dropped her off, he went home to get ready for the store himself. Neither had mentioned the proposal on the ride.

Chapter 31

As Laura entered the tea room, she couldn't help noticing the man in gray seated at a table all alone. He motioned her over.

"Miss Barranger, will you join me?"

Laura hesitated. "Who are you?"

"Jonas Hoffman."

Slowly Laura eased into the chair across the table from him. "You are the owner of the other big store. Do you have some complaint about your lunch?" She gestured at the cup of coffee in front of him. "Or have you not eaten yet?"

"I have had lunch. Quite delicious. But I came here not for the food, good as it is, but to speak to you. I want you to come and work for me, and I'll pay double whatever these miserly Parsons are paying you."

Laura's eyes widened in surprise and for a moment she couldn't speak, merely staring at him. His dark eyes seem to compel her to look at him. She dropped her gaze to his pristine white shirt, his well-fitting gray suit, and then to his hands, large hands that lay very still on the table. Finally, she managed, "What do you want me for? What am I to do?"

"Don't look so shocked. It's certainly nothing illegal. I've seen what you have done for Parsons, and I don't think they appreciate you or make the best use of your talent. Come to my office tomorrow during your lunch break and let's discuss it. I'll give you plenty of time to think about this." He smiled, and Laura felt as if the smile brought her into a different world, a world of generosity and appreciation.

He rose and left, and Laura saw her sister approaching with a plate bearing a sandwich and a slice of pickle the lunch she usually ordered. In her other hand she carried a pot of tea. She set down the plate and poured tea before she spoke to Laura. "What did he want? He's spent ages waiting for you."

Laura glanced around to make sure no one was listening and lowered her voice. "He's offered me a job, at double what the Parsons are paying."

"Are you going to accept?"

"Probably. I have to think about it."

On the way home in the carriage with Jerome, Laura didn't mention the job offer. Instead, she touched Jerome's arm, slid close to him, and said, "I didn't tell my family last night that we're engaged, but I will tonight. When do you think we should make a public announcement and set a date for our wedding?"

She felt his arm stiffen beneath her fingertips. "We can't marry until our house is ready," he said.

Laura looked around at the empty field beyond Fortune and Emma's house. "But you haven't even started on the house. Can't we rent a house?"

"I want you to have a fine house. I suppose we could live with my parents, but I'd have to have a serious talk with them."

Laura felt a chill run through her, and removed her hand from his arm. He wasn't in any rush to marry her and live with her, it was obvious. He'd been carried away by the setting in New York, when the two of them had been together having a good time, away from his family. If she accused him or even questioned him, he would deny it. She had more to think about than the job offer, and this was not the time to mention it to Jerome.

As she went into the house, she decided not to tell anyone that Jerome had proposed. Not just yet, until she was clear in her own mind that he really wanted to marry her, and wasn't putting her off for a year or more. She'd already told him he didn't need to drive her to and from work, as the streetcar line ran close to the house. Thus, she wouldn't need to see him until she'd made up her mind about Mr. Hoffman's job offer. Then she'd see what Jerome had to say.

The next morning, she went early to the store, and made sure she was all caught up on the sales records before she went to talk to Mr. Hoffman. Perhaps it would be good to be working elsewhere, so Jerome wouldn't take for granted that he could see her just anytime. Besides, she wanted always to have money of her own, and this way she could have twice as much, if she liked what Mr. Hoffman offered.

She took the stairs to Hoffman's office on the second floor, noting that there was no elevator. Well, for double the money she could walk upstairs.

He stood when she entered, and waved her to a comfortable chair, then smiled and sat back down. "Have you decided?"

"What exactly am I to do? I didn't want to discuss it at the tea room."

"I'm going to build an entirely new store, one that will attract people from as far away as Washington. I wanted to have not just clothing but everything that one might want for inside the home: dishes, bedding, decorations and so on. There would also be a jewelry section and perhaps a perfume section, and I think I'd want the café on the bottom level. I'd give you a free hand in designing the café and deciding what else would go into the store itself."

Laura's mind whirled at the possibilities. It would be a big responsibility, but one that she thought she could handle. "And before this new building is finished, I suppose I am to work in the ladies' clothing department?"

"Yes, and you will have a free hand in deciding what clothing we sell. I'm afraid I don't have a talent for picking out women's clothing."

"It sounds exciting," Laura said. "I accept."

He reached across the desk to take her hand. "I think we will make a good team. When can you begin?"

"I think it's proper to give Parsons two weeks' notice. Is that satisfactory?"

He nodded. "You may find that Mr. Parsons Sr. will not take it kindly losing his best salesperson, and he may put conditions on your leaving, but I'm willing to have you began work whenever you can."

At the end of the day, Laura went to Mr. Parsons' office to give her notice. Before she could finish speaking, he broke in angrily, "you don't need to give two weeks' notice. You can gather your things this evening or tomorrow if you can't manage it all this evening. Have you no gratitude? After all we've done for you, you're betraying our trust."

Laura stared at him, her mouth open and astonishment. Then she closed her mouth and bit her bottom lip to keep from saying the angry words that poured into her mind. Why should she be grateful to them? She had brought business to Parsons, and had improved the latest dress department as well as designing and opening the tea room. They should be grateful to her.

Mr. Parsons was not finished with his invective. "I understand that you ordered a number of dresses on the store account when you were in New York last week, I expect you to pay for them. Or you can work another week without pay and see how many you can sell."

Laura started to say she would give him her decision the next day, but she already knew what it would be. "I shall pay for them. Please deduct what you owe me in salary for the past week from the cost of the dresses. I shall pay you the day that the shipment arrives, which should be on Friday, I think, although I know that you won't be paying the seller for them for thirty days." She rose and left his office.

The cost of the dresses was more than she had in her savings account, but she could borrow the remainder from Fortune, and pay him back now that her salary would be double.

She put on her coat and walked the block to Hoffman's store and up to his office.

He looked up in surprise. "I hope you haven't changed your mind about coming to work here."

Laura shook her head. "No, but I am no longer employed by Parsons as of today. I can start tomorrow if you have any need of me. And I have a problem. When I was in New York, I placed an order for a number of spring dresses, with Mr. Parson's permission, but now he says that I had guaranteed they would sell, so I must buy them all."

"Sit down and calm down. I see you're trembling, probably with anger. Or at least I hope its anger and not disappointment or sadness at leaving Parsons. There's no problem with the dresses. I'll pay for them, and I'm sure you'll be able to sell them. You have good taste and perhaps we can arrange a fashion show and attract over the customers who used to shop with you at Parsons."

Laura realized she had been clenching her hands and quivering with anger and shock. She felt the frustration and anger leave her. Mr. Hoffman had a way of smoothing out all her problems.

After a moment he said, "What about young Parsons? What did he have to say about it?"

"Nothing," she said in some puzzlement, realizing that Jerome must have been near his father's office and heard his father's bellows of anger. She hadn't been expecting him to take her home, but he might have at least come by to speak to her sometime during the afternoon. After all, they were engaged. How could she possibly marry him now and have his father as her father-in-law, managing her life? Did she still want to marry him?

Jonas Hoffman studied her for some minutes in silence. Then he asked quietly "Aren't you tired of trying to make that boy act like a man? You need a real, grown man, a man who will stand up for you and protect you and respect you for your fine qualities." He paused looked at her with those compelling dark eyes and added, ". . . a man like me".

Laura stared at him, "what are you saying?" she managed.

"Just that young Parsons doesn't deserve you. Has he proposed to you?"

Laura nodded wordlessly.

"And did you accept?"

Again, Laura nodded. "Just two days ago."

"Then he should be almost giddy with excitement and making plans for your future even as we speak. Do you think that's what he's doing? Is he searching for you at this moment, furious that his father has spoken badly to you?"

"I don't know."

"Why don't you wait and see what happens this evening? If you go home and find him waiting for you, or he shows up, demanding to see you, and wanting to apologize and set the date for marriage, and if that's what you want, I say no more. On the other hand, if he can't stand up to his father, then his love for you is not strong enough to last a lifetime. If you want to marry him after the way his father treated you, of course I can't stop you, but I do warn you of what your life will be like. I still want you to help me plan a store. But if you're free, and can reject him with no regrets, then I would like you as a wife as well as a colleague."

Laura could only nod, dazed. She made her way out, and as she exited the building, she walked the short distance to the Parsons store but did not see Jerome looking for her. She turned back and got on the trolley.

This morning, she'd had a job at Parsons and a fiancé. Now she had a new job and if she wanted him, a new fiancé.

As the trolley clanged its way, she compared Jerome with Jonas Hoffman. Mr. Hoffman was a man much like Fortune, who made up his mind easily and who controlled his own destiny. He didn't have to answer to an overbearing father, didn't have to wait for anyone to die or retire before he could come into his own.

Laura found herself imagining sitting across the dining table from Jonas Hoffman, feeling comfortable and protected, not needing to build up his belief in himself and being on her own until one day he did. She'd made up her mind before she got home, before she even knew whether Jerome would come to beg her to marry him and to come back to the store. She didn't know Mr. Hoffman at all except for what few words they'd exchanged and the way he made her feel. If she accepted his proposal, and abrupt as it was, she'd have time to get to know him, and it might be very exciting.

Over dinner she told the family that she was going to work for Mr. Hoffman. "for more money, I hope," Fortune said, nodding his approval as he cut a piece of steak and put it into his mouth.

"Yes, double," Laura said. And a lot more responsibility."

"When do you start? Rachel asked.

"Tomorrow, Mr. Parsons told me not to come back."

"And what does your young Mr. Parsons have to say?" Emma asked.

Laura noted that her mother said nothing, as if she could read her daughter's mind and already knew the decision.

"Nothing, I haven't even seen him since this morning," she said for the second time that day about Jerome.

"Then I'll quit too," Rachel declared.

"Not on my account," Laura said. "He may fire you anyway, but if he does, you can make some demands."

"Patrick and I have been talking about leaving Parsons and setting up our own little restaurant and bakery," Rachel said, to the astonishment of everyone at the table. "We have a reputation for good food, and I'm tired of fixing the same recipes day after day. We want to expand." She looked down at her plate and added, "And he wants to marry me."

Fortune raised his glass. "This is good news. I thought I was going to have to buy that damn store and fire the man just to make sure my sisters were treated decently. Now if you need money in the short term, I'll support you until you get established. I'll pay for the wedding and save the rest of my money to buy Oak Hill."

Chapter 32

Laura made her way from the trolley to Hoffman's store with some trepidation. She hadn't been given a key to the front door nor told what time she was to show up. She felt as if she'd crossed a bridge only to look back and see that it had been burned behind her, and she was on strange territory with no way to go back.

Jonas Hoffman was standing by the open front door waiting for her.

"Am I late?" she asked, slightly out of breath from walking from the trolley. Or maybe from facing the unknown.

"No, you're actually early, and that's good. I can show you around and answer questions you have I'm sure you. I'm sure you do have some questions. We had so little time to discuss the situation yesterday. You'll know how to handle the sales, of course, but you may have questions about other things, even some about me."

Laura nodded, and let herself be led inside by the gentle pressure of his hand on her back. As she noted the day before, his store was smaller than Parsons, and there was no elevator to the second story. After they'd been seated, he studied her a moment before asking, "well?"

Where to start? She felt as if her tongue were thick in her mouth and she couldn't form words.

After a moment he asked, "Did your young Mr. Parsons show up last night?"

Laura shook her head. "My brother was very pleased that you'd offered me a job—and about the whole situation."

He smiled. "Your brother and I are a lot alike. We seize opportunities when we see them, and don't wait for the time to be perfect."

He was studying her, waiting for her to ask questions, and she knew she should. She knew so little about him, but what did she really know about Jerome Parsons, aside from the fact that he was under his father's arm?

As if he were reading her mind, Jonas said, "I've been following your career ever since I saw your picture advertising your brother's cigarette machine. And you probably have not even given a thought to me or known that I existed."

Laura managed a smile.

He nodded approvingly. "That's a start. I like to see you smile. "First, I know that I'm a lot older than you. I'm forty, and I'm well-to-do. I can easily afford to close the store and raze the building and build a new one, and that's just what I intend to do. I've taken the profits from my store and invested wisely, often in the same businesses your brother has invested in. I have a home where we can live, so we don't have to live above the store as people often do in northern cities and in Europe. I've bought land out near the site your brother and his son bought, and if you wish, we can build a house out there."

"But I haven't said I would marry you," Laura said, feeling her face flush.

"True, but you will eventually, I'm sure. I want you to be aware of the total situation, not just your job here at the store. That can change as time goes on, and probably will, but I vow to be loyal to you. You wouldn't have fitted into the Parsons world, and neither would I. We're a pair of outsiders, and they look down their aristocratic noses at us until they need us."

"Do you have family here?" Laura asked, remembering all the problems she'd had with Jerome's father, and the few words she'd spoken to his mother at church.

He had been looking at her, smiling, but now his features seem to turn cold. "Not here or anywhere, unless you count the fact that Jews all over the world consider themselves kin, not counting the converts." Then, seeing the stillness of her expression, and held her hands that were folded into each other, he asked, "Does my being Jewish affect your decision to be here?"

Laura shook her head. "No," she said, her voice scarcely above a whisper. "What happened to your family?"

"I was an only child, born of a poor family when my parents were already along in age." He paused. "Actually they were about the age I am now, but at that time in Russia and being poor, it made a big difference. The Russians went through one of their periodic attacks on us, and I saw my parents killed. I was only fourteen, and I couldn't do anything to save them, but I felt ashamed that I couldn't.

"I told myself they would understand and that I would never let it happen to me. I made my way across the continent, working at our jobs and sleeping and eating where I could, until I got passage on a ship to America. I worked in a store in New York for two years, sweeping and carrying out trash and observing how things went when I wasn't at the store. I did all jobs, and sometimes slept in a livery stable.

"I could have stayed on forever there, as there were plenty of Jews who welcomed me. But there were also plenty of stores here in Richmond where people who had gone through being beaten and seeing their world destroyed. Even though I knew I could never be one of them, I understood them. About all they had left was pride, and I could understand that too. I rented this building and eventually bought it."

Laura had been listening and watching him, trying to sort out her feelings, and unable to take her eyes off him. He had gone through so much and had come out ahead.

"Does my story offend you or shock you?" He asked.

185

"Why should it offend me? I admire you for all you have achieved."

She saw his shoulders drop slightly and as he relaxed. After hearing all this, she knew there was nothing more that he could tell her that would cause her to reject him.

"Does my being Jewish matter to you?"

"I'm more puzzled than anything else," Laura admitted. "I don't know how this affects me. What am I expected to do?"

"I won't expect you to convert, unless at some date in the future you decide to." He leaned back in his chair and said with a slight smile, "Jews have been marrying non-Jews for thousands of years. Persian King Ahasuerus married Ester who was Jewish. King Solomon either married or had an affair with the Queen of Sheba, and I suspect that Joseph had an Egyptian wife. There was no mention in the Bible of any of them burned in hell for marrying outside their religion. So, you see, it's not a new thing."

Laura shifted in her seat, almost breathless, with the enormity of what he was telling her. "Why me?"

"I admire and respect you, and I think that together we can work well together."

"That doesn't sound very romantic."

"I'm not a romantic man, nor am I well educated, if that's what you're looking for in a husband."

"I'm not educated either," Laura said. "I've had to work, and never had the opportunity to get much schooling."

"A lot of schooling is wasted time. I've read a lot, and you can educate yourself the same way. I'm a blunt man. I've stated my case. I don't have time to court you for years. I'll be a kind, loving, devoted husband. You may have a job or not, as you wish, and I will support you in fine style. do you find me acceptable?"

Laura drew in a long breath. "Yes, I find you acceptable in many ways, but there's one thing—" she stopped, embarrassed, uncertain how to express what she was thinking.

He laughed. "Don't be shy, Miss Barranger. I suspect I know what you're thinking. I am very attracted to you so that I can hardly wait for us to be married, and I will do my best to make you happy in bed and out of it."

"Oh!" she gasped. That had been just what she was thinking, and he seemed to read her thoughts. But it wasn't the kind of thing ladies were supposed to think about, much less talk about.

"Take a couple of days to think over my offer of marriage, just in case young Parsons shows up and you find him more attractive."

"I don't think I will," Laura said honestly. He had impressed her, and she wondered it she had found her true mate. Still, she appreciated that he wasn't forcing her.

"I don't think so either," he said. "Now let me show you the plans I have for the new building. Tomorrow I'll send someone over to get the shipment of the dresses you ordered and will put them in stock and see about having a small fashion show. Is that agreeable to you?"

Laura nodded. It was exactly what she had planned for Parsons.

"I have the building lot purchased and the foundation is already laid in for the new store and as soon as we have an idea of when we want to open, we'll put everything in this building on half-price sale, and together we can visit manufacturers and buy new products to stock the establishment." He stood and reached for her hand to help her up from the low chair. "Let's go see what we can sell today."

Laura felt secure with his hand in hers. He was his own man, not a son waiting for his father's retirement so he could grow up. She had decided on her future, regardless of what Jerome Parsons said or did.

Jerome came the next afternoon while they were opening the shipping carton full of dresses. Laura took a few steps toward him and said, "Good afternoon, Mr. Parsons. How may I help you?"

"Oh, for heaven's sakes! Call me Jerome."

"And you must call me Laura, of course, since we know each other so well, and this is not your business establishment." She was aware that Jonas had risen from the task and was walking away with an arm full of pastel colored dresses over his arm, giving her privacy for whatever decision she wanted to make. "I haven't seen you in a while," she said.

"I wanted to give you a few days to come to your senses and return to us." Despite expecting him to say something like this, Laura was still surprised by the elder Parsons' gall, as she knew the voice was Jerome's but the words were his father's.

"I've accepted Mr. Hoffman's offer, and your father made it clear that he didn't want me back. I doubt if you would go against your father's wishes."

"If you'd apologize to him, I think he'd be glad to have you back. You know how he is when he's angry. And we'd have to wait awhile before we could be married but you know that anyway."

"I have no intention of doing either."

"Will then, I'm breaking our engagement," he said.

Laura laughed. "You don't need to do that. I've already agreed to marry Mr. Hoffman."

Jerome's face turned a reddish purple, and his mouth dropped open, but no words came out. He turned and walked stiffly away, with as much dignity as he could manage, out of the store and out of her life.

Chapter 33

Jonas waited a few moments to give her some privacy before he stepped out from the ladies' clothing section. Without mentioning Jerome, he said, "You made some excellent choices. Those are beautiful dresses; we'll have no trouble selling them."

"We do need the customers to come looking for dresses," Laura said.

Almost as if she'd conjured up a customer by saying so, a woman appeared and addressed Laura: "Your sister told me you are now working here, Miss Barranger. I'm so sorry you're no longer at Parsons, because I enjoyed going to the tea room and then shopping, and you were always able to find just the right dress for me. I hope you can today. I want something light and airy for springtime."

"I think we have just what you need," Laura said, leading her back to the rack where all the new pastel dresses hung.

Before the day was over, she had sold two of them.

Jonas had gone to another part of the store and was busy, but at closing time he came to speak to her. "I saw in the box that you'd ordered a wedding dress. Did you plan to use that as a sample for future orders, or was it for yourself?"

"For myself. But if someone wants to buy it, I'll sell it."

"If it doesn't remind you too much of the man you are supposed to wear it with, keep it and wear it for our wedding. And I'd like you to bring in all the women in your family to try on dresses for the occasion. I'll pay for them, as my wedding gift for you."

Laura started to ask when there would be a wedding, but since they'd only discussed marriage for two days, it seemed a bit soon to bring up the subject. She lifted the lovely silk dresses and let the fabrics slither through her hand, reveling in the feel of the fabric against her skin.

Jonas himself brought up the subject. "We can be married right after Easter. That's one day I won't be going with you to church. You celebrate your Easter and I shall go to Passover."

"That's very soon, only a little over two weeks," Laura said.

"Oh? I'm eager to marry you. Do you want a long engagement, or a big wedding that takes a lot of preparation?

Laura shook her head. "We can be married in my family's parlor or at yours." She suddenly realized that he had no immediate family left alive, and probably no extended family members in the United States.

"Yours. Perhaps your sister can prepare a special dinner for us or some refreshments for the guests." He chuckled. "We might even order our refreshments from Parsons tea room."

"I don't think Rachel will be there much longer," she said. "She and Patrick have been discussing leaving Parsons and opening their own restaurant."

"Then we shall give Rachel the business, and bypass Parsons. I'd prefer that anyway. So, all we need to do is pick a date and get our license. I know a judge who'd be glad to officiate."

So, it was decided. As she rode home on the trolley, with Rachel at her side, she shared her startling news.

Rachel made an even more startling announcement. "Then Patrick and I shall be married the same day, while the food has been prepared and the judges on hand."

Laura felt as if she were living in two worlds. In one, she went about the very familiar routine of speaking to customers and writing up sales slips. In the other, her mind whirled with the enormity of marrying someone she scarcely knew, and without so much as a month's wait before she became Jonas's wife.

As Rachel was clearing the luncheon remains from the last table on Easter Monday, Mr. Parsons strode in. "At the end of today, the tea room will be closed for good, and you two will need to look other jobs."

Even though she had been half expecting this to happen, now that it had, Rachel was struck silent. Patrick came out of the kitchen, wiping his hands on his apron, and heard Mr. Parsons' remarks.

As if they had asked why, Parsons went on, "The idea of having this tea room was to increase sales of fall clothing, and it hasn't worked out that way."

"What will you do with this space?" Patrick asked.

"Turn it back into sales, as it was before."

"What shall we do with the food and supplies we have on hand and the other items here?" Patrick asked, glancing around the tea room.

"You can throw it all out in the street for all I care," Parsons said. "I plan to hire someone to strip it down and cart everything away to the rubbish heap."

"I'll remove everything and take it away for free," Patrick said.

"I don't know what you'll do with it. Most of it is monogrammed with a P, so it would only be valuable to a business whose company name began with that letter. The chairs and tables might have some value, but I'd have to keep them around until the right buyer came along. You can have it all, but you have to get it done within the next two days." He turned and walked away.

Rachel clutched Patrick's arm. "How can you possibly get it done in two days, Patrick? And what are we going to do with all this? Where will we put it? "

"I've got a few hours to figure it out. And this is a fantastic opportunity for us. We've been saying we wanted to open a restaurant, and here we have everything we need, including monogrammed napkins and tablecloths."

"But we don't have space for a restaurant," Rachel wailed. "And we don't have a wagon, and you can't do all this by yourself.

"Let me worry about it. I'll show you what kind of man you're planning to marry. Between your brother, and your brother- and father-in-law-to-be," he said with a broad smile, "I think I can make it work."

The next two days were a whirlwind of activity that had nothing to do with the upcoming double wedding. The whole Barranger family was affected, except for Fortune, who went off to his business office.

The first load was food, which went to Fortune and Emma's house, where Emma and her mother-in-law got quickly to work storing the great quantities of flour, butter, and other items that could be eaten at the wedding.

Jonas offered his carriage house for storage. "I got rid of the horse and carriage when the trolley line opened," he said. He was wearing workmen's clothing like the other men, instead of his elegant business suit, and had his sleeves rolled up and the collar open. Laura looked at his strong hands, wrists, and his exposed chest where a mat of dark hair picked out. This was as much as she had seen of his body, and she realized with a start that within two days she would be seeing all of him.

And she might be riding home from her wedding on the trolley instead of in a fine carriage.

Jonas had showed her his house, which soon would be hers. It was a tall rowhouse tucked in between two other houses, with a narrow walkway to the side that led to a garden area in the back. Jonas had made no effort to plant a garden, and only boxwoods lined the walkway to the front porch. Inside, the house had all the necessary fixtures — polished wood floors, marble fireplaces, a bathroom with ceramic fixtures, and tall with Burgundy drapes. The large kitchen, which overlooked the bare backyard, appeared equally unused.

"I want you to feel free to decorate the house to please yourself," Jonas told Laura. "Buy whatever furnishings and decorations that you wish. Living alone, and spending most of my time at the store, I scarcely paid heed to my surroundings here, and I've always had the belief that if I have something I'm not using and don't need, then someone else should have it. I found out back in Russia that belongings can be a weight holding people back. For much of my life, I owned nothing that I could not carry with me, but now is different. I want us to have a home that you feel comfortable in and proud off."

He gathered Laura into his arms and held her for a moment then kissed her before stepping away from her, still keeping his arm around her. "I have told Rachel and Patrick that they may stay here while you and I go to the Chamberlain Hotel for a few days for our honeymoon," he went on. When we return, you can start decorating. You have good taste, so I'm sure it's going to look better than it does now."

"What about the store while we're gone?" Laura asked.

"I thought about that too," he said. "Mr. Parsons thought he was punishing you and the family by firing them, but instead it will work out well for all of us. Rachel and Patrick will run the store, with everything marked down to half-price, and as soon as everything has sold, they will start moving the tea room equipment and furnishings into the bottom floor and will eventually live on the second level."

"Jonas, you've thought of everything," Laura said. "I hope it all goes as you are planning."

"It will," he said confidently.

For two days the men worked at moving items out of the Parsons tea room site. Laura and Rachel worked at Jonas's store, and on the third day Laura awoke to the realization that today would be her wedding day.

Chapter 34

Laura sat up and looked around her room, realizing that this would be the last morning she would awaken in it. Rachel sat up in the adjoining bed, stretching and yawning. "Look how late it is, Laura!" she exclaimed. "We need to hurry up and get bathed and dressed or we'll be late for our own weddings." She paused. "Can you believe what has happened to us?"

"No," Laura admitted. "It all seems like a dream, and sometimes I feel like a little chip floating on a stream that's gotten caught in a whirlpool. Things are happening that I never expected. This isn't at all the way I thought my wedding day would be, and Jonas is not at all the man I thought I'd be marrying, and yet it all feels so right. He makes everything seem right for me."

"I've known for months that I wanted to marry Patrick," Rachel said. "We work well together, and we want the same things. We'll probably never have a big house or all the luxury that you have, but I think we'll be happy, and I hope you will too, Laura."

It seemed like mere moments before Laura was descending the staircase into the parlor, looking into Jonas's upturned face. His dark eyes regarded her with what she could tell by his smile was joy. She was hardly aware of her family around her, the women wearing those silk dresses she had chosen in New York, Rachel looking as lovely as a daffodil in her pale-yellow dress, their mother in lavender, Emma in pale green, and even Patrick's mother had been given a blue dress.

Emma held the baby with little Daniel beside her, while Fortune had a hand on each of the two older children. Simon held a small silver plate on which two rings rested, and Eve stood solemnly with the basket of rose petals over her arm. The four members of Patrick's family stood together looking from one person to another of the Barranger family, as if they were attending a play, and were not really a part of the ceremony. Beside Fortune, Laura saw her brother Pete, tall and handsome and dressed as splendidly as Fortune himself.

The ceremony went smoothly, as everything Fortune planned did. Two men, one of whom Laura recognized as the reporter who had written about the tea room and about the trolley line, stepped forward. The other, she saw, had set up a camera with the black cloth covering it. There would be pictures in the newspaper the next day. Fortune liked getting publicity, and had arranged this, she was sure. The reporter held a typed paper in his hand which she assumed was information about the two couples and the families which Fortune would have prepared. He had also bought the flowers that banked the room and filled the air with the fragrance of lilies of the valley and carnations.

Later, after two dozen photos had been taken, the banquet was served at the long dining room table. Fortune, as head of the family, stood at one end of the table to give toasts to the newlywed couples. And then he lifted his glass in a toast to Emma, who stood proudly at the opposite end of the table. "To my devoted wife, Emma, will who has made all this possible."

Emma smiled in delighted surprise. Fortune had been a faithful husband, but it was usually his sisters who had received the attention. Today the spotlight had been shined upon her, and she would at least be mentioned as the hostess in whose home the weddings were held.

The white linen covered table was laid in with all the delicacies left from the tea room and more besides: mounds of chicken salad, crisp cheese sticks, deviled eggs, ham biscuits (the ham thin sliced and just salty enough with a smoky flavor), asparagus spears, soft leaves of lettuce topped by crumbled bacon and vinaigrette, and an enormous chocolate cake heavy with frosting.

Rachel had to press Patrick's hand twice to stop him from instinctively rising to clear away the used plates and cutlery, as she herself felt inclined to do. But Fortune had hired a quiet, efficient black woman who did those tasks so quickly and silently that the dishes almost seemed to disappear of their own accord. Rachel saw that Emma, at several times, started to rise and do the clearing up or serve the cake.

The sun was setting as the meal ended, and Fortune went twice from the table to look out the front door. Finally he announced, "The carriages have arrived. Much as I want to get your fares from riding the trolley, I thought it more appropriate for brides in their finery to ride in a carriage."

When there was a small lull in all the congratulations, Laura asked Pete, "Why didn't Clara come?"

"School is still in session, and the next few weeks are especially important for the students to get prepared for the next year's classes, especially the few who may be going off somewhere to school."

"It's a pity she didn't come. We could've had a triple wedding."

"She's intimidated enough by all of you—all of us—without the fanfare of all this to-do today. We plan to marry as soon as her school session is over."

"Oh, son, I'm so glad to hear that," his mother said. "Then all my children will be married, and I can die happy."

"Don't say such a thing," Fortune protested. "Today is the day to celebrate new beginnings, not dying."

As the carriages moved quietly through the darkening street, Jonas pulled Laura close to him, and she laid her head on his chest, secure and trusting. *It's like mother said,* she thought, *if I died now, I die happy. But I hope I don't. I want*

197

to live a long time, long enough to get to know this fascinating man I have married, and to give him the love he deserves.

Later, discarding her wedding finery and donning the Batiste nightgown she purchased so many months ago, she felt strange. Just across the hall, Rachel and Patrick were preparing for their first nights of lovemaking, just as she was preparing for Jonas. Was Rachel as nervous as she herself was? Probably not, she thought. Rachel and Patrick had worked side-by-side for so long, talking every day holding hands hugging each other, and anticipating this night. She had scarcely touched Jonas, and aside from what he had told her of himself, she knew almost nothing of his tastes and desires, and indeed, whether he had made love to other women.

Then he came into the bedroom from the bathroom, his nakedness silhouetted in the dim light. "No need to put that on, he said, and bent to extinguish the light before he slid into bed beside her.

He reached for her, pulling her close against him so that her breasts were crushed against his hard chest, his legs intertwined with hers, and his mouth on hers, kissing her as if her lips held the answer to all his needs. Then he parted her thighs and pressed himself into her, still claiming her mouth with his so that she could not cry out at the pain.

It was over quickly. There had been no gentleness, no words of love and persuasion.

"I'm sorry, Laura. I've been wanting you so much that I couldn't stop myself any longer. It will be better next time."

Next time! Laura felt angry and cheated. She was married to Jonas now, and would have to do his bidding. Women didn't talk much about this. When a woman was giving birth, other women came in held her hand and listened to her screams of pain, and she'd heard them compare their pain or lack of it with each other, but they never talked about this kind of pain. How often would she have to go through this? She lay wide-awake, staring at the ceiling above her.

Yet when in the night he turned to her touching her gently, kissing her lips, the nape of her neck, her breast then on down, she felt an unexpected stirring of desire. This time he touched her gently, caressing a tender spot that suddenly seemed tender no longer, but tingling with desire. When they slid together, there was no more pain. She enjoyed the gentle rocking sound and sensation and the final sighs of satisfaction.

Now she knew why women didn't discuss this a woman might give birth many times but only once in her life would she have this experience this symbol of passing from girlhood to womanhood.

Chapter 35

Laura awoke to the smell of coffee. She rolled over and sat up in bed. Jonas still slept beside her, his breath even, his chest rising and falling with an easy rhythm. She touched his arm, and his eyes flew open.

"Who? What?" Then he seemed to fully awaken and said, "Good morning, my dear Mrs. Hoffman. May I ask why you awakened me? Shall we enjoy each other once more?"

Laura laughed and shook her head. "No. Someone must be downstairs. Do you have a servant?"

"Only someone who comes in to clean." He swung his feet over the side of the bed and stood.

Laura stared at his nakedness, and then quickly averted her eyes. In the night she had managed to find her Batiste gown and put it on.

Jonas laughed. "Look all you want. You're my wife now, and everything I have is yours. Are you sure about us doing . . ." he gestured down to the bed.

"Yes, Jonas. It's morning, and someone is downstairs cooking and making coffee. You'd better put on some clothes."

Within a few minutes they had both washed and donned dressing gown and slippers and headed down to the kitchen.

Both Rachel and Patrick were there, fully clothed as if it were any workday. She was setting the table, and he stood at the stove where slices of ham sizzled in a pan of butter, and he was pressing split white roles in the fragrant butter.

"Sit down and have some coffee," Rachel invited, lifting the heavy pot from the stove. "As you can see breakfast is all almost ready."

As she poured coffee, Patrick forked the slices of left over him onto plates, followed by the warm buttered bread, and added eggs to the pan. When Patrick set the four plates down in front of each place, Jonas said, "Don't you realize this is supposed to be your honeymoon?"

Patrick laughed. "We're used to cooking, and we plan to keep on. We'll continue our honeymoon after you two leave today."

Rachel and Laura exchanged a quick slightly embarrassed look, and then averted their eyes and began to eat.

By midmorning Laura and Jonas were on the train headed southward to Newport News, along with their luggage. For the next three days, they stayed at the stately Chamberlain hotel, overlooking the Chesapeake Bay.

They walked the sandy beach, toured Fort Monroe where the Confederate president Jefferson Davis had been imprisoned, enjoyed sumptuous meals in the formal dining room, and lay in each other's arms at night listening to the soft slap of the waves below. Laura had no further pain during lovemaking, and looked forward to nightfall, when she and her distinguished looking husband could leave the other guest in the parlor or on the veranda, and go to their rooms. They slept late and had breakfast delivered to their room.

"This is bliss," Laura murmured. "I could stay here with you forever."

Jonas shook his head. "No, you wouldn't. This is wonderful for a few days, beyond anything I imagined it would be with you, but we are both born workers, and it wouldn't be long before we would be bored with this life of leisure and find our hands itching for some tasks to do. Together we can turn my house—our house—into a place as comfortable as any hotel, and began to entertain. It will be wonderful in its own way."

When they returned to Richmond, they saw a huge hand-lettered sign in front of the store: "Everything on sale half-price!" Inside, both Rachel and Patrick were busy serving customers who walked out laden with parcels. Jonas looked around. "You've rearranged things, I see. Most of this was on the second level."

"The second level is empty. We've sold it all. We move this down so customers wouldn't have to walk upstairs."

"You didn't sell my dresses at half price, did you?" Laura asked, alarmed.

"No, I'll save them for the grand opening of the new store," Rachel said. "Jonas, I think you'll find all the money in the cash box."

"Take half of it for your salary so you can set up your café."

"Thank you, Mr. Hoffman," Patrick said, "but we don't need it. We have everything we need to set up our business except fresh food, and Fortune has given us enough money for a wedding gift to get started. We've been living at your house and eating your food, and it looks as if we still have about a week left to sell out here, so we may be owing you."

It only took four days, so by the end of the week, Rachel and Patrick had moved into a two-story building that would be their restaurant, and their home.

In July, Fortune took the train alone to Pete's wedding. Emma declined to come saying she needed to be with Leticia. Fortune was concerned about the little girl, who was sickly a lot. She just didn't seem to thrive like the other children did and cried often.

As he passed through the rolling fields, he saw newly planted tobacco, standing upright, healthy and vigorous. He must remember to remind Pete to keep an eye on these farms and look for the best tobacco for the factory.

Pete hadn't especially wanted him to come to the wedding, but in the end he'd relented. "Just don't take over things and put on a show the way you did for the girls," he said firmly. "Clara is quiet and shy and doesn't want a crowd.

"Then how does she manage to teach a room full of rowdy students?" Fortune asked.

"She likes children and impresses on them how important it is to get an education," Pete replied. "The bigger ones that might give her trouble know that I will come around and see that they don't."

"If you don't want me to take care of any of the wedding arrangements, then let me pay for your honeymoon trip," Fortune offered.

"For heaven's sake, Fortune, you pay me a good salary, and Clara has been saving up the money from her teaching job, as well as helping out her parents. I'm not as rich as you are and I'll never be, and I don't want to be. You've done enough for me, for all of us. Just come to my wedding as a guest. Clara will have her parents, and mom will be there, of course. You can stand in in place of the father we know we don't have any longer. Jamie's family will be there too."

Fortune arrived the day before the wedding, in the afternoon. Pete met his railroad car, and together they went to the small house where their mother still lived.

Fortune walked over to the overseer's house where Jamie and his family lived. While the fields and fences were in good shape, green and lush with early summer growth, and the horses were still sleek and groomed, the house itself looked forlorn.

Jamie came out of the stable in work clothes, bandanna protruding from his back pocket. He took it out and wiped his face and hands free of sweat before he hugged his older brother. "I just finished plowing out the tobacco and the garden," he announced. Given a choice, I'd quit growing tobacco altogether even though I know you and Pete make a good living off it. But tobacco is about the only thing that keeps Oak Hill going."

"What would you plant instead?" Fortune asked.

"Apples, Jamie said. "The land's too steep for wheat, and I can barely grow enough corn to feed the animals, but this area is perfect for apples. I've planted a small orchard and done some grafting to try out new kinds."

"You planted on Mr. Stannard's land?"

"Yes and no. He sold me 10 acres, but he said he couldn't give me a clear deed right now inasmuch as he still owes the bank, and they have the title to it."

"When I buy Oak Hill, I'll give you your deed, and some more land besides. I owe you for being here and taking care of Ma all this time. You could've made a better living if you'd gone to Richmond like I did."

"So you still think you're going to buy the plantation?"

Fortune nodded. "What about Charlotte's husband? I thought he paid off the debts of Oak Hill."

"Here, step in the shade while we talk," Jamie said, moving back to sit down on a grassy spot and leaning back against the trunk of the tree. Fortune moved into the shade as well but stood.

"It's complicated. I think he may have paid off all of the Colonel's debts when he first married Charlotte, but things have changed. He's not the prize she thought he was. He's not rich anymore. I don't know whether it's gambling or drinking or making bad investments, but he's borrowed against Oak Hill."

Hearing this, Fortune raised his eyebrows. "Does he come here often?"

"Unfortunately, yes! Him and his New York friends show up on weekends and drink till they can barely walk straight. Then they go out claiming they are foxhunting, and ride the horses half to death, through streams and briar patch, and over rock walls. When they leave it takes me days to get the poor horses calmed down and curried, and have their scratches and sores start to heal up."

"Does Charlotte ever come? That doesn't sound like her kind of weekend."

Jamie nodded, and reached to pull a blade of grass to chew on before he answered. "She goes back and forth, and sometimes she stays here for weeks at a time. Then she'll go get that boy of hers and bring him to see his grandfather. He's a mean one, takes after his father. He whips the horses and throws rocks at them and I dare not say a word against him." Jamie shook his head sorrowfully. "I don't let my children come in contact with him if I can help it. No telling what he might do to them thinking that he's better than they are and has a right to do is he wants to."

"I had a run in with him once myself," Fortune said, remembering. "I took a stick away from him he was beating the dog with." Jamie shook his head in disgust. "Charlotte saw it but she couldn't do anything to stop me. I can understand how it is with you. Bishop might ask you to leave, but they have no control over me. At least for now."

"Charlotte is here now, but not the boy. He hates coming here." He stood, still chewing on the stem of grass. "You want to come over to the house and have something cold to drink? I'm headed that way."

"No thanks. I'm sure Ma is planning a big early supper. I'll head on back, and see you and the family tomorrow at the wedding." He clapped Jamie on the shoulder before the brothers parted. He was halfway back to his mother's small house when he saw Charlotte walking across the field. She was looking down and she hadn't seen him yet. He waited until she was closer before he waved and called her name.

She stopped walking and stood still, looking for a moment as if she might turn and flee, but then waited for him.

As he got close, he saw that she was pregnant, but he decided to wait to mention it. In fact, maybe he wouldn't mention it at all unless she brought up the matter.

"I suppose you are here for Pete's wedding," she said, without preamble "Will you be staying long?"

"No, I leave right after the wedding."

"I read in the newspaper about your sisters' weddings. You're such an important man now that it was reprinted from the *Dispatch* in New York newspapers, and probably others all over the country. And your sisters both have careers so they can support themselves if their marriages don't work. Good for them. That's what I should have done." Her voice had an unmistakable edge of regret.

"Your marriage seems to have lasted," he said.

"I stay with him because of our son. And for my father and Oak Hill. Now there is to be another child, so I'll have to stay with him. My son despises me for my weakness, and I'm sure he'll turn out just like his father, and to make some other woman unhappy in years to come." She crossed her arms and half turned away, then faced him again. "I should have married you when I had a chance, Fortune."

He waited half a lifetime to hear her say those words, and felt an unexpected tinge of bitterness. "No Charlotte. You'd always have looked down on me because I wasn't one of the chosen ones who could trace their ancestors back hundreds of years. I would always have been a farmer, and I wasn't cut out for it the way Jamie is. Leaving here was the best thing that could have happened to me, and I thank you for being so brutal with your rejection."

She bit her lip, nodded slightly and walked slowly away. Fortune watched until she disappeared over a rise in the new cut field before he turned toward his mother's home.

When Fortune went into the house, he found his mother shelling green peas, and he took the bowl from her to do the job. Her hands were twisted with arthritis, and shelling was a tedious task. Her fingers were stained from pitting the cherries that were now perfuming the kitchen as they baked into a cobbler.

"Sit down and rest, Ma," Fortune said. "You look tired."

She pulled out a kitchen chair and sat in it. Fortune pulled out one across the table from her and set the bowl of the pods in front of him, shelling briskly.

"I am tired," she admitted. "But after tomorrow, my job here on earth is done. No more looking after my children. All of you will have someone else to share the burdens with. I can die happy."

"Don't talk of dying, mom. Don't you want to live to see Pete and Rachel and Laura have children?"

"Course I do. I would like to live to see them have children and see those children grow up and marry and have children of their own, all the way down the line, but life ain't like that. There's no cutoff point where everybody would be satisfied for things to stop." She massaged her gnarled joints, gently bending each one as far as it would go. "I've got arthritis so bad I can't do much work anymore, and my eyesight's fading. I have to look carefully where I walk so I won't trip and fall and break something and be a burden on one of my children."

"You know we'll take care of you, mom."

"Course I know. I've been blessed with good children and it gives me satisfaction to know that I won't have to suffer alone. But I don't want it to be that way, being in your house. I'm ready to go, knowing I've done the best I could."

Fortune started to speak, but he could tell that she hadn't finished what she wanted to say, and he kept silent. For a moment the only sound was the peas dropping from the pod into the bowl.

"I do think about dying. And I think about heaven. Maybe when I'm there I could look down and see my children and grandchildren and know whether they are happy or grieving, or if something dreadful has happened to them. I want to see your father again, and I hope I'll be able to look back as well as forward and see my parents. I'd like to tell my mama some things I should've said when she was alive, and I'd like to give my Papa a few hugs. He never seemed to want to be hugged when he was alive but maybe heaven changes people. I'd like to see my grandmom and grandpa too. They died when I was too young to get to know them."

Again, there was silence. Fortune dared not interrupt. This was the most he'd ever heard his mother say and he listened, spellbound at her vision of heaven.

"I wonder how it will be in heaven," she went on. "Will I be old and feeble in heaven the way I am now so my grandchildren will recognize me when they get to heaven? Will I be young and healthy the way I was when I first met your papa, or will I be a child? If my parents are young, I might not recognize them, but their parents would. Or maybe we'll all have some magical way of appearing different ways to different people. It's a real puzzle."

Fortune reached across the table and took her hand. "I think heaven will be like your last possibility, that will have different ways to see people. After all, it's that way in life."

Chapter 36

After supper, they sat on the porch not talking but just looking westward toward the mountains as darkness fell and the first stars came out. The air was still and humid, and had just begun to cool off from the day's heat. Crickets chirped and somewhere Fortune heard an owl hoot and then the familiar sound of a whippoorwill.

"That one wants a mate," Pete said "It's not too late in the season; he may find what he needs."

"It's peaceful here," Fortune said as he heard one of the Stannard horses nicker in the nearby pasture.

"Always was peaceful, except for them war years," his mother said, "and that really didn't touch us a lot, not with battles, just with troops from both sides coming through stealing everything they could pick up."

"I'm glad that's all in the past," Fortune said. "The scars are beginning to heal, but it will take a long time before the South ever recovers."

His mother rose from her chair. "You boys stay up as long as you like, but I need my sleep so I'll be rested and ready for tomorrow."

Fortune and Pete stood also, recognizing a signal that it was bedtime when they heard one. Fortune carried the lamp as they made their way up the narrow wooden steps to the sleeping loft. Soon he blew out the lamp light and the brothers laid atop fresh sheets that smelled of sunshine. It was too hot for any covers.

Fortune was half asleep when Pete said from his bed, "Fortune, don't be surprised if Clara's family isn't friendly to us tomorrow. They don't want her to marry me."

At that Fortune was wide awake." Why in God's name not? What's wrong with you?"

"It's not me. They don't want her to marry anybody. She's been supporting the whole family, and now she'll be giving up her teaching job."

"She's supporting the whole family on her teacher's salary? What's wrong with her father?"

"He's a no good, shiftless excuse for a man. Probably the best time in his life was during the war, when he had a gun and could shoot people. He came home after Appomattox and married a girl half his age, little more than a child, and started fathering children."

"Do you want me to give him a job? Fortune asked.

"I got him a job at one of the warehouses in Lynchburg, but he quit after two weeks, and I have to say I was surprised he lasted that long. He's lazy and doesn't want to have anybody tell him what to do or correct him when he does it wrong."

Fortune was silent for a moment. He usually had an answer to people's problems, at least if they involved money, but he couldn't understand a man who expected his child to support him. "Are you sure you want to get into this, Pete?"

"Yes, I've given it a lot of thought and planned for a long time to marry her. I didn't get pushed into it the way you and Jamie did."

Fortune laughed. "Well it worked out well for Jamie and me. Your Clara must be different from the rest of her family."

"She is. It's like a miracle. I've told her she can keep on teaching if she wants to until we have children, and give the money to her family. And I've told her I'll see to it that her brother and sister get an education if they wanted, but I think they'll probably run away as soon as they can. Their father keeps them out of school to work on that little plot of land he has, and hires them out sometimes to other people."

"You must love her a great deal," Fortune observed.

"I do," Pete said, "and she's going to be a good wife for me."

Fortune awoke to the smell of coffee. As usual his mother was up ahead of them. She had a fire going in the cook stove, and the enameled coffee pot sputtered and spit as the coffee brewed. She slid a tray of biscuits into the oven.

"That's a lot of biscuits for just three people," Fortune observed. "Are you trying to fatten us up?"

She laughed. "No, I'm fixing food to give a basket to Clara's folks to eat on the way back home. Pete and Clara decided they didn't want to have any special dinner the way you had for the girls."

After breakfast both her sons helped prepare the ham biscuits and wrapped them as well as the cake, packing the lunch into a basket covered with a clean dish towel.

Later, when Fortune came downstairs dressed for the wedding, he saw his mother in the lavender silk she'd worn for her daughter's weddings.

"If people wear clothes in heaven, this is what I'd like to wear for eternity," she said, "though I'm not sure about the hat." She touched the brim off the light straw which had a purple band and was topped by a small bouquet of fabric violets.

"Don't you like it? Laura chose it especially for you to go with the lavender silk dress."

"Oh, I think it's perfect for today. I'm just thinking about heaven. I don't think I've ever seen a picture of an angel with a hat on."

Pete and Fortune both laughed and the three set off walking the short distance to the church, one on each side of them mother. The center aisle of the church divided the two families. Pete set down in the front pew and turned to smile at Clara. His mother set next, idly patting his hand as if saying goodbye.

Fortune stood for a moment, surveying the group. Jamie sat in the second row, looking uncomfortable in the suit that Fortune suspected he'd worn for a decade, which needed replacement. Beside him his wife and three children sat, looking with open curiosity across the aisle. The children fidgeted and nudged each other, and were quieted by Ruth, their mother.

Across the aisle Clara set on the front pew, very still, her hands clasped tightly in front of her. She turned her head and smiled at Pete as the Barrangers entered. Beside her set a grim-faced man with his arms crossed against his chest looking straight ahead. To his left set a woman who looked limp and defeated by life, and to her left a thin boy and girl in their teens.

Having been warned, Fortune was not surprised at the Hopkins family. The interesting person sat in the second pew a beautiful young woman dressed all in black.

She looked totally out of place sitting on the bride's side of the church.

When Clara and Pete stood before the minister facing each other, they exchanged a look that told Fortune instantly why Pete had chosen her. When was the last time Emma had looked at him with such adoration? Had she ever? And what about him, had he looked at her that way, signaling how much he cared? It troubled him that he didn't think either of them had ever exchanged such a look.

He was startled to hear his brother referred to as Joseph instead of Pete but his name was Joseph Peterson Barranger, and Clara was actually Clarissa.

Soon the service was over. While his mother was hugging Clara and then Pete, and sobbing quietly, Fortune made his way to the stranger in black. He held out his hand. "I'm Fortune Barranger, brother of the groom."

"Nearly everybody in Virginia knows who you are, Mr. Barranger. I'm Amelia Ames, Clara and I were roommates at the normal school when we studied to be teachers."

"And are you still teaching?"

"I am. I had just taught two years before I married, and then I went back to it after my husband died."

Fortune felt someone tugged his sleeve, and turned to see his mother signaling that he must shake hands with Clara's father. He did so, and fumbled for some appropriate words to say. He managed, "Your daughter will make a fine wife for my brother."

"She ain't got no right to be abandoning us, neglecting her duty to take care of us," Clara's father said.

Fortune stepped away. Pete moved forward carrying a basket. He handed it to Mr. Hopkins. "Our mother prepared this for you and your family. She understands that you need to leave and get back to your farm."

"By the time we get home it'll be almost dark, time to milk the cows and slop the hogs." He took the basket without thanks, lifted the dishtowel, and spotting the bottle of wine, he allowed himself a slight smile. Then he turned to his wife, who was holding on to their daughter. "Don't dawdle. You've had plenty of time to hug that ungrateful one. Go get in the wagon, all of you," he commanded.

The Barrangers followed their new in-laws, inviting the minister to join them for lunch. Clara turned and motioned for Amelia Ames to come along as well, and Fortune was glad she had. Mrs. Ames had looked so forlorn standing by herself, and the invitation showed that Clara considered herself now a member of the Barranger family.

Chapter 37

After lunch and hugs all around, Pete and Clara, Amelia Ames, and Fortune started walking toward the train station, Pete carrying their valises. Fortune looked back to see his mother standing on the porch waving to them. On the train, Amelia started into the coach car, looking for her seat, when Fortune invited her to join them in his private car. After a moment's hesitation, she did, sinking down on the velour covered seat, and smoothing her dark hair back from her face.

"How far are you going?" Fortune asked. "I neglected to ask."

"To Richmond. My aunt has been ill, and now that the school session is over, I can spend some time with her and help her clear up some bills and household matters." She indicated a small tapestry bag on the floor beside her.

"We're all bound for Richmond, so it's good that you're joining us," Fortune said, and rang for a porter to bring them five champagne flutes and a bottle of bubbly.

As he lifted his glass of champagne, Fortune toasted, "To Clara and Pete, or should I be saying Mr. and Mrs. Joseph Peterson Barranger?"

"Clara and Pete will do," Pete said, "and you didn't need to get champagne, Fortune."

"A wedding should be finished off with champagne," he declared. "Besides, I keep it in my private car. I enjoy it, and it sure beats that wine Ma makes, and the moonshine that most folks in the county drink."

"I just meant that you've already given us a big wedding gift, two nights at a top-notch hotel," Pete said.

Fortune waved his hand dismissively. "You deserve it, and soon enough you'll be back at work."

Clara drank half her glass and set it down on a small table in front of them. She leaned against Pete's shoulder and closed her eyes.

"If any of you would like to go back into the bedroom and rest, please feel free to do so." He gestured to all three.

Clara opened her eyes, exchanged a glance with her new husband, and the two arose and went hand-in-hand into the adjoining portion of the train car.

"Mrs. Ames?" Fortune asked.

She shook her head. "I wouldn't dream of interrupting the newlyweds, and besides, I want to stay awake and enjoy every moment of this luxurious ride."

"Then you should drink your champagne," he said. He noticed that she had only taken a sip and set it down. "Or perhaps you don't like it."

"I've never had it before, and I want to make it last."

"It won't be nearly as good if you let it get warm, and there's plenty more for both of us."

They rode in companionable silence for a while and then Fortune asked, "So, how long has your husband been deceased?" He saw that she took a long drink of her champagne before she answered.

"Two years," she said. She paused before adding, "You're probably wondering why a man so young died; he was only thirty. It was nothing lurid like murder or suicide or drinking. He had consumption. The doctor called it tuberculosis, but I think of it as consumption, because it consumes everything before it's over. I took care of him myself, and it was agony coming home from school each afternoon to see that he looked a bit worse than he had when I left. Eventually I had to give up my job and take care of him, and we went into debt."

"I can help you," Fortune said, "I remember what it was like to be poor."

215

"Oh, no! I'm in debt, but I wasn't asking you for help. I couldn't do that. And if I borrowed it from you, there's no certainty I'd be able to pay it back."

Fortune didn't know what to say. Most of the problems he faced were the kind that could be solved by money. He decided not to say anything more about money.

He needn't have worried. It seemed that Amelia Ames wanted to talk about her husband, and tell him everything, so he was silent.

"We wanted children, but that was out of the question. We didn't even kiss after he got the diagnosis. We went to doctors and even went to sanatoriums, but nothing worked. He just got sicker. I was ever so careful that I wouldn't catch it myself. I boiled everything he touched: the dishes and glassware, his clothing, the bedsheets and pillows. I burned the books he read. But after all that, I still may have gotten it. Or maybe I'm still just worn out and not eating right."

Fortune studied her. She was thinner than he'd noticed at church, and had faint purplish smudges under her eyes.

"Perhaps you're just exhausted. You went back to teaching, didn't you?"

She nodded. "I had to, to pay off the debt."

"Have you had any other symptoms? Strenuous coughing?"

"No, and I've put off going to see my aunt for over a year, waiting to see if I did have any of the symptoms. I'm fairly sure that I don't have it, but I still look dreadful, and people think I'm sick."

"Grief and worry can do terrible things to the human body, making us lie awake at night or forget to eat," Fortune said. "When one of my businesses is having a problem, I'll look at a plate of food and not want any of it. Your job is tiring you out too much— and I can see where it might, having to make fires, take care of sick children as well as teaching. I'll ask my sisters if either of them can find a job for you that might be less draining."

Before she could answer, the train stopped with a jolt.

"Are we there already?" she asked, gripping the armrest of her seat.

"No, it's just a short stop, but it will give us an opportunity to finish our champagne." He reached into the ice bucket container, lifted out the bottle, and started pouring champagne into her glass.

"Not so much! I feel giddy already. But I do like it, and it's generous of you to offer me so much."

Fortune looked not at her glass, but into her face, understanding the double meaning in her words. He drained the rest of the champagne into his own glass, and lifted it in a silent salute to her.

The train moved on, and the next time it stopped, they were in Richmond. Fortune was glad it was still light enough for Clara to see the city. As they alighted from the train, he waved for his carriage. "The carriage is for the newlyweds. Mrs. Ames, you and I can take the trolley. There must be a trolley line going past your aunt's house if it's downtown." He and Pete set down the luggage, then Pete helped his bride into the carriage and they rode away.

When the trolley stopped at the intersection nearest her aunt's house, Fortune set down her suitcase, and gave her his hand to assist her down.

He released her hand, then closed her fingers around some money.

"I can't take this!" She tried to give the money back, but he scrambled onto the trolley just before it began to move.

"Thank you. You're a kind and generous man." Fortune smiled at that all the way home.

At home, he found Simon, Eve and Daniel in the kitchen attempting to prepare their supper. "Where's your mother? He asked after giving them each a hug.

"She's with the baby, where she always is," Eve said. "Can you eat with us?"

"Yes. Set a place for me. What are we having?"

"Aunt Rachel brought over some chicken salad and green peas and some bread. I don't know how to get the butter to melt on the bread, and I don't know how long to cook the peas."

"Where is Maggie?" he asked. Eve replied, "She told mama that she is too old and sickly to come anymore."

Fortune looked at the bowl of peas, remembering his mother's hands shelling peas. "They are already cooked. They could be heated, or we can just eat them as they are. If you want the butter on your bread to be melted, the easy way is to put some butter in a pan, set it on the stove, and when it's melted lay the bread in it."

Fortune was dismayed at how helpless his children were in looking after themselves. Simon was 14 and Eve 11. When Rachel had been 11, she'd known how to cook, and had helped her mother serve the Bishop family. And he had been doing the full-time work of a man when he'd been 14. He'd have to talk to Emma about how they had spoiled their children. There was money now for servants, but who knew what the future might bring?

"Aunt Rachel didn't bring any cake," Eve complained.

"You don't need any cake," Simon said. "You're getting too fat."

"I am not! And you are mean to say I am." Fortune started to say something, but decided that the children needed to get used to settling things between themselves. They probably already did, and he'd been too busy with work to notice.

Emma was nursing little Leticia, and as Fortune walked in, the babies lips let go of the nipple, his eyes closed, and Emma drew a cloth over her large white breast. "Just a moment. Let me burp the baby before she goes to sleep." She lifted the baby against her shoulder and rubbed her hand along her back until she burped and then sighed with satisfaction and fell asleep. "She's a good baby, the easiest of all."

She set Leticia down in her crib, and sat in the chair beside it, rocking it gently, although to Fortune it appeared that the child was sound asleep already.

"How was the wedding?" Emma asked.

"It all went well. The family sent you their good wishes." She smiled and nodded at this. "I'm sorry about Maggie, I will look into finding somebody."

Fortune could tell that her attention was all on the baby, not on what he said, but he gave her an abbreviated version of what had happened. "Jamie and Ruth, with their three, and Ma and I were all that were there on Pete's side. Clara's parents were there and a friend of hers, a teacher, came along, but they didn't stay for Ma's lunch." He realized it wasn't quite accurate. Amelia Ames had stayed for lunch. We came back on the train, of course, and I sent them off in a carriage to the hotel. It's their gift from us." Again, he left out Amelia.

"You paid for them to go to a hotel for their honeymoon? Doesn't Pete have money enough?"

"I suppose so, but I wanted it to be a gift."

"We never had a honeymoon, Fortune," she said.

"I'll take you to a hotel whenever you want to go, as soon as you finish nursing Leticia. Or maybe you'd want to take the children along."

"It wouldn't be the same as a real honeymoon."

"True, but we can't go back. We have to take things as they are and go on from here." As he started back toward

219

the kitchen, he said, "The children have set the table and are getting ready to serve what Rachel brought over. Do you want to come and eat with us?"

"I'll be there in a minute," she said. As he walked away, Fortune noted that he had said nothing about Pete's problems, or of seeing Charlotte Stannard or of drinking champagne with Amelia Ames. He realized that Emma had not smiled at him or said she missed him or that she loved him. And he hadn't either. When had he last said he loved her?

Chapter 38

At midmorning the next day, Fortune close the ledger and pushed it aside. "I'm going out for a walk," he told his office assistant. "It's too beautiful a morning to spend it all indoors."

He walked the length of Broad Street, enjoying the warm temperature and the sunshine. He paused at the lot where Hoffman's building was going up. The cement had been poured, and the piles of new lumber gave off a familiar smell. It reminded him of the farm, where wood was always being cut and something always being repaired.

Next door was Patrick's, as Rachel and Patrick were calling their new café. The door was open and he went in. The dining area and the kitchen were ready for customers, but the café was not yet officially opened.

"Good morning, Fortune," Rachel said, coming to greet him.

"Everything looks good," he said, looking around. "And that bread you're baking smells wonderful. Are you planning to serve it anytime soon?"

"Sit down and I'll cut a slice of one of the loaves for you," she said, and in a moment returned with a plate on which lay a slice of warm bread slathered with butter.

Fortune sniffed it appreciatively before lifting it to his mouth. "No matter how much money I have, my favorite food is still this bread like mama used to make, and you're as good a cook as she is."

"I'm preparing dinner for Emma to serve tonight, but you're not supposed to know that. Just pretend that you think she did it all herself."

He laughed. "I already know your secret. Last night I caught the children trying to heat up the food you prepared for their supper. I need to take them in hand, or maybe have you or Laura take them in hand. They're so used to having servants around that they don't know how to do a thing for themselves." After a moment he added, "And Emma doesn't seem to notice anything around the house except the baby."

Rachel nodded, and sat down at the table with him. "She seems to be having a lot of trouble getting past childbirth. I hope I don't have that much problem when mine arrives."

"Are you in the family way?"

Rachel laughed. "That's such a strange expression. I'd say all of us are in the family way. We make up a unit, and every so often we let another person join our group, and they become like us. I may be expecting. It's too soon to tell for sure, so I'm not spreading the word yet."

"You certainly didn't waste any time." He finished the last of the bread, brushed a crumb from his immaculate shirt front, and stood. "Do I pay you? Or just leave money on the table?"

"Neither. I can furnish you food here for years before I pay you and Emma back for letting me live with you for so long. Now remember, compliment Emma on the dinner, and don't go home too early."

On impulse, Fortune went into a food market he passed on the way back to his office. He placed an order for sugar, butter, flower, coffee and a fresh dressed chicken, all to be placed into a basket and delivered to Amelia Ames and her aunt.

As he laid money on the counter, the clerk asked, "Is this for yourself or someone else?"

"It's a gift. Have the card read Fortune Barranger and Company."

"Oh, Mr. Barranger! I should have recognized you. Don't you want to put this on your account?"

"Not this time," Fortune said as he turned to go. Emma was strict about reading the list of items on the account, and she'd be sure to question a basket full of items.

He could have sent the basket anonymously, but while many people felt guilty about taking money, a food gift could be graciously accepted. Especially as the coffee was a special brand.

When Fortune got off the trolley that evening, he saw Clara standing at the end of the front walkway while Pete was helping Amelia Ames to alight from the carriage.

"This is a surprise," he said, approaching the group. What would Emma say about this?

As if he'd read Fortune's thoughts, Pete said, "I came over this afternoon while Clara was shopping to ask Emma if we could bring a guest, and she said it was all right."

"Well, if Emma approves, it's certainly all right with me. It's good to see you again, Mrs. Ames."

"Mr. Barranger, I want to thank you for the food basket. Aunt Alicia was terribly pleased."

"Don't mention it," Fortune said.

"Of course, I should mention it," she said. "It would be rude of me not to."

"No, you misunderstand my meaning. I have a reputation for being a shrewd dealmaker. If the word gets around that I'm giving out things, there will be no end to the people who show up asking favors."

The other three laughed, and together they went in with the rest of the family awaiting them.

Pete introduced Amelia as Clara's best friend, and Amelia pleased Emma immediately by saying, "You have a lovely home."

At dinner, Fortune looked around the table proudly. His family were healthy and prosperous. He had four children to carry on the name and the business. Jamie and Ruth had a healthy trio of children, and probably within a year or two—or even less—Pete, Laura, and Rachel would also be parents

"it's good to have all my family together," he said. He had achieved what he'd set out to do. All his businesses were running well and turning a profit. But he hadn't bought Oak Hill yet. That was still his dream. And he was concerned about his two oldest children, so it was not all perfect, but it was mostly good, and he was grateful.

He looked across the table at Amelia, who was seated between Simon and Eve, and was making conversation with them. They made their own little group, with Daniel just below beyond Eve. Everybody else was paired off.

She was talking with the children as if they were grown-ups, while the rest of the family chatted with each other, talking about their businesses.

"We are planning the grand opening of the café for next week," Patrick said.

"It's going to take us a good bit longer on the store, I'm afraid," Jonas said. "The building is coming along on schedule, but it's no overnight job. We're ordering what we think will sell, and your sister is a marvel at picking just the right things." He patted Laura's hand fondly.

"My career is about the same that it has been for the past two years," Pete said, taking Clara's hand. "But I've just married the most wonderful of wives."

"That's quite an achievement," Fortune said with a laugh. "She can tame that wild streak of yours."

"Oh, I don't want to change a thing about him," Clara said. "I love him just the way he is."

Fortune smiled. "May you have many years of happiness."

Simon and Eve, bored with the adult conversation about marriages, excused themselves and went to their rooms.

Daniel looked earnestly at Amelia. "Why are you wearing all black, instead of the pretty colors that my mommy and Aunt Rachel and Aunt Laura wear?"

"Daniel!" Emma said. "You mustn't ask such questions."

"It's all right," Amelia said. Then, looking at Daniel, she said quietly, "My husband died. When someone you love dies, a woman usually wears black."

Daniel nodded. "My bunny died, and I loved him, and I cried. Did you cry when your husband died?"

Fortune started to intervene, to stop his son from asking such personal questions, but one look from Amelia stopped him. "Yes, I cried," she said.

"My bunny was just a baby, and he didn't live very long. But he was all I had."

"My husband didn't live very long either, Daniel, so I understand," she said. "Maybe your mommy and daddy will get you another bunny or some other kind of pet."

Fortune nodded. He hadn't realized how isolated his younger son had felt, and hadn't even known about the bunny. He clearly needed to get better acquainted with his children. They needed his attention more than his businesses.

Chapter 39

Fortune gave some thought to his family situation the next morning, especially after Emma let him know her feelings about the previous night's dinner.

"Did you put Pete up to inviting that woman in black to dinner at my house?"

"No, it was all his idea. I was quite surprised to see Mrs. Ames getting out of the carriage here. And isn't this our house?"

Emma went on just as if he hadn't spoken: "She has her nerve talking to the children about what they're planning for the future, and putting Daniel up to begging us for a dog or some other kind of pet. I know who will be taking care of it, and it's not Daniel."

"I imagine it will be the housekeeper, until we train Daniel how to care for a pet. And what's wrong with asking our children what they plan to do with their future? I'd like to know that myself."

"I saw how she looked at you, as if you were some kind of hero," Emma spoke with anger, but with a touch of worry as well.

Fortune rose from the breakfast table and dropped his napkin beside his plate. "I'm going to get Eve and Simon out of bed and take them with me to the office. It's time they learned where our money comes from, and they can start having small jobs with the company instead of sitting around the house all summer, getting in your way and being bored."

Despite the children's complaints, Fortune got them to the office only a short while later than he usually arrived. He asked his office assistant to bring out several ledgers, and opened one in front of Simon. "Start looking through these, and you'll see how much it costs to keep the business going. Eve, you're a little young to be learning the business. I want you to learn to cook."

"But I'll have a servant to do the cooking, like Mama does," she protested.

"A lot of things could occur to prevent that from happening. For example, there might be a recession when all my businesses could go bankrupt."

Simon looked up from his ledger. "All of them?"

"Probably not, but times are changing, and there may not be servants willing to cook for you. They may want to go to work in one of my factories instead. Besides, your aunt Rachel and her husband both cook, and you might find that you enjoy it as much as they do. What are your friends doing this summer?"

"Visiting their kin folks, or having people visit them. A few of them talked about going to the beach, but they didn't invite me, not even to come over to the house and spend the night," Evie said glumly.

"I don't have any friends," Simon said. "They don't like me. They say I'm a rich nobody."

Fortune was saddened and surprised at the bitterness in his son's voice. "Do you brag about how much money we have?"

"Sometimes. But then they want me to give them money or buy them a treat. They say they are borrowing money, but they never pay me back, so I stopped doing it. I'm glad it's summer, so I don't have to see any of them until September."

"What about sports?" Fortune offered. "Are you good at any sports? I never was, but I had no time for things like that. I had to work."

"I hate sports time worst of all, Simon said. "I'm always the last one they choose for the team."

"We'll see what we can do about that," Fortune announced.

While he had been talking with Simon, Eve had slid one of the ledgers over to her side of the table and was pouring over the rows of figures. "I think when I grow up I'd like to be the person that writes all these figures in the big books," she said. "I like math, and I can see where all these figures end up at the bottom of the page."

Fortune patted her on the shoulder. "I'll take you down to aunt Rachel's café. She's one of the best cooks in Virginia, and she can teach you to be a good cook as well. She started out when she was your age. After you get to be a good cook, I'll have my bookkeeper show you how to keep the ledgers, and perhaps you can work for Aunt Rachel and Uncle Patrick during school vacations."

Eve's eyes shone with excitement. "A real job?"

He left Simon looking at the ledgers, his head leaning to one side, his hands bracketing his cheeks. Eve looked more like Emma, but she had clearly inherited the Barranger interest in working. Simon's attitude worried him more. Fortune knew that part of the blame, maybe even most of the blame, lay with him. He had not taken the time to spend getting to know his son.

After Fortune had taken Eve to the café and turned her over to Rachel, he went back to the office to deal with his son.

Simon stood by the window, staring out at the street below.

"I take it that you are not interested in being a bookkeeper or an accountant," Fortune said.

"No, sir."

"Do you have any idea what you do want to do?"

"Not really. I want to go to a different school, first of all. Maybe I'll be all things, I'll be an engineer and operate trains, or maybe a painter, or I'll learn how to repair cars. I just don't know, Papa. I think I'd like to try out different things. But I don't have to decide this morning, do I?"

Fortune laughed and was glad to see the forlorn look leave his sons face to be replaced by a smile. "No, son, this summer you can work in the front office here, if you think there's a chance you might like business. Or you could go and work in the cigarette factory or go stay awhile with your grandmother. Do any of those appeal to you?"

"Uncle Pete and aunt Clara will be living with her now, and there wouldn't be any room for me," Simon pointed out. "Besides grandma doesn't need me there. Nobody needs me."

Fortune wanted to shake his son in exasperation, but he recognized in that last statement a cry of loneliness. It was true that living in the city, with no farm chores, and money to pay for servants to clean and cook, a young man might very well feel useless. He himself had never felt that, but somewhere along the line he had failed to instill any ambition in his son, to make him understand where the money he counted on came from. And Emma had not even seen to it that the children learn to clean and cook and look after themselves. He passed a pad of paper across the desk to Simon. "Here., I want you to make a list of all the things you like to do and all the things you might like to try doing.

Simon took the pad and stared down at it as if he expected words to appear. "Do you want me to use a pen or a pencil?"

"A pen, I think. The graphite and a pencil smears and make a mess, and your penmanship will look more impressive with the pen."

"What difference does my penmanship make? It's just a list. I'm not writing an exam paper."

"Everything you write should be your best penmanship, son. I used to practice over and over to get my letters just so." He added with a chuckle, "You might put that on your list, too: practice penmanship."

Fortune went first to Planters Bank, where he was greeted effusively. *Now they like me*, he reflected, *now that I have enough money to buy the bank itself and don't need them. Unless they have the mortgage to Oak Hill.*

He let himself be ushered into the manager's office and offered coffee and a cigar, both of which he declined. As soon as the door was closed, he asked bluntly, "Do you hold the mortgage for the Oak Hill plantation, owned by the Stannard family?"

"I'm afraid I can't release that information now. If you had an account—"

Fortune rose and turned to the door. "Thank you," he said, not specifying the object of the thanks, and took his departure.

At Merchants Bank, he was greeted by name. The manager took his hand and clapped him on the shoulder. "What can I do for you today, Fortune?" He asked, leading the way to his office.

Fortune sank into the deep leather chair and accepted the proffered coffee. "I've come for a loan, if you have the mortgage for Oak Hill."

"We do hold the mortgage, but the interest is up to date..."

"I'm interested in buying the mortgage on that house and plantation when it's foreclosed," he said.

The manager's eyebrows lifted in surprise. "I'm surprised that you are interested in a rundown plantation. You have a beautiful new home, and more than your fair share of businesses. Why do you want it?"

"I've wanted it ever since I was a boy. I don't think it will be much longer before the mortgage goes into default. Col. Stannard has never known what to do with the place, and he's getting feeble. His daughter and her family spend most of that time at their home in New York. Be that as it may, I want you to notify me when the plantation becomes available, before you have an auction or sell it to someone else. And I want a loan to be made available at that time."

"A loan? Surely you don't need a loan, with all the businesses you own."

"My businesses are profitable and bring in the money that I will need to pay for the plantation and fix up the manor house. If I sold any of the businesses, I'd have more than I invested in the business, but that would stop the income."

The manager nodded. "I see why you are such a successful businessman, Mr. Barranger. I will let you know, and we will of course make a loan available. After all, you are one of our best customers, and you support a lot of people who are also customers, not to mention members of your own family."

Fortune shook the man's hand and left with a satisfied feeling.

As he left the bank, he met Amelia Ames. He doffed his hat and bowed slightly.

"I see you're out doing business this morning, Mr. Barranger."

"Some of it due to you." At her puzzled look, he said, "I heard you asking my children about what they plan to do this summer, and I'd already noticed that they tend to be lazy and aimless. And I can't have that. I have Simon back at the office making a list of things he might like to try this summer, and Eve is at Rachel's restaurant learning to cook. Perhaps you'd like to join us for lunch there."

"Thank you, but I'm running errands for Aunt Alicia and I must get back in time to fix her lunch. I'm glad that you took my remarks kindly, rather than being offended."

"Your conversation with Daniel is the most troubling. I realize that he is a lonely little boy who needs a pet, though I don't think he's old enough or responsible enough to try to train a puppy, and I doubt if Emma would permit that. A large dog might be too much for him to handle. So, you see my problem."

"Since I caused the problem at least partially, perhaps I can suggest a possible solution. What about a house-broken dog.?"

"I'd have to have a pen built and a doghouse."

"Not for this dog. Aunt Alicia has an Irish setter who is gentle as can be, and who is a bit chubby from lying around the house and needs to be walked and played with."

"That sounds ideal. But why does your aunt want to get rid of the dog?"

"Oh, she doesn't. I just thought that Daniel could come over and get to know her and learn to care for her, while letting her sleep at my aunt's home each night. Then when he's older, he could have a dog of his own."

"That does seem to be the answer to my problem," Fortune said. "I'll certainly give it a try."

"I'm glad to do anything for you, Mr. Barranger, to pay you back for what you've done for me." She smiled and stepped to one side, extending her hand. "It's been a pleasure to see you again, and I'll expect to see you and Daniel one day soon."

Fortune realized that he was smiling as he strode down the sidewalk nodding to people he met. Mrs. Ames seemed to affect him that way.

At the office, Simon handed him a long list. Fortune folded it and put it in his breast pocket. "I'll look at this over lunch. Now let's go see what your sister has learned to cook today.

Even though Patrick's was not officially opened, customers found their way in anyway, so the dining area was about a third full. Rachel came out wearing an apron, and said in her best grown-up style, "How may I serve you two gentlemen?"

Simon started to laugh, but Fortune kicked him under the table. "What are your specialties today, Miss Barranger?" Fortune asked

"Aunt Rachel says we are only offering chicken salad sandwiches and lemonade today, and the sandwiches are made with bread aunt Rachel made herself. And I've learned to make white sauce. It doesn't have much flavor, but aunt Rachel says that we can add cheese to it, or chipped beef, or brown it more when we're starting and turn it into gravy. Isn't that something? And tomorrow I'm going to learn to make biscuits. Now, I must bring your food and help serve others."

"Your sister is going to be a sales lady for sure," Fortune said to Simon. He took the paper from his pocket. "Now let's look at this list and see what you are going to become . . . 'Write a book. Play the piano. Be good at sports. Have some friends. Learn to build something. Have a girlfriend. Learn to fight. Help people. Become a doctor.' " Fortune put down the paper, and studied his son. "If you did all this, it would take you half a lifetime. Let's look at the things that you might do right now, and be thinking about becoming a doctor or an architect or musician in the future. Some of these we can combine. Which one of these is most important to you?"

"I want some friends. How did you go about making friends, Papa?"

Fortune shrugged. "I don't suppose I really have friends, except for my two brothers, but you need someone your own age, not waiting around until Daniel grows up. We could send you to the farm to live with Uncle Jamie and Aunt Ruth. They have a son a year younger than you, but that won't help you much when school starts again here. I never had time to do most of the things you have on your list, and men my age seem to hunt and fish for fun. Hunting and fishing on the farm were ways to get food, not

233

necessarily fun, especially if we didn't find some game. Walking around with a gun and talking to other men strikes me as a waste of time frankly, I enjoy business."

Fortune stopped, realizing that he was talking about himself, instead of helping his son.

He went back to the list. "Maybe we can combine sports and making friends. Which sport interests you??"

"I'd like to learn boxing, so I can defend myself, but that won't make any friends. Nobody would even know I was good at boxing until somebody pushed me or hit me. I want to do something so they respect me and I won't have to hit anybody."

Fortune nodded approvingly. "That's good. I've never had to hit anyone to defend myself. People respect me."

"Because you have money. But they don't respect me for that. They just take advantage of it."

"People don't respect me because I have money. They respect me because I know how to make money. That's a big difference. What sport do the boys at your school play?"

"Baseball. And the bigger ones play football."

"Baseball it is. Is there someone who is fairly good at the sport who would be willing to come and teach you?"

"You mean you'd pay somebody to teach me?"

"No. He must be willing to spend time with you, with a possible reward at the end, like a trip the two of you could take maybe to a fair or a battlefield or a show."

"Well, there's Robert Tyler. He goes to our church. You can ask him on Sunday."

Fortune shook his head. "No. You must ask him. Think ahead what you're going to say. You'll have to complement him on how good he is and tell him you know you won't get to be as good as he is, but you'd like to learn from him. You can tell him that if he's a good teacher, they'll be a reward at the end."

Simon nodded. "I'll need some equipment."

"Fine. You can ask him to go with you to the hardware store or wherever you find baseball equipment and help you choose it. Now, let's finish our lunch. I want to see your uncle Pete before he and Clara leave. Would you like to go along with me?"

Pete and Cara had just finished lunch at the hotel and were getting ready to leave.

"Pete, I want you to send mom back here. Tell her we need her."

"You just want to give Clara and me a chance to be alone for a while, don't you, Fortune?"

"That too," Fortune conceded. "But I do have a need of her, and it will give her a chance to see the girls and their husbands, since they didn't get to the wedding."

"Mom may not want to come on the train all by herself," Pete pointed out. "She's always had you with her."

Fortune turned to his son. "Simon would you be willing to go and escort your grandmother back on the train? You'd only need to stay overnight."

Simon looked startled. "You trust me?"

Fortune nodded. "Then it's all arranged. I can't get away right now. I have a lot going on. We'd better hurry and get Simon's things together and meet you at the station."

Chapter 40

Simon felt awkward sharing the train car with Uncle Pete and his new wife. He didn't know what to say to them, and apparently, they didn't want to talk much anyway. And he thought it would probably be worse with his grandma.

But he didn't have to worry about what to say. She talked a blue streak, hugging him and saying how glad she was to have him, and even gladder to have him on the way back once she found out that she was to go to Richmond. They had eaten on the train, and it was almost dark by the time they arrived. Simon wondered where he was to sleep, especially as grandma had not expected him. But she seemed used to dealing with a lot of people in the small house. She had made up the big bed for uncle Pete and aunt Clara, and she was to sleep in the tiny little room next door. Simon had the sleeping loft all to himself.

She awoke him by calling out early in the morning, "Get yourself up and come on down, Simon! Are you going to sleep all day?"

By the time Simon came into the kitchen, grandma was pulling a sheet of biscuits out of the oven, and the kitchen felt stifling hot. Aunt Clara flipped fried eggs neatly in the frying pan, and then lifted one out onto each person's plate and took them to the table just as uncle Pete came in with a pale of fresh milk.

"Sit down and eat, Simon," his grandmother commanded, pointing to his place. "You're gonna need a big breakfast, cause I'm going to keep you running all day long, getting things ready to take back to your folks."

She was right. He was sent to pick cherries, to gather eggs, and to go out in the cow pasture where dew berries grew wild, and pick as many of those is he could find. It was hot sweaty work, but at least he didn't have to dig the new potatoes or slop the hogs or feeding and milking the cows.

Uncle Pete did that. After they'd eaten the mid-day dinner, his grandmother said she needed his help a little bit longer before they went for the train.

While he held a small baking pan, she pulled up small plants of all kinds, wrapping them in newspaper as she finished with each variety. Straightening, she swiped her hand across her sweaty forehead, and said, "Take that over to the water bucket and poor enough water to soak that newspaper good and wet, and set it in the shade until we are ready to go."

"What's all this?" Simon asked, eyeing the heap of bundles that lay ready for the journey.

"Good fresh food you can't get in Richmond — butter and eggs and cherries, as well as new potatoes and half a ham. Your Papa wouldn't take anything when he went, saying it wasn't fitting to take things on a bridal journey, but he wasn't on the bridal journey."

"We can buy food at the market in Richmond," Simon protested wondering how he was going to carry everything.

"Not like this. The red earth of this county makes food taste special."

Simon didn't have to carry it all. Uncle Pete and aunt Clara each picked up an armful, leaving Simon with only the box of wet plants. These weren't food, and he wondered what they were for.

When they reached the train station, a porter jumped down and helped Uncle Pete carry the parcels into the special car. Simon let himself be hugged by Pete and Clara, and then followed his grandmother on to the train. Just as it began to move, she leaned out and called, "I'm leaving it all to you to take care of my animals, and water my plants."

Simon thought now that he was home, he'd be able to sleep late, but he was wrong. He was awakened by his grandmother tapping on the door and saying pretty much the same thing she'd said the day before: "Get yourself up and come on down to breakfast. You can't sleep all day. We have work to do."

Simon groaned and set up, swinging his feet out of bed and onto the floor. He washed up and put on the same clothes he'd worn the day before. He didn't know what his grandmother had in mind, but she seemed to find work that got people dirty.

Downstairs, he found the family seated around the table. He slid into the empty place and accepted the plate of ham, eggs, and hot buttered biscuits that his grandmother handed him.

"Thanks, Grandma Lorena, that looks great."

"Eve made the biscuits. They are a little ragged around the edge, but before you know it she'll be making biscuits good enough to win a prize at the fair."

As he ate, Simon glanced around the table at his family. His father was dressed as he always was, in a business suit minus the jacket, which Simon knew would be hanging in the coat closet by the front door, waiting to be donned just as his father left. He had a snowy white napkin tucked into his collar so his clothing stayed pristine. Grandma was neatly dressed in a calico dress with the sleeves rolled up. Her hair was braided and coiled atop her head, out of the way and neat. Eve was also neat, ready to go to work for Aunt Rachel. His little brother Daniel had tousled hair, and his shirt was wrongly buttoned, so there was some shirt hanging below the last button.

His mother didn't usually come to breakfast, but this morning she sat with the baby in her lap, reaching around the squirming infant to her plate. "I can't eat and hold the baby," she complained. "Maggie usually brings my breakfast to the bedroom."

Lorena stood and reached for baby Leticia. "Here, let me have her. There's no reason why you have to hold that baby in your arms all the time. She needs to get used to some of the rest of her family." She took the baby, and after a startled moment the infant let out a cry. Grandma Lorena laid Leticia expertly against her chest, and as she gently rubbed the baby's back, Leticia stopped crying.

Emma ate hastily, took back the baby and started toward the bedroom, the sash on heard dressing gown trailing along after her.

"Don't go back to bed," Lorena said. "Have yourself a nice bath and bathe my little grandbaby too. When the woman Fortune hired comes, I'll have her change the sheets and do some of the deep cleaning that you haven't been able to manage while you've been busy with the baby. You can take her outside in this nice fresh air."

Simon saw his mother's back stiffened. She was angry, he could tell, but she didn't say anything back to Grandma Lorena. Not many people did.

In the silence, Daniel said, "Look, Simon, I dressed myself. And Papa says I can go see a dog today."

"Good. Before you go, let's take care of that last button so your shirt is all nice and even."

Fortune rose and dropped his napkin on the table beside his empty plate. "I'm going to have lunch at Rachel and Patrick's. Today is their grand opening. Any of you who want to join me, be there at noon." He walked to the bedroom door and called in, "Emma, do you want to come down for Rachel's grand opening at noon?"

"We'll see," she said.

Fortune, Eve, and Daniel, holding his father's hand, set out for the trolley. Simon watched them go and waited to find out what he'd be doing during the day.

"Bring me all those dishes, and you can either wash or dry. We can leave the cherries until later this afternoon."

"That's woman's work," Simon protested

His grandmother turned from the dishpan of hot soapy water. "Young man, get that idea out of your head! Work is work. I had three sons before I had my two girls, and my boys learned to help out in the house as well as outside. So, jump to it and we'll have time to do the gardening before we head downtown."

"Gardening? But we don't have a garden."

"Exactly, but you and I are going to create one. And that's supposed to be man's work, but I've done it myself many a year." She handed him a hot wet plate to dry.

They were soon outside, Simon carrying the box full of plants.

"Where does your father keep his tools, his hoes and clippers and things?"

Simon shrugged. "I don't know that he has a hoe."

"Of course, he does. Everybody does. It may be rusty and dirty and as old as the hills, but we'll have to make do. If we can't find one, we'll buy one this afternoon. Or maybe two so we can get other people to help us dig as well. Right now, we're going to heel in some of those plants until we decide where in this wilderness back here we're going to plant them.

Simon set the box of plants in the shade of one of the two trees on the property. "What does 'heel in' mean?"

"Let me find that hoe, and I'll show you." She walked to a door set into the wall beside the back steps, and opened it. "Lord goodness, just look at the mess in here! This could do with a lot of cleaning, but we'll leave that for another day. Your young eyes are better than mine, so come in here and let's find what we need."

Simon stepped into the dark dank area and brought out two items that looked like those he had seen at the farm.

"Good boy. She took the long handled one. "This is a garden hoe. We use it to cut down weeds and make dirt into hills where we plant things, and even to kill snakes if we see one."

"Snakes? Out here?"

"Most likely not. Snakes like places that are cool and wet. Maybe in there where you found the hoes, but his hot as it is here, snakes have probably headed for the river over there." She ignored Simon's look of alarm upon realizing he had been sent into a possible snake den.

She set aside the hoe and took the short handled implement that was pointed at one end and flat at the other. "Some people call this one a grubbing hoe, and some people call it a mattock. No matter which, it's what we use for digging holes and trenches and cutting into the roots of things that get in our way. Now take it and dig me a little trench there in the shade, about six feet long and two inches deep."

Simon took the grubbing hoe and struck deep into the earth, throwing himself off balance.

"Here, let me show you. It doesn't have to be a fierce attack on the soft soil, just like this. She demonstrated, producing a yard-long trench. She handed it back to Simon. "Now you do the other half."

When he'd finished, she showed him the plants she had brought. "These are zinnias and these marigolds. I had a lot of both of them. Once they take hold, they'll bloom until frost. These are chrysanthemums, two different colors. These are watermelon plants. I was thinning out mine, and just thought I'd bring them along and give them a chance, but I wouldn't count on them. They don't have much root. We'll take these two back in the house. This one is coleus and these are sultanas. They can grow in a pot in the house or outside, and will root just in a jar of water. This last is Sweet William. Just take a smell of it. It will make a nice bouquet for your girlfriend someday."

"I don't have a girlfriend, and I may not ever."

"Of course you will, a tall good-looking boy like you. And smart too, if you just get past the idea of what's woman's work and what's man's." Simon laughed and helped her cover the roots of the plants that were lying along the edge of the trench, with just their roots down inside it. "I brought along some clippings from my rosebushes. They'll need some grass cover that still lets in the air. I doubt if there is anything like that in that horrible storage house. For the time being, we'll put those in a glass of water." She straightened from her task. "All right, now, how big do we want this garden to be? Start walking until I tell you to stop."

Mystified, Simon did as he was told.

"Stop! Now, turn right and walk to the other side of the house until I tell you to stop again." She came with the grubbing hoe and dug out a bit of turf to mark the point, then followed him to the next and dug another small patch. "Do you think your mother has a measuring tape in her sewing kit?"

"I'll go look," he said. He returned minutes later with paper pencil and a limp frayed tape, so used he could barely read the numbers. "All right, measure where you walked, and add up each side of the fence. That's how much fence we're going to need. You can do math, can't you?" Simon nodded. "I can do it, but I don't much like it."

"You don't have to like something for it to be useful. Now, when you finish that, let's figure how many bricks we'll need to make a walkway through our garden, and we'll plan on putting a gate at the very back, so allow for that."

Simon's head was spinning with figures, and he had little idea whether he was getting too few bricks or enough to pave the whole driveway.

"All right, put the two hoes away, and let's get ready to go down to Rachel and Patrick's restaurant. We don't want to miss out on the grand opening, and if I know Fortune, there'll be newspaper reporters ready to take pictures. You want your picture in the paper, don't you?"

Simon wasn't sure about that, but he went in to change into his good clothes.

Simon admired his grandmother. She reminded him a little of the principal at school. She knew what needed to be done and assigned people their part. He might have to do a lot more work than he wanted to, but he liked the sense of order and of a shared goal.

When Amelia Ames opened the front door of her aunt's house, Fortune was surprised to see that she was wearing pale green, not black. Her dress was a soft cotton fabric, whose name he didn't know, but it didn't matter. The dress was green like young leaves in springtime, and it seemed to float as she walked.

"You're not wearing black anymore," he said, and then wished he hadn't said it.

"Yes, this is much cooler than the heavy black dress. And it's time." She led the way down the hall, paused at an open bedroom door, and said, "Aunt Alicia, the Barranger boy, Daniel, is here to see Brandy. And you."

A reddish gold Irish setter lay sleep on a braided rug beside the bed. At their approach, she leapt up and growled. Daniel jumped back, clinging to his father's trouser leg.

"It's all right, Brandy," Amelia said in a soothing voice. The dog lay back, head on paws, and regarded them warily.

"She doesn't see many people," Amelia apologized. "It will take her awhile to accept you, Daniel, but then she'll lick your face and show you she loves you. Come here and take my hand." As Daniel edged forward, she took his hand in hers, and bent down in front of the dog. "Good girl, Brandy. Good dog."

The dog's tail moved slightly, and she regarded them with golden brown eyes as she sniffed Daniel's hand. Then, as if deciding that he was acceptable, she stood and lifted her right paw.

"Go ahead, Daniel, Fortune urged. "She wants to shake hands."

Daniel took the silken paw in his hand, and Brandy reached down and licked his hand. "She likes me, Papa," he exclaimed. "Just look."

"So, you have a friend now," Fortune said. To Amelia he said, "I'll come and get him just before noon, in time for lunch at Rachel and Patrick's restaurant. You're welcome to join us, if you wish."

"Thank you, but I can't be away from Alicia very long. Can you order some lunch for Aunt Alicia and me, and I'll bring Daniel on the trolley and pick up the food?"

"If you prefer that, that's fine. And I'll pay for your food in return for you at training Daniel in dog care. A deal?" Without waiting for her agreement, he said to Daniel, "Do just what Mrs. Ames tells you to, son."

As Daniel followed Amelia and Brandy out to the tiny fenced backyard, he asked, "Is your aunt dead? She's lying very still, just like my bunny was."

"No, she's just asleep."

"Will she die?"

"Yes, someday, but we don't know when."

"Will Brandy die?"

"Yes, everyone and everything will die someday," she said wistfully. "But thinking too much about that will never make you happy. Instead, think how much you and Brandy will enjoy playing together, and how much your mother and father love you."

Daniel was silent as he digested this.

Amelia stopped on the small screened back porch.

"This is Brandy's water bowl, and that is her food bowl. The water bowl is very important, especially in hot weather. She could live for a week or more without food, although she wouldn't like it, but she could only live a few days without water. So when you have a pet, always remember to make sure its water bowl is full."

Daniel nodded. "Why are we going outside?"

"Dogs need to be outside several times a day, and they need to run around and get some exercise."

As if to prove the truth of her words, Brandy ran in circles in the small grassy area, paused to urinate quickly, and ran some more. She stopped beside a tub off soapy water and backed away suspiciously.

"Dogs need baths, just like human beings do, but not as often. If we don't give her a bath, she'll smell bad, and nobody would want to be around her. But she doesn't understand all that. She just knows she doesn't like a bath. I'll hold her still while you take water from the tub and pour it over her."

Brandy accepted this unpleasant event, and stood still, her eyes locked onto Amelia in condemnation. Daniel poured the warm sudsy water over her and helped rub the soap through her reddish-gold fur until it was soaked.

"Now take the pitcher of water will and hand it to me." Amelia trickled the water down over the over the dog's head and down her spine. "Now watch out," she warned.

Daniel stepped back, but not far enough. Brandy shook vigorously, spraying him with water, and he laughed in surprise and pleasure.

Brandy slid along the grass, first one side down and then the other, and then stopped in front of Amelia, who reached out to rub her down with an old towel.

"Now she's ready to play some more," Amelia said, rolling a ball along the grass. Brandy brought it back and dropped it beside Amelia. "Now you," she said, handing the ball to Daniel.

He rolled it only a few feet and Brandy fetched it and stood in front of him holding it in her mouth.

"She wants you to play. Take the ball and throw it a bit further." While Amelia put away the bath equipment and went inside to care for her aunt, Daniel played with Brandy until they both were exhausted. He lay down on the grass, enjoying the warm sun. Brandy licked his face, and then dropped down on the grass beside him and went to sleep.

Amelia called them in and ask Daniel if he'd like her to read something to him. Daniel nodded. "And sometime, I'm going to learn to read to myself."

Amelia smiled. "Of course, you will, and we can start today if you want to. Once you learn to read, you can never be lonely again."

By the time Amelia and Daniel reached the café, the rest of the family had gathered, and a newspaper reporter was arranging the group for a photo. "Little one, on your father's lap. Ma'am, you can stand just behind Mr. Barranger."

"Oh, I'm not family," Amelia protested, stepping back into the crowd, many of whom were pushing forward with curiosity to see who was being photographed.

After lunch, Fortune accompanied his mother and Simon to a lumberyard. He looked at the figures Simon had written down. "This may not be enough, so we we'll order extras of everything." To the lumberyard owner, he gave his name, placed the order and arranged for it to be delivered on the following Monday.

"Can you and Simon take the trolley back to the café and see to getting Daniel and Eve home? I have to get to the office. I still have some other business I must take care of."

Chapter 41

Simon awoke with aching muscles. Surely his grandmother wouldn't have him digging anymore on a Sunday. But then dread overtook him. He had to talk to Robert Tyler—not just talk to him, try to make friends with him. That was worse than digging.

There was no dodging it. Throughout the service, Simon had glanced at the Tyler family from time to time, and when the last hymn had been song and the last amen said, Fortune led his family out of their pew and approached the Tylers.

"Good morning Dr. Tyler, Mrs. Tyler," Fortune said, extending his hand. "I'm Fortune Barranger, and this is my wife Emma. I'd like to get to know you better."

"I know who you are. Everybody knows you, but it's good to get to be closer acquainted. You've chosen the right day. We can talk while we eat the picnic lunch outside."

Mrs. Tyler stepped forward and took Emma's hand briefly. "I'm Natalie Tyler. I'm in charge of the Altar Guild, and we could use your help."

Emma hesitated, and started to say that she was too busy with the baby, but she felt the pressure of Fortune's hand on her back and nodded. "I'll do what I can. You'll have to show me how."

"Gladly, though there is not much to learn. And we do appreciate the fine basket of food you sent over this morning."

Emma's mouth dropped open in surprise, but before she could say she hadn't sent it, she felt Fortune's hand pressing her back again, and realized that he must have arranged it with Rachel. "I hope you'll enjoy it," she said.

"This is my daughter Eve, and my son Simon," Fortune continued. "Our sons probably already know each other, as they go to the same school."

"Don't you have a younger one as well? I thought I'd seen him with you."

"Yes, Daniel is five, and we have a newborn daughter. The two younger ones are at home with my mother, so Emma would have a chance to get out of the house and attend church. He nudged Simon forward. "I think Simon has a favor to ask of Robert." Simon wracked his brain, trying to think of what his father had told him to say, but nothing came. "Will you teach me to play baseball? You are so good at it, and I'm not."

Robert looked surprised. "All right. You want to meet at the schoolgrounds tomorrow?"

"Can you come to our house instead?" Simon asked, horrified at the thought of being seen learning and making mistakes before everybody he'd. He'd had enough of that already. "We have a big empty backyard, and my father can give you some tokens to ride the trolley."

"Well, sure. I can come over."

And so, it was settled.

In the shade of the ancient oaks behind the church, the food was spread on long wooden tables. Emma wanted to stay near Fortune's side, but she saw that the group seem to be divided, men together and women together at the other end of the table. She stood awkwardly, balancing a plate of food. Like the other women, she set her glass of tea on the table and reached for it periodically.

"Your fried chicken is delicious, Mrs. Barranger," Mrs. Tyler said.

For a moment, Emma thought of merely saying thank you and taking credit for it, but that would be unfair, and it might get her on the committee for cooking church dinners. "I'm glad you like it," she said. "But thanks are due to my sister-in-law, Rachel, she and her husband Patrick are running the new café, Patrick's."

Rachel had been listening, waiting. "We made the potato salad and chocolate cake, and my niece Eve made the biscuits."

"Oh, so the café is a family business, then," Mrs. Tyler said. "What else do you serve?"

"Whatever our customers request, within certain limits, of course," Rachel said, thinking rapidly of the potential. "We are available for weddings, afternoon teas, debutante parties, and other events."

"Oh, that's good to know. I'm a good cook, but I would gladly turn the job of arranging an event over to someone who can do it better than I."

Emma gave a little laugh. It was a relief to hear someone admit to not being the very best at women's activities. Fortune's sisters were so capable, that she felt unequal to anything they could do.

"I'm not even a good cook," she admitted. "I cooked for years for my father, and then for Fortune and me. When we finally could afford it, I was glad to turn everything about the house over to a servant." She stopped, realizing that she'd said too much. Not everyone had servants as she did. She made herself continue: "Both of Fortune's sisters are good at business. You've probably purchased clothing from Laura when she worked at Parsons, and she and her husband are soon to open a grand new department store, Hoffman's."

"Yes, indeed, Miss Barranger always seemed to find the right dress for me," Natalie Tyler nodded to Laura.

"Yes, and I want to have a fashion show soon," Laura responded. Would you possibly consider modeling for me?" she asked Mrs. Tyler.

Mrs. Tyler looked surprised and pleased. "I'd love to, if you think I'm a suitable model."

Laura looked around, taking in other women who had been listening and edged closer. "I think you'd be fine, Mrs.

Tyler. And I can use half a dozen more women and some girls, and little children, since we're planning to have specialty area for children."

Fortune had been right, Laura thought. These people were not friends yet, but they might become friends. Probably they would have been friends sooner, but hesitated to approach the Barrangers for fear they would be seen as wanting money from Fortune. She realized too, that she and Rachel had given so much of their time to their jobs, that they had not participated in the kind of gatherings that many Virginia women did.

She glanced at the gathering of men at the other table, half expecting to see the Parsons, but they were absent from the gathering. Patrick stood awkwardly beside his father-in-law, but Jonas seem to be enjoying himself. Then she heard the question she had been expecting: "You're Jewish, aren't you? What do you make of our service?"

"Three quarters of your Bible was written by Jews— Moses, David, Solomon—and Jesus was a Jewish rabbi, so I feel quite comfortable here," Jonas responded.

Laura felt a sense of pride and relief wash over her. Of course Jonas felt comfortable here. He made himself at home wherever he went.

Patrick helped Rachel gather up the picnic leftovers, she felt suddenly queasy.

"What is it, honey?" He asked. "You look pale."

"I think I'm pregnant," she said. "Already."

"Do you think you can manage to get home on the trolley, or should I ask for carriage?"

"Of course, I can manage on the trolley. I'll be all right in just a moment. This is a normal occurrence, not an illness. Ma went through it five times, and she's still all right."

The next morning at breakfast, Jonas passed the *Dispatch* across the table to Laura. "You'll want to see this," he said.

"Oh, did Patrick's get a good write-up for their opening? And did they use the photo?"

"Probably yes to both your questions, but the restaurant didn't make front page news. He tapped the headline.

Laura read: "Well-known merchant dies." The details followed: Jerome Parsons Senior had died suddenly at his home on Sunday morning.

"Your suitor will now be in charge. You could have waited just a few more months for him."

Laura slammed the newspaper on to the breakfast table, causing cups and cutlery to rattle.

"And why would you say such a thing? I don't regret for a moment marrying you instead of Jerome Parsons."

"You waited for him for years," he stated. "You must have cared for him."

"Only because I hadn't met you," Laura said, reaching across the table to take his hand. When she saw the look of love that passed across his face, she knew she had said the right thing. She went on truthfully, "The moment we met, I felt an unbelievably strong attraction for you, and it was you, not me, who suggested waiting a few days to see if Jerome would stand up to his father and insist on being married. At that point, I knew it didn't matter what he said or did. I wanted you."

"My beloved Laura, I will spend the rest of my life trying to make sure that you never regret your decision." He stood, pushed aside the breakfast dishes, and pulled her into his arms.

Laura knew that for today, her mind would not be on choosing items for the store.

Chapter 42

Before he left for work, Fortune took Simon out to the backyard to demonstrate making a fence. He brought out two sawhorses from the storage area, laid one of the long narrow boards across them, and measured the height of the fence post. "Have you decided how you want it to look? Do you want it to be pointed at the top, or flat?

"which one do you think looks better?" Simon asked.

"This is your fence. You decide. I'll make one for a pattern, and you measure carefully and use that for each one after."

"What if I make a mistake or break one?"

"You probably will make some mistakes. People always do, but you don't stop. We can always have the pickets farther apart if we run out of lumber, or we can go buy more. Until you're dead, there's almost always a chance to repair the mistakes you've made." Fortune padded his son on the shoulder, but he realized it was himself he was talking about. He felt that his life was going well, and especially after yesterday, he thought that applied to his whole family as well.

His father's demonstration had been quick and efficient, but when Simon tried, the saw seemed to buck and jerk in his hand, not pull smoothly through the wood as his father's had done.

"Always start exactly at the tip, and give yourself enough room so that the saw doesn't cut into the sawhorses. And watch your fingers. Now give the saw a smooth even pull."

Simon's first effort was a lopsided picket, because he had let the pattern slip. He got a pencil from his father's desk, and traced the original onto the wood. His father had not mentioned doing that, but it seemed logical to Simon, and he was proud of himself for thinking of it. He worked slowly and carefully, and by the time Robert arrived at midmorning, he had produced two usable pickets.

Robert arrived, trudging slowly as if reluctant to fulfill his promise. However, when Simon led him through the house and out the back door, he said, "Gee whiz what a big backyard! It's almost as big as a farm. We just have a tiny little space behind the house, and there are houses on both sides, so close you could almost touch the one next door." His voice was tinged with envy. Seeing the pile of lumber and the sawhorses, he asked, "Is your father building a fence?"

"No, I am," Simon said proudly.

"Can I saw something?"

"After we've practiced playing baseball," Simon said, realizing that he now had a skill to trade with, however newly acquired it was. "Thanks, Robert."

"Okay. Put on your glove. And please call me Robbie. Now, step back about four feet and watch me carefully. If the ball comes at you up high, you do this. If it's somewhere between your shoulders and your knees, catch it like this, and let your hands move back with the ball, to slow it down and keep you from getting an injury to your hand. If it comes in low, like bouncing on the ground, scoop it up with your glove and take it with the other hand and throw it." He demonstrated the positions.

"But I'm too close," Simon objected. "Nobody's going to throw me the ball if I'm that close."

"True, but you have to learn the positions a bit at a time. Then we'll get farther apart. And after you're really good at catching the ball, we'll practice hitting."

Over and over, Simon caught balls coming at various angles. When he missed a highball, Robbie said, "if you see it's coming high run back and turnaround before it gets there. If it's over your head, it's gone."

Simon was so exhausted from catching the ball and from sawing, that he was relieved when his grandmother called the boys to come in for lunch. They washed up and set down at the table for fried chicken, and chocolate cake left over from the church picnic, and glasses of cold lemonade."

"Boy, this is good," Robbie said, "and no vegetables. I hate vegetables, but my mother makes me eat them."

"I don't like them either," Simon said, although he did like vegetables.

After lunch when the boys went back outside, Robbie said, "Now I want to saw some before we practice hitting."

Proud of his newfound skill, Simon said "All right. Now take it a little bit at the time, the way you just taught me. Why don't you practice on this picket that I messed up. Put it up on the sawhorse, and hold it down with one hand or put your knee to hold it down and saw the end off. now, look where you are sawing, and maybe draw a line and then very slowly pull the saw back toward you."

Robbie did, but brought the saw down to abruptly, and it bounced off the wood. He tried again, but pressed down too hard on the wood, so that it tightened on the saw. When he jerked back on it, he almost fell to the ground.

"I forgot to mention watching your fingers," Simon said. "It's a good thing you didn't cut yourself. Try again."

"I'll try again tomorrow. Right now, let's see if you can hit the ball. Stand with your back to the house, closer to me, so if you hit it, it'll go way out in that empty field. Now stand with your knees bent, hold the bat to the right about even with your waist, and swing the minute you see the ball leave my hand."

Robbie stood close and tossed easy balls, and on the 5th pitch., Simon hit one. "I did it!" He exclaimed.

"Yes, but by that time you would have struck out." Robbie said. "You're just practicing now, but in a real game, don't swing unless you think the ball is coming right in the place you want to hit it. If it's too far to one side or too high or too low let it go."

"It's an awful lot to learn," Simon said. "I'm not sure I can do it."

"By the time school starts, you'll be a good player, and I'll be a good fence maker. You'll see," Robbie said.

The next day, Robbie arrived smiling and ready for work, just as Simon was finishing breakfast. It was the opposite of his reluctant arrival the previous day, and Simon felt now that they were equals. He made sure Robbie talked to him more about baseball each day before they went to fence-making. His father provided a second saw, and two hammers and boxes of nails, and showed them how to attach the pickets to the heavier fence frame. Cutting the horizontal frame pieces was harder than making pickets, and it had to be exact for the back part of the fence where the gate must match. They painted all the pieces, marked the fence line with taught strings, and dug ditches to hold the fence.

"Are we going to pour cement around the fence posts?" Simon asked his father after the ditches had been dug.

"No, the next owner of the place may not want to have a big garden."

"Are you going to sell the house?" Simon asked, dismayed that someone might tear down the fence he and Robbie had worked on so long and so proudly.

"We never know how our life may change," his father said, "and you may decide to do something fancier, now that you know how to use the saw and hoe," he concluded.

Simon was somewhat consoled. And they still had to lay the bricks for the walkway, and two separate the flowerbeds his grandmother wanted laid out.

Robbie joined in all of it, making sure that bricks were firmly set in the dirt, and helped pour the sand that filled the cracks in the walk, and formed the paths between each bed.

Soon it was all done, and grandma Lorena supervised the planting and instructed them how to care for the plants.

Then she announced that it was time for her to return to the farm.

Chapter 43

Emma had come to count on her mother-in-law being there to look after the house and stay with baby Leticia while Emma shopped. She hated leaving the baby for even a short while. It was her last, she was sure, and she wanted to prolong her time with the infant.

But she had promised Fortune and the ladies at church that she would join the Altar Guild and get to know some other women. So, while her mother-in-law was still there, Emma hired a carriage to take her to church.

Two women greeted her pleasantly, giving their names as Susan and Mattie.

"I'm Emma," she said, realizing if she were to be the friend of these ladies, she must be called by her first name.

Mattie removed the altar cloths and handed them to Emma. "We take turns laundering these." She reached for a fresh set. "You might as well get broken in right away. Do you think you can launder these and bring them back to church on Sunday?"

"I can—" Emma started to say that she could have her servant take care of the laundry, but she realized that perhaps these women did not use servants, and finished, "I can take care of it."

They finished the preparations quickly, and Susan said, "That's all there is to it. Can we put you on the schedule?" When Emma nodded, Susan went on, "You might be interested in some of the other things we women do. We have a culture club. We take turns writing a paper about something we're familiar with and read it at the next meeting?"

Emma was startled. "I—I don't know anything I could write about. All I've done is keep house for my father after my mother died, and then marry Fortune and have children.

"I suppose you could write about what it's like to be married to a wealthy businessman," Susan said briskly. "or you could pick a title or a subject, study up on it, and then educate the rest of us on it. Do you garden?"

"Yes," Emma lied. "We're laying out a garden right now."

"That would be interesting to me," Mattie said. "We also have a book discussion group. Each month we choose a book and everybody reads it, and we talk about it. Do you read a lot?"

"Not as much as I'd like," Emma managed.

"I'm sure you miss those school days when the professors expected you to read a great stack of books and write papers about them. That seems so long ago," Maddy mused."

Emma felt that she had been thrown into deep water and didn't know how to swim.

"I didn't go away to school," she admitted. "After my mother died, I had to take her place as the housekeeper."

"How did you meet your husband?" Susan asked.

"He worked for my father." Emma saw the two women exchanged a glance, and she thought they must be wondering what Fortune had seen in her. She knew she wasn't beautiful, and she put on weight with each of the children's births, and she had often refused Laura's advice on dressing.

After a moment's silence, Mattie said, "Well, we don't have any rules that say you have to have gone to college or even to a finishing school or junior college. In fact, we don't have any rules at all, we just expect our ladies to read the book and be honest about it.

"We try to read serious books on subjects that our husbands might be interested in. They don't want to hear about the house and children—at least most of them don't— and if we don't keep up, they may take an interest in some pretty young woman who's working in their business or office."

Emma had a quick vision of Amelia Ames. As a teacher, she surely would be reading as many books as she could afford.

"What do you think, Emma?" Susan asked. "We can certainly keep you busy. The book group is on Monday, culture group on Wednesday, and Altar Guild on Saturday morning. You don't by any chance play the piano or organ, do you?"

"No, thank goodness," Emma said. "I couldn't handle anything else."

Mattie and Susan laughed then Mattie said, "I'll send you a list of the books we have chosen for the rest of the year. We won't expect you to participate the first month, since it's in just a few days. And it will be several months before it's your turn to present a paper, or to have it at your house."

Emma left with an arm full of wine-stained altar cloths and a sinking heart. What must they think of her! This was going to be much more difficult than she had expected.

Laura had no difficulty in making friends, although she knew that many who sought out her company were mainly eager to model an outfit for Hoffman's grand opening, in return for a discount on that item. Her best friend would always be her sister Rachel, who was right next door, but it was good to know many people as she walked through the store checking to see if things were in place, she thought how good her life had become. She had the very best husband possible for her, a man she loved and worked well with.

Grandma Lorena walked along the sandy paths between the garden beds, squashing a bug here and there, or pinching off an unwanted bit of greenery. Coleus and sultanas grew in the shade of the elm; tomato plants, already full of small green fruits, hot peppers and sweet potato plants occupied separate beds; and on the other side zinnias, marigolds, and scarlet sage were already blooming in profusion.

"I'm real proud of you two boys," she said to Simon and Robbie. "You've done as good a job as most men would do. But your job is not over. You've got to keep the weeds pulled, kill any bugs you see eating on things, and that means you have to lift the leaves of the tomato plants and look underneath. Tomato worms can eat up your plant in no time. And make sure you water everything regularly. These summers get hot, and your plants can die in no time. Now come on inside and have some lemonade and cake. You've earned it, and it's the last you're getting from me."

"When are you going home, Grandma?" Simon asked.

"Tomorrow morning early, if your pa can arrange it to go along on the train with me."

Simon paused, a fork falloff chocolate cake in midair. "I went before. I can go with you again."

"I don't see why not," she said, brightening. "You did just fine before. We'll ask your father. He'll probably be glad not to have to go himself again so soon."

"Can I go too?" Robbie asked.

"If it's okay with your father and my father," Simon said.

As they boarded the train the next morning, Robbie asked, "where are our tickets?"

Simon laughed. "We don't need tickets. My Papa owns the railroad."

"What about lunch?" Robbie asked. "My father gave me some pocket money to buy lunch."

Grandma Lorena padded the basket on the seat beside her. "I packed a few things to eat,"

"Or we can ask the porter to bring us something," Simon said proudly.

"Or you can do both," grandma Lorena said. "Boys your age are always hungry, even if you haven't been building a fence today."

At the Oak Hill stop, the boys carried the packages Laura had sent: smooth sheets for the beds and fluffy towels to replace the worn-out scratchy cotton ones.

Robbie looked across at the Oak Hill mansion and asked, "who lives there?"

"Old Mr. Stannard," Simon replied. "Calls himself Colonel this long after the war. He must be 100 years old. My Papa says he's going to buy that house one of these days. Maybe he's waiting for the old man to die."

"Why would he want it?"

Simon shrugged. "I don't know. The house is not nearly as good as the one we live in, but Papa says he can fix it up so it will be one of the finest houses anywhere."

On the return as the train neared Richmond, Robbie said, "I can't wait to tell the guys at school about riding on the this train, in the special car—" then, seeing the look on Simon's face, he added, "with you."

The next day was hot and humid, and after tossing the ball back and forth a few times, and taking turns hitting, they both lost interest in the game, and sat in chairs in the shade drinking lemonade.

"I miss your grandmother," Robbie said.

"Me too." After a few minutes of silence, Simon added, "It's a good thing we finished the fence before the weather got so hot. It's too hot today to work, or even play ball."

"Let's go get in the river," Robbie suggested.

Simon shook his head. "Mama's father drowned in the river, during the flood, and I'm not supposed to go near the water."

261

"Just because an old man drowned doesn't mean you will," Robbie said. "You're a scaredy-cat."

"I'm not."

"Prove it. We don't have to get in the river, just walk that way and look at it. It's boring just sitting here."

So, Simon let himself be persuaded. As they set off across the field, Robbie asked, "Does your father own all this land?"

"Most of it. But the part where we were walking belongs to a man my aunt Laura was going to marry. Then she married uncle Jonas, and I don't think that other man would want to live that close to us anymore."

"Well, if he's not here, he can't object if we walk across it."

They were exhausted by the time they broke through the protective line of trees and shrubbery to the riverbank. The water swirled below them, breaking over slippery moss-covered rocks and dropping into a whirlpool. They bent down to pick up rocks and clods of dirt to throw into the water. Suddenly the bank gave away, and they plummeted into the whirlpool. Simon went into the deep and murky water, but popped up after a moment, still caught in the whirlpool. Robbie was nowhere to be seen. Looking around for Robbie, Simon didn't see the overhanging tree branch until it was almost upon him. He grabbed it and swung himself up. Gasping for breath. He caught a glimpse of Robbie being carried by the water toward him. He grabbed Robbie's shirt with one hand, holding onto the tree limb with the other. For second, he lost his grip on Robbie's shirt, then grabbed again and got hold of the limp arm.

Inch by inch, he crept along the tree branch, dragging Robbie until they were beyond the edge of the whirlpool. He let go of his friend, dropping him on to the sand, and letting go of the tree limbs so that he too could fall on to the sand.

He shook Robbie, who seemed to be dead. He had heard his father talk about how you had to push the water out of a drowning person, so he rolled Robbie onto his stomach, and straddled his back, pushing down on his friend.

Water poured from Robbie's nose and open mouth, and he gurgled and gasped. "Get off me!" He said, choking out the words.

Simon got off and rolled Robbie onto his back. Robbie set up and then promptly vomited

"I thought you were dead," Simon said.

"I thought so too. You saved my life."

"But we can't tell anybody about it," Simon said with regret.

"What do you mean?"

"We broke the rules. I'm glad I was strong enough to save you, and it's all because we've been working this summer. But we could both have drowned, and no one would even know where to go and look for us." Tears sprang to his eyes as he realized the enormity of what he had done, and he dashed them aside with the back of his hand.

"Can you walk? Can you climb up on the riverbank?"

"If you'll help me," Robbie said.

After a few struggling attempts, the boys scaled the bank, and stood leaning against a tree, panting for breath.

"We'll have to stay out in the sun until our clothes dry, Simon said. "And you look terrible. How are we going to explain that cut on your forehead and the black eye you have?"

Robbie touched his forehead and stared at his bloodied fingers. "I'll say you hit the ball hard and I was running for it and slipped and fell and hit my face against an old tree stump." He grinned. "We'll be friends for life, bound by a secret."

"Friends for life," Simon repeated.

Chapter 44

For the first time in what seemed like years, Fortune considered his family situation with some satisfaction. As this summer went on, members of his family seemed to be, as the saying went, "healthy, wealthy, and wise." Maybe not all of them had all three, but overall his life and theirs seemed to be going smoothly. Emma had begun going out to meetings with ladies from the church, though she had skipped a few. Both of his sisters and his brother Pete seem to have made good marriages. His own marriage he would not have called happy; it was simply the way he and Emma lived. Maybe it was the way most marriages were after fifteen or twenty years.

He and Emma spent little time together and had few words with each other. She spent most of her time playing with the baby, doting on it, to the exclusion of her three other children. However, Fortune thought he had done well with the children this summer. Simon had made a friend and had become good enough at baseball and construction that he wouldn't have idle time to stray into bad habits. The boys seemed to like gardening as well, thanks to his grandmother.

Eve was enjoying working at the bakery, and could handle the mathematics of adjusting recipes with no trouble. She was also showing the beginnings of what might be a career in business. It was too soon to tell what skills and interests Daniel would develop, but he certainly was enjoying caring for Brandy the dog, and according to Amelia Ames, Daniel had quickly learned to read and was asking her for books suitable for children several years older than he.

And he, himself, enjoyed taking his small son out each morning, talking with him, and getting to see Amelia Ames each day.

His well-arranged existence began to unravel one morning late in August.

When Amelia opened the door, she said, "Aunt Alicia died in the night. I've sent for the undertaker. Can you take Brandy and Daniel to your house?"

"Of course, and I'm sorry about your aunt." Fortune's mind was working rapidly. It would take time to go back to the house with Daniel and the dog, and how would Emma handle it when they got there? She would just have to accept it, he thought.

Daniel looked from his father to Mrs. Ames. "Can I have Brandy? Aunt Alicia doesn't need her anymore?"

Amelia Ames knelt to Daniel's level. "Aunt Alicia is dead, and she can't take Brandy with her. She wants you to have Brandy. You will take care of her, won't you?" Daniel nodded, and bent to stroke the head of the dog which laid on the rug beside the dead woman's bed, not moving or making a sound.

At Daniel's touch, she opened her eyes and looked at him, then rose to her feet, head and tail down. "Is she sick?" Daniel asked.

"No, she's grieving, but she loves you too, and she'll get over it," Amelia said. Turning to Fortune, she went on, "I know I'm leaving her in good hands. I've sent a telegram to the principal of the school where I taught to tell him I'll be returning." She laughed shakily. "Aunt Alicia always arranged things just so, and she managed to die just in time so I'd have a chance to get back my teaching job. I'll be boarding with someone, so I can't take the dog with me." She turned back to Daniel, and said, "Brandy is yours forever."

Fortune wanted to ask her more questions, but this was not the time. She could decide what to do about the house after the funeral, and after she'd spoken with the lawyer about her aunt's estate. His job now was to get Daniel home and tell Emma what had happened. Amelia had already gathered Brandy's belongings into a bag, which she handed to Fortune.

When Fortune told Emma, she said, "It's probably for the best. It's hard taking care of a sick person."

Fortune started to ask when she had ever cared for the sick person.

Emma went on, "She'll inherit the house, won't she?"

Fortune nodded before he could say anything more. Emma continued, "So we can take the dog back after the funeral."

"I expect she'll sell the house. She's going back to her teaching job, and she's given Brandy to Daniel." Fortune saw a look of relief, almost a smile, on Emma's face at the mention that Amelia would be leaving, to be replaced by distaste at mention of the dog. "I won't have a dog in the house!"

"We'll get her a doghouse and put it out just inside the fence, but for now, she'll be staying in the house, in Daniel's room, and her food and water bowl will be on the back porch." Fortune spoke firmly, seeing the worried look on Daniel's face.

Emma's mouth tightened, and Fortune knew he would hear more on this issue, but it was settled for now. As he turned to go to the office, Emma said, "death and disaster go in threes. I wonder who will be next."

"That's just a superstition," Fortune said, but he left with a sense of foreboding.

The day of the funeral was humid and hazy and as Fortune looked at the sky, he hoped the service would be over before the thunderstorm hit. The only mourners were a few older friends of Alicia's and the Barranger family. Emma had declined to attend. "She wasn't a friend of mine, and besides, Leticia is fretting and running a fever. She's cutting teeth." Fortune said, "She's been sick a lot, hasn't she?"

Amelia followed the priest down the center island of the church, walking all alone. Daniel turned back to look, and whispered, "She should have brought Brandy too. Brandy loved Aunt Alicia."

"Dogs don't understand death," Fortune said. "Brandy wouldn't know what to do at a funeral, and she'll be happy with you." After the short service, Amelia handed the house keys to Fortune. "Thank you so much for agreeing to put the house on the market and arrange for sale of the contents."

He took her hand. "Are you sure you don't want anything that's in the house? I can arrange to have them put it in a warehouse until you need them."

"I packed a few things in a trunk and had it sent to the train station, but I don't have a home, so I have no place for most of the things."

"Would you like company as far as the train station?"

She shook her head. "I have to get used to the way things are. You've been a true friend, and I can never thank you enough." She withdrew her hand and walked away. Fortune watched her walk away, her back stiff in the same black dress he had first seen her wear.

As Fortune and Daniel got out of the trolley, lightning struck nearby and thunder shook the ground around them. Hand-in-hand they ran for the house.

Moments later, Daniel ran from his room. "Brandy's gone!"

"She must be somewhere in the house, Fortune said. Simon helped him look for the dog. "Maybe the thunder scared her and she's hiding under a bed," the older boy said.

But after a search, Fortune went to the master bedroom and confronted Emma. "Did you let the dog out?"

"Yes. She kept whining and pacing around all over the house."

"She's not familiar with this place, and you were supposed to keep her inside. Daniel's heart will break if anything happens to that dog. We're going out to look for her, if it takes the rest of the day and half the night."

Daniel was sobbing on his bed when Fortune went in. "She's gone! Something bad has happened to her."

"We're going to find her. I think I know where to look. Put on your raincoat and get an umbrella. Simon will come with us to help look."

"She may have gone to the river," Simon suggested. Fortune gave him a puzzled look. "Why would she do that? No, let's go back to where she used to live. And if she's not there let's go to the church." He envisioned the dog scratching at the new grave. "Bring her leash, so she won't run away from us again."

They found Brandy, wet and dirty, lying against the front door of Alicia's house, howling in a low mournful voice. As Daniel approached with the leash, she struggled to her feet, and then collapsed.

"She's hurt! She's bleeding!" Daniel gasped. Fortune approached, laid his raincoat on the porch floor, and quickly wrapped the sleeve of it around Brandy's nose so she wouldn't bite him, then gathered her onto the raincoat and up in his arms. The dog whimpered with pain.

"Is she going to die?" Daniel asked.

"No, we're going to take her to the doctor right now."

"Who or what hurt Brandy?" Daniel asked. Emma did, Fortune thought. Aloud, he said, "Maybe some other dog got in a fight with her, or maybe she got kicked by a horse or hit by a carriage or the trolley."

Later, taking the bandaged dog home, Fortune got the wooden box his mother had brought plants to Richmond in, and lined it with small baby blankets. When Emma protested, he said "We can buy more baby blankets if you have more babies. For now, this dog needs it. She's got two broken ribs and a broken left leg. I'll take her outside first thing every morning and the last thing at night. In between, you're going to have to carry her out in your arms and bring her back in, just as if she were a baby."

Emma opened her mouth to protest, but Fortune went on, "If this dog doesn't pull through, or if you ever let anything else happen to this dog, I'm taking the children and moving away from here so you can have your precious house without any dogs in it."

The next morning when Fortune went in to take Brandy outside, he found that Daniel had taken the pillow and blanket from his bed and was lying on the floor beside Brandy's box. Fortune reached for the dog, who whimpered softly, awakening Daniel.

"It's all right. We'll be back." When he brought Brandy back in, he brought in a bowl of water and food, and the leash. "I think you'd better keep Brandy in here, even while we're all at home. When she gets better, you can start taking her walking around the house and outside. That leg needs to heal."

"Papa, can we pray for Brandy the way we pray for sick people at church?"

Fortune hesitated. This was a touchy topic, not one he was prepared for. He couldn't promise that God would do anything specific, but he didn't want to discourage his sons belief in God in prayer. "Yes, you can pray that Brandy gets well. But if she dies it means that God decided Alicia needs her more in heaven than you do."

Daniel didn't answer, and Fortune wondered if he had said the right thing.

School started, and Simon and Eve were quickly involved in school activities. Simon came home to break the news that he'd been the second person chosen for the baseball team after showing the other boys how well he could play. He had friends, and some of them even offered to buy him treats. Eve was in a new grade, in her new school, and making friends. She liked her teachers, especially the math teacher, and was soon earning As.

Daniel reported at dinner that Brandy had gotten out of the box all by herself and gone to scratch at the door. "She's going to get well," he predicted happily. "Maybe Aunt Alicia has a new dog in heaven. Can we take Brandy to her grave so she can say goodbye?"

"Don't be silly!" Emma said.

"Of course we can," Fortune said, with a threatening glance at Emma. She turned away from Fortune and began to spoon food into Leticia's mouth.

And so, on a windswept Saturday morning when Brandy was finally able to walk again, Fortune took his two sons and the dog to Alicia's grave. He was pleased that Simon wanted to go along. Simon had helped care for the injured dog and had watched with deep interest as the veterinarian removed the stitches and changed the bandages.

Daniel held Brandy's leash and followed as she walked all the way around Alicia's grave. At the end, she put her paw on the dirt, which had begun to sprout grass, and then turned and looked up at Daniel. He patted her, and said, "we're ready to go home, Papa."

That night, as he got into bed with Emma, Fortuned asked, "What do you want in your life, Emma? I know you are unhappy."

"I want it to be like it was at first, with you and my father coming home every night."

"We can't go back," he said flatly. He remembered her slipping into bed beside him every night, slipping into his

271

arms, willing and eager to make love to him. She had been happy to be pregnant, happy to marry him, but she'd never wanted him to own the businesses or do anything that took him away from home for even a night. "We're not young and poor anymore, the way we were then. We can afford to have Christmas dinner at the hotel this year if that will please you."

She said, "No, I would rather have it at the house."

"If you're sure, find out what the hotel would have charged and I will write you a check for that amount. In fact, I'll do better. After you've decided on your menu, buy whatever you need and put it on my account, and buy yourself whatever you want for Christmas." He almost said that Laura could help her choose, but stopped himself just in time. Instead, he said, "I'll pay Mrs. Watkins to do the cleaning. And if you want to invite your friends from church to have lunch or tea with you, I'll pay for that as well." He realized that he was handling this conversation with his wife in the same way he would handle a business discussion, but it was the way he was used to dealing with people.

"I may invite them. We're supposed to take turns being the hostess, and I haven't had a turn, but I don't feel comfortable with them. They all know so much more than I do," she admitted.

"Well, read the book, whatever the latest one is. And if you don't understand it, let me have a look at the book, and we can discuss it beforehand." He saw by the way she tightened her jaw that he'd said the wrong thing, so he added, "I never got far in school, you know, but I read a lot of books that belonged to Col. Stannard and he used to discuss them with me." If she wanted to read the book, she would, and if she didn't, then she wouldn't. He could only go so far in helping her to make friends.

He changed the subject. "Are you going to tell me what your menu is? Or will it be a surprise for me on Christmas Day?"

"I'll decide later. I'll probably tell you."

"And another thing, Emma. Leticia does cry a lot. I'll make an appointment with Dr. Tyler to have a look at her."

"Why don't we wait until after Christmas, and see if she gets better?" Emma asked.

"I think we've waited long enough," Fortune said.

A week later, he announced at breakfast, "Get Leticia dressed for going outdoors. We have an appointment this morning with Dr. Tyler."

The doctor looked puzzled as he ran his hands over Leticia's body, looked in her throat, and wiggled her spindly legs. "This is a frail child, way underweight for a one-year-old. She has all the signs of being undernourished, and yet I know will you can afford to give her ample food, and probably are doing so. She needs to get more exercise, learn to crawl and pull herself up and walk. And I found her throat strangely irritated, as if she regurgitates her food frequently. This might point to a blockage in her digestive system and she has what I believe are two broken ribs. Has she had a fall?" He looked from Emma to Fortune.

Fortune looked questioningly at Emma. "I don't see much of the child, being at work most of the day.

Emma shook her head. "No," she whispered.

"Could an older sibling have played with her too roughly? Or accidentally rolled over on her?" Emma shook her head again.

"What do you suggest we do?" Fortune asked.

"Make sure she is not left in the hands of careless or irresponsible people. Get her out of the crib and put her on the floor—under supervision, of course. Most important, see that she is gently burped after feeding. And she has cut teeth. Give her solid food, a bit at the time, and make sure she does not regurgitate it. Bring her back to see me in a month, say, January fifteenth."

Fortune was silent in the carriage. When they were home, Fortune said, "I don't know why you've been mistreating this child, but it's got to stop. It's no wonder the child is crying a lot. She's hungry and in pain. I'll stay home this afternoon and feed the baby and make sure the food stays down. Leticia will be in her crib from now on, at least until we can get her a bed of her own. Tomorrow I'll hire Mrs. Watkins to be a nursemaid to stay here every day and care for the child until my mother can get here."

Emma had not spoken as he laid out his plans, not protesting that the doctor was wrong or that she wasn't to blame.

"Well, you think your mother can handle every problem, don't you?"

"No, but she may keep this problem from getting any worse."

That afternoon, Fortune scanned the list of what Dr. Tyler had said they must do and what they should feed little Leticia. She hadn't learned to chew yet, so he had to give her mashed food for a while, as well as milk. Milk from the icebox, brought by the milkman, was all right, but canned evaporated milk would be better. She shouldn't have a lot of food at once, but just a little bit many times a day, until she got better, and used to eating solid food.

Fortune crumbled bread into a bowl, and poured warm milk over it, then spooned a bit of it into Leticia's mouth. Apparently, Emma had been feeding her this, at least, for she accepted it, and smacked her lips. Afterward he put her on the floor in the parlor, on her stomach, and watched as she raised herself up on hands and knees, wobbling as she moved forward. By the time Simon and Eve got home from school, Fortune had opened the door to Daniel's room, and let her crawl inside. She was a smart child, Fortune thought, smart as all his children were. She just hadn't had a chance to show it.

Leticia touched Brandy, who lay asleep on the soft rug. The startled dog awoke and looked at Daniel, then turned and licked Leticia, who giggled with pleasure.

At bedtime, Fortune put Leticia in her crib and got in bed himself on the side of the bed nearest the crib. Emma came in from the bathroom, dressed in a long flannel gown, got in bed on the other side, and turned her back on him.

Grandma Lorena came two days later, finally deciding that she could travel all alone in Fortune's private carriage cars. On the way from the station, Fortune told her that Emma had been neglecting the baby. He couldn't bring himself to say she'd been mistreating Leticia. "You did well by the children during the summer, but they seem to be slipping back into their lazy ways, and Daniel needs attention."

"I'll do what I can, son, and I'll try to tread lightly, but you know I've never been one to hold back what I think. And I know Emma doesn't really want me around. No woman likes to have another woman in her home, especially in her kitchen or telling her how to bring up her children"

The next morning after Simon and Eve had left for school and Fortune for work, grandma Lorena took the bib off Leticia and lifted her from her high chair.

Emma reached for the baby. "Give her to me. She needs a clean diaper and a bath."

"I can tell that, and I can take care of bathing and diapering. I raised my five from babies, all the time while canning, gardening, and helping with the crops. Fortune tells me you've taken on a lot of jobs at church, and you have a book to read and a party and Christmas dinner to plan and shop for yourself. Now you get out of that robe and put on some decent clothes and go set yourself down in the parlor and read that book. I'll take care of the children while you do what Fortune wants you to do."

"You can't tell me what to do."

"I know you don't like me, Emma, and you never have, so I'm going to speak plain to you and you'll probably like me even less. So be it. I'm telling you this for your own good. I want my son and my grandchildren to be happy, and right now, they're not. Simon and Eve don't bring their friends home to stay overnight. Before long, they'll be going away to school, and they may not even want to come home. And Fortune may not either."

"He doesn't love me. He already stays away until late in the day and sometimes stays away for two or three nights at a time."

"He has to go and see about his businesses. They are all over Virginia and in other states as well."

But is he planning to leave me? I can't stand that. He's all I've got! He doesn't love me," she repeated.

"No, he's not planning to leave you, at least not yet. He's been loyal to you because he's a good man. But he is a man, and he's smart and rich and very good-looking for his age. There are many women who would like to be in your footsteps, and some of them may try."

"What can I do?" Emma asked, defeated and alarmed.

"For right now, go read that book. Then this afternoon go downtown to Hoffman's and have Laura pick out several dresses for you. You might also find out who does her hair. Right now, I've got to tend to the baby. I've got my hand on a wet diaper, and she's squirming to get down on the floor." Lorena walked off to take care of Leticia.

She found Daniel in his room, lying on the floor beside Brandy, reading aloud. She put Leticia down on the floor next to Daniel and moved to a chair near them. When Daniel finished reading the short book, she said, "that was fine. I'm sure Brandy enjoyed the story too. Does your mother know you can read?"

"She doesn't like me. She screams at me and Brandy."

"Well I don't think she will do that to you anymore," she said. "At least, I hope not. Now come here and read to me."

He came and stood by her chair, book in hand, but he looked down at his little sister on the floor, a frown increasing his face. "Leticia is not supposed to be on the floor. She might get dirty."

"You watch her while I go for cleaning cloths. We're going to clean up your room so she won't get dirty. You can also pick up your toys. And pick up the clothes off the floor." Daniel worked, cleaning and putting away his things. Once he was finished, Lorena praised him.

As Lorena sat back in her chair, Leticia crawled over and pulled at her skirts. Losing her grip, the baby sat down on the floor, but reached again for her grandmother's skirt, and succeeded in pulling herself up right. When Simon and Eve came home from school, Simon asked, "Where is mama?"

"Downtown doing some shopping. Simon, I want you to help Daniel give Brandy a bath. He's learned what to do, but he can't handle the job by himself. Eve, watch Leticia while I help Simon carry the tub of soapy water outside. She's crawling now, and can get into trouble. Then I want both of you to clean your rooms, so if you want to have a friend each come over and spend the night tomorrow night, you won't be embarrassed about your room."

"Papa pays Mrs. Watkins to do that," Eve said.

"It's time you learned to look after yourself. Before you know it, you'll be going away to school, and there won't be a Mrs. Watkins to pick up after you. Now get going. "

After a startled look from Simon and Eve, and a happy smile from Daniel, the children set about their tasks.

When Emma came home, she spotted Brandy curled up on a towel in front of the dining room fireplace. "What's that stinky dirty dog doing in here?" She demanded

"She's not stinky and dirty, mama," Simon said, taking Daniel's hand in sympathy. "Daniel and I gave her a bath this afternoon, but she's cold and needed to get warm."

"And I cleaned my room, mama, and got rid of all the hairs Brandy doesn't use any more," Daniel said. "Come and see."

The three children followed her into Daniel's room, where she stood just inside the doorway and glanced around. "Good, Daniel," she said, turning back.

He ran for one of his books. "And I can read too, mama," he said, holding up the book for her to see.

"That's good, Daniel how did you learn to read?"

"Mrs. Ames taught me. She said I was smart enough to learn to read already." Emma said nothing.

"We cleaned our rooms too," Eve said.

"Mrs. Watkins would have done that."

"That's what I told grandma," Simon said, "but she said even I would soon be living away at school and we needed to know how to take care of ourselves no matter how much money Pop has."

It was, Emma thought, just as grandma Lorena had said: the children would leave her.

Just then Fortune came home and had to be shown the clean rooms as well. At a signal from his mother, he praised the children and turned to Emma. "You look nice, my dear. I'm glad you bought yourself a new gown."

Emma was in a good mood the rest of the evening.

Chapter 45

On December 23, Jamie and Ruth arrived on the train with their three children: James Jr., Martha, and Edmund. They brought along so much food along with their baggage that Fortune had to hire two carriages to get everybody to his house. There was a whole smoked ham wrapped in a pillowcase, a bushel of apples of several kinds, mostly winesaps, a bushel of sweet potatoes in a burlap bag stuffed with turnip greens and another full of turnips, as well as three pounds of fresh butter and five pounds of fresh sausage.

"I don't know what we're going to do with all this," Fortune said. "Emma has been shopping for days, with Mama and Eve."

"Well, it will all keep," Jamie said. "We thought you might like to eat some of the kind of food your poor relatives still eat in the mountains."

"That's the best kind of food there is, and I thank you very much."

"We just killed hogs, and I salted down most of the meat except for what I gave Pete and Col. Stannard. Most of the sausage rolled up and hung in the smokehouse, but it hadn't smoked enough to bring it along."

"How is Col. Stannard?" Fortune asked as the carriages began to move.

"Feeble. And a little touched in the head, I think. Sometimes he calls me Yank, like a Union soldier, and threatens to shoot me."

Fortune laughed. "I wouldn't worry. He's such a poor shot he probably couldn't hit the side of a barn."

"Oh, I don't know. I don't want to put it to the test."

"Does he still have Bessie?"

Jamie shook his head. "That poor horse finally went to her reward a few years ago. She must have been thirty years old."

"Do the Bishops come often, or is Col. Stannard all by himself?"

"Charlotte comes once in a while, with the little girl; she's a toddler now. Haven't seen the husband or that worthless boy of hers in a coon's years."

"How's the apple business? I see you brought a basket full of beauties."

"Making more money off apples than we ever did off tobacco. I'm shipping them every which way to stores and canneries, on your railroad, of course." Jamie laughed. "I'm thinking of opening a canning business of my own. Could you finance me?"

"Probably. It depends on how much you need and when. I'm still counting on buying Oak Hill, and I've got the bank's promise to loan me whatever I need. I could add you in on that."

The children were distributed into their cousins' rooms, while Jamie and Ruth were sent in a carriage to Jonas and Laura's house for the night. After breakfast the next morning, Fortune took the six children for a trolley ride to Hoffman's, where Jamie and Ruth were waiting for them and Laura.

"I'll be your best customer today," Fortune announced. "New suit for each man and boy, a new dress for each woman or girl, and Laura, choose a new dress and coat for mama, and of course Emma gets a dress as well as you and Rachel and Ruth. Do you have baby things? Leticia is beginning to grow out of her baby things." He handed each of the children money. "Buy a gift for yourself, or to give someone else if you want to."

"That's too much, Fortune," Ruth protested.

"Not a bit of it. You brought us an awful lot of food, and you've been looking after the land I plan to buy. And Jamie, you stayed and worked the farm while I came here and earned so much. After the shopping, go to Patrick's café and have lunch. Rachel will put it on my account. Then take the trolley to our house."

"And what do we say?" Ruth asked.

"Thank you!" The children chorused.

The visiting children were so excited that they begged to stay longer, but Jamie said, "Three nights away is enough. Uncle Pete is having to do all of our jobs while you were gone, looking after the animals as well as taking care of Aunt Clara."

Fortune was thinking of how it might be arranged for the younger children to stay longer while James Jr. returned with his parents, but it would be complicated, and not fair to the older boy. Then a frown from Emma cut short his plans.

"It's been good to have all of you here," he said, "but I understand how it is on a farm. There's no telling what Pete's done with all the milk, or if he even milked the cows as often as they should have been." He laughed. "Taking care of animals has never been Pete's favorite job."

On Christmas morning all the children took turns walking Brandy until the dog was happy to curl up and sleep during Christmas dinner.

The next morning, as Eve finished drying the last plate her grandmother handed her, she asked the question she'd been wanting to talk about: "I heard Jim and Simon talking last night about doing something to girls. They were whispering and laughing."

"Your brothers are just like all the rest of the boys and men in the world, hoping and planning on how they can get on with female. That's the way men are their whole lives.

Sometimes they use sweet words and promises, and sometimes they force a woman. You don't want it to happen to you in any case until after you're married. Then it's a good thing, because that's how babies are made, and you don't want to be diapering babies for ten more years."

"Martha said all boys are like that," Eve said, "but I didn't believe her. It sounds awful, especially the bleeding."

"It's a woman's lot," her grandmother said. "Having babies can be a wonderful thing. It's something man can't do."

"I think I'd rather not," Eve said.

"You may change your mind, but in the meantime, I'm going to tell you girls have to make sure it doesn't happen to you until you are married and want it to happen. You should be going to school and to parties and having fun. You should get enough schooling that you can get a job and take care of yourself if you have to." She poured out the dishwater, wiped out the dishpan and put it away.

Martha had joined Lorena and Eve in the kitchen. Lorena gathered the two girls to her and explained how best to keep themselves safe.

"First of all, keep your clothes on and don't be alone with a boy or man. They'll surely try to persuade you to take off those clothes. They'll want to take you riding a horse or walking in the woods or going up into somebody's attic to look for something. Then they'll try to touch your breasts or your lady parts down there." She pointed, and both girls looked down to themselves.

"What he wants is to get his man part into your lady part. What you do is kick him right between the legs if you can, but it's hard to kick when you're wearing a long dress. Second-best is to hit him there with your fist. Not with your open hand, or he'll get the wrong idea. He's very tender there, and if you hit him just right and hard enough, he'll leave you alone and grab himself and be in terrible pain but he'll leave you alone, and that's your chance to get away."

When she finished, both girls looked at each other in solemn silence.

"Both you girls are pretty and smart, and some men will fall in love with you for yourselves and want to marry you. Be careful if they seem too interested in what your father's house is worth or how much money your father has." She drew them against her, one arm around each girl, and kissed them. "Now go on and have fun."

The children wanted one more ride on the trolley before they left, so Fortune arranged that Jamie and Ruth, along with their baggage and all the gifts, should go to the station in a carriage, while the children went on the trolley.

"And Emma, my dear, you must go in the carriage as well, and take Leticia with you," he said. "She's still a bit young for the trolley."

"I'll just stay home with her," Emma said.

"Nonsense, my dear! You deserve to get out of the house, and the fresh air will do you and Leticia a world of good. But if you insist on staying home, I'll ride in the carriage and hold Leticia."

Emma saw that she really didn't have a choice. Leticia was used to riding to church in a carriage, and soon would insist on going along with her older sister and brothers on the trolley.

At the station, after hugs all around, and Fortune watched part of his family depart on his train. He remembered Jamie's parting words to him: "Everything went well over the holidays, thanks to you, Emma, and your children. May it be so in the new year."

But it was not to be. Winter wore on in the typical Virginia way: a cold snap in January that froze the edges of the James River and stopped construction on the houses next to Fortune and Emma's; deep snows in February that soon melted, only to be replaced by another snow, and a long, wet March.

All Fortune's businesses were running smoothly: people still smoked cigarettes, rode the train and trolleys, and ships still needed coal. Emma was so busy with the church groups that Fortune finally decided to hire Mrs. Watkins full-time to do housework and to look after the younger children. Simon and Eve were doing well at school and making friends.

His only worry was his extended family, due to a letter from Jamie.

"Everybody here is poorly. All but Pete and me. Ruth and Martha got over it pretty quick, whatever this ailment is, and the boys were only sick a couple of days. I wanted to take Ma to the hospital in Charlottesville, but she refused. Said she had been through winter sickness more than one time, and this one would pass on too. I checked on Col. Stannard, and sent for Charlotte, but he recovered, and she went back up north. Hope all of you are well."

Two weeks later, another letter arrived: "Thanks for the doctor. We all survived, even Col. Stannard. Mama and Clara still a little weak. Mama says she might not have pulled through if it hadn't been for that nice coat you bought her to keep her old bones warm in this cold weather. Hope all of you are well."

He told Emma of the letters' contents and his relief that everyone seemed to have recovered.

"I'm glad you didn't go up there to take care of your family, Fortune," she said. "It would have been just like you to do that, and you'd have probably caught whatever they had. It's bad enough that so many people here in Richmond are sick, including some of my friends, but we haven't caught anything."

"You might consider staying home so you won't risk catching anything."

"They are my friends, and I like going out to their houses or to Rachel's café, or shopping. You wanted me to make friends, and I have, so there you are."

A week later, Emma got sick. She coughed continuously, keeping Fortune awake, and he was glad that Leticia was now in the nursery, away from catching her mother's illness. By morning, Emma was gasping for breath and her body was wet with sweat.

When Fortune called Dr. Tyler to arrange to have Emma admitted to the hospital, the doctor hesitated. "The hospital is full, and even some of the doctors and nurses are ill. She might get better care at home."

"I don't want Emma to come in contact with the children, especially our youngest, and my sisters are both pregnant, so it would be a mistake for either of them to come to help out, and I'm no help at all as a nurse."

"Do you have household help? I seem to remember that you do."

"Yes, but I want her to take care of the children and I don't want Emma infecting the children."

"Give her hot tea with honey to ease her cough, and if she's able, have her give herself a sponge bath. I'll see what I can do. Don't touch her yourself, keep her glasses and dishes separate from the ones the family use, and wash your hands after you have touched anything that she has used."

Dr. Tyler called back later that day to say that he had arranged a room for Emma.

Fortune helped her to dress, and arranged a carriage to take her to the hospital. By the time they arrived, Emma could barely walk.

The next day, a telegram arrived from Jamie: "Ma died. Burial Saturday."

Fortune put the telegram down on his desk with a shaking hand. She shouldn't have died so soon. She was only sixty. Once that had seemed very old to him, but now it seemed that her life had been cut short. Resolutely, he turned to making the necessary arrangements. First a telegram to Jamie: "I will buy a suitable coffin and send it to you tomorrow. Will also arrange for flowers, and put notice in newspapers."

When he called the newspaper, the reporter said, "Mr. Barranger, you are too important for your mother to just have a standard obituary. It's got to be an article. I'll be right over."

In the interim, Fortune called both his sisters, and made sure everyone had suitable clothing that was fit for the funeral.

That would be no question of Rachel going to the funeral, as she was due to have her baby just any day now. Laura would want to go, and she could look after Leticia. And keep an eye on Daniel.

When Fortune told his children about their grandmother's death and plans for the trip, Daniel said, "Brandy should go too. Brandy loved grandma just as I do." Fortune was about to say that dogs didn't go on trains or attend funerals, but he saw the anguished pleading in his young sons' eyes. And it would erase the need for arranging any care for Brandy. Having a private car made things easier. He nodded, to the astonishment of Simon and Eve.

Fortune picked up the copy of the *Dispatch* off the front walk on the way to the train station with his children. The headline read, "Mother of noted businessman Fortune Barranger dies." He knew that the newspaper editors were only interested in his mother because she was his mother, but he was dismayed that his name was mentioned in the headline of the article. The article was accurate, but he didn't need to read it. He passed it across to Laura once they were seated in the train car.

She read the entire article out loud: "Mrs. Lorena Adams Barranger, mother of businessman and investor Fortune Barranger, died on April 5. She is also survived by two sons, James Barranger, orchardist and farm manager of Oak Hill estate, and Joseph Peterson Barranger, a tobacco buyer and warehouse owner; also, two daughters, Mrs. Jonas Hoffman, co-owner of Hoffman's department store, and Mrs. Patrick Martin, co-owner of Patrick's café. Mrs. Barranger is also survived by seven grandchildren. A lifelong Episcopalian, she was involved in church activities and was an avid gardener."

She shook her head. "Rachel and I just lost our identities as far as the newspaper was concerned. We're only mentioned as the wives of our husbands. And what about all this mention of businesses, Fortune? It reads like a business article."

Fortune laughed. "Newspapers like to write up my business connections. And they did give the time and place of the service, so our neighbors and friends will know to attend."

The lacquered wood coffin dominated the main room of what had been Lorena's home. She lay on the satin pillow, dressed as she had planned in her lavender silk dress and lavender straw hat.

"Grandma doesn't look dead. She looks like she just went to sleep," Daniel said. "And she must be cold; she should be wearing her new coat."

Fortune put his arm around his sons' shoulders. "It's warm and pleasant where Grandma is going. She would want that coat to be used by someone else here." He turned the boy and dog away from the coffin as it was closed and moved out onto the wagon to go to church.

Fortune was astonished at the packed church. Besides his mother's children and grandchildren, there were some of her nieces and nephews whom he had not seen in so long he hardly recognized them, neighbors who had filled the tiny kitchen with bowls of potato salad, baked apples, meatloaf and other food for the guests. Then there were some of his business associates, many of whom had sent flowers, to judge by the array of color flanking the altar. His mother would have been pleased.

A feeling of emptiness overwhelmed him on the train journey home. He was now the older generation, forty years old, with his children about him. Eve had curled up on one of the velour seats, next to Laura, who held the sleeping Leticia in her lap. On the opposite side, Brandy lay curled up on the floor with Daniel's feet just touching her. Simon stared out the dark window. Fortune was proud of his children, and confident now that they would turn out all right, thanks in large measure to his mother. He would never again be able to ask her for advice, or call on her to solve a family problem or tell her how much she had meant to him.

As soon as he got home and saw to it that the children were settled in their own rooms and that Brandy's needs were taken care of, he said good night to Laura as he dropped her off, and then had the carriage take him to the hospital to see Emma.

She sat up in bed, her hair's drag late and unwashed, a satin nightgown slipping off one shoulder.

"How are you, my dear? I won't kiss you, in case you are contagious still. What does Dr. Tyler say?"

"Much you care!" She said. "I saw the newspaper article so I know where you've been, to your mother's funeral, and I'll bet you took the children along." Before Fortune could answer, she went on, "you should have been here with me! You couldn't do anything for her. She's dead, but I'm alive, and I needed you."

"Emma, be reasonable. Of course, I went to my mother's funeral. And I couldn't have done anything for you anyway. The doctors and nurses are what you need, not a husband sitting around watching you. I can see that you're still sick, and you probably need rest. I know I do. So, go to sleep, and I will come and visit you again tomorrow, I promise and I'll soon be taking you home, after you're well."

She hadn't even said she was sorry about his mother.

Chapter 46

Emma came home, gaunt and demanding, with dark circles underneath her eyes.

Fortune decided to walk to work instead of taking the trolley. It would take much longer, but he needed the time to think, away from business problems, and the exercise and fresh air would do him good.

Why was Emma like this with the children, and with him? She was filling them all with guilt and keeping them uneasy. If only he could ask his mother what to do. Last summer, and again at Christmas, she had come and straightened things out, and left his household and family in better shape. But that was all past. It was his job now, and he wasn't sure how to handle it.

He tried to think about Emma as she'd been when he first met her. She had no family beyond her father, and never knew the responsibility of looking after brothers and sisters. When she lost her father, Fortune became her only family. Her father had come home every night; Fortune couldn't, and didn't. He was the wrong husband for her, but she'd never let go of him to seek for another, just as she wouldn't let go of the children, and yet she couldn't show them love.

How had his mother and Amelia Ames managed to win the love of his children, when their mother could not? By teaching them something useful, something they could be proud of. Something that had make them feel independent, but Emma did not want them to be independent.

By the time he arrived at his office, he had thought of something that each child could share with Emma and he was going to make damn sure it happened. School would be out soon, and the two older ones needed something to occupy their summer with. Daniel could get started right away. Satisfied, Fortune turned his mind to his businesses.

A quick look at the report his assistant had prepared showed that all was well financially. He wanted to do something to be a memorial to his mother, and he had to give some thought to Jamie's plans for a large orchard and a cannery. There was money available, more in the bank than he really liked keeping in the bank. Should he put the money in more real estate or in expanding the trolley line, or look for some other investment? He tried to think of something he could do would please Emma. He'd discuss it with her, he decided.

When Fortune arrived home, he knocked on Simon's door and found his son studying for his final exam. Simon looked up in surprise, and pushed his book aside. "Am I in trouble, Papa?"

"Not that I know of. Are you?" Without waiting for an answer, he went on, "your mother is in a disturbed condition, as you undoubtedly had noticed this morning. Your school ends in two more days. I want you to read whatever books she's reading for her group, and discuss them with her."

"What if she says no? She always does."

"She won't this time. I'll see to it. Now, go back to your studying. I know you've done well so far in school, and I want it to continue, so you'll be prepared to go off to college."

Next, he asked Eve if she would like to learn to knit.

"Yes, Papa, but who's going to teach me?"

"Your mother knows how. Ask her, and I'm sure she'll be glad to teach you. And Eve, touch her hand while she's teaching you, and let her touch yours."

Eve nodded, with a puzzled look. Fortune was uncertain how to handle his next effort. He first told Daniel to get Brandy ready for a walk, and then went to Emma's bedside and threw back the covers. "Get on some outdoor clothes were going for a short walk. You need to take some exercise or you'll end up spending the rest of your life bedridden."

After a flash of anger, she asked, "Are you going walking with me?"

"Yes," he said with enthusiasm he didn't really feel. After she was almost finished dressing, he added, "Daniel and Leticia are coming along too. It's a family outing while Simon and Eve a studying."

Out in front of the house, he positioned them on the walkway covered with crushed oyster shell. "Daniel, can you take mama's hand with your left hand and hold Brandy's leash with your right hand?"

"Me?" Leticia asked.

"You'll take papa's hand. We'll go down and back, and then I'll take Daniel's hand, and Leticia can take mama's hand." it almost pained Fortune to see the joy in his children's eyes. He realized that he as well as Emma had neglected these two younger ones.

The procession moved slowly with Emma taking halting steps, Brandy pausing to look back for instructions from Daniel, and Fortune slowing his footsteps so that Leticia could match his stride.

His plans for his older children to get to work with their mother failed. At supper three nights later, Simon announced, "Papa, mama doesn't need me or want me to read with her. Her book group is not meeting during the summer. They're going to the beach."

"And we can't go," Eve added.

Fortune put down his fork and turned to his wife. "When were you going to tell me this, Emma?"

"Soon, we're getting away from husbands and children." Before he said anything more, she added, "and you can't stop me."

"I wasn't thinking of stopping you, Emma. I would, however, have appreciated being told as soon as you decided, so I could make plans for the children." He realized that he and Emma had just crossed a line in their marriage. There would be no turning back. The children sensed it too, even the youngest, as they looked from father to their mother and back again.

"When will you go?" Fortune asked.

"July first. I'll be staying two weeks. Mrs. Barksdale has rented a cottage for the entire month, so if we all get along well, I may stay the whole time."

Chapter 47

The day before Emma was to leave, Fortune received a telegram that changed all of their lives forever: "Baby born. Clara died. Pete berserk. Jamie."

"We must go as quickly as possible," Fortune said, showing Emma the telegram.

"I'm not going. You go. It's your family." She folded another garment and placed it in the open suitcase.

Fortune walked out of the bedroom and called the children together. From now on, he would consult them about what they wanted, and he alone would make the final decision, without Emma.

"Aunt Clara is dead, and Uncle Pete needs my help. I need to depend on you to take care of each other. I don't think this is a good time for you children to go, so I want to leave you here with Mrs. Watkins. I'll pay her extra so she can stay overnight, every night. Can I depend on you to obey her and help her? If anything bad happens, call Aunt Laura and Uncle Jonas, and if they can't come and take care of things, then call Aunt Rachel and Uncle Patrick. Would you do that?"

The children nodded solemnly.

"I'm almost sixteen, Papa; you can count on me."

"And I'm almost thirteen, and I can cook and help Mrs. Watkins," Eve said.

"I'll be six before Christmas, and I'll take care of Brandy," Daniel said, reaching down to touch his dog. "Could Brandy go to Uncle Pete's?"

"I don't think so," Fortune said. He called both his sisters, packed a bag and left for the train with great trepidation both at what he was leaving behind and what he would face ahead.

Jamie met Fortune at the station and told him what had happened. "Clara had the baby—a little girl—and at first everything seemed all right. Pete was just crazy with happiness, and kept telling her how much he loved her. Then she seemed to get weaker and weaker and just faded away. Pete had set by her bed day and night until finally he fell asleep, and when he woke up, she was dead and cold. She hadn't been able to nurse the baby, and Ruth has been taking care of it, bringing it to be with Clara during the daytime and taking it home at night."

"You said in your telegram that Pete has gone berserk."

"He stands outside the house screaming and crying and beating his head against the house. I tried to get him to calm down and gave him a drink. He grabbed the whole bottle from me and drank it almost without stopping, and then collapsed. We were able then to take Clara's body out of the house and prepare it for burial. Now Pete has come to, and he says he won't look at Clara or the baby and is going to kill himself. He's damn near succeeded already."

"I'll talk to him," Fortune said.

"Maybe he'll listen to you, and maybe not. You're our last hope."

Fortune found Pete slumped against a tree, reeking of alcohol, vomit, and urine. His clothes were a stinking mess. Fortune had to make himself get close enough to speak to his brother. He motioned Jamie to hold Pete up, and fetched a bucket of water from the well, throwing it over his brother as they lifted him to his seat on a bench.

Pete jerked free. "What the hell you doing?!"

"We're going to get you cleaned up and in some decent clothes in time for the funeral," Fortune said.

"Not going," Pete mumbled.

"You must go and say goodbye to Clara," Fortune said quietly.

"Can't see her like this. She was so beautiful."

"She loved you, more than I ever saw a woman love a man," Fortune said. He remembered the way they had looked at each other on their wedding day, with a love so searing it was painful to watch. He had never loved anyone to the extent that Pete and Clara had loved each other, and he never wanted to. "And she left you a daughter, a part of herself and you. You've got to take care of yourself for the sake of that child."

"Don't want to see the baby. It killed Clara." His head lolled to one side, and he seemed about to fall asleep.

Together, Fortune and Jamie maneuvered their brother into the house. The bed had been stripped and the mattress removed. "Let's put him on the springs. At least if he vomits again, he won't mess up any more bedding."

Jamie began stripping off the filthy clothes, dropping them in a heap on the floor. As he pulled off the last stinking sock, he gathered the bundle, and holding it at arm's length stepped outside. "I'm going to burn these," he announced.

When Jamie returned, Fortune was still struggling to dress the unconscious man. With Jamie's help, Pete was dressed and sitting up, but he dropped back onto the bed springs.

"Might as well leave him there," Jamie said. "Based on the way he's acted the last few days, he'll be asleep for hours. We need to do a little bit of cleaning ourselves up and get on to the church."

Jamie didn't ask where Emma and the children were, and Fortune didn't say.

The tiny church was packed. Ruth and the children sat on the front row, with space left for Jamie, Fortune and Pete. Across the aisle, just as at the wedding, sat Clara's family looking awkward and out of place. Behind them were what Fortune assumed must be Clara's former students as well as neighbors he remembered. At the back he saw Amelia Ames dressed in black, holding Pete and Clara's baby. He walked back to her and said, "I don't think Pete is coming, so there will be an empty seat on the front row. Please come up with the baby. She's family, and you were Clara's best friend."

Throughout the service, Fortune kept glancing out the door, hoping that Pete would awaken and change his mind. But the service ended, and the family was surrounded by people offering sympathy, and others guiding the crowd out to the churchyard for the burial. Clara was buried beside her mother-in-law in a plot down the hill and behind the church, half hidden by trees and boxwood. A few people lingered to speak to Fortune and Jamie's family, but most headed for shade and where a makeshift table had been set up which was spread with food.

As soon as he could pull himself away from the crowd, Fortune went to the house to check on Pete. He was gone!

After Fortune sent Jamie, Jamie Jr., and two of Jamie's farm workers in search of Pete, Clara's father approached him.

"I hear tell your brother don't want this child, Clara's baby. We'd be willing to take care of it, seeing as it's half Clara's side. Course, we would need a bit of money to pay for what it would eat and wear and so on."

"My brother is so grief stricken over Clara's death that he's out of his mind. When he recovers, he will surely want his child." Fortune wasn't sure just what Pete would do if and when he recovered his senses, but he couldn't imagine anything much worse than turning this baby over to this shiftless family. Clara had escaped from it, and he would not send her child back to it. "It's kind of you to offer, but my sister-in-law has been caring for the baby for the past few days, and she will undoubtedly continue to care for it," he made himself say in a calm businesslike tone.

"I just thought . . ." Clara's father said.

Fortune didn't let him finish the sentence, but turned away, looking for Amelia Ames.

He found her at the edge of the crowd, holding the baby up against her shoulder, supporting its head as expertly as if she herself had been a mother before. "I'll hold the baby while you get something to eat," he offered.

She shook her head. "I'm not hungry. I'm glad you're not giving the baby to Clara's parents. I promised her I wouldn't let them have her, but of course, you're the head of the family and it's up to you to decide what's happening to her now that Pete has gone."

Before they could talk further, Jim ran up to say, "Uncle Fortune, one of the Bishops' prize horses is missing. You want me to take the other one and go after Uncle Pete?"

"No. He's had a head start, and he'll either ride the horse to its death or it will throw him and someone will find the body. He's not coming back. That I'm sure of."

Fortune began pondering what would be needed to care for the baby. She may well have lost both her parents. Ruth had to look after her own family as well as help Jamie with the farm work. There was no question of asking Emma. He couldn't trust her with her own baby, much less someone else's. He looked again at the gentle way Amelia Ames was holding the infant. "Would you consider being a full-time nanny for the baby? I'll pay you well."

She nodded. "I want to take care of the baby. I came two days ago and was with Clara at the last. I promised her I'd be the baby's godmother and take care of it until your brother finds someone else to love and marry."

"I'm talking about a permanent arrangement. I doubt that Pete will return," Fortune said sadly. "Even if he does, he said he hates the baby, and that's not a good start for fatherhood. How did you feed the baby? Ruth said that Clara was too weak to nurse."

"I washed and dried a pair of white cotton gloves, then soaked one of the fingers in milk and put my finger in the baby's mouth and she could suck the milk. It took a long time, because I had to keep re-soaking the glove."

"Very resourceful. One of my sisters may be able to nurse the baby a bit. I'd like to take her with me tonight. How soon can you come to Richmond?"

"I can go immediately. I was planning to go as soon as Clara had recovered her strength, and all my worldly goods are in a small trunk which is in the little room where I stayed to be close to Clara."

Fortune was bone tired. He'd slept badly on the train last night and today's events had been worse than he had expected. He considered having his private car stay in place overnight, but he could sleep as well with the train moving as stationary. He assisted Amelia in boarding and then handed up the small box that served as a bed for the baby.

He boarded, and as he turned back to wave farewell to Jamie and Jim, he saw in the distance a horse returning to Oak Hill, without a rider, reins or a bridle. Pete had simply managed to mount it in the pasture, dressed in his church clothes. He probably hadn't made it far before the horse had thrown him.

Any other time, he would have searched for his younger brother, but this time, he had troubles of his own.

Chapter 48

The house was dark and quiet when he unlocked the front door and stepped back to let Amelia enter with the baby. He motioned her to go into the master bedroom and waited while the carriage driver hoisted Amelia's box onto his shoulder and brought it inside the front hall. After he paid the driver and locked up for the night, he went into the bedroom to make sure that Emma had left things in shape, and saw that Amelia was already asleep, fully clothed, with the baby sleeping on a pillow beside her.

He went into the parlor, quietly took off his shoes and lay down on the sofa, pulling an ottoman up for his feet. This wasn't the best place to sleep, but it was better than the bags of grain he'd slept on in Mr. Brown's warehouse those many years ago. If he couldn't sleep, he could at least get some rest. The night air was still and humid, and he could hear crickets chirping somewhere.

When he awoke, it was full daylight, and his son Simon stood over him. "Are you all right?" Simon asked. "Do you want some breakfast?"

Fortune sat up and wiped his eyes. For a moment he couldn't remember why he was sleeping in the parlor. Then he heard the faint mewing of the baby.

"Why did you bring Pete's baby's here? Is he coming too?"

"No, he's not, he's gone away, and we're going to take care of your new cousin." He rose, stretched, and started toward the bathroom to get ready for the day, when Simon asked, "What is Mama going to say about that?"

"'Is mother here?"

"No, sir."

"Is Mrs. Watkins here?"

"No, Pop. Eve I talked things over, and we decided we needed to start taking care of ourselves and Daniel and

Leticia. Mama seems a little . . ." he paused, ". . . a little strange, like she doesn't want to be with us."

Fortune embraced his oldest son. "I'm proud of you. Can you help me get Mrs. Ames's trunk into the bedroom? She will undoubtedly need some of the things inside it. As soon as we've all gotten our morning baths and are ready for breakfast, we have a lot to talk about."

Fortune delayed leaving for the office until he could get his family settled at least somewhat. Business could wait for a little while. As far as he knew, each of his enterprises was functioning just as it should, but his family was in trouble.

"Children, Mrs. Ames is going to be staying here for a few days until we can get her settled in a house of her own. You may call her Mrs. Ames or Aunt Amelia, as she's taking care of your new cousin, Clarissa." With a quick glance at Amelia, he went on, "When the baby is a little older, Mrs. Ames can take care of Leticia."

"Can I go too? And Brandy?" Daniel asked. "Brandy and I like Aunt Amelia."

"We'll see, you'll be starting school soon and maybe Brandy can go over there each day, so she won't be lonesome for you while you're away." That seemed to satisfy Daniel.

Simon and Eve looked at their father expectantly while Amelia was busy feeding the baby with the milk-soaked glove. "Eve, do you want to continue working in Aunt Rachel and Uncle Patrick's café, or take care of Leticia for a while? Or maybe Aunt Rachel's baby?"

"I want to work in the café. They pay me money."

Fortune nodded. "I can always give you money whenever you need it, you know that. But I'm glad to see that you are willing to earn some on your own."

He turned finally to Simon. "And what are your plans? You'll be turning 16 soon."

"I want to go to William and Mary or Hampton-Sydney College and I've been studying so I can pass the entrance exam. Robbie has already been accepted at VMI."

Fortune stared at his son in surprise. Somehow while he'd been busy with business and with concern over Emma, Simon had taken steps will that would affect his life and career. "Don't you want to go to VMI also? You and Robbie are such good friends, I thought you might go to the same school."

Simon shook his head. "VMI is for soldiers and engineers. I think I want to be a doctor."

"That's a fine profession, son, but it's a very difficult one. Have you talked with Dr. Tyler?"

"Yes. He says I should spend some time working with him next summer, after I've had a year of school under my belt and have had some experience with other subjects."

In the kitchen, Amelia smiled across the table at Fortune. "Children very quickly grow up to be their own people. Yours are turning out wonderfully." She sighed. "I want to get into my own house soon. This is a lovely house, but I don't think it's a good idea for me to be here when Emma returns. She is returning, isn't she?"

"As far as I know. She said she'd be away two weeks definitely, and perhaps a full month. Your house needs a bit of cleaning, and it should be ready in two days. I rented it to some students and I'm afraid they left a mess. If you'd like to take a drive out with the baby and the younger children, we can go at noon. I have some things to take care off at the office this morning, but I can make a trip back here and be at the office again."

Fortune arranged for the carriage to pick them up, as he didn't think the trolley would be suitable for a newborn. As they climbed in, Daniel asked, "Can Brandy come too?"

"Yes, I think she might enjoy the ride. Jump in," Fortune answered, fairly sure that Daniel would not go without his dog.

When they approached the house, Amelia exclaimed, "But this was Aunt Alicia's house. I thought you sold it." She eyed him suspiciously. "You sent me money."

"I bought it. I thought it was a good investment, and I still think so."

Brandy stood up in the carriage and whimpered excitedly, recognizing her former home.

"I think this will do fine for all of us," Amelia said.

Once again, Fortune thought that he had settled his family problems. He returned to his office and spent a productive afternoon working. He was about to leave for the evening when Jerome Parsons arrived.

He waved aside Fortune's offer of a cigar or drink and came right to the point. "I'm engaged to marry Miss Elsa Freeman. You may have seen the engagement in the newspaper."

Fortune shook his head. "I've been involved with family matters."

"We plan to live with my mother, and you probably would be uncomfortable having us living close to you anyway, so I no longer want the lot I bought from you."

"I've been expecting you. You made a down payment, and the final payment is due next month."

"I'd like my down payment back," Jerome Parsons said, his voice dropping at this steely gaze Fortune put on him.

"Considering how your family treated my sisters, I don't think you should expect any return of your down payment, especially since it's kept me from selling that lot to someone who might have the money up front."

"I'll be willing to settle for half of what I paid you."

"I can manage that," Fortune said, he reached in his desk drawer, drew out his checkbook and quickly wrote a check, passing it across to Jerome. Jerome rose and extended his hand. And how is Laura?"

"She's due to have a baby just any day.

"And the rest of the family?"

"What can I say? I have a fine family." He wasn't about to go into any details and wondered whether Parsons knew that Emma was away with friends. "And congratulations on your marriage, Mr. Parsons. I hope you'll be happy."

As Jerome Parsons left, Fortune reflected that this was a matter that had almost slipped his mind, but now he didn't have to think a bit about it anymore. The price of building lots had gone up, and he could make a tidy profit on this one, with its expansive view of the river.

Laura had her baby that night. Rachel went to be with her sister, taking along her own baby.

A week later, when Fortune arrived home from work, Eve was sitting at the bottom of the front staircase, looking pale. "I have to tell you something, Papa. Just you, not the family," she said in a slightly wavering voice.

Puzzled, Fortune led the way into the parlor and slid the pocket doors closed, shutting off the rest of the family. "Now tell me what's wrong, honey?"

Her words came out in a rush. "I'm sorry, but I can't work at the café anymore. Uncle Patrick touched me here"— she touched her breast—"and here." She pointed toward her crotch. "He said if I told anybody, I would be sorry, but I'm telling you anyway."

"What did you do then?"

"I hit him down there, just like grandma told me to." Her face lost the stricken look, and she laughed. "And he screamed and bent over and held himself there, just like grandma said he would."

"You were right to tell me, dear," Fortune said, putting his arm around his daughter's shoulder. "I'm proud of you for defending yourself. After supper, will go have a talk with your Aunt Rachel."

Fortune and Eve found Rachel at home, putting her little son to bed. When Fortune told her what Eve had said, her face paled and she said, "I don't believe it." Eve looked stunned. "Why would I make up something like that? He told me not to come back to work ever, and you know I'm a good worker."

Rachel burst into tears. "I do believe you. I just don't want to believe that Patrick would do such a thing, to a child! It was bad enough when I caught him kissing one of the waitresses who was working in my place. Patrick said it was because I was putting all my attention on the baby and not on him, and he needed a woman. But a child!"

"What are you going to do about it?" Fortune asked.

"I don't know. What do you think I should do?"

"If he did this twice that you know of, how many times has he done something like this when you didn't know? And if he's done it only twice, how do you know he won't keep on? Is that the kind of man you want for a husband? For the father of your children?" Fortune demanded relentlessly.

"But he loves me and little Matthew, and he said it wouldn't happen again."

"But it did," Fortune pointed out. "Personally, I'd like to beat him to a pulp, but that's against the law. If word of what he's done gets out, it can ruin your business, so that's another reason for you to get rid of him."

Rachel wiped her eyes with the back of her hand and leaned limply against her son's crib. "How can I manage without him? How can I run the café with a small baby to care for?"

"You can hire Mrs. Watkins to look after the house and Matthew," Fortune suggested. "We don't need her, now that the Leticia is two, and Amelia Ames is here to take care of

Pete and Clara's baby as well as Leticia. You know I'll support you financially if you need it."

Leaving Eve with Rachel, Fortune went downstairs into the restaurant. Chairs were upended atop the tables, and Patrick was just mopping the floor.

"What can I do for you, Fortune?" He asked. "We're closed, you know. Folks around here tend to eat early."

"I need to have a word with you. Actually, quite a few words. Rachel knows what you did to Eve this afternoon."

Patrick looked for a moment as if he might deny it, but Fortune went on. "She said you had done something worse earlier, but at least thank God, it wasn't to a member of my family, as this is."

"What do you want me to do?"

"Get out of Richmond, and out of Rachel's life."

"Where do you want me to go?"

"That's your decision, and you have twenty-four hours to make your decision and have your things packed up ready to leave. How much money did you put into this restaurant do you estimate?"

"I've worked hard here for two years."

"So has Rachel. So, no actual money invested." Fortune made it as a statement, not a question. He went on, "I'm taking the books with me tonight and I'll have my assistant look them over. Come to my office tomorrow afternoon at four, and if there are no discrepancies in the finances, I'll be writing you a check, more than you deserve, but I don't want there to be any difficulty with closing the restaurant and paying the bills. If you harm Rachel in the meantime — in any way worse than you have already destroyed her trust — I'll see you in jail."

He went back upstairs to get Eve. She was showing Rachel what she had done to Patrick. "Grandma showed me what to do to stop a man from doing something you don't want him to do."

"She showed me also, years ago when I had a problem almost like yours."

"Did you hit the man where it hurts him?" Eve asked. Rachel shook her head. "It didn't come to that, but Ma saw to it and sent me here to Richmond." Fortune suddenly felt angry and sad for his daughter and sisters, having experienced the worst of men in such a way.

This year has been awful so far, Fortune thought. *There have been two deaths, and God only knows what happened to Pete. And now this!*

Chapter 49

Fortune felt as he once had when he and Jamie had been burning off a piece of land to make a plant bed. The fire had gotten out of control, and they had beaten it down, only to see flames licking up in another spot.

He reread the document he had prepared and which Patrick had signed, renouncing all his rights in the café, the building, and any finances from any member of the Barranger family. He had agreed not to seek custody of their only child, Matthew.

Fortune called his lawyer to arrange a legal separation for Rachel, to be later turned into a divorce on the grounds of desertion. Next he called the Rector to set a date for the baptism of the three babies. Patrick had wanted Rachel and the baby Matthew to join the Baptist Church, but he now had no say so in that.

Amelia was settled in with the children and Brandy. When Daniel began first grade in September, she would have the extra daytime job of looking after Brandy, as well as Leticia and baby. Fortune could not make himself refer to the infant as Clarissa.

After closing the café and crying for three days, Rachel dried her eyes and hired a painter to take down Patrick's name, and replace it with one that read "Rachel's Café." Matthew's crib was placed in a corner where a potted palm had stood and where he could be watched and tended. Eve helped out with cooking, and Fortune paid Simon and Robbie to be waiters and to clean up after closing time.

When Fortune was sure that the café could continue to function, he called up Zachary Todd, the *Dispatch* reporter who had so often written business news articles about the Barranger enterprises. He would be sure to take a photo and get all the names included, which the boys and Eve would

like, and Fortune suspected that the reporter had had his
eyes on Rachel for several years.

Rachel announced that she couldn't afford any new
napkins just yet and would use the old ones, provided the
monogram could have a tail added to make the "P" into an
"R". Robbie's sister Sarah volunteered for the job, and
prepared for the interview by making a large chocolate cake
from her mother's recipe, and assigning Eve to make hot
bread and tea.

When Mr. Todd asked about the change in
management, Rachel said, "I am legally separated, but don't
put that information in your article. Just say that I was the
co-owner and am now the sole owner."

"I'll keep that information to myself, and for myself,"
he answered. He put down his notebook to enjoy a slice of
cake.

Emma did not return until the last day of July, and
made no comment about the empty house or the absence of
her children until everyone was seated at dinner. "I enjoyed
my stay at the beach," she said. "I see that all of you
managed well without me, so I shall feel free to make more
trips."

Fortune had moved into the nursery, sleeping on a
narrow single bed, leaving the elegant four-poster to Emma.
They lived in a state of tense civility, speaking to each other
only when absolutely necessary. How long, he wondered,
could this go on? If only he could put a definite end to the
situation, the way he had done for Rachel, but he knew
without asking that Emma would never give him a divorce.

One of his family problems changed, but was not
solved, when a letter arrived from Pete: "I joined the Army.
We are going to the Philippines. I put you down as nearest
of kin."

So he was alive, at least for now. He must have ridden the horse only as far as the nearest stop on the train. He might get killed by the rebels he was sent to fight against, or he might get lost in the jungle and die, or have malaria or some other tropical disease.

Simon left for William and Mary College a few days after his friend Robbie left for the Virginia Military Institute. Daniel began first grade at a nearby school, taking the trolley to and from it. Brandy and Leticia spent their days with Amelia, coming home at night and on weekends.

At his office, Fortune often looked up at the portrait of Sir Thomas Dale. It was one of several portraits from the 17th century that he had purchased, not for his home but for his office, and he looked to them for inspiration. They were men who took risks, solved problems, and didn't really care if they were liked or disliked, leaving it to history to judge their achievements. Visitors to Fortune's office sometimes looked at the portraits and asked if he were descended from any of these fine gentlemen. "Only in spirit," he'd reply.

He had read in Col. Stannard's books of the founding of Virginia and America, and he admired Sir Thomas Dale above all the other early Virginians. Dale had saved the colony in the "starving time," when the settlers were ready to give up and return to England. There had been no gold, silver or pearls lying about at Jamestown, as they had fantasized, and they were gentlemen, considering themselves too good to work. He sternly established the rule "no work, no food."

His problems, he knew, were minuscule compared to what Dale had faced, but they were nevertheless troublesome to him. He had money in the bank, and more arrived every day. Should he invest in streetlighting, or more trolley lines? Other cities needed them as well as Richmond.

He had even been approached by a salesman to invest in a horseless carriage company, which they were now beginning to call motorcars.

"Trains and trolleys are a very efficient way to move people and goods," Fortune argued.

"Trains and trolleys are limited to where the rails run," the salesman had replied. "What happens when some people live some distance away from the tracks? The only way you could service everyone with trains and trolleys would be to have a track running to every home in America."

"I hadn't thought of it that way," Fortune responded. "But there aren't roads going to all the houses either. Sometimes people have to walk or ride a horse to get to their homes."

"These motorcars are expensive now, and are just expensive toys for rich people who live in the city. But once they buy a motor car, they will want to go more places outside their city or to another city. The roads will come, because people will demand them. In fact, Mr. Barranger, there are more roads than you think. There are corduroy roads and stagecoach roads. They are rough, but the Scots have developed an easy way to turn a dirt road into a paved road."

Fortune considered the facts and purchased stock in the manufacturing company as well as investing in a sales company for motorcars. But he wasn't ready to buy a motor car for himself.

He still had a substantial sum sitting in the bank waiting to be invested in something. He wanted to discuss Jamie's plans for a cannery before he invested in it.

Then he knew what he would buy next. The bank manager called to say that no further payments had been made on the Oak Hill loan, and the plantation was thus for sale.

On a Saturday, Fortune took the train to Oak Hill, carrying with him his checkbook and a receipt from the bank showing that he had paid off the mortgage, and was therefore the owner of the estate.

He walked slowly from the train station, enjoying the first glimpse of the manor house. It was a sunny day in late November, with the cloudless blue sky above the fields where crops had grown. The house and the fences, he saw, were more dilapidated than he remembered—but the last time he'd been here, he'd been more concerned with Pete and the baby than with real estate.

He had hoped to catch Col. Stannard in a lucid frame of mind, able to understand the implications of the papers. He stepped up onto the columned front porch and rapped on the heavy paneled door. The frail old man who opened the door to him looked worse than Fortune remembered. From somewhere back in the house, he heard Charlotte callout, "Who is it, father? We aren't expecting anyone. Is it a man from the bank?"

When Charlotte saw him, she said, "Do come in, Fortune. Father, you remember Fortune."

"Of course I do!"

"Then don't let him stand out on the porch on this chilly morning. Invite him in."

Col. Stannard looked as if he might argue, but he stepped back so that Fortune could enter. Fortune took off his hat and held it in his hand but kept on his coat to ward off the chill in the parlor, where a small fire put out a weak heat into the room.

"Do have a seat, Fortune, by the fireplace." She was wiping her hands on a white dish towel and turned back for a moment to take off her apron and return the towel to the kitchen. "I would offer you something to eat, but I'm afraid Ruth hasn't brought over anything today."

Probably because the bills have not been paid, Fortune thought. He waved his hand dismissively. "I ate on the train."

Charlotte seated her father, and sat down beside him, extending her hands toward the feeble flames.

Fortune took this as an indication that he too should now sit. He had learned his etiquette lessons well.

After a moment's silence, Charlotte said "I was very sorry to hear of your sister-in-law's death. The few times that I saw her, she seemed a lovely person."

Fortune nodded. "She was indeed. And I hope that the horse my brother Pete borrowed without asking did not suffer any permanent damage from what I assume was a wild ride."

"I wasn't here then, or I would have attended the funeral and spoken to your family. Your brother Jamie told me about the borrowed horse, and since he takes care of the horses, I left it up to him to tell you if anything was owed for damages'

Col. Stannard suddenly stood and said, "I must go and see to Bessie. Those Yanks sometimes steal our horses."

"Father, Bessie has been dead for years. The horse you have now is named Mary. She is old too, but you can go and rub her down."

Fortune exchanged a glance with Charlotte, and she nodded. "Sometimes he gets like this, going to check on Bessie and talking about what happened in the war." She sighed. "I take it this is not a social visit."

"No, I came to let you know in person that I have paid off the loan that was about to be foreclosed on your plantation. Oak Hill is mine now." He saw a startled look in her eyes, a sure sign that she was not expecting this.

"But the bank has been good to us all these years, letting us pay the interest and rolling over the loan."

"But you haven't even paid the interest for a year, despite letters from the bank warning you."

"So, you're taking advantage of us! How could you do this? After all that Papa has done for your family!"

She had leapt to her feet, but Fortune waited until she sank back in her chair before going on, "You should be glad that I'm the one who bought Oak Hill instead of someone else. I'm prepared to be generous to you. You and your father may continue to live here until the end of March. I plan to make a number of changes both on the house and the surrounding land, and weather doesn't usually permit that kind of work in winter. You may of course move out at any time prior to that that if you choose.

"If you decide to remain until the end of March if no damage has been done to the house or grounds when you move out, I'll give you an extra thousand dollars so that you can settle somewhere else. I take it that you see the need for someone to care of your father, and it's not my position to say whether you should take him to New York with you or remain here with him. I'll hire someone to live here in the house and see to his daily needs. Frankly, I think his living alone would be a danger to himself and others."

"I don't think my father would do well in New York, and I'm not sure anymore just what I would do there. My son is off at school, by his father's choice. My daughter and I have the house to ourselves most of the time, as my husband is away a lot." She looked down, avoiding his eyes.

"I understand that house also is heavily mortgaged, but you have no worry that I plan to buy that mortgage. New York is not my place. I do go there occasionally on business, but I plan to make my permanent home right here. If you and your daughter need a place to live, the small house that my mother owned will be available."

314

"Me, live there? You're trying to get even with me for rejecting you all those years ago, aren't you?"

"Not at all," Fortune said easily. "Living here married to someone who thought I was beneath her would have kept me poor in every way. Instead, I am one of the twenty richest men in America now, or so the newspapers tell me. I don't dwell on the past, and I don't waste time trying to get even or get revenge on anyone. I put my attention on earning money and enjoying it. Now, shall we go out and see what your father has done with the horses?"

She blinked a few times, then rose to follow him outside. He continued, "As to the horses, I assume they are your husband's, and he may want to make some arrangements for them elsewhere. If they are a financial burden to him and to you, I'm quite prepared to take them off your hands and have Jamie continue to care for them. My children and my nieces and nephews will enjoy riding them."

As they went outside, they saw Col. Stannard trying without success to stop one of the horses by grabbing its mane. He was thrown to the ground, and pulled himself to a sitting position as the horse raced off across the pasture. "Damn Yankees! Steal our horses! I won't let you take me alive and send me to prison." Fortune started toward the old man, but it was too late. Col. Stannard pointed the gun at himself and pulled the trigger.

Charlotte gathered up her skirt and ran beside Fortune to where her father slumped. Fortune had no idea, given the condition of the old man's body, that he'd be alive, but for Charlotte's sake, he picked up a limp wrist and checked for a pulse.

When he turned to her, shaking his head, she collapsed in a heap next to her father's body. She began sobbing hysterically, her shoulders shaking violently. He reached out to her, but she pushed him away, consumed with grief and despair. Fortune pressed a handkerchief into her hands, then backed away from her and allowed her to cry as much as she needed to.

An hour later, they had walked back to the main house. Fortune had called a local doctor to see to the Colonel's body, and Charlotte had recovered enough to talk with him.

"Do you want him buried here on the plantation, or at the churchyard?" he asked as gently as possible.

"Here, if you don't mind. There's a fenced off area back by the woods, where my mother is buried. There is already a tombstone for them both, and for my baby brother who was born dead." She began to cry again and Fortune waited for it to pass.

Once her tears had subsided, he said, "I'll make the funeral arrangements, unless you prefer to take care of that yourself."

"You do it, please," she said and slumped back against her chair, sobbing.

If he had wanted revenge, this moment was it. Charlotte Stannard had two children, but only one of them was likely to be worth a damn, she had lost her father and her home, and her husband spent his time drinking and gambling, as well as beating her.

Fortune realized just how far he'd come from the brash young man who had asked Charlotte to marry him. He didn't feel anything like revenge or satisfaction; he felt horror for how suddenly Charlotte had lost her sole remaining parent, worry for how her son might turn out, sympathy for her loss of her home on the same day as her father, anger at the husband who didn't seem to care for her, and sadness for the loss of the Colonel's life, so needless and violent.

This was the fourth death in less than two years of someone who affected his family, he thought. Who would be next?

Chapter 50

When Fortune arrived home and told Emma about the purchase, she said, "Well, you should be satisfied now. It's what you planned to do your whole life. Now you have a real excuse to see Miss Charlotte Stannard whenever you want to."

"Don't be silly, Emma. I've seen her a number of times when I had to be back there looking after someone in the family. Besides, now she associates me with her father's death. As of the end of March, she will be leaving there. In the meantime, if I need to go there for any reason to make arrangements for the improvements I want to make at Oak Hill, you are certainly welcome to go along with me. You could have gone every time I've been there."

"You're spending a fortune on that plantation," Emma commented.

"And I shall spend more in improving it and building what I want there. I paid for the plantation itself, but I've earned it. And haven't I spent enough on you and the children? I paid you back what you loaned me to get started in business, and I've put money regularly into your account. I built you this house just as you wanted and you had a free hand in furnishing it. My sisters are working to earn their own living, and I've never asked you to do that, so what more do you want from me?"

"Promise me you won't sell this house. I don't want to go to Oak Hill. I never have."

"I know that, and you are welcome to stay here. Simon is already off at college, and Eve soon will be also. The younger children will move with me to Oak Hill."

"You're taking my children away from me! You've been trying to ever since they were born."

"You are perfectly welcome to come and live with us. I am establishing our residents at Oak Hill."

"If you loved me, you would stay here with me," she whimpered.

"And I may say that if you loved me and your children, you would go with us. You're obviously not happy no matter what I do, Emma. Is there anything you want that I can supply?"

To his surprise, she said, "Buy me a motorcar."

"Why do you need a motorcar?"

"It's not a question of needing one. I'm the wife of one of the richest men in America, and I shouldn't be seen riding the trolley. And carriages are old-fashioned. Everyone who matters now drives a motorcar."

He laughed. "But you don't know how to operate one any more than I do."

"Then you will have to pay for lessons for me as well as purchasing it."

"If that will make you happy, I'll do it without any question. And I may buy one for myself as well." She shrugged and nodded, then walked away without a word of thanks.

For New Year's Eve, Fortune arranged a huge party, renting the ballroom of the Jefferson Hotel. He asked Emma to issue the invitations, Rachel to plan the menu and provide the food, and Laura to choose appropriate ballgowns for all the women and to buy tuxedos for himself and Simon. Eve was allowed to choose her own ballgown, with her Aunt Laura's advice.

Fortune hired an orchestra to play for the event, and arranged for the entire family to have dancing lessons. Mrs. Watkins would be taking care of Leticia and the babies as well as Brandy.

"Are you inviting the reporter from the *Times-Dispatch*?" Rachel asked. "If you don't want him there to represent the newspaper, I would like him to be my guest."

"He's already on the guest list. He's given us a lot of good publicity over the years, and this will be a special event."

"Are we inviting the Tylers?" Eve asked.

"Of course. They are friends and our children are friends. We're also inviting the mayor and his wife, and politicians and businesspeople."

"You're spending an awful lot on this," Emma protested. "How can you afford it, after buying the plantation and two cars?"

"I got a special deal by buying two cars and agreeing to be photographed driving one—which, by the way, I need to learn how to do. As for all the officials, they will be good for business."

"Does everything you do have to pertain to business?" Emma asked.

"No, of course not. I am inviting many friends from church as well as the minister and his wife. Do you need some help in addressing the invitations?"

"I can manage."

"Then you know who our guests are. You must also keep track of who accepts and who does not. I predict that we'll have many acceptances. This will be a way of introducing us to top society in Richmond as well as a farewell party of sorts. I plan to have a different kind of gathering at Oak Hill."

He didn't tell her that he had invited Amelia Ames.

The week before Christmas, the cars were delivered, and the salesman went out instructing first Fortune, and then Emma, on how to drive. Despite wanting the car, Emma proved hesitant about driving it, and Fortune suspected that she had merely been testing him as to whether he would buy her car. Simon asked to learn to drive as well, and proved to be an excellent driver. Fortune

320

arranged to store the cars at a warehouse near his office until a suitable space could be built for Emma's car. His would be driven to Oak Hill by Simon.

Eve caught her breath with excitement at the site of the ballroom decorated for the New Year's dance. She scanned the huge room as they back as the family entered, looking for Robbie Tyler. She felt very grown up in her emerald green taffeta dress with a square cut neckline.

Fortune had a florist send each of his sisters, his wife, and Eve a corsage for the occasion. Eve would have preferred a gardenia to the carnations that made up her corsage, but aunt Laura said gardenias were too sophisticated for a 14-year-old. They could come later.

Eve saw Robbie and waved, although she knew that was not considered ladylike, but she didn't care. She wanted him to see her, and wanted to dance with him. Her first dance would be with her brother Simon while her parents danced together. Then Simon would dance with his mother and Eve with her father. After that she would dance with Robbie as many times as she could manage.

"You look lovely, Eve," he said, bowing slightly, hampered by his VMI uniform with its high collar and fitted jacket.

"Thank you, Robbie. And you look handsome in your uniform."

"May I have this dance? I'm not a very good dancer but I'll try."

"I'm a good dancer," Eve said. "Papa paid for lessons for all of us, and the teacher said I have natural ability. If you want to go off to a quiet corner, I can show you the steps he taught us, and then I'm supposed to follow whatever you do."

He laughed. "You are so much like your father, confident of yourself, and not hesitant about speaking up."

"That's a compliment, I think, so thank you," she said. "Papa says you never know what you can get until you ask, and then you must work for it."

Later, as they were dancing together, Eve said, "I'm going to marry you when I get old enough, Robbie."

He laughed. "By the time you're eighteen, you'll probably have half a dozen proposals. Young men will be lining up to court you and marry you."

"Would you be one of them, Robbie?" She asked pausing in dancing to look up at him.

"Of course, you can put me on your list. but you may change your mind before then. You're only fourteen, and you haven't even started going out with suitors. And I predict that your father is going to be a stern judge of who marries his oldest daughter. He may be planning to marry you off to some European nobility, or at least the son of a rich powerful colleague of his.

"Do you have a girlfriend already?"

"No, Freshman at VMI don't have time to even think about girls. We spend all our time studying and drilling and polishing things and keeping our beds and uniforms neat."

"Good," she said. "You may think I'm just a child now, but I do know what I want."

"You're very pretty, Eve, and you'll probably be beautiful by the time you're eighteen. You will probably enjoy being courted by all the eligible young man in Virginia, and even beyond. I'm pleased that you would even think of marrying me. Any man would. Just don't limit yourself. Now, let's enjoy dancing and have some punch and food. I'm sure you have other names on your dance card, and some girls have probably already put my name down."

"I want to be your partner for the last dance of the evening, Robbie," she told him.

He wrote his name on her dance card and said, "Please call me Rob from now on."

As he had predicted, Eve had many partners, but she kept looking over her shoulder to see who Rob's partner was. She was surprised to see her father dancing with Mrs. Ames and from the look on her mother's face, she was sure that she hadn't sent the invitation.

As midnight approached, Eve looked around for Rob, and saw him crossing the floor toward her. He held out his arms to her, and she went into his embrace.

"I've trod on many a foot tonight," he said, "but you seem to know just what I have in mind, and follow easily." As midnight came, the dancing stopped, and Rob pulled Eve into his arms for a soft gentle kiss. She responded with an eagerness that surprised him. As they drew apart, he said "Keep me in mind, Eve, and try not to kiss too many men."

"But you told me to enjoy the courtship of lots of other men," she laughed.

He laughed as well. "You're right, I did. We shouldn't even be thinking about what may happen five or more years down the line anyway," he said. "Let's just enjoy this moment. Your father really knows how to put on a swell party."

He might say that they shouldn't think so far into the future, but Eve knew that she would think of him. She just wouldn't talk about it anymore to him or anyone else. It would be her secret, while she worked out how to bring it about.

Fortune had confirmation nearly every day that the richer and more important you became, the more eager people were to give you deals on things. His family had become celebrities of a sort, and purveyors of merchandise and services wanted to be associated with them. it was almost like being royalty, when items could be advertised as "by the order of her Majesty the Queen."

The discount on the motorcar was just the start. There were photos in the newspaper of Fortune and his wife dancing to the music of the orchestra, which was prominently shown, and later the orchestra leader told Fortune that he was refunding him part of what he had paid, since numerous people had come seeking the orchestra's music for their own parties.

But being noteworthy had its downside too. People came seeking favors from him, asking him to donate to causes, or to serve on various boards. He was already on the vestry of the church, where he actually attended meetings and thought that he might be useful. Other organizations often wanted his name to appear on the letterhead of their stationary, to give some note of popularity to the calls.

Then he was asked to appear on the board of the Jamestown Exposition. "But that's several years ahead," he said. "Well not until 1907, to be exact."

"But it will be a tremendous project for the state of Virginia," the representative said. "Land must be cleared, pavilions built, a paved area added, and of course a railroad line laid to the site. We are counting on you to add the line to the site. It should be good business for you as well as attracting visitors and making it easy for them to arrive."

"You can count on me. I'll have it done in plenty of time. I don't think I have time to help with the planning or supervision of any of the other projects. After all, I do have businesses to run."

"We want to have you as co-chairman or honorary chairman, whichever you prefer. And we want a special favor from you, Mr. Barranger. It's known that you have a collection of portraits of famous early founders of Virginia. May we borrow those for the duration of the exposition?"

"Of course. I'd be honored to have my artwork shared on that occasion."

"Do you by any chance have any paintings of events in our early history, perhaps dealings with the Indians, or early activities that the settlers participated in?"

"No, but I'll be glad to commission such paintings."

The exposition was to be built at Norfolk, and Fortune already had railroad rights to the port, where his coal was shipped to foreign countries. Large numbers of visitors would be arriving by land and sea. He wanted to make sure that those who arrived by land came on his railroad. He would need several passenger cars suitable for carrying families with their picnic baskets and luggage. He could arrange a series of day trips from Richmond.

The trolley would have to come from the railroad to the exposition site, with an additional trolley line running from the harbor, and he envisioned a slow smaller trolley, perhaps a small train that would circle the entire site from inside, so that those who didn't feel up to walking could see the exposition from the comfort of the trolley. There was already boat service on the Chesapeake Bay, so he saw no possibility for profit there, but his trolleys definitely would pay off, and by agreeing to loan his paintings and serve on the board, he had gotten the opportunity to build with plenty of time allowed.

He had a few other ideas he planned to take up with the board. Visitors would need food, and if Rachel felt up to the job, she could make a tidy sum by selling sandwiches, cakes, and drinks. Souvenirs too, and Jonas and Laura would have time to design and order coffee mugs, glassware, banners, and other mementos of this historic occasion.

Meanwhile, he needed to find the right painter. The resulting work had to be real art, not just the quick works that were used to advertise his cigarettes and other businesses. They had to be historically accurate, as well as fitting, so his painter had to be willing to do research and to actually go to the original Jamestown site.

Fortune placed an ad in the *Dispatch*: "Painter or painters wanted to depict the early settlement of Jamestown." He added his address as well as his phone number. In the next few weeks, he talked to three painters, looking at each one's work and finally choosing Adam Hoffheimer.

"I will need to see some pencil sketches of scenes that you think appropriate, such as the Jamestown church, showing every day activities such as the growing of tobacco, felling trees and turning them into lumber, grinding corn, and so on," he told the painter. "Show regular people not just governors and soldiers, though a soldier or two would be all right."

"How big do you envision these paintings to be, Mr. Barranger?"

"As big as you want them to be. They can build the pavilion to fit your paintings instead of fitting your paintings to the pavilion."

"Will I be allowed to sign my work, and let it be known that I am painting them?" Hoffheimer asked.

"Yes, of course to both. A worker should be proud of his work, and an artist should be proud of his art."

In the midst of his planning for the exposition, a telegram arrived: "Joseph Peterson Barranger missing in action, believed to be dead."

Chapter 51

Fortune decided to go to Oak Hill on March 31 and see personally that the house and grounds were in good condition as the Bishops moved out. Simon was still in school, but Eve decided to go along with him and spend time with her cousin Martha. The day was windy, but warm and lovely.

Fortune also intended to talk to his brother Jamie about his plans for a cannery. Fortune realized that he did not want a cannery anywhere on the grounds of the Oak Hill estate. He would thus have to buy Jamie a separate farm, and until the new orchard came into production, apples from Oak Hill would have to be transferred to the cannery site.

Eve and her cousin Martha were tossing a baseball back and forth outside the mansion, while Fortune went inside with Charlotte Bishop to make certain that the house was still in the same condition as it had been in November.

A young man with wavy blonde hair and blue eyes walked up to the girls and asked Martha, "Would you like to take a walk with me through the woods?"

She had just picked up the bat ready to hit balls that Eve tossed at her, but she dropped it and walked toward the young man, nodding.

"Who are you?" Eve asked.

"Julian Bishop the fourth, the son of the woman your father stole this plantation from."

"He did no such thing! My father never steals anything. He paid good money for it. Martha, don't go with him."

In answer, Martha let Julian Bishop take her hand, and the two started walking away toward a wooded area.

"He's terrible! He hits dogs and horses with sticks. My father has seen him do it."

"You're just jealous because he wants to walk with me instead of you," Martha said over her shoulder and kept walking.

As soon as the pair reached the woods, Eve picked up the baseball bat and ran after them. Even though Martha had been rude and nasty to her, she was still family, and Eve was sure that Julian Bishop was up to no good.

A path led through the woods toward a stream, and she followed it, but she wasn't sure if they had turned off and gone into some hidden spot. Fortunately, leaves had not come onto the trees yet, so only evergreens could hide them.

Up ahead on the path, she heard Martha scream, "Stop! You're hurting me!"

Eve ran toward Martha's voice, and saw her cousin lying in dead leaves thrashing and kicking helplessly at Julian, who had her pinned down and sat astride her, one knee between her legs. Her panties lay torn on the ground beside her, and her skirt was shoved up above her waist. Julian had his hand over her mouth, and as she tried to bite him, he grabbed up the panties and stuffed them into her mouth, then grabbed both her hands and held them above her head. With his other hand he had opened the fly of his trousers.

So engrossed was he in his assault, that he didn't notice Eve's approach.

She swung the bat hard and heard it crack against his arm. Eve stood a moment, astounded at what she had done. Then she screamed, "Hit him like grandma showed us, Martha!"

When Martha did nothing, Eve approached the young man who was holding his arm, unaware that his genitals were still exposed. Eve kicked him solidly in the crotch and was satisfied when he let out a scream and doubled up in pain.

"Get up, Martha, and pull your skirt down. Take your panties out of your mouth. Now, let's get back to the house before he stops hurting and starts trying to get even with us."

"He'll only want to get even with you," Martha said. "I didn't do anything to him."

Eve grabbed Martha's hand, and started back toward the house. Martha looked over her shoulder. "Is he going to be all right?"

"I don't know, and I don't care. You shouldn't care either. He was trying to rape you, just like grandma warned us men might do. You should be thanking me for coming when you screamed. What if I hadn't? He might have done his dirty deed, and got you pregnant."

"Then he'd have to marry me, wouldn't he?"

Eve paused in the middle of the field, almost back to the house, and turned to her cousin. "Don't be stupid! Now, let's get back to the house where my father can take care of the situation. I think I broke Julian's arm, and his mother is not going to be happy about that, any more than Julian is. I'm going to tell Papa exactly what happened and what I did, and that I heard you scream that he was hurting you. You did, and if you deny it, I'll never speak to you again in my life."

Fortune and Charlotte were just emerging from the mansion when the girls ran to the front door, out of breath. Eve told her father what had happened, and he nodded. "I'm proud of you for defending your cousin," he said.

"I don't believe any of this!" Charlotte said. "Why would my son have anything to do with a country girl like this, when he can have the best girls in New York?"

Julian limped into the front yard.

"If I have a baby, you're going to have to marry me," Martha declared.

"Of course, he's not. His father and I don't want to be supporting him the rest of his life. I'll see that he goes to prison instead." Fortune said.

"I'd rather go to prison," Julian declared, and Eve saw by Martha's stricken look that a part of her had hoped Julian truly liked her.

"There won't be any baby, unless it's somebody else's. I didn't get far enough for that. That bitch" — he turned on Eve — "broke my arm with the baseball bat. This bat." He held it out.

Eve took it from him. "Thanks. I was trying to make sure Martha escaped, and I forgot to pick up the bat." Julian glared at her.

"If there are any broken bones, I'll pay the doctor's bills," Fortune said. "Here, let me have a look at it."

Julian jerked away. "She also kicked me in the nuts."

Fortune managed to stop himself from laughing. Instead, he said, "Let that be a lesson to you, young man. Girls and women must be wooed and persuaded, not raped." He turned to Charlotte. "Everything seems satisfactory in the house, and I don't believe you've left anything behind. If you have, I'll see that it gets shipped to you."

He turned at the sound of a child's voice. "Ma'am, you didn't look in the closet where I was hiding, don't leave me!"

A flaxen haired child that looked so much like Charlotte ran to take her mother's hand. Charlotte said, "Of course I would not leave you my darling, you are my treasure." Charlotte took the little girl's hand and said to the others, "Eliza, this is Mr. Fortune Barranger and his daughter and niece."

Fortune bowed and the girl said hello, while a seething Julian started to walk toward the train station.

Fortune said to Charlotte, "I can't imagine that you or your family will be visiting us here anytime soon. In a year or so, after I have made the additions I plan to Oak Hill, perhaps I'll issue an invitation to one of the gatherings I plan."

Fortune kept both girls close beside him until the Bishops had boarded the train and it began to move. Only then, with the last of the Stannard line gone, did he feel that Oak Hill was finally his. From the angry expression on Martha's face, he wasn't sure that the Stannards had gone completely, at least in her mind. He'd have to warn Jamie and Ruth to keep an eye on her. Girls her age sometimes did silly things, like running away to be with some undeserving boy.

As he walked back to his new house, Fortune mused over the different ways Charlotte reacted to her two children. Little Eliza looked a lot like her mother and not at all like her brother. There was also something in her features that was unlike either of them. Was it a gene inherited from a distant relative or had Charlotte had an affair with someone other than her husband? He hoped she had. She had little enough happiness in her marriage.

At the front porch, Fortune turned and looked about him, envisioning how Oak Hill was going to look. He'd had an architect draw up plans for enlarging the mansion. Its original design was a central hall with two rooms on each side, and the same upstairs. He envisioned it as it soon would be, with a wing added on each side containing four rooms each. He would be adding a total of six bathrooms, and a modern kitchen. The main front portico would stand as it was. He'd always liked that, with its tall white columns that stretched from the front porch to the roof, with a balcony in the center above the front door. The floor of the front porch itself would have to be redone, its rotten boards pulled up and replaced by flagstone or slate.

His nephew Jamie Jr., now going by Jim, joined them, looking over Fortune's shoulder at the drawings he held unscrolled.

"I think I'd like to be an architect, designing rich people's houses," Jim said. Say, you can put me in touch with all those rich people you know."

"Only if you deserve it," Fortune said. "You'll need to go to the University and study architecture."

"Thomas Jefferson designed houses in courthouses all over Virginia, and he didn't have a degree from a university in architecture."

"No, he didn't have a degree from a university, he designed the University itself, as you should know," Fortune observed, referring to the University of Virginia. "He also played the violin. Are you planning to do that?"

Jim laughed. "I'm not sure I'm going to the University. Papa wants me to stay and run the apple business along with him."

"You'll do better at whatever kind of business you go into, even if you decide to stay here and grow apples, if you have a few years at the University. It will expose you to new ideas and to people who have good ideas."

"But you didn't go to the University, and just look at how rich you've gotten to be, Uncle Fortune."

"From the time I could read until I left Oak Hill and went to Richmond, I was reading every book I could get my hands on. I never liked Col. Stannard, because he was living on pride instead of accomplishments, but he let me read his books, and for that I'll be forever grateful. If I'd had a degree, I might have become successful even sooner.

"Instead I worked, as do my sisters and your father. Work and education both help you to be ready for an opportunity when it comes along. So, in answer to your first question, you want to go to a university to study something useful. Then I'll be proud to recommend you to my friends.

"I'm planning to invite my friends and colleagues who lead the city, as soon as I can get the house in shape for visitors and get started on other projects," he continued. "I want to have telephone service into the mansion, new church, a race track, greenhouse, pastures for my horses and places for people to park their own motorcars."

"Where is your motor car?" Jim asked.

"In Richmond. Simon drives when he's home from school to places outside the city. I confess I prefer having someone else drive me in my motor car instead of myself so I can get work done."

That night he and Eve stayed in the home that had been his mother's. The next morning, he went to see the farm that Jamie thought would be useful for growing apples.

Later, as they walked over the sloping land, Fortune said, "Well, it's convenient to the railroad. Other than that, I'm no expert on land. That's your specialty. Jamie, have you had any tests done by the new agricultural college at Blacksburg? Or do you just know what kind of land it takes for an orchard?"

"A bit of both," Jamie said. "Are you going to loan the money or will we share the business?"

"I'm not in the business of lending money, in fact, I owe a bit myself. I'm keeping my cash for the additions I want to make at Oak Hill. You should keep your cash for operating expenses and building the packing plant and cannery. And, of course, planting trees."

"We will need a contract, wont we?"

"Yes. We'll never need a contract to be good brothers to each other, but contracts will make sure we're also good business partners to each other."

Chapter 52

Fortune reveled in seeing his life's dream materialize. By the end of the summer, the mansion house had tripled in size. He decided to increase the front porch, as well as the balcony above, adding miniature balconies to the front bedroom windows. Once the building was finished, he had the entire exterior painted white, and dark shutters were hung at all the windows. It was stately and grand, just as he had imagined it would be.

Inside, each of the bedrooms had its own fireplace, and a ceramic tile bath was shared between each pair of bedrooms. Downstairs, what had been a bedroom was joined on to the dining room to make a banqueting hall, with a dining table that could seat eighteen. The two rooms across the hall were joined into a large parlor, which could serve as a ballroom if the carpets were removed. The central hallway ran to the back of the house, where he replaced the wooden door with an all glass one, giving a magnificent view of the Blue Ridge Mountains beyond. To one side was a powder room and his office; opposite was a gleaming efficient kitchen where meals could be prepared to feed a crowd.

What could he do with the small house he'd grown up in? The mansion house commanded a hilltop, while the small house occupied a smaller hill, and was barely visible from the mansion. Eventually, he decided to turn it into a miniature of the mansion. It had originally been a long house, with beaded weather boarding applied on the outside, and tongue in groove boards inside. He had the whole exterior painted white and a columned portico added in front.

Inside, he stripped away the bead boarding in the big front room, exposing the logs. The big fireplace, where cooking had once been done, became the focal point of the room. He boxed in the stairway to the loft, and added a bathroom and a sparkling new kitchen. He had originally thought of moving the house to some inconspicuous spot, or perhaps turning it into a garden shed, but his final product pleased him. This could be a guest house for someone who wanted to be secluded from the mansion. Or he might make it his office, or perhaps one of the children might marry and want to start out in a small house before moving into the mansion and eventually inheriting it.

During the summer, he hired Simon as well as Jamie's son Eddie to build a garden. One sweltering mid-summer evening, he decided to have a swimming pool and pool house installed. For his own enjoyment he wanted a formal boxwood and rose garden as well as a greenhouse that could supply fresh flowers for the mansion year-round.

The estate was far from complete according to what he wanted done, but he decided it was time to invite the whole family to Oak Hill instead of to the house in Richmond. Here was space for everyone, so he didn't need to have part of the family in a hotel.

Besides the family members, he invited Amelia Ames. She would, of course, be bringing little Clarissa, and would be looking after Leticia as well. Rachel invited her friend, the reporter, and Fortune made certain the two had bedrooms in separate wings of the house, so there would be no reason for gossip.

Jonas and Laura closed the store on Monday, as did Rachel the café, and the group spent Sunday and Sunday night at the mansion. Eve invited Sarah Tyler, and Simon of course invited Rob, but Rob had to go to summer camp as part of his military training. Eve felt left out, especially as Simon spent most of his time with Sarah.

Fortune urged Emma to come along, and she agreed, but announced that he must not think that this would be repeated. She just wanted to see what all the fuss was about.

Fortune had ordered food brought in on the train, but everyone had to pitch in and help setting up and cleaning after meals, and when they left on Monday afternoon, they left behind masses of sodden towels rumpled sheets and pillowcases. Fortune had looked on this as a rehearsal for inviting important dignitaries from all over the state, and he was glad he done so. He realized that if he were going to entertain anyone beyond the family, he'd have to hire a housekeeper and workers to keep the grounds clean and the fireplaces well-stocked with wood, and of course someone to do laundry and see that all the beds were made and fresh towels and soap were in all the bathrooms.

On a fine autumn morning, Fortune was enjoying the crisp mountain air, and the panorama of color that showed itself every year. Of his family, only young Daniel had chosen to come along this morning. He trailed along beside his father, occasionally tossing a stick for Brandy to fetch. Even though it was a Saturday and classes were not in session, his older children had weekend plans. Simon was studying chemistry and biology, and often spent weekends in the lab, but this weekend he was back in Richmond spending time with young Sarah Tyler. Fortune had little doubt that the two would someday marry, and he approved the match.

Eve was working in Rachel's restaurant, and he approved that too. She was determined to marry Rob Tyler, but in his case, his studies and military requirements kept him too busy for much social life. Jamie's family had kept close to the estate. Jim had enrolled at Virginia Tech, and while he was home on the weekend, he joined Martha and his younger brother Eddie helping to pick and pack apples. Jamie's family seemed content, and Fortune wondered if Jamie and Ruth even knew about the narrow escape Martha had had with that wild arrogant Bishop boy.

Life is like a kaleidoscope, he thought. With each turn of the year or some event, the pattern changed. But in real life, people were not imprisoned within the kaleidoscope, but came and went. Children were born, people died, and other people came into the pattern for a while and then moved away, as the Stannards had. He himself was at the center of the kaleidoscope pattern, that one all the others depended on, and called on when there was a problem.

"I like it here," Daniel said, interrupting his father's reverie.

"I do too," Fortune said. "And it's going to get better as more and more things get built according to these plans." He tapped the sheaf of papers he held in his hand, drawings of the greenhouse and Italian garden, which were coming along nicely, and of the proposed racetrack and viewing stands.

"Look," Daniel said, pointing. "There's an old man on crutches coming to see us."

Fortune looked where Daniel pointed in the direction of the train station. A man on crutches, one trouser leg pinned up where a leg had been, was lurching toward them on crutches. It took him a few seconds to realize that this seemingly old man was his brother, Pete. Fortune ran toward him. "You're alive!"

Pete stopped, unfastened the pack strapped to his back, and dropped it to the ground. "Just barely."

Fortune hugged his brother, being careful not to throw him off balance, then picked up the pack and said, "Welcome and sit down and tell me what's happened to you." At the doorway of the little house, he went in and fetched two chairs, helping Pete to sit in one of them.

Pete looked around. "I hardly recognize Oak Hill. It's pretty obvious that you have bought the place and fixed it up. So, tell me about the family."

"After you've told me what's happened to you," Fortune said. "But first, why don't we have something to eat and drink? Daniel and I were about to have lunch." Daniel frowned in confusion over the lunch plans he was totally unaware of.

"When we come for the weekend, we usually sleep in the mansion, but I'm sure there's food in the pantry here, things that keep, and I know there's a jug of cider just on the verge of turning hard, if it hasn't already. It should give you a little kick." Motioning to Daniel to follow him, he went inside and, in several stages, brought out a third chair, three plates, and three glasses of cider. "Jamie is producing apples faster than he can sell them, so he's turning a lot into cider. Daniel, did you find the cheese and bread?"

"Yes, Papa. Right here. And I found some ginger cookies too."

"The garden is full of late vegetables, which we'll pick and take back with us, and of course there are apples. If I'd known you were coming, I'd have had Ruth cook something for you. Why didn't you let me know you were coming? The last I heard was a telegram from the government saying you were missing and presumed dead."

"After the way I acted when I left, I didn't think you'd want to have anything to do with me," Pete said.

"You are my brother, and this will always be your home, as long as you want to stay here."

"If you are my papa's brother, then you must be my uncle," Daniel said, studying Pete. "But I remember my uncle with two legs, and you have only one."

"Daniel! You mustn't mention things like that."

"Don't scold him, Fortune. Children are observant and curious, and he can't help noticing that I'm missing a leg, or at least part of it. I'm used to stairs and questions. You're probably wondering yourself what happened to my leg."

Fortune nodded. "Well, yes."

Pete finished his cheese and bread and drained the last of his glass of cider. "My unit was sent out to capture the Philippine rebel Aguinaldo. We were captured in an ambush. All of us got sick. My leg had gotten shot up and got gangrene. When we were rescued along with the others to the hospital I wanted to die. I tried to peel off the bandages so I would bleed to death. A brave nurse stopped me and stayed by my side day after day to make sure I didn't do anything so foolish again. Without her I would have died, but now at least I can get around with crutches."

"Then we owe her a debt of gratitude."

"She wanted to come along, but I told her I had to come first and get the lay of the land. Is there anything here for me to do to earn a living? I don't want to be a burden."

"Yes, you can manage the work that I'm having done here, pay the workers on a regular basis, and make sure that things are done properly," Fortune said promptly.

Pete smiled. "I can get an artificial leg, but in the meantime, they'll give me a wheelchair. I'll send for Mildred. She can push me around until I get better at walking."

"Mildred? That's the nurse? What's her last name?" Fortune asked.

"Sherman, and she's from Ohio. She may be related to the Sherman that Southerners hate, but we don't talk about the past. She's a lot like you, Fortune. She says it doesn't matter what people's ancestors did, only what the people who are alive right now are doing."

"Even if I didn't like her, I'd pretend for your sake, and make her feel welcome. You sound as if this is a serious business."

"I told her I'd marry her if I had a way to make a living, so she can give up being a nurse in a military hospital. We may even have children." He reached for an apple, bit into it, and chewed thoughtfully and then asked, "What happened to my daughter – Clarissa?"

Fortune saw that it took some effort for Pete to say the child's name. "Amelia Ames adopted her. I pay her a salary to take care of Clarissa as well as Leticia."

"So she has a good home," Pete said with relief. "Could I see her?"

"Only as Uncle Pete," Fortune said firmly. "She thinks of Amelia as her mother, and probably me as her father. If you're going to marry Mildred Sherman and have children of your own, you should start out fresh."

"My children are growing up so fast. Simon is thinking of becoming a doctor. He comes home regularly on weekends to see Sarah Tyler. Eve is in her first year at Sweet Briar, studying economics, languages, art, and music. I promised her a year in Europe when she finishes. Jonas and Laura are expecting another baby, and she says that she is giving up the store to be a full-time mother, though I suspect she may go on buying trips even if it means taking along two toddlers. Rachel is running her café alone and is waiting out the time for her divorce to become final so she can marry her reporter. Zachery."

"What happened to Patrick?"

"She found out he was fooling around with other women, and girls."

Pete raised his eyebrows, understanding Fortune's meaning, but not asking for details.

"Jamie has a new farm. The whole family works in the apple business and it is going great guns. Say, Daniel, can you refill our glasses, son?"

Daniel hopped up and said, "Maybe Brandy and I will go to the garden to see what we can harvest. I like picking things."

"That's a fine idea, son. You're a good little farmer."

After Daniel left, Pete asked, "I didn't want to say anything with Daniel around, but how are things with you and Emma? I noticed that she's not here."

"She stays at our house in Richmond, going to meetings, reading books, shopping, and eating herself to death. I give her money every month. She's independent. She's told me that she wouldn't mind if I want to have an affair with someone, but I wouldn't do that. It wouldn't be fair to the reputation of the woman concerned."

"The other woman is Amelia Ames, isn't it?"

"How did you know?"

"The way your voice sounded when you said her name, talking about her looking after Clarissa. And the way you and she looked at each other the day of our wedding, at the church and on the train. Emma must know too." He gave Fortune a sad smile. "What are you planning to do about it?"

"I don't know."

Chapter 53

That afternoon, Fortune sent a telegram to Mildred Sherman on Pete's behalf:

"Am home, all is well. Can you come here by Christmas?" Fortune stopped to ask, "Do you want to sign it 'Love, Pete'?"

"No. 'Love, J. P.' That's how she thinks of me, as that is the way my property was all marked, Barranger, J. P."

Ruth and Jamie were not quite as quickly forgiving as Fortune, but after they'd heard his story, they insisted that he must stay with them instead of in the little house.

"It was once adequate for ma and pa and the five of us," Fortune said with a laugh. "Now I fixed it so it's not even suitable for a married couple, if one of them is on crutches."

"Married couple?" Ruth and Jamie asked in unison.

"Yes, I'm going to marry the nurse who saved my life and gave me a reason to go on living," Pete said.

"Well, congratulations are in order," Jamie said, slapping his brother on the shoulder. "Fortune, since Pete will be managing your renovations here, I think we can call him the farm manager, and he can move into the house we're in now. Ruth and I have been talking about having a house of our own anyway, and the one we are living in belongs to you."

"It will take a good while to build you a house, so you needn't be in a real rush to move out. Pete and Mildred can live in the mansion. That will give him an incentive to fulfill his first job, hiring a housekeeper."

"We're not planning to build," Jamie said. "When we looked at the farm, we were concentrating on the land itself, but there's a substantial house on the property which is standing vacant, and there are several outbuildings. The outbuildings are a little shabby, but the house is in pretty good shape. Of course, it needs plumbing for bathrooms and a decent kitchen, but I think we can get it done in a month."

"You might be surprised," Fortune murmured, thinking of how long projects at Oak Hill could take.

"A lot of what we're having done is inside, when it's likely to be cold and wet outside. If I pay good wages, I think I can hire some people away from going hunting."

Fortune had to admit that it sounded like a solid plan. "Remember, I'm not pushing you to move out," he told Jamie. "There will be room enough for Pete and Mildred as well as all my family over Christmas." Later he reflected that sometimes things solved themselves. The manager's house would soon be vacant, and it had been Jamie's idea, not his.

A few days later, a telegram arrived from Mildred saying she hoped to arrive by Christmas Day.

"This means I've got just over a month to get my artificial leg and learn how to walk with it," Pete said. "Fortune can you take me to the UVA hospital?"

"I have the car here, but I don't drive well. Even Emma does better than I do. Still, I'm the only choice right now. All the younger generation who know how to drive are in college, and Jamie is in the midst of the apple shipments at the same time he's trying to get his house in order by Christmas. So, I'll give it a try."

At first, Fortune crept along trying to get accustomed to the unfamiliar feel of the motor car. It was a chilly early November day, and he and Pete were wrapped in overcoats and war hats with ear flaps, and fur-lined gloves. Fortune would have liked to be wearing his good suit and his new Homburg hat, but it might have blown off in the breeze from the open car. A few other cars passed them, hooting for them to move over from the center of the road.

"Motorcars must have a future, since other people are buying them," Fortune said. "These drivers passing us can't all be as rich as I am."

"Are you going to invest in a motor car company?" Pete asked.

"I already have, so it's probably a good investment although there might be too many companies making cars right now. Every man who can use a wrench seems to think he can build a motor car."

At the University of Virginia hospital, Pete was fitted with an artificial leg. When he tried to walk, he moved jerkily but soon gained confidence in his gait.

On one of his occasional visits to the Richmond house, Fortune told Emma about Pete's artificial leg and how well he was taking to it. She said, "It's always your family you're concerned about, isn't it? You don't care what's happening to me. What if I need to go to the doctor?"

"I feel sure if you called Dr. Tyler, he'll come here to the house," Fortune said wearily. "If you are seriously ill or have an accident, he could probably arrange for you to go to the hospital. Or, you could call Jonas. He's become something of the patriarch of the family while I'm away, and he's a fine trustworthy man. He's also bought a motor car and learned to drive it, so he wouldn't have to use yours."

"Dr. Tyler says I have heart trouble."

"Does he know you're drinking?" He asked, noting that she seemed to keep a small glass of bourbon always in her hand, taking sips from time to time.

He said a drink a day might be good for me." She curled her hand around the glass, so that for a moment he could not see the contents.

"One drink, yes, but you're drinking a lot more, and eating more than is good for you as well."

"So what if I am? Why should you care? You're never here. What I do is none of your business or Dr. Tyler's."

"Are you happy like this, Emma? Don't let pride stand in your way of coming to Oak Hill with me and the rest of the family."

"I haven't been happy since my father died, and you let him drown." She swallowed the rest of the bourbon and set the glass down on the table with a click.

"That's wrong and unfair, and you know it, Emma," Fortune said. "I almost drowned myself trying to save him, but it was hopeless. He was swept away so swiftly that there was no chance for him. What would you have done if I had died the same day?"

"I'd have found a husband who would have been home with me every single night." She got up and went to pour another glass of bourbon.

Fortune said, "You could still find someone else, Emma."

"You'd like that, wouldn't you? Go through humiliation with everyone knowing that you deserted me."

"All our friends and family know that we're living apart, Emma. I only stay here occasionally, and our children know that we don't share a bedroom anymore. Nobody dares criticize you because of the money." She said nothing but took another sip of the bourbon.

He sighed. "I think we have talked enough for one night, Emma. Good night."

The next time he met Amelia she asked, "Will there be any problem about Clarissa, now that her father is back?"

"No. I've made it clear to Pete that you adopted Clarissa, and you are the mother she's known. He abandoned her and has no rights to her. And if you look at the adoption papers, you'll find that I had myself listed as the adoptive father."

She looked startled. "I never read them. I thought it was all just a lot of legal language, and put the papers away in my cedar chest."

"Children need something and someone they can count on, no matter what. Clarissa can count on you — and me.

He invited Emma out to lunch the next day, and she accepted, seemingly pleased. She was not drinking, he noted, for he detected no smell of alcohol, but he saw that her hands shook's slightly as she held the menu.

After they'd ordered, Fortune asked, "What would you like for Christmas this year? I can't top the car I gave you last year, but I'll buy whatever you like within reason. I never know what to buy for you, but if you'll give me some suggestions, I'll choose one of the items."

Emma said, "A new dress, perfume, a piece of jewelry, a new coat. Any of those will do, so long as you choose it. What would you like? I never know what to get you since you have everything.

Not everything, he thought. "Nothing that needs wrapping," he said to her. "I want you to come and spend Christmas with me and your children at Oak Hill. Even just Christmas Eve and Christmas Day and that night. It would mean a lot to the children and me if you would."

She nodded. "We'll see."

After spending a day in the office checking over the books and making arrangements for Christmas bonuses for all his employees, Fortune took the train to Norfolk. He wanted to check the progress of the trolley lines from the port to the site, as well as the one inside the site. The trolley line that led from the railroad to the site was being used to carry building materials to build the Pavilions — not just his, but all of them. He'd earned money from that enterprise as well.

Back in Richmond, he met with the artist for the Jamestown paintings. He spent another night under the same roof with Emma before going out west to the coal mines.

He had not told the manager he was coming. He liked to catch his managers and other employees off-guard. If they knew when he was coming, they could always put up a good front. He didn't send any spies or attempt a disguise. That would have been foolish. His arrival was enough to send them running to make corrections of any lapses and operations. They never knew when he might come or send someone else to check up on the operations. Fortune grew depressed as the train neared the mining town. Puddles of water stood on the bare earth where an early snow had come and melted, and bits of it still clung in the hollows. The colors of autumn had gone if they had even been here, and at the edge of town a mound of coal waiting to be shipped towered over the small houses. As soon as the train stopped, he sent the first man he saw for the manager.

The man arrived almost at a run, obviously apprehensive at Fortune's presence. "Is something wrong?" He asked.

Fortune thought about what Christmas must be like here. During the years he had owned the mine, he'd paid good wages, and periodically checked on the safety and functioning of the mine, but he hadn't come at this time of year, and it gave him an entire to new outlook on the people who had labored to help make him rich.

"I hope there's nothing wrong," he said. "Please ring the bell to summon everyone who is above ground."

As he waited for the miners and their families together, he looked around at their pale faces and gaunt bodies. There was much in the world that he could not change, not even in his own personal life, but here he could make a difference, at least for a short while.

As a child he had been poor but at least he had had the bit of money his father distributed to the children after the final sales of the tobacco crop. These children didn't have anything.

"Wes," he said to the manager, "carry a notebook like mine to note decisions I make and problems that I see. I'd like you to stand nearby and write down the same thing and afterward we can compare notes. If I come back later and find that my instructions have not been carried out, there will be hell to pay for somebody."

The mine manager nodded, understanding, and poised his pencil to write. When the last stragglers appeared, Fortune announced, "In addition to your regular pay you workers will receive a Christmas bonus. The bonus will be paid to the worker's wife or mother, to make sure you men don't spend it on moonshine." This brought laughter from the crowd.

"The mine has proved to be more profitable than I expected, which means you deserve a reward. Then perhaps you'll want to work just as hard in the coming year to get a reward next year. I want to give everyone a half bushel of apples, turnips or turnip greens, two gallons of milk, and two dozen eggs. There will also be a chicken for every three people in a family."

Looking up from his writing, he saw children shivering. He went on to say, "And each child will receive a pair of shoes. and will also receive a jacket and a book suitable to his or her reading level." People reacted in astonishment, mothers and fathers hugging their children. There would be food and gifts for Christmas.

He thought about the fur coat he was planning to buy for Emma and the gowns he had bought for her and his sisters over the years, clothing worn only a few times each. With what he was spending on his family, he could outfit the whole town here. "Each man will have a new shirt and pair of trousers as well as new boots, and each woman will have three yards of fabric to make a dress, a wool hat or a warm shawl, warm gloves, and a pair of shoes." He decided that he would add in some cigarettes for the men or a chew of tobacco, and bottles of hand cream for those women's chapped hands, but he needn't mention everything.

"In case you are thinking this may not be fairly distributed, I plan to send my son and my nephew along with the shipment of things and they will have my list and check off everyone. As the items are distributed a stamp will be put on each hand so that no one can come through the line twice." Fortune knew that unless someone close to him was responsible, managers might take the food and clothing and sell them instead of giving them out as he had indicated.

He raised his hands. "I also plan to build you a hospital, but that will take time and certainly won't be done by Christmas. Now, a Merry Christmas to all of you. You'll be receiving the items the week before Christmas, if I can manage to get them all here in time." He turned to indicate that he was finished talking, and heard a cheer rise from the crowd. "Let's compare our notes," he told the manager, "so there will be no misunderstanding and no mistakes when food and money are distributed. You will have the same Christmas gift from me as all the other men."

As he boarded the train, Fortune's mind was already busy with how he might manage to fulfill his promises. The manager had given him a list of the employees, with the names and ages of their children. Laura and Jonas would have to guess at the right sizes, but they could throw in a few extras just in case. The food would be no problem. Jamie could furnish the apples, of course, and Rachel had access to large quantities of food at discount prices. Shoes and work boots would be the most difficult to supply.

At the bottom of the list for Laura he added a note to buy Emma a full-length fur coat. He thought about a poem he learned back in school: "As grandfather Ray said on Christmas Day, if you want to be happy, give something away." As much as he was giving away, he thought he should be happy for the year to come.

Chapter 54

Mildred arrived on December 22. Within moments after the train stopped, she appeared at the door, waving and smiling. "JP, stand right there and let me look at you," she called. Relieving Pete of the necessity of running toward her and possibly falling at her feet, she stepped down from the train unaided, and ran the few steps toward Pete, arms outstretched for an embrace.

The porter set down a single suitcase, and Fortune reached for it. "Is this all?" He asked, pressing money into the Porter's hand.

She turned briefly toward Fortune. "Yes, that's it. At least for now. A truck will be arriving someday. I took the fastest train so I could get here before Christmas, but my trunk is coming by freight. The military doesn't let us have much in the way of belongings, and most of what I had was suitable only for the tropics, so I left it behind."

She was candid, and not the least bit shy, Fortune noted. And she was sturdy, not thin and frail like the delicate Clara. Not tall and big bosomed and narrow waisted like his sisters, and not portly like Emma. Just sturdy.

She caught Fortune looking at her, and asked, "Do I pass muster, Mr. Barranger?"

Fortune laughed. "More than pass. I'd give you an 'A.' Welcome to the family." He extended his hand, and she shook it firmly.

Fortune considered who would sit where in the car. It would be difficult for Pete to get into the back seat, and it would be ungentlemanly for him and Pete to sit up front with Mildred in the rear where the wind was stronger. "Do you drive, Miss Sherman?" he asked.

"I learned to drive an ambulance, so I think I could manage this car if need be."

Fortune said, "Then I think I'll walk the short distance to the house. The walk will do me good."

"So, would you like to drive, or shall I?" Mildred asked Pete, picking up Fortune's signal and saving Pete's pride. Pete said, "It's only for a short distance; we're in sight of the house. Why don't you drive, sweetheart?" Fortune helped Mildred into the car with one hand and turned towards the mansion.

At the mansion, Fortune held the door open for Pete and Mildred, and reached back for her suitcase. He wasn't sure at the moment where to put it.

Pete had hired a competent housekeeper, Mrs. Burton, who ushered them into the dining room where she had laid the table for lunch. "Seeing as it's such a pretty day, I wondered if you might want to eat on the back porch and enjoy the view. Although to me, that fire in the fireplace feels good."

"This is fine, Mrs. Burton, and I assume you have hired extra help for the next few days."

She nodded vigorously. "My daughter and my daughter-in-law will help with the cooking and serving and take care of all the laundry after that."

Fortune remembered when his own sisters had been the ones willing to serve and be housemaids to earn extra money. His mother too, of course, had cooked and cleaned here for the Bishops who had too much stiff-necked pride to even pick up after themselves. Times had changed.

Mrs. Burton had prepared roast pork, turnip greens, cornbread, and baked sweet potatoes.

"This is quite a change from the tropical food we've had in the Philippines, but it looks a lot better than what we nurses got served in the mess hall." Mildred tasted the turnip greens and cornbread doubtfully, but ate with determination.

"We won't be living in anything nearly this luxurious," Pete warned.

"I don't need luxury, just a comfortable place with a roof over our heads and indoor plumbing so I don't have to go outside in the cold to an outhouse."

Fortune and Pete laughed together. "You don't have to worry about that. I just wanted you to be prepared for what our home will be like," Pete said.

"When will we be married?" Mildred asked.

"We could go to the county courthouse and get the license tomorrow, and then talk to the minister about when we can have the ceremony," Pete said.

"Can we be married at the courthouse?" Mildred asked.

"Yes, I suppose we could, if you don't want a church ceremony."

"How far away is it?"

"Twelve miles, I think," Pete said.

"Will what do you think, JP? Do you want to go get this wedding over with this afternoon, so we can start living together with a clear conscience?"

Pete nodded, and then broke into a big smile. "I'm glad I shaved and dressed up a bit for my wedding."

Mildred rose from the table. "Give me five minutes to put on something clean out of my suitcase. Then let's put up the cover on the car. The only wrap I have is this flimsy coat I bought in San Francisco."

As the couple left, Fortune sat alone drinking coffee and enjoying a slice of the apple pie that Mildred and Pete had been too busy for. He liked Mildred. It was easy to tell that she'd been used to giving orders to nurses and sick soldiers—and probably to young doctors as well—and seen to it that those orders were carried out. She'd bring new blood and a new attitude to the family, a woman who tackled life's problems with the same gusto that she had attacked food she didn't especially like. She was the best thing that could have happened to Pete, and he'd almost guarantee that pretty soon everybody in the family would be calling Pete "JP."

He called Laura to ask her to buy Mildred a coat.

"What kind of coat?"

"A warm one, maybe gray, with fur collar and cuffs. Poor Mildred didn't realize how cold it can be in the mountains of Virginia at Christmas time."

"What size is she?"

"Not as tall as you are. About Emma's height, but much trimmer. About Amelia's size, I'd guess."

"If we don't have gray, and I'm thinking maybe we don't, I'll send dark green or red or whatever is in stock. It's almost Christmas, and people are buying winter clothing as gifts. I'm putting Jonas in charge of seeing that everything gets things wrapped and put in the railroad car. I think I may have the baby tonight." That was a pause, and he heard her groan. Then she came back on the line. "What's this Mildred like, Papa?"

"A commanding general, with short brown curls and a big smile. You'll like her, I'm sure, she'll be the making of Pete, or JP, as she calls him."

The week before Christmas, Simon, Rob, and Jim, following Fortune's instructions, took the train filled with Christmas gifts to the coal mine. In a lightly falling snow they distributed the gifts. Jim was in charge of food, while Simon gave out the children's gifts, and Rob had the hardest job of all, helping people squeeze their bare and sometimes dirty feet into new shoes.

The children and the women all put on their new jackets, which was a good thing, since it was beginning to snow. "It's as cold as the mischief," Jim said. "They got their jackets just in the nick of time."

Meanwhile, Simon opened up the last area of the railroad car, where they had stowed the bolts of fabric for the women. Some of them had begun to look a little concerned, as if perhaps their fabric had been forgotten. The women's eyes got big with pleasure when they saw the new fabrics and bright colors, not hand-me-done homespuns.

"I don't know how Laura found so many different kinds of fabrics, but there were no two alike, and there were three left over, so that the last woman had some choice. She even sent two patterns in each size, and thread of all colors."

"Was there anything left over, or did we plan exactly? Besides the fabric, I mean." Fortune asked, enjoying the boys' excitement and telling of how they had coped with the distribution plan.

"Yes, Papa there was some left of just about everything. Laura had allowed for their being several people in each size range. At the end, we asked if there were any widows there, women whose husbands had died in the mine. And we gave them all the leftovers to barter for what they do need from their neighbors."

"And at the very last, we gave the women hand cream, and there were almost tears flowing at the site of something feminine. The men got their twists of tobacco or cigarettes, and each child got a small peppermint candy. All in all, sir, I'd say that the people in your mill town will now love you forever."

"I'm always pleased when I get thanks for something I've done," Fortune said. "People who say thank you are more likely to get something the next time around as well. But that's not why I give thanks. I feel that God blessed me by allowing me to be prosperous, and to have such good children. In a way, I'm paying back a little of what I have received."

He paid the three young men, and they pocketed their money with thoughtful expressions.

Chapter 55

Eve wrote to Rob, being careful to wait a week after his letter came before she answered. Aunt Rachel had suggested she play hard to get, and a little jealousy never hurt. So she wrote, "I spent the weekend of mid-term in Charlottesville with my roommate, Christina, and met her brother Howard. He is nice, but not as nice as you. We went to the football game." She treasured Rob's reply, "Watch out for that Howard."

She was looking forward to seeing Rob at Christmas and could hardly pay attention to her classes thinking of him.

Jamie had bought a pickup truck to haul apples from the orchard to the processing plant, and the cider mill and canned apples to the rail line for shipping. This, and a horse-drawn wagon, were used for the move from the manager's house to their new house on the apple farm.

Jamie took advantage of all the available labor the young people presented. While he and Ruth and Eddie stayed at the new house deciding where to put furniture, Jim drove the truck and Pete the wagon. Eve, Sarah, and Martha were put to wrapping dishes and glasses and other small items in newspaper, then packing them in apple crates while the young men loaded tables and chairs, and rolled up rugs.

Martha climbed up on a small wooden stepladder to take down curtains. She unfastened one end and called, "Eve, you're tall. Come here and hold this end of the curtain rod. Rob can you help me down. She let go of the curtain and reached down to put her arms around Rob's neck, and as he reached up to take her around the waist, she slid down the length of his body. "My goodness, Rob, but you're strong."

Eve stood paralyzed, holding the end of the curtain rod with the fabric draped dripping onto the floor. Rob let go of Martha and moved the stool over to the other end of the window. He climbed up quickly and took down the second half of the curtain, handing it to Eve without a word. She felt her face grow hot with anger and humiliation. Rob was smiling at Martha and ignoring her.

Jim walked in and, possibly sensing the tension in the room, suggested, "Hey, Rob, you and I can take down the curtains without bothering the girls. That way they can get busy folding and packing the linens and things like that."

Martha shrugged and asked, "Where is the broom?" When Jim responded "It hasn't been packed yet," Martha went into the kitchen and began sweeping. After a few minutes, she called, "Rob, can you find me a dustpan and bring it in here?"

Jim turned from taking down the last curtain, and walked toward the kitchen. "How would he know where the dustpan stays? Here it is, in plain sight, where it always has been." He handed it to her and went back into the parlor to help with the last small furniture items.

When the last item was loaded, Martha said, "Eve, why don't you and Sarah ride in the front of the truck with Jim, where it's warm. I'll go in the wagon. Rob, can you help me up?"

As she started to climb up, her skirt caught on the tailgate, and it exposed her legs above her laced up boots. Rob looked away, and Jim called out, "For heaven's sakes, Martha, you've been climbing into wagons since you were a toddler! Get in so we can finish this job today." He got in the truck and slammed the door. Simon climbed up into the wagon beside Rob and Martha, but as the truck drove away, Eve saw that Martha was snuggled against Rob. She felt tears sliding down her face, and she hated Martha as much as she hated Rob at that moment.

When the last few items were moved into the house, Martha took Rob's hand and called out, "Let's go down to the creek and look for some mistletoe."

Rob turned back and said over his shoulder, "Are you coming, Eve?"

"Nobody needs to go down by the creek," Jim said. "Just look up. There is mistletoe growing in that big oak just to the left of the house. Let me get my rifle and I'll shoot some down for us. He went into the house and came back with the rifle. The group followed him toward the oak tree. He aimed, fired, and a bunch of mistletoe fell at his feet, along with the smattering of debris and bark. Simon took a turn, and then Rob, and each managed to clip a small piece of mistletoe.

Martha picked up a bunch of mistletoe and had started toward Rob, when Pete took control of the situation. He slid down from the wagon and handed the reins to her. "Young lady, I know you can handle horses, so how about helping your parents by rubbing down the horse and putting it away. Maybe your little brother can help you."

To Jim he said, "Can you get this old truck turned around and take the rest of us back to the mansion so we can get dressed for supper? Then you'll still have time for that date I think you have tonight. You take a bunch of the mistletoe with you if you think you need it. Eve and Sarah, let's get some mistletoe to take back to the big house. We never know who might want to take advantage of it. Can you girls sit in the back of the truck so your crippled old uncle can sit up front?"

Everyone scurried to do as Pete asked. Rob got in the pickup truck and with a smile reached a hand to help Eve up. "You seem to have forgotten how to help a girl up," she said, "but I'm all right." Simon helped Sarah up into the back of the truck, and climbed in beside her. The truck rumbled across the field to the main road to the Oak Hill mansion. As soon as everyone got out, Jim turned the truck around and sped off.

Eve strode toward the house, not looking back. Rob caught up with her, grabbed her hand, and turned her around to look at him. "What's wrong, Eve?"'

"Martha that's what's wrong! You had your hands all over her." When he didn't answer, she went on, "I even saw you kissing her in the wagon, right in front of Simon."

"We were just having fun," he protested.

She jerked her hand free. "Just having fun? You humiliated me. Even her brother saw what was going on, and tried to stop it twice. And if you'd gone after mistletoe, there's no telling what might have happened."

"What was I supposed to do when she asked me to help her down from the stepladder or help her into the wagon?" He asked.

"You could have done nothing," Eve said. "She knows how to get into a wagon or a pickup truck better than I do. She's grown up on a farm. You could have gotten up on the ladder yourself instead of helping her down the way you did."

"You have no right to be telling me what to do. We're not married, or even engaged," he objected. "And you remember, I told you that you might meet someone and want to go out with them instead of me."

"So, you want to go out with her?"

"I didn't say that, Eve, and that's not what I mean."

Simon and Sarah darted past and went inside, pretending they hadn't heard the quarrel.

Rob reached to take her hand, but Eve crossed her arms over her chest. "Go on," she said, "if you have some explanation."

"I told you, it was just in fun. I don't care for her."

"Well, she doesn't care for you either. She's doing this just to spite me."

"Why would she do that?"

"She's set on Julian Bishop, the son of the people who used to own Oak Hill. I stopped him from ... attacking her in the woods. The way she acted and talked to me later, I think she might have wanted him to succeed. She thought if she was carrying his baby, he'd marry her, but I don't think so, and neither did Papa."

"That works for some people," he said with a shrug.

"That's why my parents married," Eve said. "And they're both unhappy."

"But if they hadn't married, I wouldn't have you, and I wouldn't have Simon as my best friend."

"Do you have me? You weren't acting like it."

"I thought I did. Don't you care for me, Eve?"

"I'm not so sure anymore. If I can't trust you when I'm looking right at you, how will I ever trust you when we're apart?" He raised, then dropped his hands as he made a feeble noise of protest.

Eve stalked into the house, and avoided meeting his gaze during lunch. She felt on the verge of tears, so she pushed back her plate with most of her lunch not eaten, and asked if she might be excused before dessert. Her father nodded, but had a worried look, easily aware that some trouble had arisen for one of his children.

Later, Sarah waylaid her brother as he was preparing to go out hunting with Simon and Jim. "Rob, you acted a fool today. Eve's worth ten Marthas. I won't even say what I think of her."

"Don't you start in on me. I've had enough of being told that I did wrong," Rob said. "But this morning Eve didn't seem to mind."

Sarah responded, "You didn't even look at her to see her face. She can hide it from some people, but not from me. She acts calm, as if she doesn't care, but you've hurt her badly."

"I'll make it up to her. I brought her a Christmas gift, and I didn't bring one for Martha."

"That's not good enough. I called Papa, and he said he thinks we should come home tomorrow and not stay over until Christmas Day. I can't stay without you, so you've spoiled my Christmas too. I wanted to be here with Simon."

"So, everybody is meddling in my business."

"When you have a problem with Eve Barranger, it's not just your business anymore, Rob. It affects all of us." She turned and went back in the house.

Rob went with the men on the hunt, but his mind was not on hunting. When it began to snow, the group decided to end the hunt, although only Jim had killed anything, a wild turkey. Simon drove Sarah and Rob to the train, and Eve let Rob kiss her on the cheek, but not on the lips, and only lightly put her arms around him to say farewell.

Soon after the departure of the Tylers, the train from Richmond arrived, bringing Emma, Amelia, Leticia, and little Clarissa. Simon drove the ladies and children from the train to Oak Hill, despite Emma's declaration that she could drive and they would be more comfortable, but he smelled the alcohol on her breath, and suspected that she'd been drinking during the entire journey.

It continued snowing during the night, so that on the morning of Christmas Eve, the world around Oak Hill was an undulating sea of white snow. Mrs. Burton and her daughter had stayed overnight, wisely deciding not to attempt travel in the mountains during a heavy snow, and set about cooking for the group. Simon went out to take care of the horses, grumbling that Jim and Ed had moved away at a very inconvenient time.

With no reason to get up early for church services, or to take a walk, most of the family slept late. Fortune always arose early, the habit of a lifetime, and was finishing up breakfast of sausage eggs toast and coffee when Amelia came in with Clarissa.

"Good morning, Clarissa," he said. "It's good to see you again."

Fortune rang the bell for Mrs. Burton and ordered milk for Clarissa and more coffee for himself and Amelia. She chose bacon and eggs for breakfast, and oatmeal for the baby. Pete, Mildred and Emma did not appear until noon, and skipped breakfast altogether. Simon came in from the stable, stamping snow off his boots on the back porch, his face red with cold. When Eve came down at midmorning, she and Simon took their younger brother and sister out to make a snowman, forming small balls and rolling them in the snow until they had picked up enough of the wet snow to be almost immovable.

They assembled the snowman just outside the dining room window so it could be viewed while everyone was having lunch. Afterward, Fortune went upstairs and came down with a large wrapped parcel and handed it to Daniel. "This should be opened today while there is still snow. Everybody else must wait until after breakfast tomorrow morning." Daniel ripped off the wrapping and found a sled. "oh, boy! Thank you, Papa."

Daniel and Leticia donned their outdoor clothing again, and Amelia even went out for a brief ride on the sled. Fortune was pleased to see that Simon volunteered to pull, and Brandy leaped along beside Daniel, enjoying the snow. Eve joined Amelia and Mildred in popping and stringing corn, and fashioning garlands of greenery – with a little help from Pete – to festoon the banister of the main staircase.

The day before, Fortune and Daniel had walked out on the farm in search of the perfect Christmas tree. They cut it, dragged it home, and Fortune nailed a cross of wooden strips to its base so that that it could stand in the parlor. For extra support, he wired it to one of the wooden bookshelves.

The women decorated it with colorful glass balls imported from Europe, which Laura had sent. In the late afternoon, everyone sat in the parlor, admiring the decorations. They ate popcorn and drank hot cider.

"Let's sing Christmas carols," suggested Pete. "Eve, can you play?"

"Not very well, and I'd rather not," she said. "Mrs. Ames is really good at playing."

As everyone turned to look at Amelia, Mildred said, "I will hold your daughter while you play," and reached out. Amelia met her eyes, and knew that Mildred was well aware that this was Pete's child. She handed the baby into the outstretched arms and went to the piano. When they had run through all the Christmas carols that everyone knew, Amelia rose from the piano stool and took back Clarissa.

"She's a darling," Mildred said, "and you're obviously are a very good mother. I hope Pete and I have children," she concluded softly.

Since there would be no church services because of the snow, Fortune reached for his Bible and read the story of the nativity. As he finished, he looked around with satisfaction at his family. He was concerned about the shadow of sadness on Eve's face, and he couldn't help noticing the tremor in Emma's hands, and the trips that she had frequently made upstairs, returning with a scent of alcohol.

Still, most of his family seemed to be all right. "Off to bed, children," he announced. "And remember, no gifts will be opened until after breakfast tomorrow."

Christmas Day began with a brilliant blue sky and sun sparkling on the snow, which quickly began to melt. The snowman still stood guard outside the dining room window, on the shady side of the house. The family had their breakfast of hot chocolate or coffee, ham biscuits, and hot buttered rolls spread with strawberry jam. Then they trooped into the parlor, heaps of gifts spread across the floor beneath the Christmas tree. Simon read off the names, and Daniel delivered the gifts to the recipients. "No one opens gifts until everybody's is delivered," Simon announced.

"That would take all day," Leticia complained.

"You have all day," Simon said, and continued his self-appointed task. Finally, everything had been disbursed except for three large boxes, which Simon delivered himself. Then, it was as if someone fired a pistol to start a race. Everyone began untying ribbons removing and refolding it, or in some cases ripping it off and dropping it on the floor. The givers were thanked over and over, especially Fortune. Soon the floor was littered with red tissue, white tissue, and multicolored stiff papers as well as tangles of colorful ribbon. Everyone turned then to the ladies who had each received a large box.

Mildred opened hers first, and drew out a dark green wool coat with Astrakhan for collar and cuffs. "It's lovely, Fortune, thank you so much. Now I can keep warm in this weather along with the rest of the family."

Amelia opened hers next, and found a red wool coat and a similar style as Mildred's, with ermine collar and cuffs. "Thank you, Fortune. You have excellent taste."

"It's Laura who has the good taste," he said with a laugh. "I just have the money."

Emma was last, and she opened her box to discover a full-length fur coat. "Ooh!" She exclaimed as she rose to try it on and model it, and in so doing lurched forward and fell against her husband.

Mildred leapt up. "You must be ill," she said, placing a supporting arm around Emma, coat and all. "I've noticed how you're trembling. You may have a temperature. Let me help you upstairs and I'll bring you something cool to drink and see if I can find some pills to help you sleep this off."

"Stay here!" Emma objected, but her voice quavered and lost its force. "I'm all right."

But she clearly wasn't, and everyone watched as Mildred expertly guided her upstairs.

Chapter 56

By the time of the midafternoon Christmas dinner, Emma had come back downstairs, although Fortune could tell by the hard line of her lips and the way she gripped the stem of her glass, that she was neither happy nor well. Still, she had made an effort to be with the family.

Fortune gave his usual short blessing to begin the dinner, wanting to enjoy each food at its best temperature. Over dessert, though, he wanted to open up to his family about what was in his heart.

"I do appreciate all the socks and handkerchiefs and ties you have given me, but I thank you even more for the things you have given me that my money could not have bought. First, I want to thank Emma for making the journey to be here with the family for Christmas, although I know how much she dislikes Oak Hill."

Emma looked up at him and gave a brief smile, then returned to her coffee, the cup shaking and clicking as she said it back in the saucer.

Fortune went on quickly, wanting to take attention away from her tremors. "I want to thank Mildred for bringing Pete back to health and bringing us back here to us, and I want to thank Pete for bringing us Mildred, a valuable addition to the family. Our family has added one more member this year, with the birth of Jonas and Laura's second boy. They are now making their own holiday traditions. Jamie's family is celebrating their first Christmas dinner in their own home, and Rachel is spending the holidays with Zachary Todd and his family, to which she will soon belong. Families change, growing and decreasing all the time.

"But I digress, and I can see some eyes glazing over in boredom. Simon and Eve, thank you for helping Jamie's family move, and Simon, thank you in addition for going to the coal mine and developing compassion for those who are not as blessed as we are. Daniel, you are doing well in school and in caring for Brandy, and I think from the way you feel about Oak Hill that you will turn out to be the child who takes over the plantation eventually. Leticia, you have learned to read early, and read me an entire book of yours."

He paused, took a sip of coffee, and looked at Amelia. "And I especially thank Amelia Ames who has cared for a bevy of Barranger children and now has one of her own, Clarissa."

By the time Fortune finished his speech, everyone was smiling, except for Emma, who glared at Amelia.

After dinner, Simon took Eve aside to hand her a small gift. "This is from Rob, of course. I saw you looking at the bare space beneath the Christmas tree after I had distributed all the gifts, and I knew you were wondering what had happened to it. I thought you might prefer to open it in private."

Eve nodded, and carefully opened the package. Inside was a silver locket with a tiny picture inside of Rob in his VMI uniform. Then she saw the card she'd almost overlooked in the wrapping that read, "think of me when you see this." She bit her lip to hold back tears. Of course, she would think of him, whether she looked at his picture or not.

"Do you have a gift for him? I can take it to him."

"Yes. I knitted some socks for him that match his uniform. What did you give Sara?"

"I gave her a ring with a topaz set in it, her birthstone. After I graduate, I'll have a diamond set in the ring, if she accepts my up my proposal. I think she will."

Eve was silent for a moment, envying Simon and Sarah. If only she could be as sure of Rob as Simon was of Sarah. "And what did she give you?"

"A stethoscope. She knows I'm planning to be a doctor, and I've been using an older one her father had."

Eve hugged her brother. "Simon, you and Sarah are meant for each other, and I hope you'll be happy for a long time. You're such a good person."

He stepped back. "Between you and Papa, I'll have a swelled head. And, Eve, you're a good person too, and I think you'll get even more so as you get older."

Emma announced the next morning that she would return to Richmond that day. Fortune drove her to the station, and as they waited for the train, he said, "Thank you for coming to Oak Hill, Emma."

"You already thanked me. When are you going to return the favor and come to Richmond to be with me?"

"I don't know. With the telephone connection and telegraph hooked up here, I can do most of my business straight from Oak Hill. I do occasionally need and want to visit businesses and check up on things. I'll let you know when I'm coming."

"How long is Mrs. Ames staying?"

"She and the children will be back the day before school starts again in January. Simon will be coming on the early morning train on the thirtieth to be with the Tylers for New Year's Eve. Eve was invited too, but she and young Rob had some kind of breakup."

"She didn't mention it to me," Emma said.

"Nor to me either, but Rob and his sister left suddenly, and she's been moping around ever since. I know that departure had nothing to do with Simon's girlfriend, Sarah, her name is. If I could get my hands on young Rob Tyler, I'd give him a good thrashing."

"Fortune, you can't solve everybody's problems in the family," Emma said, shaking her head.

"Yes, but I keep trying, and more often than not, I succeed."

Chapter 57

When the telephone rang before seven, Fortune picked it up in the darkness with trepidation. It was bound to be trouble. Nobody made social calls this early, or even business calls, unless there was a problem that the person on site couldn't handle.

"Papa, there's been an accident," Simon's shaky voice came over the line.

Fortune felt a sudden jolt of fear. "Are you all right, son?"

"Yes, Papa, but . . ." there was a long hesitation before Simon could continue, "Mama's dead."

Emma! Fortune pictured her in a flash as she'd been that first day he'd seen her, driving the carriage to bring lunch to her father. He drew in a deep breath. "What happened? Did she fall downstairs?"

"No Papa, she ran her motor car into the trolley. I was on the trolley from the station, and we had to stop and get off and walk around to where the police and the trolley operators were clearing up things. Then we had to get on another trolley beyond that. I didn't know then who it was, but when I got home, a policeman was standing at the door. They had taken mama to the morgue."

He drew in a hitching breath. "I don't know what to do, Papa."

"Don't do anything you don't have to, Simon. I'll be there as soon as the train can get me there."

"Papa, this might be a time to use your motor car. You could almost be here before the next train even leaves there."

"You are right about the time, but I'm not a very good driver, and we don't want to have two accidents in the family in one day. Still..."

"Get Jim," Simon suggested. "He's a good driver."

Fortune bathed and dressed hastily, with a token effort at shaving. He decided not to get Jim, but to drive himself. The fewer people who knew about the accident at this point, the better. He tapped on Amelia's door, and when she answered, told her only that Emma had had an accident and he must go to Richmond. "Just tell the children I had to go to Richmond. They are used to my being away. I'll call you later when I know more myself." He hated having her or anyone else see him at less than his best, but that couldn't be helped today.

He got the motor car started with no trouble, and was soon on the highway. The first few miles he regretted that he hadn't asked Jim to drive, but he grew more confident. He was glad that the snow had melted and the temperature was above freezing, so there was no ice on the highway. There wasn't much traffic, either. The few people who owned motorcars were probably still asleep or having a big breakfast. He was grateful that the sky was overcast even though it looked like more snow, but at least driving east he didn't have the sun in his eyes.

As he drove, he thought about funeral arrangements. Emma would be buried at the church in Richmond, not at Oak Hill. There would have to be an announcement in the newspaper, and he'd have to do what he could to control the story.

Fortune arrived to the Richmond house to find Simon sitting at the table in the kitchen, drinking coffee with Dr. Tyler. He rose and ran to his father, throwing his arms around him.

"I called Dr. Tyler," Simon explained. "We've been to the morgue and identified mama. I brought home her rings and pearl necklace. She was wearing the fur coat you gave her at Christmas. It will have to be . . . cleaned," he concluded.

Fortune understood.

"I wrote the death certificate to say cardiac arrest," Dr. Tyler said. "I had been treating her for a heart problem, mainly due to her weight, and it's possible she was already dead before she hit the trolley."

"Thank you," Fortune said "I hope you'll be willing to say that, if it comes down to an investigation."

"I don't know where she had been, any more than you do, Fortune," Dr. Tyler said. "Or what she had been drinking, if anything."

Fortune cleared his throat. "I want to quash any suggestion that she had passed out from drinking. I know that she did drink, but I don't want the general public to know about her private life, and I don't want her children to be ashamed of her. The public will be interested in her partly because of our wealth, and she would have hated that. The newspapers will be interested in her death, of course."

"I've called Zachary Todd, Papa," Simon said. "He should be here soon. We can shape the story so that it's truthful without saying too much." Privately, Fortune wondered if Emma had not deliberately put on her fur coat and driven out on a cold night, intending to kill herself and embarrass him and the family. He pushed those thoughts down, and got up to pour himself a cup of coffee just as Zachary Todd knocked at the door.

Todd shook hands with the men, accepted a cup of coffee from Simon, and sat down at the table with his notebook open. "I'm glad you called me. If there are any whispers or gossip going around, my story in the newspaper will be the official one, because I'm the only one who is actually interviewing the people closest to Mrs. Barranger.

After half an hour of talking and scribbling, Todd said, "Here's what I propose publishing. Tell me if you have any changes, or if I've gotten the right tone as well as the information."

He read: "Mrs. Emma Brown Barranger, wife of the wealthy businessman and philanthropist Fortune Barranger, died early December thirty-first in a motor car accident.

"Mrs. Barranger was returning home shortly before daybreak from visiting friends overnight, and it is believed that she had a heart attack and died before striking one of the cars of the Richmond trolley line. Mrs. Barranger had been treated recently for heart problems by local physician Dr. George Tyler.

"Riders on the trolley noted that Mrs. Barranger drove out from a street without stopping, and appeared to be slumped in her seat. There were no skid marks indicating an attempt to stop."

After Todd and the doctor left, Fortune called Oak Hill and spoke with Amelia: "I can tell you more now. Emma was driving and ran into the side of a trolley. Dr. Tyler says she may have had a heart attack. I'd like you to come on the train tomorrow or the next day and bring the children. They will need to have suitable dark clothes for the funeral, which Laura can help them choose.

"I'm sorry that I had to take the motor car, so you and the children will have to use the horse and carriage to get to the train station, and Pete and Mildred will have to use it as well. I don't think Jamie has had time to get a phone installed at his new house, so if Pete and Mildred want to drive over in the carriage and tell them about Emma, that will be all right. I don't expect them to attend the funeral, as the weather is very uncertain for traveling, and they only saw Emma on a few occasions. Mildred, of course, has seen her only at Christmas, and she and Pete will probably welcome having Oak Hill all to themselves for a while."

"I'll do just what you've asked," she said, and Fortune felt some of his tension subside.

"I know I can count on you, Amelia. I always have. This will be a difficult time for the children, and they'll depend on you to see them through it." He wanted to say more, but when he paused, she said, "We'll see you sometime tomorrow, or if the weather is bad, the following day." Then, before he could say more, she hung up.

Fortune turned his mind to funeral arrangements. This was more difficult than Ma's had been. She'd arranged everything ahead of time herself, whereas Emma had left him a mess. Besides, the death of a wealthy man's wife was bound to attract attention, good and bad. There would be a certain number of ghoulish lawyers who will line up for a peek at the deceased in her coffin. He wouldn't have that. Emma's coffin would be closed. Choosing a coffin and deciding on flowers would be easy. He went to the funeral home where Simon sat waiting for instructions on how to help his father.

Should he have a private funeral and private burial? Or would the newspapers think he had something to hide? They might anyway, because of the closed coffin, but that could easily be explained by the fact that she had been involved in an accident and suffered severe facial damage. Would friends be calling at home, or should they arrange to have visitation at a funeral parlor? Or maybe a reception after the funeral. By invitation? Or open to all comers?

He might consult Amelia about this. She had gone through the death of a spouse. But she had known he was going to die, and Emma's death had come as a complete surprise. Moreover, Amelia wasn't one of the wealthiest people in America.

Simon was watching him. "Is there anything I can do to help, Papa?"

"Yes." He started to tell Simon what he had been thinking, but his son stopped him. "Papa, you were talking to yourself, and I could hear you. If we have a service for the family only, some of mama's friends will be very upset to be left out. Do you know their names and addresses? Because I don't."

Fortune shook his head. "I see where this is going. The Tylers aren't family either, but they are as close as people can get without being birth kin."

"And some of my college friends might come, but an invitation to them would sound like a command."

Fortune laughed. "All right. We'll announce the place, time and date in the newspaper and let whoever wishes come."

"I think the reception should be after the funeral," Simon continued. "It's tempting to have a reception before the service, as it puts a time limit on the reception, but that can be a bad thing too. If we had it the night before, people would have to make two trips, and if they are from out of town, they would have to stay overnight. If we have the funeral at two in the afternoon and the reception at three, with the burial later, people can take the late train home or if they are from Richmond, they can get home before dark, or even return to the office, in the case of your employees or managers."

"You're a good logical thinker, son. Your Sarah is going to get a good solid husband, and you show consideration for others, which is a good quality for a doctor. I'd make one correction to what you said, though. I plan to close all my businesses in and around Richmond for the day in Emma's honor."

"That's good, Papa. Now, where should we have the funeral reception? And I suppose you plan to have the burial later and in private."

"About the burial, yes, private. Yes, later, depending on the weather. I don't want people standing outside in snow or sleet or rain. The reception should probably be at a hotel, maybe the John Marshall."

Fortune rose and set his coffee cup in the sink. "I don't know what arrangements Emma had made with Mrs. Watkins, but I think we need to have her on hand every day from now through the funeral and probably a few days more as well, to see to storing the food that people undoubtably are going to bring, and to keep the coffee and tea flowing. I wonder how many we plan for at the hotel?"

"Tell them one hundred. Then we can judge by how many flower arrangements arrive as well as cards and phone calls — and with food, of course — and we can increase the number. The important thing is to reserve the space. You should go notify Mrs. Watkins now."

Simon was still flushed with pleasure, both at his father's complement, and the mention of Sarah. "Do you think it will be all right if I go to see Sarah tonight, or would that be disrespectful to Mama?"

"By all means, go. Nothing that you or I or anyone else does now can help or hurt your mother. I think it would be too much if I were to go out for New Year's Eve, but you will be at the Tylers' home, so go and enjoy your evening."

Fortune realized that he was utterly fatigued, from the stress of the event and the drive from Oak Hill to Richmond. Let midnight come. It was just another hour, no different, really, from the one before it and the one after.

He slept late, not awakening for all the firecrackers and bells ringing to announce a new year. He picked up the Dispatch from the front steps on New Year's Day.

Over coffee, he read the announcement of Emma's death. He folded the newspaper carefully so that the story showed, and laid it on the hall table in the front door. Phone calls began to come in before noon, the first from the priest at St. John's. Fortune met him at the rectory, and set the date and time for the funeral and what might be said at Emma's service. After alerting the funeral home, he called Zachery Todd. We need a follow-up article." "I know," Todd said. "I will come over soon."

Todd arrived just as Simon came home and together the three men discussed what more should be said and not said. After a bit Todd read what he was going to put in the article.

"Mrs. Barranger is survived by her husband; two sons, Simon Barranger and Daniel Barranger; and two daughters, Eve Barranger and Leticia Barranger. Both her parents predeceased her.

"Mrs. Barranger was a member of St. John's Episcopal Church, and was very involved in church and literary activities.

Todd put down the notebook. "What do you think?"

"I think it's just right," Fortune said. "Just add the funeral arrangements." He turned to his son. "What do you think, Simon?" The boy nodded.

"Do you want to add anything more about the accident?" Todd asked.

"No, we don't know if she was visiting friends overnight," Fortune said. "We don't know where she had been and why she was out in the very early hours of a winter morning."

"But it's vague enough that no one can prove where she was, or challenge what we said. Each set of friends will think she was with someone else." Fortune leaned back in his chair and put both hands on the table. "Go ahead and send it out to all the newspapers you think would be interested."

"We'll keep the telegraph lines busy, and we may put out a special edition this afternoon," Zachary Todd said.

Fortune rose and shook hands with Todd. "Thank you for coming and writing this. You're a real friend of the Barranger family."

"I plan to become a member of the Barranger family."

Fortune stopped the newsman. "Should we add some explanation for why Emma was here alone? Maybe we could say, Mrs. Barranger had returned early from the Oak Hill estate, while her husband and children remained there for the remainder of the holiday."

"That sounds fine," Todd said.

After Todd left, Fortune called Amelia at Oak Hill. "The funeral will be on January fourth at two in the afternoon, so you and the children should plan on arriving on the second. We'll need to buy appropriate clothing for the children."

He paused, uncertain how to phrase his wishes for the rest of the family. "Tell Pete and Mildred that I want them to stay and look after things will until I come back to Oak Hill. They will probably appreciate a chance to be alone as newlyweds. As for Jamie's family, if any of them come over to Oak Hill, of course tell him about Emma's funeral. I don't think Jamie has a phone in his new house just yet, and I wouldn't expect you to go out in the carriage in the cold to tell them. If they do know about Emma's death, tell them that I don't expect them to come here just for the day, especially if weather is bad, and they'd have to make hotel reservations. We can't have a house full of guests at this time."

He paused again and then added, "I especially don't want Martha to come. She and Eve have had a run-in, and while it will blow over eventually, I don't want any conflict right now. I realize I'm putting you in a bad session about notifying Jamie. Don't take the blame. Tell them just what I said, though you might leave out what I said about Martha."

"You can count on me," she said. "I'll handle it."

"I know I can always count on you. I'm looking forward to seeing you and the children again." He thought about saying that he had missed them, but it had only been a day.

By the time Fortune hung up the phone, Simon was ready with a list of other things they needed to do.

"I'll call my office manager and have him notify the others."

"How do we avoid the voyeurs who go to famous people's funerals?" Fortune asked. "I don't want this funeral to turn into a circus."

Simon laughed. "Voyeurs mainly stand outside and watch who comes and how they addressed. They are interested in seeing famous people. I doubt if any of them want to sit through an Episcopal funeral service, and they won't have a peek at mama's body, since you already decided to have a closed coffin, and it will be covered with the pall as well."

Fortune nodded "You knew that your mother and I were not getting along well?"

Simon met his father's eyes. "We all knew except maybe Mrs. Ames. And Eve and I also knew that she was drinking heavily, and of course Uncle Pete's wife caught on to that right away." Uncomfortable with the subject, he shifted topics. "Say, I'm hungry. I haven't eaten anything all day. Let's see what's in the icebox."

In the kitchen, he turned back from the open door of the icebox to announce "There's nothing here but a large half-eaten fruitcake, one of Aunt Rachel's."

"Let's see what's in the storage area," Fortune said. When he opened the door to the storage room beneath the kitchen, he was assailed by the smell of apples. Enough light came in from the open door that he could make out a box of apples, a bushel of turnips and one of potatoes, and a large wheel of cheese and a wooden box. A wire basket filled with eggs, a ham and a side of bacon hung from hooks. This was probably Jamie's Christmas gift, which Emma had not mentioned, and which she obviously had not been eating.

"We can have some eggs with ham or cheese or bacon, but there's no bread," Fortune said.

"Let's go to Aunt Rachel's, if she's open," Simon said, backing out of the larder. "I'll drive, and we can stop off at the hotel on the way back to make the arrangements for the reception."

Rachel welcomed them to the café. She seated them at a table for four, and sat down with them, bringing her son Matthew to take the fourth chair. "Zachary told me about Emma, I'm sorry, and shocked about the way it happened. What can I do to help?"

"You could suggest a menu for the reception, although the hotel may have its own menus for funeral receptions," Fortune said. "Between us, I think Simon and I have taken care of everything else. It's a bad time of year to have a funeral, because of the cold. The ground may be frozen so we can can't dig a grave, and it may snow or sleet or rain on that day, but we don't choose. I would hate to have all those carriages and horses outside in the cold, so I'm thinking of running a special trolley from downtown to the church and then from the church to the hotel and back."

"That's a fine idea," she said.

"And I do need to buy some groceries. There's nothing in the icebox. Emma must have planned to stay longer at Oak Hill and changed her mind." Or else knew that she would not be eating at home anymore, he thought.

"Don't buy much," Rachel advised. "In the next few days you're going to have a kitchen full of food. I'll send you home with enough leftovers for tonight and tomorrow, or you can join us for dinner tomorrow. We are having Laura and Jonas, and I'm sure she would like to hear all the family news. It gets really noisy when David comes over doesn't it, Matthew?" She asked, turning to her little son.

Matthew nodded, looking from Fortune to Simon and back to his mother.

"Thank you, but I think we should be at home. Once people read of Emma's death and the newspaper, there will be phone calls for sure, and maybe even people dropping by."

"I do miss having Amelia taking care of the little ones," Rachel said.

I miss her too, Fortune thought. Aloud he said, "I'm sure she'll be willing to take care of them the day of the funeral. We all count on her so much."

They left with the basket full of food, and by the time they stopped by the hotel to make arrangements and arrived home, the sun was setting. Simon washed up and left for the Tylers, while Fortune put the food away and went to bed early.

Fortune awoke to a weak winter sun, so pale it scarcely made a shadow across the bedroom floor. He had slept in the big four-poster for the first time in months, no longer having to avoid touching Emma. For a moment he puzzled over why he was there and Emma wasn't, and then the knowledge came flooding back. He felt heavy from all the sleep, but rested.

He looked at the clock: almost eight thirty. No wonder he was rested; he had slept almost eleven hours. He put on a dressing gown and slippers and examined the array of food assembled on the kitchen table. There on a plate covered with waxed paper lay half a dozen pork ribs with fat congealing on them. A small Mason jar held two servings of string beans, and side by side were loaf pans, one half filled with macaroni and cheese, and the other with meatloaf. All that was familiar, the fare he and Simon had shared for lunch the previous day. There was a bag of oranges and a bunch of celery which he remembered buying on the way home. Then there was a pan of light rolls, a large jar of what proved to be potato and onion soup which he tested with a fingertip, and two slices of chocolate cake, each wrapped in waxed paper. Surely Rachel's basket had not held all that.

He found a jar of honey from Jamie and Pete's apple orchard. When Simon came down, Fortune had already eaten two buttered rolls with honey.

"Happy New Year, my boy! Get yourself a plate for the rest of the rolls and join me in here."

Simon went through to the kitchen, and came back in a moment bearing his food. He sat down beside his father, both with their backs to the fireplace. "Why is it so cold in here?" "As near as I can tell, your mother either turned off the furnace or failed to add in some coal. These are good yeast rolls, by the way, but I don't remember that Rachel had bread like this yesterday."

"She didn't. Sarah made these, as well as the chocolate cake. Her mother made the potato and onion soup. I brought them in last night. I knew we had some food here, but I had complemented Sarah and Mrs. Tyler on the dinner, so I couldn't refuse to bring home what they urged on me."

It was a nearly one in the afternoon when the first knock came at the front door. Fortune and Simon had gotten the furnace started and the house had warmed up. They had heated water for sponge baths, dressed ready to receive any guests, and were just sitting down to lunch.

The caller was Mrs. Watkins. "Mr. Barranger, I was so sorry to read in the *Dispatch* about Ms. Barranger's death. She gave me yesterday and today off, but I had to come to let you know why I wasn't here to cook you some food. Do you want me now?"

"You can have your day off just as you planned, but thank you so much for coming and offering. I will need you tomorrow and every day from now on just as you have been working for my late wife."

She twisted her hands together in front of her, her thumb rubbing across her fingers. "'I didn't actually do much cooking for her lately. She was . . ." she paused, and then went on with determination, "sick a lot. She ate so much cake and candy it's a wonder she didn't die of the sugars, and she liked macaroni and cheese a whole lot. Miss Rachel sent it over sometimes. Mainly I just looked after her. I never thought she would die like this. I wonder what I could have done different."

Fortune saw that tears were about to flow, and patted Mrs. Watkins's hand. "Please don't think it was your fault or that you could have done more." He knew that she was hinting by her emphasis on the word "sick" that Emma had lived mostly on alcohol as well as sugary treats and food brought home from Rachel's café.

"Thanks for being here today, Mrs. Watkins. Now, let's finish our lunch. That chocolate cake looks so good I almost had it for breakfast."

Simon drove to the train station to meet the family. Amelia and Clarissa rode in the motor car along with the luggage, while Eve, Daniel, and Leticia took the trolley.

The time before the funeral was a flurry of activity. Black suits and dresses were purchased or unearthed, shoes were polished and gloves located. Visitors arrived bearing gifts of food, and a delivery man came with flower arrangements and baskets of fruit. Fortune and Simon answered the door and the telephone, and Eve listed in a notebook who had brought or sent what, and began writing thank-you notes.

Amelia took Leticia and Clarissa to stay at her house, in the hopes of giving them a feeling that everything might still be normal.

And then it was time for Emma's funeral.

Chapter 58

Eve stepped back from helping Daniel with his first necktie. "You look fine. Now, eat something so your stomach won't growl during the service."

"I'll eat something, but no more chicken salad. Not even Brandy wants chicken salad anymore. Why don't people bring a turkey with dressing and gravy?"

"A turkey would take up too much space in the icebox, and it makes a mess. Sandwiches are ready to eat, and they don't have bones." Eve explained.

"All right. I guess I will have a pimento cheese sandwich and a big piece of chocolate cake," Daniel said.

Eve started to protest, but then relented. At least he'd have something in his stomach, and besides, she didn't want any more chicken salad either. "Brush your teeth after you finish eating and put your dishes in the sink. Mrs. Watkins has enough to do without picking things up after you."

"I know. You've already told me that before." Eve felt a pang in her heart over how sad her little brother looked.

She went to check her appearance. Her dress was black velvet, with sleeves that came to just below the elbow, and a neckline cut in a Vee. She had filled in the Vee with a bit of black lace, held in place by a pearl and onyx pin of her mother's she touched the pin as she turned before the mirror. Was it too fancy? Her mother had always chosen big pins that attracted attention, as this one would. She decided to leave it on. After all, it was the only jewelry she was wearing today.

She put on her new coat, cut in the same Princess line as Mildred's and Amelia's. She'd have preferred red like Amelia's, but that was out of the question for a funeral, and aunt Laura assured her this coat was smart looking and would give her years of service. She perched her black feathered hat at a becoming angle on her head, and secured it in place with a long pearl tipped hatpin. Pulling on her black leather gloves, she went to wait for her father.

As Eve took Fortune's arm to walk down the center aisle of the church to the front pew, she glanced around as unobtrusively as she could at the gathering. The church was filled to the very back with men in dark suits and women in black coats and hats much like her own. Her mother's lady friends occupied the second pew, and at the end of the row sat a gray bearded man without a topcoat. Something about him looked vaguely familiar, but she couldn't place him."

Where in this mass of people was Rob? Or was he here at all? It was wrong to be thinking of Rob at her mother's funeral, she told herself sharply, and turned her attention to her mother's coffin, which stood at the front of the church covered in a purple Damask pall. Beyond it were banks of flowers, filling the sacristy and overflowing it. Simon and her father had transferred the flowers from the office and most of the ones from the house here to church. Their fragrance made her feel faint.

She knelt for the prayers, stood to sing the familiar hymns, and listened to the reading from the Book of Common Prayer. It didn't seem real, more like a stage play.

Finally, it was over, and they processed out the front door and to the black draped trolley half a block away. The spectators outside had stood in quiet respect, and then dispersed as the mourners left the church. The trolley moved slowly toward the hotel, passing through intersections and passed other trolleys on sidetracks without stopping. At intersections people stood silently in the cold showing their respect. At the hotel she joined her father and brothers in their family reception line. She stood next to her father, as people moved past murmuring words of consolation. She sensed her father stiffening as the shabby man she'd seen in church shook his hand and said, "I'm Emma's cousin."

"Please get something to eat and drink, and let's talk," her father said. The man obediently went toward the buffet, and as soon as the line had finished, Eve joined her father in seeking him out. She was as curious as her father. Who was this man? Was he indeed her mother's cousin, and therefore a relative of hers? Why had she never heard of him or met him before?

"You may be thinking that I'm trying to fool you just to get a good meal," the man said frankly once they had all sat down with their lunch. "But I'm the only kin from her father's side of the family, and there is none from her mother's. Emma disowned me years ago because I was drinking and running around and she was ashamed of me. She never wanted me to come to the house, but she did send me money from time to time."

"I didn't get your name," Fortune said cautiously.

"I didn't say it yet. It's Percy Poindexter." He glanced around at the well-dressed crowd, and then down at his own suit, which hung on him as loosely as clothes on a scarecrow. "Do you want me to leave?"

"Not at all," Fortune said. "I'm intrigued that Emma kept your existence a secret all these years. Now I can't help wondering what else she kept secret and took it with her to the grave. Well not quite to the grave yet," he amended, remembering that because of the cold weather Emma would be buried later.

"Do you need money?"

Poindexter shook his head. "I changed and bettered myself in spite of Emma."

Fortune smiled slightly. "So, you have a job?"

"Yes, sir. I work in your cigarette factory."

Fortune laughed. "You're a wily one getting money from me at work and from Emma. Did she know about your job?"

"She knew I had a job, just not where. She kept on sending me money so I would stay away and not embarrass her."

Fortune extended his hand. The other man set down his cup of punch and shook the offered hand. "I grew up poor," Fortune said. "Since you're kin to my children, you're welcome to visit us sometime. Just let us know ahead of time. We may be at Oak Hill. Now, if you'll excuse us, we have a lot of people to speak to. Stay as long as you like and eat as much as you want."

As she followed her father and brothers, Eve looked back over her shoulder at the man who was once again helping himself to a plate at the buffet. He looked something like her mother. That's why she thought at church that he looked familiar.

Simon raised his hand in greeting to a lanky young man across the room, who started in their direction. As he reached their side, Simon said, "Eve, I'd like you to meet a classmate of mine, Steve Merrill."

He bowed and smiled. "It's a pleasure to meet you at last, miss Barranger. Your brother has been singing your praises, and you are as pretty as I imagined you'd be."

Eve smiled. "Mr. Merrill, you do know how to flatter a girl. When I get him home, I'll find out just what Simon has been saying about me. I should say that he's been singing your praises too, but actually, he hasn't. Of course, it could be that our mother's death came in such a shocking manner that it has wiped away his ability to say anything."

"I quite understand, Miss Barranger. He did say that you were always honest and spoke your mind, and sometimes that made you some enemies. I appreciate honesty, though I want to be your friend not your enemy."

"Are you in pre-med too?"

"That I am. Years of slogging still ahead of us. Are you planning to go into medicine as well?"

"Probably not," Eve said. "One doctor in the family is enough. Business will be my career."

"You'd run an enterprise." He said in admiration, then added, "and a very attractive one. You should be planning to marry and have children."

"I can do both. Both of my father's sisters have run businesses as well as having husbands and children. I like math and dealing with money, and I'm good at it."

"You do speak your mind, just as your brother said, but you've not made an enemy of me. I admire you. Would you like to sit down over there by the palm and let me fetch you a plate of food and some punch? What would you like?"

Eve saw Rob Tyler coming forward "I am tired of standing and by this time the food will be mostly eaten so I will just have a bit of whatever is left. Preferably, no chicken salad. We've been inundated with the stuff."

When Steve left to fetch her plate, Rob approached and said, "Eve, I've been trying to talk to you. I'm so sorry about your mother." He looked even more handsome in his dark suit then she remembered seeing him in his uniform.

"Thank you, Rob. How have you been since I last saw you?"

"I kept waiting for you to finish talking to the tall guy. Is he someone special?" There was a tinge of jealousy in his question and Eve gloried in it. "I just met him, but he seems very nice."

"Eve, can we forget what happened before Christmas and be friends again?"

"Yes, of course we can be friends."

"I'm going back to VMI tomorrow. Will you write to me?"

"As often as you write to me," Eve said, adding to herself, and with just as much affection, no more. She saw Steve Merrill approach balancing two plates, each of which had a glass punch cup perched in it in the center "Thank you, Steve. You're so kind. Rob, do you know Steve Merrill?" she asked, knowing full well that he didn't.

Rob bowed stiffly. "It's good to see you again, Eve. Nice to have met you, Mr. Merrill."

She watched Rob walk away and thought, *now he maybe knows how I felt. And I don't have to act foolish as Martha did.*

Chapter 59

When Fortune drove over to Amelia's house to pick up Leticia, he thanked Amelia, and asked if she would be willing to move into his house.

"You and your children need some time to be together there, and to get used to not having Emma."

"We haven't had Emma for a good while," he said. "You know that."

"I have known that there was a strain in your marriage." She touched her finger to her lips and then pointed at Leticia, who was looking from one to the other.

To the child, she said, "Leticia, look around the house and make sure you have everything. It's starting to snow outside, and you may not be able to come here tomorrow."

Fortune had noticed a few flakes falling, not the kind of snow that would keep anyone from traveling, but he admired the way Amelia handled Leticia, sending her off on an errand so they could finish their conversation.

"We'll talk about arrangements later," he said. "I'm considering sending Leticia to school, if anyone will accept her at her age. She's only five, but you've taught her to read and do simple math, and I wager she's ahead of most in the first grade. Eve and Daniel will continue to live in Richmond until the end of the school year and I will continue to spend most of my time at Oak Hill."

He paused, and then, taking her hand, said, "And of course I want to marry you after a suitable amount of time has passed. It won't be long."

Amelia's eyes widened in surprise. "'Of course'?! Fortune, that is no way to propose to a woman. You make it sound like closing up a business deal."

"It's not business by a long shot, but it is the most important deal I'll make for the rest of my life," he said with feeling "When you marry me, say in about two months?"

She looked at him with scrutiny. "Do you love me, Fortune? And don't say of course."

"I fell in love with you the day I first met you, at Pete and Clara's wedding, but I could do nothing about it. Emma refused to give me a divorce, and I would never have put you in the position of being my mistress. I respect you too much."

"I love you as well, for the fine man that you are, kind and generous," she said.

Fortune responded, "My love for you goes deeper than that, but that's a good start and I hope yours will grow. I have to say, though, that I have never loved as Pete and Clara loved, nor do I want to. I'm sure that if Pete had died first, Clara might have done something equally as crazy as what Pete did out of grief.

"Loving one person to the exclusion of everything else in life is just asking for trouble. When that person is gone, you're left with nothing and might want to give up. I want to see my children grow up healthy, successful and happy, I want to keep investing in sound businesses, and I want to live at Oak Hill and build up the area with hospitals and schools. What I'm saying, Amelia, is that while you wouldn't be the only thing in my life, you would come first."

She responded, "Thank you for your honesty. I know I would never put myself in the situation Pete did with Clara. I want to be part of your life and the children's also and I would never ask you to give up the other things you care for. You wouldn't be the kind of man I would respect."

"Then you would marry me?"

"Yes, but isn't it a little soon after Emma's death?"

"Emma is as dead as she will ever be. Whether we marry now or later will never bring her back.

Leticia came in and found her father's arms around Mrs. Ames, his lips on hers. Fortune disengaged herself from Amelia's arms and said to his daughter, "I was just saying a special goodbye to Mrs. Ames. It's snowing and we may not see her tomorrow."

Leticia asked, "Can I give her a kiss too?" "Of course you can," Amelia said and bent down to the child's level. She touched her finger to her cheek. "Kiss right here." As Fortune picked up their bags and took Leticia's hand, he turned to Amelia and smiled. She smiled back, and he felt his spirits lift.

As they walked toward the motor car, he noticed the snow was coming down heavier. He would probably not see Amelia the next day. His body tingled at the thoughts of having her beside him in bed. He had waited three years and he could wait two months more, but it would take all his self-control not to spread the good news. He had to plan when and how to tell his bereaved children what was about to happen.

He drove home carefully, especially past the spot where Emma's accident had cost her life. He doubted the official version, a heart attack, but was grateful that Dr. Tyler and Zachary Todd had helped to quiet the rumors otherwise.

He pondered all that he had to do in the next few months, in addition to getting married. Pete and Mildred had to furnish the manager's house and move in, but that would not concern him beyond advancing Pete money on his salary as manager. Jamie's family were comfortably ensconced in the renovated house at the orchard, and while they might be miffed at not being invited to Emma's funeral, it might stir Jamie to get a telephone installed. Aside from his financial interest in the orchard and apple processing facilities, Jamie's family were set, and he need not be concerned about them. Rachel would soon be marrying her fiancé, and Laura had Jonas, that sturdy forthright husband to take care of her for life.

As to his immediate family, he intended to start by clearing out all Emma's clothing and belongings. That done, he needed to talk with his children about their future. Simon would soon graduate from college and begin medical school. Eve was doing well in college and in the spring she would have her coming-out party. When he arrived home, he found Eve and Simon reading quietly by the fire in the parlor, while Daniel was lying on the hearth rug beside his beloved dog. They greeted their father with gentle smiles.

Mrs. Watkins walked in from the kitchen wiping her hands on a towel. "I heard you come in, Mr. Barranger. I would like to go now so I can get home before the snow gets any worse."

"Of course. Simon can drive you, and I would like to give you all the food that has been left here. I am sure the children can spare the chicken salad." Even Mrs. Watkins laughed at that.

"I for sure can find some hungry people out where I live who would like the city food. Thank you." She accepted the money Fortune pressed into her hand.

Eve and Simon made several trips carrying food from the kitchen through the house and out to the motor car, which sat in the driveway gradually being covered with snowflakes.

Fortune awoke the next morning to the smell off coffee and bacon. He must've overslept, tired out from the stress of the past few days. Mrs. Watkins must already be here. He pushed aside the draperies at the bedroom window and looked out at a snow-covered world. There were no car tracks indicating that Simon had gone for the housekeeper, nor any footprints indicating that she'd walked from the trolley line. Then who was cooking?

In the kitchen he found Eve standing at the stove, lifting slices of bacon from a pan of hot fat. Daniel was setting the table in the dining room.

Eve turned from the stove. "Good morning, Papa. You can pour the coffee. Simon can you break eggs into the fat and dish up the fried apples? I'll go up and see if Leticia has dressed herself."

She met her little sister coming down the stairs. "I told you I could dress myself, Eve. Miss Amelia taught me how."

Eve served up the food onto plates and handed two at a time to Simon. Soon the family moved to the fire in the dining room fireplace.

"What are we going to do with those things in the storage area: apples, sweet potatoes, and turnips?" Simon asked. "And how long have they been there?"

Fortune shrugged. "We'll eat some of them. Uncle Jamie must have sent them while we were all at Oak Hill and your mother was here alone. She didn't want to bother Mrs. Watkins to cook those things just for her," he concluded, putting as good a face on it for Emma's sake as he could.

"I could make pies out of the apples and sweet potatoes, if we had any flour or lard for the crust," Eve said.

"Bake some of the sweet potatoes and apples, and boil the turnips. And there is a ham hanging in the storage area as well. After the snow melts, I promise you we'll go have a good dinner at Aunt Rachel's, and you can have whatever you want. Or we can buy a roast of beef—" he looked at Daniel and smiled then continued, "or a turkey and some cornmeal to make the cornbread stuffing with a fried egg."

After breakfast, Fortune summoned his children into the bedroom and opened its closet doors and wardrobes. "These were your mother's, of course. Help me decide what to do with them." Eve went to the closet and began moving dresses on hangers from right to left. "These dresses are all kinds of sizes," she announced with amazement. "I don't remember ever seeing mom wear a lot of these, and nearly half of them still have the price tags. The ones in small sizes must be over ten years old. They're out of style."

"Why would she buy so many clothes?" Simon asked.

"We'll never know," Fortune said. "And I don't think they would fit any of the women in the family. Eve, would you like to try on some of the ones she never wore?"

Eve shook her head. "I don't really like them. And the ones small enough for me have been hanging here so long that the fabric is almost rotten. Why don't we ask Mrs. Watkins when she comes back if she knows anyone who can use them?"

"Or we can give them to the church ladies, friends of mama's. They are always looking for clothes for the poor people," Simon said.

Fortune opened another section of closets and discovered hatboxes stacked one on top of the other, almost to the ceiling, with racks of new boots below, of all styles and colors. In other spaces there were gloves and scarves, and lacy underthings that Fortune couldn't imagine Emma wearing, at least not in his presence.

Eve said, "I could use some of the gloves, and I might want some of the hats. But everything else here is simply not for me."

"That's it for the clothes, then," Fortune said. "We'll have them moved out within a week or so. Now, on to her jewelry."

He opened the top drawer of her jewelry cabinet and took out velvet covered boxes and small chests. He dumped the contents out on to the bed, spreading them apart with his hands.

"Take turns, starting with Simon, then Eve, Daniel, and Leticia. Each of you choose one item you'd like to keep it for yourself or in the case of you boys to give these to your girlfriend or wives." He never knew Emma had a collection of jewelry that rivaled the clothes.

He watched as his children made their choices. No matter what each one chose no one would be cheated because this jewelry had cost a tidy sum.

"Sarah will love this ring," Simon said, holding up a ruby ring with a diamond on either side. I will give it all to her, but not all at once, a piece each year.

"I'll wear these pearls to my coming-out party," Eve announced. We all have to wear white dresses and pearls, so no one looks richer or finer than anyone else."

Daniel held up an amethyst pin, "I want to give this to Miss Amelia. She wears purple a lot."

"I want to give her something too," said Leticia.

Fortune didn't think Amelia would feel comfortable wearing Emma's leftovers. We'll go together sometime soon and buy Miss Amelia a piece of jewelry that she will like that is her very own."

Over the next weeks, the snow melted and the family resumed their regular routines. Simon returned to college for his final term, Eve returned to Sweet Briar, and Daniel to fourth grade. They rode the trolley together, as they had for years.

Leticia asked him, "Papa, are you going to take me on the trolley every day now or will I have to go by myself sometimes?"

"What do you mean?""

'When momma felt sick, she said I should go get on the trolley." A grimace crossed his face at the thought that his little girl, small for her age, had been forced to ride alone on the trolley, not staying home with an indifferent mother. Did Amelia know about this? Leticia could have been kidnapped.

He took Leticia's hand and said, "From now on I will take you on the trolley when I'm here, but if I have to be away on business, I will make sure that Mrs. Watkins rides with you. You are precious to me, and I want you to be safe."

As they left the house together, he asked, "Did Miss Amelia know you rode the trolley alone?" "No, Mama said I shouldn't tell anybody, not even you. It's all right to tell you now that she is dead, isn't it?"

"You are right to tell me everything," he said.

As they waited for the trolley, Leticia said, "It would be much easier if Miss Amelia moved into our house."

"Maybe that will happen one day." Fortune couldn't tell her that he too longed for Amelia to join them.

On February 14, he sent roses and a Valentine card to Amelia with a single word above his signature: "Soon."

When he went to pick up Leticia later that day, he asked Amelia, quietly so the children didn't hear, "Do you want a fancy wedding and reception? I can afford whatever you want."

"Not at all. I had that once, and that's enough. I just want to be your wife."

"Would March fifteenth suit you?"

"The Ides of March," she said. "Yes. With that date we will always remember our anniversary."

"Rachel and Zachary are getting married on March 8 at the courthouse. Will that do for you? Or do you want a priest?"

"The courthouse. If we chose a church, we'd have to talk to the priest, and I don't need to explain to anybody why I want to marry you."

Fortune laughed. "Then it's set."

The *Dispatch* had a notice of the marriage of Barrangers and Todds, with no mention that Zachary was one of their own reporters or that the bride had been married previously and divorced. The following week there was a simple notice headed "Ames-Barranger," with only the names of the couple and the date of their wedding. Readers could easily have overlooked either notice, and that was how the Barrangers wanted it.

When Fortune offered Amelia a diamond ring, she shook her head. "The wedding band is enough. But I do want something: a new bed, with new mattress, pillows, sheets, blankets, and bedspread. Also new towels for the bathroom. I don't mind living in Emma's house, although I prefer Oak Hill, but I want everything in the bedroom to be a fresh start for the two of us. I don't think that's asking too much."

"Not at all. I was ready to buy a diamond as big as a Partridge egg. Go down to Hoffmann's and pick out anything you want and I will pay for it."

Fortune insisted on immediate delivery of the purchases, and had the old bed loaded onto a wagon for Mrs. Watkins.

That night, as he slid into his new bed beside his beloved new wife, he knew true peace and comfort. Their bodies were warm and yearning between the fresh sheets, covered by soft blankets. "Being with you like this is what I have longed for," he said. "I wish it could be like this for the rest of our lives."

"But we know it won't," she said. "Our children will go their own way and we'll get old and sick. Anything can happen. I don't think we'll be poor, at least."

"No. You took me for richer or poorer, but it's almost guaranteed that it will always be richer. I have to many businesses that are profitable. Even if one or two failed, we would still be rich."

"No more talk of money or business. We must enjoy every bit of happiness we have, every day." She kissed him gently, and he pulled her against him, cutting off any more conversation.

Chapter 60

The first interruption in their comfortable routine came with a phone call from Jamie, talking so fast and with such anger that Fortune could barely understand him. "Martha has run away. She left a note saying she was going to New York, probably to see that Bishop bastard. Who else could it be? We've got to go find her."

"I assume that 'we' means you and I."

"Yes. You know how to do things and find people there. I wouldn't know how to start. When can we go?"

Jamie arrived in Richmond later that day. He and Fortune set out for New York, arriving the next day. Through Fortune's colleagues they located the Bishop home, and had a carriage driver take them there.

Charlotte herself answered the door, her eyes widening in surprise at seeing them. She stepped back to let them enter, and Fortune noted that while the house was located on a very good street, it was shabby inside, and there appeared to be no maid in sight. This confirmed Fortune's suspicion that while the Bishops had had money at first, Charlotte's husband had wasted it in some way—drinking, gambling, or just failing to work and invest. But he needed to focus on Martha and not on Charlotte's financial situation.

"Is my daughter here?" Jamie asked.

"Why would your daughter be here? I don't even know her," Charlotte said, confused.

"Your son does. Can we speak with him?" Fortune asked.

"I put him out after we had an argument. He was just lying around doing nothing when he should be getting a job and making something of himself. He's taken rooms near the college, and his father gives him an allowance, against my wishes. As long as he has just enough to get by on, he won't be forced to get a job. He'll spend his time hanging around the college, pretending he's still a student."

"I want to talk to that young man!" Jamie said.

Fortune put out a restraining hand against his brother's chest. "Mrs. Bishop, do you have an address where we can find your son? We'd like to take Martha back home."

Charlotte stood went to a desk by the window, wrote the address and handed it to Fortune. "You may be wasting your time. My son is very likely not in, and the girl could be anywhere. Foolish girls come to New York all the time, thinking they're going to live the upper-class life, and the lucky ones go home and find a nice man to marry them."

Fortune thought by the tight lines in her face and the tone of her voice that she was talking about her own experience. He thanked her and guided his brother out to the street.

They found the address, walked up two flights of creaking wooden stairs, and knocked on the door. He heard running footsteps inside, and the door was flung open. At the site of her father and uncle, Martha's bright smile faded.

"May we come in?" Fortune asked, easing his foot against the door before she could close it.

"Damn right we're coming in!" Jamie declared.

She started to block it but both men pushed against the door and went in. Fortune glanced quickly around the shabby room, noting the sagging bed pushed up against one wall, the tiny table and two chairs, one pulled out at an angle where Martha must have been sitting. On a shelf above the single burner cooking unit was a collection of mismatched crockery and cutlery, and a saucepan with a spoon standing in it. Beyond was what he assumed would be a tiny bathroom.

The floor was stained with years of who knows what kind of spills, and a single soot-grimed window looked out onto an expanse of brick wall. A curtain on a wire across one corner of the room formed what was the only visible storage area. Much of what hung there, he thought, was Julian's, as Martha had brought nothing with her.

What did the poor girl do with her time while the young loafer was away all day? He noted the yellow cover of a trashy novel spread open face down on the table. She must have been thinking that Julian was coming home early for some reason when she opened the door to her father and her uncle. As if reading his thoughts on the dismal state of her living quarters, Martha said, "We are going to move into a much better place when Julian gets a job."

Jamie said, "Come home. All is forgiven. You can come back home and you'll have your own room and we will arrange for you to go to college, if that's what you want. You don't have to work in the apple processing plant if you'd rather get a job somewhere else."

"I don't need to be forgiven!" she flared. "I want to be here to marry Julian. It's my life!"

"You've broken your mother's heart. She hasn't stopped crying since she read your note."

Fortune thought that Jamie's mention of Ruth's tears might change Martha's mind, but he was wrong.

"I love Julian and he tells me all the time that he loves me. We are going to get married and some day we will live in a big house. I will never work on a farm again. Can't you give me your blessing?"

In answer Jamie took some money from his pocket and handed her two folded bills.

"Is this a wedding gift? Thank you," she said stiffly.

"No, it's money to pay your way home when you need to."

Fortune placed two more bills in her hand. "Hide this, put it away where Julian can't find it."

Jamie put his arms around her and gave her an awkward kiss. "At least write us my sweet little girl."

401

Fortune could tell from her unrelenting silence that even if he had her captured and brought home she would only run away again. She had to come to the realization on her own how bad Julian was. Fortune prayed that the realization would come before Julian injured or killed her.

Once he returned home, Fortune told Amelia everything, glad to have a wife he could confide in to share his problems and frustrations as well as his joys and successes.

She took his hand. "My dearest, you can't keep the whole family happy all the time. Trying to control young people is like trying to stop water from running down a rocky hillside. It chooses its own way and makes its own trench. Just be glad it wasn't Eve who ran away to be with that boy."

"Eve has more common sense. She has a good head on her shoulders, and she never trusted the Bishop boy, and tried to warn Martha."

"I know I should not speak ill of any member of your family, but I have never cared for Martha. She is headstrong and behaves in a far too seductive manner for a young lady. Her flirtation with Rob at Christmas time was what caused the rift between him and Eve."

"I knew something was afoot, but she closed up and wouldn't tell me what it was. If that young man breaks her heart, I'll give him a thrashing."

"No, you won't, because you're a gentleman. Moreover, he's half your age and has spent four years practicing to be a soldier. He'd not take kindly to a thrashing. Trust Eve to take care of this herself. I suspect she's already gone a long way toward paying him back for his indiscretion in December."

Chapter 61

Eve sat at her desk holding two bundles of letters, one from Rob and the other from Steve Merrill. The top letter in each bundle was an acceptance of the invitation to her coming-out party, which her father had decided to call the Richmond Debutante Ball. She knew he had a right to call it whatever he wanted, and to make the rules and decide who got invited, for he was paying the major part of the cost.

She headed down the stairs to see Amelia, whom she could not think of as a stepmother and who had said she felt that Eve was the younger sister she never had. Her father was away at Oak Hill and the younger children were already in bed.

She found Amelia in the parlor reading a book, which she put down at the sight of Eve.

"She patted the Queen Ann's chair that sat next to hers and Eve sat down.

"Problem?" Amelia asked.

"I invited both Rob and Steve to the ball, and both accepted," Eve said glumly.

"Most girls would envy you having two young men vying for you. Your father has also invited his business partner's sons. The whole idea of the ball is to introduce young ladies to eligible young men."

"How am I going to decide between them?" Eve fretted.

"You don't have to, dear. If you can't decide, neither one is the right man for you."

"Did you ever have to decide between two men, Amelia?"

"I wasn't as witty and charming as you," she said with a smile to Eve. "And I had no brother to introduce me to his friends.

"I met my husband when I went to an isolated place to teach and boarded with his parents. I saw him at breakfast, dinner and on weekends. I fell in love with him and he proposed. After he died, I never thought of marrying again until I met your father, but he was already married. I decided I would remain a widow. I had experienced marriage, and I had little Clarissa to love and care for."

"But how do you know which one to marry? And how do you know that you are in love and it is not a passing thing?"

"You just do," Amelia said. She sipped her tea, and poured a cup for Eve before continuing. "You have to feel comfortable with him, and trust that he will be faithful to you. You have to feel excited just to be with him, as if he is the most important person in the room and you can't wait to have him hold your hand and kiss you and take you in his arms. It's a wonderful feeling. It changes after you're married, but then a different kind of love develops."

Eve went back up to her room, propped herself up in bed, and settled in to read four months' worth of letters from her suitors. She had written them almost identical letters each week, for her news and thoughts were the same, and it was interesting to see how they responded.

Rob wrote every Sunday evening, and described his daily routine. In the second letter he announced that he would only be writing about school if there was something unusual to report. He ended with "Thinking of you. Yours truly, Rob."

In one of her letters she told him about Martha's running away and about her father and Uncle Jamie trying to bring her home.

"I haven't thought about her since my foolishness at Christmas," he responded. "You have forgiven me for that, haven't you?"

"I have forgiven you. I told you at mama's funeral. Remember?" Eve wrote.

Rob's last letter was an acceptance to the debutante ball. He concluded, "in return, please attend my graduation. I'm looking forward to seeing you on both occasions. Yours, Rob."

Eve tied the bundle of letters together and scanned those from Steve Merrill.

He wrote a great deal about his classes and the grades he was receiving. "Good enough, I think, to earn me a place at med school."

He wrote that he was glad she was at Sweet Briar as he could see her next year if he was accepted at the University of Virginia medical school.

Steve's letter accepting the debutante ball invitation was as effusive as his other letters, and as romantic: "I look forward with the greatest anticipation to holding you in my arms and dancing with you. I know that you and I will each be dancing with others, as that is the point of such an occasion, but my thoughts will be only on you. Faithfully yours, Steve."

Eve put both packets of letters into her desk, and tried to sleep, but her thoughts were on the debutante ball. Would she have some sign or some feeling that would tell her which of these young men was meant to be her husband? Or would she meet someone else entirely? "Wear white kid gloves and pearls around your neck," she murmured to herself, "and be glad you don't have to choose either one tonight."

The next night Eve was dressed in white with long kid gloves, ready for the ball. Amelia fastened the pearl necklace about Eve's neck. "You look lovely, my dear. You will have more than two men falling in love with you."

"I'll try to stay calm and not accept any proposals tonight," Eve said with a grin.

Amelia was dressed for the event in a blue beaded gown appropriate for a married woman.

"Are you ready? Now, let's be going," Fortune called up. He had left the older car at Oak Hill, and had bought a much larger, roomier car that easily accommodated the four of them with space to spare.

Eve's evening was made, as young men lined up to sign her card. The first dance was with her father and then Rob stepped forward to claim her. "I am also honored to have the last dance with you," he said.

When the dance began, Rob pulled her into his arms and murmured, "You look lovely, Eve, and you smell lovely too."

"That's the most romantic thing you've ever said to me, Rob."

"You're a good dancer, and you feel just right in my arms."

"You're a good dancer too. I wish I could dance all the numbers with you."

"I took dancing lessons, just in case the uniform didn't do the trick with women, so now I have two advantages over some of your suitors."

He held her in the regulation dancing school position, one hand firmly on her back, the other clasping her hand in his, though perhaps a bit closer than an instructor would have approved. He guided her expertly through intricate steps of the waltz, and Eve felt the way she thought Cinderella must have felt, dancing with the prince.

Her next partner was Steve Merrill. After a moment of awkwardness, he began dancing with determination. "I couldn't help noticing the way you danced with that guy Rob," he said. "I've been busy studying for my final exams, but last weekend my mother had me roll back the rug and practice dancing so I wouldn't look a complete fool."

"She's a good teacher to have taught you so well in one weekend," Eve said, trying to ease his nervousness.

Steve pressed on. "Not only is he a good dancer, but he's got the uniform. Women go for a man in uniform, don't they?"

Eve laughed. "Some, yes. But I'm more interested in someone's character and personality."

"Good. Then maybe I stand a chance with you. I must tell you that I've fallen in love with you, but it will be years before I can support a wife."

Eve realized that he had guided them to the edge of the dance floor and stopped dancing. She was so shocked she hadn't noticed. "I don't want to marry for years," she said. "I want to finish college and meet a lot of people, and travel, and have a job, before I settle down with a husband and children."

"Then we will both be ready at about the same time," he said. "Will you attend my graduation?"

"Of course, I'll be there. You and Simon are both graduating that day—assuming you both pass all your exams."

"Yes, I know you'll be there. I mean, will you pretend that you are my girlfriend? You'll be the prettiest girl there."

Eve nodded. "What will your mother say? Maybe she's already picked out some girl for you."

He shook his head and said, "I don't think so. Not yet, anyway. Not until after medical school. Say, let's finish this dance, shall we?"

After that, there was a bevy of young men she hadn't met. She flirted with them but promised nothing.

Halfway through the evening, Rob came back and took her in his arms. "Eve, all of the young men in the ballroom are vying to dance with you or talk with you. Have you had a lot of proposals?"

He made it sound lighthearted, like a joke, but Eve sensed a serious undertone to his question. "Only one," she said. "All the others complemented and flattered me, with a variety of motives, to call on me."

He said to her, "You're my girl and we are going to be married someday. I love you, just as you knew at thirteen I would. You're the only girl I ever said that to."

Rob was expressing words she'd never heard him say, and had in fact wondered if he ever would say them. "So, are you really asking me to marry you, Rob?"

"Yes, will you?" Rob said.

"Yes, Rob. Just not yet. I need to finish college and Papa has promised Sarah and me a trip to Europe."

"Even if you didn't have plans, we'd have to wait for several years, until I get a promotion so that I could support a wife. Let's go out for a breath of cool air." He took her hand and lead her outside.

She wanted Rob to kiss her, and was delighted when he did. It was as wonderful as she had imagined it would be for five years. It was a long kiss that left her almost dizzy. "We'd better get back," she said, and they walked in silently, touching each other's arm as they headed back to the dance.

As they finished the dance, Rob said, "Cancel the rest of your dances. Pretend you have a headache or something."

"I can't do that. My father has spent a lot of money on this, and the young men who sign up for dances deserve their chance. You had my first and you will have my last, and you somehow got this extra one that we just finished."

"Oh, all right," he said grudgingly. "I only want to dance with you, but if I must keep on dancing with others, I will, if you insist. I leave for VMI tomorrow morning. Will you attend my graduation? I want you to see me have my lieutenants' bars pinned on. I want you to be proud of me."

She said, "I am proud of you and I always will be."

The next morning Eve sought out her stepmother. "Did the debutante ball help you make a decision about your dilemma?"

"No, it just made it worse! Steve talked about how he couldn't support a wife until after four years of medical school and Rob proposed!"

"Did you accept Rob's proposal?"

"Yes. He said he loves me, and I know that I love him. How can I let Steve down easily and two others who asked if they could come to call? Not only that, both Steve and Rob both invited me to their graduation ceremonies. What shall I do?"

"Well, if you accepted both invitations you will have to go. And I wouldn't worry too much about the other two potential callers. People sometimes make vague mentions of visiting when they don't mean to. That said, don't be alone with any of them where you might be put in a compromising position. In four years, you may change your mind about all of them. Now go thank your father for the party."

Chapter 62

Once again, Fortune's life seemed to be running smoothly. There had been no more trolley boycotts, no mine explosions or accidents, and no worker strikes, although they were happening in other states. The cigarette business was still profitable, although his cigarette rival Buck Duke had also gotten cigarette rolling machines, and the resulting competition had cut into the profit.

Pete was proving a good choice to manage Oak Hill. He was good at math and at managing money, which seemed to run in the family. He was supervising several sets of workers at once, as the racetrack was taking shape and a bigger stable and a greenhouse were built. Mildred had decided to continue her nursing career and had gotten a job at the medical school in Charlottesville.

On a personal level, he was happy with Amelia. He loved her body and soul, especially treasuring the time they spent together at Oak Hill. When she had told him that she was expecting his child, it was all he could do not to whoop in delight.

Simon had been accepted at the medical College of Virginia, his first choice so he could be with Sarah frequently. Fortune suspected the two were would marry long before Simon had qualified as a doctor, but he would help the couple with finances, and Sarah would make him a good wife. Eve would be back at Sweet Briar college, albeit frustrated by her academic requirements.

"Papa, why do I have to study such useless domestic subjects? I want to study something useful that will help me in business."

"You have opportunities that I never had. I'll always be rough around the edges, but you can learn to be an elegant, well-educated lady."

Eve had studied the expected subjects for a young lady: needlework, flower arranging, decorating and this summer was studying Spanish while Rob was at military camp.

He added, "As my daughter, you will meet governors, members of Congress, musicians, writers, artists, and rich businessmen and you'll be able to hold your own."

Whether she married Rob or not, she was quickly becoming a well-educated young lady that any father could be proud of.

With his two oldest away, the rest of his family could move to Oak Hill. Daniel had always felt at home there, and soon Leticia and Clarissa would come to love it as well. Amelia, he now knew, could be happy anywhere.

Two of the Richmond houses were in Emma's name, and she had left them to the children in her will. Fortune sold them and set up separate accounts for each child, dividing the money equally. He put the furniture in storage, since Oak Hill had already been decorated. He offered the house that had been Amelia's to Simon, rent free, during his time in med school. "You can rent out some of the rooms to other students, if you wish," he told Simon.

"I'd only rent to Steve, but since his mother lives here in town, he'll probably live at home," Simon shrugged.

Fortune regularly had lunch at Rachel's Café, and invited Laura and her little boys to join them. Laura was also looking after Rachel's son Matthew, and planned to care for the baby Rachel and Zachary were expecting as well.

"What will we do without you?" Rachel asked when he went for lunch on the last day he was in Richmond before the final move. "It's ironic, Laura and I both left Oak Hill to come here and live with you, and now you're leaving us and going to Oak Hill." She laughed. "But don't count on us coming to Oak Hill to live with you. Not this time."

Fortune chuckled with her. "Do you miss working at the store?" he asked Laura.

She shook her head. "A bit, at first, but not anymore. I am devoted to Jonas and our children, I'm happy being a wife and mother, and I'm happy right here in Richmond."

As he set out for Oak Hill, Fortune reflected that of all his family, only Jamie was not prosperous and happy. True, his apple-growing and -processing business was turning a profit, while Jim had graduated from Virginia Polytechnic Institute and had quickly found a job as an agricultural extension agent in a nearby county.

Jamie was disappointed that Jim was not working alongside him, but he hadn't given up hope that his oldest son would come home to work with the apples after a few years. If not, then perhaps Eddie, now in high school, would become the family businessman. Jamie and Ruth grieved over Martha, not knowing if she were dead or alive. They had written her many letters, but received no replies.

The call came to Fortune one day in late summer as he worked at his Oak Hill office. There were no pressing business matters, so he had left the Richmond office in charge of his assistant. He answered the phone himself. "Fortune Barranger. How may I help you?"

"Are you the man that owns railroads?" The voice was unfamiliar, and definitely not Virginian.

"I own railroad lines in Virginia and have shares in other railroads," he said warily. "Is there a problem?"

"There is a young woman here, says she's your niece and that you'll be good for the cost of her ticket. She looks like she been in an accident . . ." the man paused before adding, "all beat half to death."

"Yes, I'll be responsible for her ticket to Richmond, Virginia. Put her in a private car, or at least in a private compartment, so she can get some rest and not be stared at.

If you can arrange this to my satisfaction, there'll be a good tip in it for you."

"Yes sir, I can see to it." He turned away from the phone for a moment, then was back. "The young lady said thank you. Least wise, I think that's what she said. She's crying and blubbering, and her mouth is swelled up really bad, and bleeding. I'll see that she gets taken care of." Fortune got the man's name, employee number, and station, as well as the number of the car that Martha would be on.

After he hung up, Fortune set drumming on his desk with clenched fists. He seethed with anger. It wasn't the railroad employee's fault, of course. It was that Bishop bastard. Fortune had no doubt Martha had not been in a bad accident, but had been beaten by Julian Bishop. At least she was alive, and with God's mercy and all the medical care he could arrange, she would pull through.

He pondered whether to tell Ruth and Jamie, or to wait until he had seen for himself how bad off Martha was, before they got to see their daughter. He had seen injured men at the mine, and sometimes the site of a maimed body was enough to make even a strong man pass out. Not yet, he decided, and instead called Simon.

"Son, I have an important favor. Martha has been beaten. She is on the train from New York. Can you meet her and help her? I don't know exactly what her condition is. You may have to help her off the train, and if you think she needs to be in a hospital, get her admitted. I'll be there as soon as I can."

"Maybe I should ask Dr. Tyler to go along."

"No, the fewer people who know about this and see her like this, the better. If you take her to a hospital, admit her as Martha Bishop, which she may be, but I doubt it. We don't want any publicity about this, much as I'd like to have that worthless boy sitting in prison."

"I'll do what I can, Papa."

After he hung up the phone, Fortune went to tell Amelia where he was going and why. "Just tell the children I had to go to Richmond."

Fortune consulted his watch and knew the railroad timetables from memory. Much as he hated driving, this was an occasion when it was necessary. With any luck, he could be in Richmond before the New York train arrived. He called Simon again to wait for him at the station unless Martha was in dire need of medical treatment, in which case to leave a message at the station about where he and Martha would be.

He had acquired driving experience, and felt confident behind the wheel, but he still resented the lost time that he might have used to good purpose on the train. He arrived at the station just as the train pulled in, and he saw Simon in the crowd. Steve Merrill was with him, and they carried a stretcher.

Few people paid any attention to the event or to Fortune himself.

While Fortune was relieved to see she had been provided private quarters, he was stunned by the sight of his niece. His son Simon less so, as he had seen numerous injured bodies before.

Martha lay curled in a fetal position, barefoot and in a torn dress. Both eyes were swollen almost shut, with dark bruises beneath them. Both cheeks were swollen and bruised, blood on her face from cuts in two places. The arm that lay atop her was swollen and discolored. She tried to stand, but Simon pressed her back gently, and Steve managed to get her onto the stretcher amid her moans of pain.

They waited until departing passengers had gone, and whistle had blown that the train was ready to move southward, then carried Martha gingerly down the steps.

414

Without waiting for his father's instruction Simon climbed into the larger car and said, "I'll drive, Papa; you've already driven enough for one day. Steve, can you drive my car and follow us?"

Fortune was pleased at how his son took charge. Before driving off, he lifted Martha's head enough to give her a sip of water. During the whole time, she had not spoken but she accepted that she was being treated well by people who cared for her. Tears seeped from her eyes and ran down the sides of her blood-stained face. Without consulting his father, Simon drove to Dr. Tyler's office, and he and Steve carried Martha inside on the borrowed stretcher.

After a quick startled look, Dr. Tyler asked, "Who is this, and what has happened to her?"

"My niece, and she's been beaten by her husband."

"Have you reported this to the police? Do you plan to press charges?"

At this question, Martha stirred, and shook her head no.

"She was living in New York," Fortune explained. "I don't think she wants to go back to testify. As much as I'd like to see the man punished, we won't be pressing charges."

"A pity," Dr. Tyler murmured, his fingers gently pressing Martha's swollen face, and then her arm. "The arm's broken. I can set it here, with help from Simon. A broken nose, I can't do anything about. Come in and I'll clean her up before I begin treatment."

She was taken to a curtained area. They heard several moans and some soft soothing sounds. Dr. Tyler administered ether, and he and Simon began work on the injured girl. While they were working, Fortune had Steve drive him to Hoffman's, where he bought a loose dress and some shoes, guessing at the size, and buying slightly larger than he thought she might wear. For things to wear before she made the trip to Oak Hill, he bought a robe and slippers.

415

Martha was brought out unconscious, with a plaster cast on her broken arm, and stitched-up areas on her face neck and chest. "I had to pick glass out of the skin on her broken arm," Dr. Tyler said. "That monster either hit her with something glass, or threw her against the glass in a window or door. She's lost a lot of blood.

"She also had bits of glass and other debris in the soles of her feet. I don't know how far she walked, but she must have been in shock. She will recover, but it will take time, and let's pray her wounds don't get infected. I cleaned them the best I could while she was under, and poured on the iodine. For now, just let her sleep, and give her water when she awakens to help get her system back in shape."

Fortune insisted on paying double the doctor's usual fee, and decided that Martha should stay for the night at Simon's house, while he went to a hotel.

"Papa, I'd like you to stay here, if you don't mind, so we can take turns watching her and sleeping. I have classes tomorrow, and I assume that you are planning to drive her back to Oak Hill."

Martha was moaning and occasionally attempting to lift her arm as if to ward off a blow.

The next morning, Fortune found Simon in the neat kitchen preparing breakfast. To his surprise, Martha set at the kitchen table, sipping a glass of tomato juice. Much of the swelling in her eyes had gone down, though her nose was still swollen, and her face was a mass of stitched up cuts.

Fortune set down, accepting a cup of coffee and a plate with buttered toast and a poached egg. A plate with the same food was in front of Martha, untouched. "Do you want to stay on here for a few days, or go home?" Fortune asked. "I'm surprised to see you up so early this morning. I suppose it's the resilience of youth."

"I want to go home and get in my own bed and hide," she said. "But I know my family will hate me. I've brought shame on them."

"You'll find parents can be very forgiving. They love you, no matter what. But they thought you might be dead, since you didn't write."

She put down her fork and looked up, startled. "But I did write, even when I didn't hear from them! Do they know that I'm here?"

"No. I wanted to see for myself what the situation was. We can talk on the way and you can decide if you want to hide out for another few days, or if you want to go straight home and face the music."

"Riding in the car may be hard on her," Simon interjected.

"We can go in my private car and we can talk as we travel."

"What about the motor car?" Simon asked. "Won't you need it at Oak Hill?"

"We'll put it on the train," Fortune said. "Flatbed train cars that carry logs and lumber can also carry motorcars."

Once they were comfortably on board and the train began to move, Fortune turned to his niece and said firmly, "All right, it's time you talked. I want to know the whole story."

"I don't feel like talking. I'm in pain, and I feel sick."

"Your father and I lost two days and the cost of a hotel to find you in New York. Right now, I'm losing a day's work as well as Dr. Tyler's fee, plus the money I paid the railroad agent to get you here. I don't like putting my time and money in a bad investment, and so far, you've been a bad investment."

"Stop it!" She recoiled. "I'm not an investment, I'm a person! Can't you see I'm plenty upset and ashamed?"

"And well you should be," he said sternly. "You didn't have even the grace to write your parents."

"I'm telling you, I did write and they never answered," she protested.

Fortune shook his head. "I can attest to at least one letter they wrote, because I mailed it myself from Richmond just in case the problem lay with the local post office." The meaning of what Martha said dawned on him and he relented somewhat. "I assume, then, that your man destroyed your letters to and from your parents, so you'd be isolated and dependent on him, essentially his prisoner. Is that what happened to your money as well?"

She nodded, and he saw that she was close to tears, so he proceeded cautiously and gently. "Was this the first time he beat you?"

She nodded again. "Well, he did take a hand to me when I accused him of taking my money. But that time he just hit me once, and later he apologized and said he'd give me back my money when he found a job and that we needed it to buy food."

"Why didn't you leave then?" Fortune asked, shaking his head.

"He said he was sorry he'd hit me, and that things would get better, and I believed him. They did for a while, but then..." her voice trailed off, as if she were recalling the incident.

"Eve tried to warn you about him."

"I know," she said miserably. "I thought she was just jealous, because Julian kept telling me how beautiful I was, and he had such good manners, and was from New York."

"Well, it can't be helped now. What brought on this beating, and why was it the one that made you leave?"

"He told me I had to go out and get a job as a waitress, and I told him I couldn't, because . . ." she hesitated, looked down, avoiding his eyes, and finally went on, "because I'm going to have a baby."

Fortune sighed deeply and passed his hand across his forehead. "That's worse than a broken arm," was all he could say.

"I thought he'd be pleased about it."

"Men are usually pleased to be fathers only if they have a means to support a child, and are married to the mother." Fortune was about to ask if Bishop had married her, but decided to let her talk without interruption.

"He hit me in the face, and in my belly. I threw up on my shoes which I was about to put on. He picked them up, went outside and threw them down the trash chute. I couldn't get past him, he hit me again and again, and the signet ring he had on cut into my face.

She had begun rocking slightly back and forth. "He threw me to the floor, and that's when he broke my arm. He began kicking me, and I could feel ribs breaking. Then he started kicking me in the belly and screaming at me. I curled into a ball the best I could, and tried to protect myself with my hands and I think he broke some of my fingers then." She extended her hands, and Fortune saw that several fingers were swollen and purple

"I thought he was going attack again, but then he stopped and left. I didn't know if I would die or if he was going to leave me there or if he might come back and kick me some more. I waited until I thought he was out on the street or had gone farther away, before I tried to get up.

"I knew my arm must be broken, because I couldn't use it. I inched my way over to the door, and pulled myself up with the other arm. It took me over an hour make my way to the station. If it happened here someone would have offered to help but in New York they either didn't notice me or ignored me.

She stopped talking and clutched at her belly, wincing with pain.

Fortune was silent. The anger he had felt toward her had fallen away completely. Yes, she had made a terrible choice of man and run off with him, but she had been punished enough. More than enough. After a few moments of silence, he asked, "What do you want to do?"

"I want to go away where nobody knows me and have the baby and put it up for adoption."

He replied, "That will take a little time to arrange. What about today? Shall I take you home?"

She shook her head. "Not until I look better and feel better."

Fortune noticed that beneath the cuts and bruises, her skin had turned pale, and she looked as if she might vomit at any moment. "Do you think you can make it to the bathroom?" He asked, but by the looks of her, he knew the answer was no. He grabbed a towel from the tiny lavatory, and handed it to her just in time she retched, but little came up.

"You don't want your parents to see you like this, and I don't want my children to see you. When we get to the Oak Hill station, I'll call Mildred and ask if she can take care of you overnight."

"I've been such a fool! I don't deserve your kindness, Uncle Fortune."

"No, no, I'm happy to help where I can. Did that scoundrel marry you?"

She said, "We got a license, but we had no ceremony."

"Well, that's the first bit of good news I've heard in this whole situation. That means we don't need to go through the New York courts to get a divorce, and he has no claims on you or on what you might inherit. I don't think he would dare come looking for you. If he does, I'll have him arrested and thrown into jail." *Or something even worse,* he thought darkly.

"I don't want to ever see him again and I don't want to bring up his baby as It might look like him."

When they arrived at the station he decided not to call from there, there might be curious listeners, always eager for news of his family. He took a blanket from the sleeping car, bundled her into the motor car and drove to Pete and Mildred's house. When Mildred saw Martha, she gasped with shock at what had happened, but she managed a kind smile.

"She doesn't want to face her parents until tomorrow," Fortune said.

"Of course she can stay here," Mildred said, guiding Martha inside. "I will take care of things; just leave it to me".

The next morning, when Fortune went back to Pete and Mildred's house, she met him at the door. "We have one less problem to worry about today. She lost the baby in the night.". She will begin to look and feel better a little bit each day."

"You're a good woman, Mildred. Pete is lucky to have you."

She smiled. "And you're a good man, Fortune. We are all lucky to have you."

Chapter 63

Eve and Rob exchanged long letters with each other. His were often filled with frustration at his duties at Fort Riley Kansas, while hers were family news and her college experiences. They addressed each other as "my dearest darling," and were always filled with loving expressions.

Eve wrote that Martha had returned from New York, and was working at a store in Danville while she decided what to do for the rest of her life. Rob wrote that being in the Army was just like VMI all over again, except that now he was one of those in charge, but his duties were light. "We have no war to fight right now, so we practice all the strategies and battle positions of what happened in the past. There are rumors that we may be sent to some island, like your Uncle Pete. I don't know we you need to settle matters in places outside the United States, but as they say, 'ours is not to question why.'"

She wrote back in French. "I will probably be able to use French when Sarah and I go to Europe next summer, but in years to come, I might find Spanish much more useful. When you and I are married, you may be sent to one of those places you mentioned, and I would have to use Spanish to buy food and probably read the local newspaper.

But before the month was out, her plans for Europe were dashed. "Papa and Amelia are going to have a baby! The timing is almost unseemly, but Papa is acting as proud about this as if he had won a prize or been invited to the White House. I am learning more and more that what other people do can change my life no matter what I do."

She wrote, "When the French professor comes around to look at our work, he puts his hand on my shoulder. I don't need or want him to give me good grades, I want to earn them. I am intelligent, and I spend my free time studying. Fortunately, for Spanish I have a pleasant middle-aged woman from Cuba, who does not touch me or any of the other students. She just teaches."

Rob wrote back that when he got leave, he would come to college and attend her classes, if he were allowed to, making it clear that she was engaged and "not to be trifled with. I'll show that prof. that you belong to me."

Soon she wrote, "Aunt Mildred and Uncle Pete—or JP, as she calls him—are also expecting a baby. What is going on in my family?"

Rob wrote that he was being promoted to first lieutenant and would have leave in early December. "I will not, alas, be with you for Christmas, my darling."

She did not add that she was still receiving letters from Steve Merrill. He had just written that he would like to see her during the Christmas holidays.

Rob had promised that after spending a few days with his parents, he would take the train to Oak Hill and borrow one of her father's cars to drive down to Sweet Briar. Eve hoped against hope that he might arrive that evening, but knew the sensible thing was to drive down early the next morning, gather her luggage, and drive back home. But romantics are often not sensible.

Eve could hardly eat or sleep the night before his arrival, and when she saw him from the window of her French class, without waiting for permission, she leapt from her seat and ran outside. She knew that students and professors alike would be watching from the windows, but she didn't care. She and Rob ran toward each other and embraced with unashamed passion.

He looked down at her and said, "You need to go back in and finish your class." She told him it was almost over, letting him lead her back inside. They entered and the Professor said, "Miss Barranger, introduce us to this amorous young man?"

Eve did, concluding with the words "my fiancé."

"We French of all people understand romance and it is far more interesting than conjugation of verbs," he said. "Class dismissed!"

Days followed in almost delirious happiness. To Eve, every moment was precious, a memory to be stored up for when he was once more away from her. Oblivious to the cold, they kissed as they sat in the viewing stands of the race course, watching grooms walk horses around the track. They kissed in the steamy warmth of the greenhouse where he plucked a gardenia from a row of glossy plants. They kissed in the chapel Fortune had just had built, imagining themselves standing before the altar to be wed. And that night they kissed sitting by the fire, her head on his shoulder and his arm protectively around her as they discussed their futures.

"I may be sent to the Mexican border, down by the Rio Grande. Outlaws keep coming across, robbing ranches, and stealing horses and shooting their owners. Or maybe I'll go to Panama."

"What will you do there?" Eve asked drowsily, not really caring what words he used, only reveling in the sound of his voice.

"Panama is a new country and we own part of it. We're building a canal there, going from one ocean to the other. We need to make sure nobody kills the workers or blows up the canal."

"That sounds dangerous," Eve said sitting up suddenly.

"My darling, it will mean a lot of standing around on guard, or possibly sitting in an office."

It was almost a relief when Eve stood by the train that was taking him away. She had so longed to give in and make love to him, but remembering what had happened to Martha stopped her. She was safe from temptation until he returned on leave or she visited him.

Looking over the financial records of the cigarette factory, Fortune noticed that sales were down. This was puzzling, for the cigarette factory had always been his most consistent income producer. Once people started smoking Barranger cigarettes, they were usually customers for life. He was too well known to go around asking people why they didn't buy Barrangers, and besides, he was enjoying spending time with Amelia and the children. What he needed was a spy.

He sent for his nephew Jim. He knew that ever since he had rescued Martha, his brother's family felt beholden to him, and he was not shy about getting some payback. He had looked after the whole family in one way or another, for years, and never asked for anything in return. Now he would.

When Jim arrived, Fortune told him, "I want you to go to a tobacco store where nobody knows who you are, and browse the cigarettes. In the end I want you to buy a pack of Barrangers, but beforehand, look at other brands, and ask the shopkeeper what he recommends. Then offer cigarettes from your pack to people riding the trolley or waiting to be served in a restaurant. Ask them how they like the cigarettes and then come back and tell me. I will pay you well."

"I'm on Christmas leave, uncle. I'll do it as a favor to you."

Jim was back in two hours. "I didn't need to go to a café to get my answers. A ride on the trolley was all it took. The men who accepted my offered cigarettes took a few puffs, and then threw it to the floor of the trolley and ground it out with exclamations of how bad it tasted. Two others offered me their cigarettes—Buck Duke's brand—and said they had switched from yours because they weren't as good as they used to be.

"So, I went to your factory and examined the tobacco that has been bought so far this season. It's trash, Uncle

Fortune." He paused, as if uncertain about what he would say next. Then he stood as straight as he could and looked at his uncle. "I stopped production."

Fortune drew in a deep breath, aware of the enormity of what had happened to his business. "You did the right thing. Let's go see if we can track down who sold that tobacco"

As Jim drove, Fortune talked, detailing all he planned to do. He scribbled as much as he could as he rode, balancing his notebook on his knee and holding on to the car with the other hand.

They stopped first at the cigarette factory, where workers stood about idly, wondering what to do.

He motioned for the factory manager to accompany him to the tobacco storage area. With Jim at his side, Fortune had the manager tear into hogshead after hogshead of tobacco. With the exception of a few bright leaves atop the pile, all the rest was inferior. He straightened from his examination and faced the manager. "Couldn't you tell that this tobacco is not what we had been using all these years?"

"Yes – yes," the manager stuttered. "But I thought maybe you were trying to save money, and it's not my job to question. I just keep the machinery going and the workers working. You're going to be spending a lot of time fixing this matter.

"Do you have shops and businesses that order from us?" The man nodded. "Of course."

"I want to know which farmers sold us this tobacco. The warehouse name and a code number are on a card attached to the burlap cover." He pointed at it.

"Good. Jim, take the tags off the first five hogsheads you can lay your hands on. How many warehouses are we dealing with?" He asked, turning again to the manager.

"Charlottesville, Lynchburg, and Danville." He pointed to the tags and identified a warehouse in each of the cities.

"Only one batch from Charlottesville. Most from Danville, Lynchburg second. Used to be we got tobacco from all over the southern part of Virginia, but Mr. Wright said it was easier to deal with the ones close by.

"Is Mr. Wright the only buyer we have now?"

"Yes sir. You hired him less than a year ago."

Back at the city, Fortune went immediately to the bank, and put in writing that no further funds were to be issued to Mr. Billy Wright under any circumstances. At the main office, he called the warehouses in Lynchburg and Danville to tell them that they were not to deal with Mr. Billy Wright any further.

He cut the list of cigarette buyers in two and sent Jim to one location and his office manager to another, with identical telegrams to be sent to every buyer on the list, stating that they should return any Barrangers they had in stock and that the price they had paid would be refunded within thirty days of receipt of the unsold cigarettes, in their packaging.

Fortune himself composed a public statement. There was no avoiding that grave situation. It was more than a matter of money; it was his good name. Once a person or business has been besmirched it would take years to build back trust. After he had cleared up the situation, he would have to make special offers and even give out free cigarettes just as he had done in the beginning to win back customers.

When Jim came in, he asked, "What's next? And what do we tell the factory workers?"

"Call the factory and have the manager tell the workers to show up tomorrow as usual. I gather from the records that we were only running one shift now." He sighed. "I should have paid more attention to the cigarette factory instead of the upcoming Jamestown Festival. This might even affect what I do or am asked to do at the festival. Tell the manager that we will pay all the workers their usual

427

wages until further notice. At least until the end of the year, when we will assign them different tasks."

"What else?" Jim asked.

"Now you can resign your job as extension agent and come to work for me. I've seen that you are a good worker and astute observer, as well as smart and efficient. You're the kind of man I can depend on."

"I accept, Uncle Fortune, sir. I've always wanted to work in your business, to work my way up, possibly becoming your second in command. But I thought it would go to one of your children."

Fortune shook his head. "It's pretty obvious that Simon is going to be a doctor, and Eve, while she has as good a head for business as you do, will become the wife of a military officer – and fairly soon I suspect. I thought your father would turn the apple business over to you."

"He thought so too, "Jim said, "but apples are just . . . apples. You have enough different enterprises that make your business very interesting. What are you going to do about the office manager and the factory manager?"

"Give them a good talking to, and then it will be your job to keep an eye on them." Jim laughed at this.

Fortune said, "You've put in a long day. Do you feel like driving up to Oak Hill after we've had something to eat?"

"Yes sir. And from now on, I should probably refer to you as Mr. Barranger instead of Uncle Fortune. And I'd like to be referred to as Randel, my middle name, instead of Jim. Don't you think Randel Barranger has a good ring to it?"

Fortune agreed. "Tomorrow we're going to some tobacco warehouses in Danville to have a look at the books, and then I want to find out just how much Billy Wright was paying the farmers. Fortunately, the tobacco markets are still open into January, with just a few days off for

Christmas. I hope I can press family members into being tobacco buyers for the short term.

"I still know how to tell bright leaf from trash, and I'm sure you and your father and Pete do also. Eddie can drive Pete. With all of us buying, we should be able to get enough to produce at least a few cigarettes in the new year. Tomorrow, I'll send Pete to the bank to pick up enough money to cover what we buy."

"What will you do about Billy Wright?"

"Fire him, of course. With no notice, no recommendation, and no severance pay. He's made enough from me. If he argues with those terms, I'll have him charged with fraud. By that time, I'll have the records to prove it."

Jim, now Randel, asked, "Are we going to look for him tomorrow?"

"No, I think he will come looking for me. And I think I'm actually looking forward to that meeting. I don't like being cheated, and I never cheated him."

Chapter 64

By closing time the following day, Fortune had determined that for every fifty dollars paid to farmers, Billy Wright had charged Barranger Industries one hundred dollars. He had talked to the banker at Farmers Bank who had been his friend for years early that morning and had gotten access to Wright's account. Perhaps it wasn't legal, but neither was the way Wright had earned the money. The banker agreed that would be no withdrawals from that account for the next forty-eight hours, to give Fortune time to see the deposit record for himself.

Assured of that, he wanted his team to buy enough high-quality bright leaf at the tobacco auction to keep the factory running for a week. They were armed with cash and instructions to bid as high as necessary to get the best bright leaf on the floor in each warehouse, with delivery for January 1.

Fortune had just returned from the bank, armed with pages in his notebook that listed dates and amounts of deposits into Billy Wright's account, when Wright himself came in, his face red with anger.

"Have a seat," Fortune said, gesturing toward a chair.

Wright remained standing. "You've told all the warehouses I'm not buying for you. Are you firing me?"

"Yes, before you can do any more damage. Immediately, and with no recommendation or severance pay."

"Then you'd damn well let me have my own money. The bank stopped me from taking any out today. You have no right to do that. I'll sue you."

"Most of it is my money," Fortune said, "money that you stole from me. A subpoena is on the way to the bank even as we speak, giving the bank manager permission to put a hold on that account."

"You can't prove that I stole it!"

"Actually, I think I can. My new vice president of Barranger Enterprises, my nephew Randel, and I spent a busy two days tracking the money the farmers received for that tobacco. Of course, warehouses were involved too; in addition to the usual fee you paid them a five percent bonus if they cooperated but you threatened to stop buying at their warehouse if they didn't play along." The fraud had gone beyond Wright, of course; it had to. "We interviewed several farmers who are willing to testify against you, if it comes to that."

"Those sniffling wretches! They were happy to get anything for that tobacco." Wright's nostrils flared as he breathed deeply. "So, what are you going to do?"

"First, I'd like to know why you did this. Didn't I pay you a fair wage? Better than most other places?"

"You have so much. Why shouldn't I have some of it?"

"You have to earn it."

Wright half rose from his chair. "You're a greedy, tightfisted old son of a bitch. I suppose I should've been grateful that you gave a job to someone who wasn't related to you?"

"I treat people with honesty and fairness, and I expect honesty and fairness in return. I give extra rewards to those who work hardest." Fortune wasn't going to address the charge of nepotism. After all, what was wrong with keeping wealth in the family?

"What I took was just a drop in the bucket," Wright said sulkily.

"On the contrary. I have done a quick tally, and you stole more than what I invested in my first business twenty-six years ago."

"But I didn't hurt anybody!"

"You hurt the company. We lost many customers because the tobacco quality dropped so much. Barranger cigarettes might never recover the good reputation we'd had in the market, and that might put other peoples' jobs at risk. All because of your greedy behavior." Fortune felt himself growing agitated and took several deep breaths before addressing Wright again.

"At first, I thought of letting you keep a portion of the money you stole from me, since I should have been more alert and noticed what was going on sooner. However, you have shown no contrition and have not even said you were sorry, so I'm keeping the total amount you embezzled."

Wright leapt from his chair. "You can't do this!"

"If you're thinking of attacking me, there is a policeman standing just outside the door. I have arranged for an arrest warrant if necessary. In addition, if you are thinking of taking some kind of revenge on me or my family in the future, the arrest warrant is undated and can be filled in at any time."

Wright slumped back into his chair, defeated. After several moments, he arose and walked to the door. There, he paused and turned back. "What are you going to do about the warehouse managers?"

"We were easily able to determine which warehouses in each city had been in on the scheme with you, and I personally notified them that we will not send our buyers there anymore. They will lose far more in the future than they made in the past.

"A bit of advice, Mr. Wright: the hardest path can become much easier if you just keep walking it. You're a strong young man and I can probably find you a job on the railroad lines shoveling coal into the engine boilers. It is hard labor, but it's honest labor and the pay is fair. Of course, you won't handle money so here would be no temptation to steal, and it might give you time to think."

Fortune wondered if Billy Wright would admit to himself that he had been wrong and change his ways. He was obviously intelligent, to have planned and carried out his theft for so long. With a better attitude, he could have made his way up in Barranger Enterprises, and if he admitted the errors of his ways, Fortune thought he might still make a good employee, especially one shoveling coal.

Fortune decided to have an early lunch at Rachel's Café, then arrange for the trash tobacco to be destroyed. He suddenly realized that getting rid of something might be as difficult as acquiring it in the first place. He walked onto the factory floor and announced that anyone who wanted the poor tobacco could have a wagon load if they brought a wagon the next morning along with a pitchfork for loading, or even that afternoon if they could arrange for transport on short notice.

The workers looked at how much tobacco could be taken away. "What would I do with a wagonload of tobacco?" one of them asked.

"Spread it on your fields," Fortune said. "Tobacco sucks lots of nutrients out of the land so this is a way of putting it back. If you don't have fields, put it on your garden plot and you can save some to burn next summer when mosquitoes come. You can give it to your friends for rolling their own cigarettes or take it to some warehouse to sell if you can find some sucker who wants it. Regardless, I don't want my name attached to it."

"The tobacco that is left will be burned. There is a suitable area between here and the woods. Fortunately, it's been a wet month, so the fire is not likely to spread. All the same, I'd like half of you to go out and scrape back any fallen leaves, and make a dirt berm around the fire area. When you finish, you can have the rest of the day off. I've had tools sent over—rakes, hoes and an axe or two." As the outside team of workers went out, the others looked to Fortune for instructions.

433

"Your job is to sort the bright leaf from the trash tobacco and to put aside those good bundles. Look for lemon yellow leaves in the bundles. If there's only one good leaf in a bundle of twenty or so, pull it out. Is that clear? Put the good tobacco to your right."

By noon the next day, they were ready to take the remaining tobacco out and start the burning. It was a day without wind to whip the flames or rain to put them out and stop the burning. As each batch of tobacco was tossed into the fire, flames crackled and shot straight up into the still air, then died as the tobacco was consumed. When the burning was all over, only pale ashes remained. The smoke hung around the ground in a fragrant blue haze. Fortune reflected that even poor tobacco smelled good when it was being cured or burned.

On the following day, as Fortune had calculated, cartons of the returned cigarettes began to arrive. Before any cartons were cut open, he selected two workers to stay and sent the others home for the day. As they were leaving, he announced, "Anyone who takes any of these cigarettes will be fired. I don't want a single cigarette existing made of this inferior tobacco with my name on it."

To the two remaining, he said, "If this burning can be done efficiently and honestly, you will have a bigger bonus. It's cold outside today. We are going to take the boxes to the burn area. Smith, take this knife and cut this carton open and hand me the invoice inside. Richardson, count the packs of cigarettes and give me the number, then take the packs of cigarettes from the carton and throw them onto the fire. We'll repeat this until all the cigarettes have been burned, and I'll be with you the whole time." Fortune had lived by the adage, if you want a job done well, do it yourself. It had served him throughout his working life.

In the days leading up to Christmas while the Virginia warehouses were open, he acquired enough bright leaf to keep the factory running for the next six months. Fortune felt confident that in the first few weeks of January they could acquire the remainder he needed.

This business was the first setback he had had since the flood that had killed his father-in-law and had almost taken his own life. Since the cigarette factory and the coal mine would be closed between Christmas and New Years and the work would slack off in preparation for the Jamestown Exposition, he would have time to go over all the records with Jim during the holiday. *Randel*, he corrected himself. How long would it take to get used to calling his nephew Randel? Together they would make sure no other problems were overlooked as this one had been.

Yes, he thought, *the next year will be much better.*

Chapter 65

Fortune surveyed the dining room table on Christmas Day, reflecting on how different each Christmas was from another. The traditions remained the same: finding and decorating the perfect tree, the special foods his family enjoyed that might seem unappealing to others, and attending church on Christmas Eve. The church service this year had been held in the little chapel he'd had built at the edge of his plantation, replacing the ramshackle one where Pete had been married twice and their parents and Clara had been buried.

The people who were seated around the table had changed as well. Last year Emma had sat at the foot where Amelia now sat, and he was sure that he wasn't the only one to recall Emma's last holiday with the family. Rob had been sent for duty in Panama, leaving Eve forlorn. Simon had stayed in Richmond working at the hospital partly to be with Sarah, and had only arrived on the train late the night before. He knew he was wanted and expected at the family table, but his thoughts were elsewhere. He had already called Sarah this morning.

Despite being pregnant, Mildred was still working part-time at the hospital in Charlottesville and was too tired to come for dinner. Simon and Eve volunteered to take dinner to her and Pete after everyone else had eaten.

The biggest surprise was Martha's arrival. She had taken the train and walked to Oak Hill just as her parents and brothers arrived at the mansion.

Ruth was the first to react. She enfolded her daughter in a hug, and tears sprang to her eyes. "Baby, I didn't know you were coming. You didn't say you were. But I'm so glad you did." There were hugs as the family was ushered into the vast dining room. Even Eve hugged her cousin. A place was set at the able for Martha, and everyone sat down. No one mentioned Martha's still very vivid scars.

As a fruitcake fragrant with bourbon was brought in, Simon asked "What have you been doing, Martha?"

There was silence at the table. Then she said, "I'm studying to be a beautician. I'm not pretty anymore, but I'm learning how to make other people pretty."

She exchanged a quick glance at Fortune, which only he noticed. He had known about her studies as he was paying for them.

Neither Laura nor Rachel had come for Christmas. Both Hoffman's department store and Rachel's Café were open on Christmas Eve. With small children they did not come at Christmas, but would come in the summer when the children could play outside, splash in the shallow end of the pool that Fortune had installed and even ride horseback, seated in front of an adult rider.

After the meal was over, Simon and Eve took food to Mildred and Pete, while Martha and Ruth helped clear the table and Amelia set up a game of Chinese checkers to play with the two youngest children. Eddie went with Daniel out to the back porch to see about Brandy, who was frail and sick. She raised her head enough to lick their hands, and her tail moved slightly in greeting.

"She's going to die, isn't she?" Daniel asked, though he knew the answer.

Eddie nodded. "I'll help you move her inside by the fireplace, where she always liked to be, now that dinner is over," he offered.

"Thank you, "Daniel whispered." Tears slid down his face unchecked. He wiped them away with the back of his hand and then bent to pick up his end of the box that formed Brandy's bed. "I'm too grown-up to cry," he sobbed. "But I love her. I've had her since I was five."

"I'd cry too if I lost a close friend," Eddie said. "She can hardly move; she will be better off when she is out of pain."

"She'll go to be with Grandma Lorena and Aunt Alicia. But she'll be leaving me and I will miss her so." The two boys spent the afternoon sitting on the floor by the fireplace with Brandy between them, gently petting her golden fur.

When Fortune, Jamie, and Randel came back from their walk around the estate, Randel announced, "I'll be over tomorrow to start going over the records, Uncle Fortune."

"And I will be over to help with Brandy," Eddie told Daniel.

Daniel sat by Brandy's box until he fell asleep. Amelia tiptoed in and covered him up where he lay. When he woke up the next morning, he reached to touch Brandy and screamed when he felt her stiff, cold body.

As good as his word, Eddie came over bringing an apple box to serve as a coffin, and helped Daniel bury his beloved dog. They fashioned a cross and carved Brandy's name on it. Eddie offered to help pay for a real tombstone later.

Fortune tried to console his grieving son. "When spring comes, we will get you another dog." And like everyone the world over who has lost a beloved pet, Daniel cried out, "I don't want another dog! I want Brandy back." Fortune let his son grieve, knowing that he would want another dog someday.

On the 27th, two guests arrived: Christina Bentley to be with Eve, and Steve Merrill to see Simon, although Eve suspected and dreaded that Steve might be coming mainly to see her. Fortune had given Mrs. Turner two days off, and the family ate leftovers, supplemented by other things that Eve cooked. Randel came over every day and he and Fortune sat in the office pouring over the records for four hours or more.

The first day at lunch, Eve noticed that Randel and Christina were smiling at each other, and he asked her questions about her home, her train journey, and her classes.

So much for foisting Steve off on Christina, Eve thought. Sure enough, after the men had gone back to work Christina confided to Eve, "Your cousin Randel is really handsome. Is he engaged to anyone?"

After dinner that night, Steve volunteered to help Eve clear the table and wash dishes.

"But you are a guest," she protested. "I like being around you," he said with a shrug and a grin. They worked well together and quickly finished the task. Then, as they walked toward the parlor, they passed under the chandelier from which hung greenery and ribbons.

Steve pulled Eve into his arms. "I'm going to pretend that's mistletoe up there, but I don't really need mistletoe as an excuse to kiss you."

He kissed her so passionately that Eve felt almost dizzy with excitement and responded to him. Then guilt washed over her. Steve could not help but take encouragement from her response. *If only Rob were here*, she thought, *I wouldn't have done that*. She must avoid Steve for the rest of his visit.

She was down early to prepare breakfast the next morning and had made the biscuits, cooked bacon and spooned applesauce into small bowls, when he came down.

He offered to help and she accepted as formally as she could, giving him bowls of applesauce to put on the table. He had finished when Christina came in, also offering to help. Eve worked better alone, but she decided that her guests wanted to feel useful, so she gave them tasks like putting out butter, jam, and honey while she waited for the right time to start the eggs.

Just than Randel came in. "I came over for some of cousin Eve's biscuits. She's a master bread maker. But that bacon and coffee smell wonderful, too. Turning to Christina, he asked, "Do you have a cooking specialty?" She blushed and shook her head. "We have a cook, but I plan to learn." The two began talking about favorite foods and memorable meals.

It was interesting, Eve thought, to see two people falling in love so obviously. Randel had never come over for breakfast before and at college, Christina had not been an early riser.

Had she and Rob ever looked like that when they were first falling in love? Of course, she couldn't remember a time when she hadn't been in love with him.

More members of the family trickled in for breakfast, and Eve was kept busy. After the meal, she pulled Simon aside and whispered, "Take Steve hunting, or riding, or just walking around the plantation. He's always around me, wanting to help."

"He loves you."

"But I love Rob. You know that."

"Well, I've heard that it never hurts to have more than one man in love with you, just in case."

"What do you mean, just in case? Has Rob said something to you that I don't know anything about? Are you keeping something from me?" She asked, her worry rising.

"No, of course not. But he's in the army. Things happen. He could be killed." Seeing the stricken look on Eve's face, Simon left to take Steve walking. As she went back to work, Eve told herself not to worry about something that might never happen.

That afternoon, when Fortune and his nephew stopped work, Randel stayed on, talking and sipping a glass of wine until Eve announced that supper was ready. Seeing that he was reluctant to leave, she asked, "Jim — oh, I mean Randel, would you like to stay and dine?"

"Don't mind if I do," he said, and joined the family at the table. As Randel was leaving, Eve asked if Martha would like to come over the next day and practice what she was studying.

The pair did not arrive until after breakfast. Randel, after smiling and greeting Christina, joined Fortune in the office. Martha had brought a cloth bag full of combs and curlers, bottles of setting lotion and little jars of cosmetics "I'm glad you asked me to come over," she said. "I was hoping you would."

"We studied all day yesterday," Eve said. "Today we just want to look like beautiful ladies." She lowered her voice. "And I've missed you." Martha smiled at this. "Me too."

She moistened Eve's and Christina's hair with setting lotion, then deftly swirled locks of hair into curls and secured them with hairpins. While they sat by the fireplace drying their hair, she lightly moistened Leticia and Clarissa's hair and formed long corkscrew curls around her finger. When the older girls' hair was dry, she piled their hair atop their heads in a queenly design, leaving curls on each side to frame their faces.

She added color to the lips and cheeks of the older girls, despite Eve's protest.

"Just a touch," Martha said. "I won't make you look like clowns." She darkened their eyebrows with a bit of charcoal and blended it with her fingertip.

The girls admired themselves, turning this way and that before the mirror. Eve admitted to herself that Martha's studies were more useful, and more likely to earn her a living, than the classics she herself was pursuing.

After lunch, Steve turned to Martha and said, "You're a lot better now than when I last saw you. I'd hardly have recognized you."

She flinched as he pushed aside her overhanging hair, exposing all her scars, and touched one of them. "Dr. Tyler did a good job considering the situation. Surgeons now can do more to improve the look of the scars. I am going to become a surgeon, you know." She pulled her hair down once more to cover part of her face.

"Oh, don't worry, I wouldn't operate myself. It will take me years to become skilled and qualified. I meant that I think we can find doctors at the medical school who would operate on you as part of a lesson for surgeons. When you have finished your study program, notify me and I will see about making the arrangements for your surgery." Martha looked embarrassed and muttered a quick "thank you."

When it was time for Christina to leave, Randel said he would take her to the station.

Simon was about to say the station was so close that she would not really need a ride, but Eve kicked him under the table just in time. Christina said, "Oh, thank you! You are so kind, Mr. Barranger."

When it was time for Steve's train, he asked Eve to go with him and she agreed. After all, it would be rude to refuse. When they heard the train approach, he embraced her and gave her one soft kiss. "You're going to make some man a marvelous wife, Eve Barranger. Just not me, I fear."

"No," she agreed. "And you are going to make some woman a marvelous husband, just not me." Moments later, she waved goodbye as his train left.

Chapter 66

On January 1, Eve thought, *Mama has been dead a year.* She was sure other members of the family were thinking the same thing, but no one mentioned it, though they went about their day quietly, lacking the usual holiday exuberance.

The closest Fortune came was when he gave his New Year's toast: "May this new year be better than the previous one."

Simon returned to medical school, and Daniel returned to military school. Back at Sweet Briar, Eve wrote Rob: "Steve Merrill came after Christmas to visit Simon. I thought Christina, my roommate, might be attracted to him, but she fell for my cousin Randel, who is now Pop's vice president."

She also received a letter, from Randel: "I have been too busy with business to write or visit, but I would like to take you and your roommate Christina out for dinner on Valentine's Day. Will the school permit it?"

When she read the letter to Christina, she added, "I'm fairly certain you're the one he really wants to take out on Valentine's Day."

Randel arrived with Valentine cards for both girls, and a big bouquet of red roses from the Oak Hill greenhouse. Over dinner, Eve let her thoughts wander, as Randel told Christina about his job and his travels to the various Barranger Enterprises. Christina responded with smiles and repetitions of "how wonderful" or "how interesting." The words mattered little; their voices said, "I love you."

Christina received several letters from Randel. Then in late March, one came that she read and turned to Eve and read it aloud: "I think I will succeed at this job and be able to support you. Will you marry me?" Christina clutched the letter to her bosom. "Will you be my bridesmaid, Eve?"

"Of course. Has he set a date for the wedding?"

"Don't be silly; that's up to me," Christina said with a grin. She read again from the letter. "Please be warned that I will be traveling often but I will be with you as much as I can."

Eve envied Christina. If only she could see Rob as often as Christina and Randel would see each other.

Fortune and Randel visited the sites of all the Barranger Enterprises so that Randel would be familiar with each and that he would be introduced as the person in charge. "The trolley lines aren't as profitable as they used to be," Randel reported.

"Is someone cheating me?"

"No. People are buying motorcars. In our family alone, you have one, I have one, uncle Pete has one and my father has a pickup truck."

"Yes, but we have money. Most people can't afford a motor car. And some people prefer horses and carriages."

"True, but surely you've noticed more and more cars on the streets when you visit Richmond. Also, autos can go anywhere there is a road, but trolleys are limited to where the tracks have been laid. Soon, I think we'll have a fleet of autos that can go all over the city and people will ride those instead of the trolley limited to its tracks. In fact, you might consider selling off your trolley lines if you get a good offer."

"I'll think about it." Fortune was impressed by his nephew's long-term thinking.

Despite Randel's fondness for automobiles, they took the train to the coal mine. "The weather can be bad in March," Fortune said, "and roads in the mountains are poor. Besides, gasoline stations and repair garages are few and far between." Randel conceded, though he pointed out that those things would increase in number as more people drove autos, and fewer rode trains.

"I'm not selling my railroads," Fortune said. "We may lose riders, but railroads will always be the most economical way to haul coal."

When they arrived, Randel looked about the mine town. "It's different," he said. "The hospital and school look good."

"Yes, but it's difficult to get doctors and teachers to come here."

"I haven't been here since the year Simon, Rob and I came and distributed your gifts. Are you still doing that?"

"No, I set up a store that is run by Mr. and Mrs. Barns. "He is an injured man who lost his arm and can't work anymore. People like to deal with the man, but Mrs. Barnes is the brains behind the operation. At Christmas I give every woman here a voucher good only at the store, so their menfolk can't buy liquor. And I have a spy who lets me know if the store's prices get too high."

"Some of the houses are shabby," Randel said bluntly. "I'm selling them. The shabby ones are still rental. People don't take care of something unless it belongs to them, and it takes me as much money and effort to keep up a few houses as it does for an entire factory."

Fortune introduced Randel all around, and the two boarded the train again. As the train began to move, Fortune looked back. "I've done what I can to help these people. I hope that by the time machinery begins to replace workers, these people will have enough education to make it somewhere else."

The cigarette factory was running full speed. New cigarettes were sent to the buyers to replace the poor ones. Fortune had placed ads in newspapers and magazines touting the return to the original high quality of Barranger cigarettes, and had seen to it that articles appeared in leading publications detailing what he had done to ensure top quality, without mentioning the corrupt tobacco buyer.

A free cigarette was offered at tobacco shops for customers to try.

Their last stop was the site of the upcoming Jamestown exposition. As at the other sites, Randel was introduced, and both men talked to workers. Fortune was pleased with how the project was coming along. "It will be finished in plenty of time, and just as I planned it."

Randel looked around at the busy scene. "What's the point of this?" he asked. "Do you think this trolley loop will turn a profit? And the pavilion itself is a big outlay with no way of earning back its cost."

Fortune patted his nephew on the shoulder. "Not everything is meant for financial profit." After a satisfied glance around at the project, he started back toward the train, talking as he walked. "We're not descendants of the first families of Virginia, but pride in ancestry alone can't pay a mortgage. I started with nothing but my own intelligence and determination to get ahead. Now I'm one of the richest men in America, and the whole family is prosperous and respected.

"I want more than that; I want us to be considered one of the finest families in Virginia. So far, we are headed that way. Members of the House of Delegates and of the Senate, and heads of schools and hospitals have called at Oak Hill to ask me to be on various important boards. I have accepted a few of these positions and donated to those I did not accept. I recommended Jonas for the Chamber of Commerce; your father is now on several agricultural commissions; and Mildred is an honorary member of the state version of the Red Cross."

Randel asked, "Am I supposed to donate and serve on boards too?"

"Not right away. You're being paid a salary, and what you do with your money is your own business. You can save it, spend it, donate it or invest it. I think you know which one I prefer," he said with a smile.

On the train, Fortune said, "I'm glad to be heading home to be with Amelia when the baby comes. Would you be willing to drive us to Charlottesville?"

It was a good thing Randel agreed to drive. Only four hours after they arrived at Oak Hill it was time to take Amelia to the hospital. Early the next morning she gave birth to a son they named Gerald.

Just before noon, Mildred was also rushed to the hospital in labor. By evening she had delivered twin boys, and was wheeled into the same room as Amelia. She was in amazingly good health and good spirits, and the next morning announced that the boys were to be named Theodore and Thomas, Ted and Tom for short.

Newspapers splashed the news across their front pages: Three new Barranger sons in the same day. Accompanying the articles were photos of the four parents and their three offspring.

The births were reason enough not to chaperone Eve and Sarah to Europe, but Fortune still felt guilty. He asked Ruth and Jamie to go but they had no interest in leaving Virginia. He offered to hire one of the teachers at Sweet Briar as a chaperone, but the girls opposed that. Eve enrolled in summer school, so that she could graduate sooner, and thus marry Rob sooner. Sarah also enrolled in summer classes so she could become a nurse in two years and help pay Simon's medical school. Fortune counted on paying the full cost of his son's medical education, but at the same time, he thought it was good for the younger generation to take on responsibilities.

He thought women as well as men should have an education, and he wanted his daughters to stay in school as long as they could, until they earned their diplomas or degree. He included Sarah in this, as he was sure she'd become his daughter-in-law.

He had tried talking to Simon and Randel about waiting until they were at least 25 before marrying, but he could tell that his words fell on deaf ears. Eventually, Fortune realized that he and Jamie had very little reason to delay their sons' marriages. The brothers had married at younger ages and with far less education and prospects than their sons. Fortune wanted Simon to marry at Oak Hill, but the site was the bride's choice, so it would be at St. John's Church in Richmond.

Eve resumed her studies in languages and economics and added classes in education. Rob wrote how he missed the cool temperatures and colored leaves of Virginia in the autumn. Panama, he wrote, was hot and humid. He thought the education classes were a good idea. "Panama is American, after all, at least the canal zone. If you come here, you may be able to find a teaching job, although I know that in your heart you will always be a businesswoman."

She wrote back: "What do you mean 'if' I come to Panama? I miss you so much, I thought of taking a train to Texas and down across Mexico and Central America but that is a little frightening. It would be better to go to Norfolk and take a ship to Panama or, better still, if you could take a ship here.

"Christina talks constantly about wedding plans. They plan to marry at Christmas time, and I have promised to be her bridesmaid, so I'll go with her to Charlottesville.

"Another family wedding is afoot, although you probably know more about this than I do, as the bride is your sister. Simon, like most men, is not interested in wedding details, so I only know the most basic information."

448

Rob wrote back, "I shall pay attention to every detail of our wedding. Do you want an arch of swords? I'm sure your father will want the ceremony to be held at the church he has built at Oak Hill, and that is fine with me. He has made it convenient for guests to travel there, but I may invite so many of my fellow officers that the church won't hold them plus all of you Barrangers. I shall have a special gift for you at Christmas time, or when I next see you."

This letter in particular made her smile. However, as Christmas approached, Rob's letters ceased. "Are you ill with malaria?" she wrote, worried. "If you are, have someone write me on your behalf."

On December 26, she made herself smile on the arm of Christina's brother Archie. The Barrangers filled the groom's side of the church, though not every family member was there. Amelia and Mildred stayed home with their babies, while Jonas was the nanny to his own children and Rachel's. Zachary accompanied the sisters and took wedding photos.

At the reception, Eve danced with Christina's brothers and cousins, feeling disconnected from the festivities. She could hardly wait to get home to see if there was a letter from Rob. There was none.

A week later she still had not heard from Rob, as she joined the family for the trip to Richmond to Simon's wedding. She was again a bridesmaid, and this time she walked to the front of the church on the arm of Steve Merrill. As they walked Steve squeezed her hand tight against his side and looked at her with a wistful smile.

Afterward, as they marched to the back of the church, she saw Rob sitting in the back pew. She squeaked with delight, forgetting decorum as she threw herself into Rob's waiting arms. When they could talk privately, she demanded, "Why didn't you write to me? I sent a telegram, thinking you might have gotten malaria!"

"I was hoping to come to the wedding, but when my leave was granted, it was too late to write you, and I wasn't sure even then that I'd be here in time for the wedding. Your telegram must have arrived after I left Panama. Let's not dwell on it. Kiss me," he said sliding a ring on to Eve's finger. "This makes it official that we are going to get married, which you all along knew would happen someday. Would you prefer late May or July?"

"What's wrong with June?" she asked.

"We don't want to conflict with the Jamestown Exposition." Eve had forgotten all about it in the rush of excitement, but now she realized he was right.

The Exposition was Fortune's party. It opened on a hot day in early June 1907, with banners flying, a band playing, and crowds surging to see the attractions. The entire Barranger family was gathered at the Virginian pavilion, where dignitaries and regular citizens formed a semi-circle around the pavilion.

The Governor stepped forward placed his hand on Fortune's shoulder and began to speak. "Mr. Fortune Barranger is one of the foremost citizens of Virginia and even the entire United States. He was a poor boy from one of the poorest parts of the state. Armed only with his intelligence and will to work hard, he reached the pinnacle of American finance. If he had had an education, he might even have become a governor." He paused for laughter.

He went on: "His entire family is exceptional as well. Mr. James Barranger is the premier apple producer in Virginia and Mr. Joseph Barranger has served his country in the military, nearly losing his life in the process. Mrs. Laura Barranger Hoffman and Mrs. Rachel Barranger Todd have run successful businesses off their own before becoming mothers.

"Not only has Fortune Barranger become wealthy and given to his family, but he has benefitted the State of Virginia and her citizens. He has built hospitals, clinics, and schools. These portraits of early Virginians are on loan from his private collection and he commissioned and paid for these four murals depicting Jamestown that will become the basis of a fine arts museum here in Richmond so they can be enjoyed into perpetuity. Thank you, Mr. Barranger, for all that you are and all that you have done." The Governor turned to Fortune and applauded, and the rest of the crowd followed suit.

The Jamestown Exposition was Fortune's opportunity to be recognized and praised for his accomplishments. Eve's wedding was a day to show off his oldest daughter and Oak Hill.

The wedding had been postponed until late August to allow Eve to complete her summer school studies. The day opened clear and sunny and blessedly cooler than the week before.

Activities began soon after dawn. More than two hundred chairs were set up on the vast green lawn, and a trellis had been built and covered with roses. In the small guest house that had been Grandma Lorena's home, a glittering array of wedding gifts was locked away safely at night and guarded by day. Most of them would be left behind in storage, as Rob said they didn't suit a soldier's life in Panama. Private railcars arrived, and motor cars brought even more guests. Fortune had arranged for a harpist, flutist and a tenor soloist to provide music. Waiters and waitresses stood by in splendid costumes.

As Eve walked with Fortune toward the Rose decked trellis, he reflected, *this is how a wedding really should be.* He knew that photos and thousands of words about the day would appear in the nation's newspapers. He felt a pang of sadness at Eve's marrying, but she had been planning for this for years, and he had known that it would come. If not, her heart would have been broken.

Guests helped themselves at the buffet and took seats at white damask covered tables. Carvers stood ready at baked hams and huge beef roasts, and servers added to plates sautéed vegetables, sliced ripe tomatoes, fried oysters, and crusty hot rolls. On each buffet table stood a watermelon basket carved from a whole melon, and filled with balls of cantaloupe and honeydew, sliced peaches and pineapple the groom had brought from the tropics. Champagne was served and toasts spoken before the huge wedding cake was cut.

When the festivities were over, Eve had changed from her white silk wedding dress to a blue linen traveling costume. She and Rob walked hand-in-hand to the waiting private train car that would take them to Richmond and on to the Chamberlain Hotel for a brief honeymoon.

Watching them go, Fortune wished that he might hold this day in his hand and keep it perfect as it was. But he knew he could not protect her from the problems and tragedies that would surely come into everyone's life. That day he took his wife's hand and looked down at her with a smile reveling in his own present happiness. He wondered if she might be thinking the same thing.

Two weeks later, Fortune and Amelia received a letter from Eve: "We have arrived here in Panama and are settled in our own little house. No one here knows I am your daughter and I plan to keep it that way. I want them to like me not because you are rich and famous but for myself and what I can do. Here I am merely Eve Tyler, the lieutenant's wife (soon to be captain, he thinks). Thank you from Rob and me for giving us such a beautiful wedding day."

Chapter 67

Fortune thought January 1, 1915, a fitting time to take stock of his finances and his life in general.

He and Amelia both had gray hair and the beginning of wrinkles. They were grandparents and doted on their youngest child. Gerald, at nine, was fascinated by numbers and showed signs of becoming a businessman when he grew up.

Simon and Sarah were tending miners and their families at the clinic Fortune had built. Martha had opened beauty salon there, to the delight of the miners' wives and daughters. Simon wrote that their friend Steve Merrill had been coming to the clinic to help out one week each month and would soon come to live permanently. He seemed to be courting Martha.

Eve had done well in marrying young Rob Tyler. He was already a major in the army and kept up on world affairs. He told Fortune of the coming need for steel for tanks, weapons, battleships and airplanes. So, Fortune bought a steel mill and invested in both an iron ore mine and in the railroad that hauled the ore to the mill. That meant an increased need for coal, so he bought part interest in another coal mine.

All his new ventures were paying well when he and Amelia, along with Jonas and Laura, had gone on a long-delayed trip to Europe in 1911. He had gone to see the Krupp works, and noted that the Germans were producing steel and its products as fast as America, or even faster.

The only bad part of Eve's marriage was she and Rob had no permanent home. They moved from one military base to another, and when Rob was sent to the Mexican border in 1910 to fight Pancho Villa, Eve and little Ann had come to Oak Hill to live.

Fortune had given Simon money for a house, so he gave Eve the same amount. As he had noted years before, Eve had a good head for money and business. She put the money into stocks, closely watching her investments, and was becoming a wealthy woman. Eve and Rob, along with Ann and their new son Jason, were at Oak Hill for the holidays, awaiting news for Rob's next posting. Now that war had begun in Europe, the American military was readying itself for war as well, just in case.

Fortune was especially proud of Daniel, the shy sensitive boy who loved his dog Brandy more than he cared for most people. Instead of being a doctor like his older brother, he had become a veterinarian. He'd found a Golden Retriever puppy, and now he bred Golden Retrievers and looked after the growing stable of racehorses at Oak Hill, which were becoming noted throughout the state. He built a small office on the estate and looked after neighbors' animals three afternoons a week and in emergencies. Of all Fortune's children, he planned to live permanently at Oak Hill. His cousin Eddie had married the daughter of another apple grower and planned to live on the land.

Despite her early neglect and mistreatment, Leticia had blossomed into a lovely young woman who was studying to be a teacher like the woman she knew as Mama. Clarissa, in high school, was showing talent for art. Pete and Mildred had never made any claims for her, simply reveling in their twin sons.

Leticia announced in October that she was bringing home a friend that would be just right for Daniel. She didn't tell Daniel for fear he would shy away. She told Fortune that "Eliza's mother grew up at Oak Hill." Realizing who this friend was, he was prepared to dislike her, but he found her pleasant and down-to-earth.

Her flaxen hair, fair skin, and graceful walk reminded him of Charlotte, but she had none of her mother's haughtiness. When he saw the adoring way Daniel looked at her as she snuggled one of the puppies, he knew that his son was falling in love with her. And when he saw how Eliza looked at Daniel when he helped her mount her horse, he knew she was falling in love with him as well.

At dinner the first night, Eliza said, "Oak Hill is so much grander than how my mother described it."

Fortune smiled. "Well, I have made a few additions and changes since I bought Oak Hill. How is your mother?"

"She stays to herself since my father died."

Fortune nodded. "You have a brother?" he asked, wondering how he could accept as a member of the family the beast who had beaten Martha.

"I did. He was killed." Before Fortune could ask how, she went on in a low voice: "He spurred his horse to jump a fence. The horse reared and threw him off, then he reared again and his hoofs came down upon Julian and killed him."

"I am so sorry," Daniel said, touching her hand.

Fortune could not bring himself to be sorry. It was a fitting way to die for someone who had abused animals even as a child and it solved a problem. Had the horse been abused itself and gotten revenge?

When Eliza came again to Oak Hill after Christmas, she asked to speak privately to Fortune. "You probably expect your children to marry rich people. I'm not. My mother lives in a tiny apartment, and I'm at college on a scholarship."

"Neither of my two older children married for wealth but for love," he told her gently. "You love Daniel, and it's plain that he loves you, but you must promise not to take him away from Oak Hill."

"Why would I do that? I love it here!"

455

"Would you want to have the wedding in New York?"

"No, at that sweet little chapel you built."

Fortune smiled with pleasure and extended his hand. "I'll be delighted to have you as a daughter-in-law." He added, "and when your mother comes, I'll arrange for her to stay at our guest house. It used to be Daniel's grandmother's home."

He thought of the irony of it: his family would be in the mansion and Charlotte would be in the sharecropper's cottage. And they would soon share grandchildren.

So on January first, as Fortune stood at the head of the giant table to give his annual toast to the new year, he felt not just happy but truly fulfilled.

"Welcome a new member of our family, Eliza, who will marry Daniel some time in the new year!" he announced, as the family cheered.

"And may the coming years be as happy and prosperous for us all. Even more importantly, may we grow ever closer and love each other more every day."

Acknowledgments

I wish to express my appreciation to my editor, Catherine Cantieri, my publisher Joe Perrone, Jr., and my husband, Jerry Liedl, who has read over this book more times than he would like. My thanks to my daughter Catherine Cantieri, who formatted it and designed the cover.

Thanks to my sister Margaret, who shares my love of Virginia's history and its people. She brought me to the house that inspired Oak Hill.

A Note From the Author

I want to say a huge thank you for choosing to read this book. If you enjoyed Fortune's Way, I would be very grateful if you could tell your friends and family. A word-of-mouth recommendation is incredibly powerful, and it helps me reach out to new readers. You could also write a product review. It needn't be long, just a few words, but this also helps new readers find one of my books for the first time.

To find out more about me, or to send me a message, you can check out my website, *www.emileehines.com*, or my author page on Amazon.

Also by Emilee Hines

Fiction

Burnt Station

Callie's Choice

The Castle in the Wilderness (with Catherine Cantieri)

The Christmas Dance

A Place to Love

The Prince and the Passion

The Proposal

Shadows on a White Wall

Voting for Love

Non-Fiction

East African Odyssey (A Memoir)

Til Death Do Us Part

Virginia: Mapping the Old Dominion State through History: Rare and Unusual Maps from the Library of Congress

(Mapping the States through History)
It Happened in Virginia: Remarkable Events That Shaped History
(It Happened in . . . series)

Virginia's Remarkable Women: Daughters, Wives, Sisters, and Mothers Who Shaped History
(Remarkable American Women series)

Mysteries and Legends of Virginia: True Stories of the Unsolved and Unexplained
(Myths and Mysteries series)

Virginia Myths and Legends: The True Stories behind History's Mysteries
(Legends of America series)

Speaking Ill of the Dead: Jerks in Washington, D.C., History
(Speaking Ill of the Dead: Jerks in History series)

Old Virginia Houses series

Along the Fall Line

Harbors

The Heart of Virginia

The Mountain Empire

The Northern Peninsulas

The Piedmont

Shenandoah

www.ingramcontent.com/pod-product-compliance
Lightning Source LLC
Chambersburg PA
CBHW022237020726
47496CB00004B/951

9 781734 675061